RAVE REVIEWS FOR CHRISTINE FEEHAN!

New York Times Bestselling Author
Romantic Times Career Achievement Award Winner
Five-time Pearl Award Winner

"Christine Feehan is a magnificent storyteller."
— *Romantic Times BOOKreviews*

"If you have a taste for intense relationships and the darker side of fantasy, it's hard to do better than Christine Feehan."
— The Romance Reader

"Feehan has a knack for bringing vampiric Carpathians to vivid, virile life in her Dark novels."
— *Publishers Weekly*

"Feehan never fails to deliver the sexual tension or romance....For a different and utterly satisfying vampire romance, this Dark series sets the bar pretty high."
— Roundtable Reviews

DARK CHALLENGE

"The exciting and multifaceted world that impressive author Christine Feehan has created continues to improve with age. By introducing this new band of Carpathians, she is setting the stage for more exhilarating adventures to come."
— *Romantic Times BOOKreviews*

"WE SHOULD NOT BE DOING THIS," DESARI SAID DESPERATELY, DETERMINED NOT TO ALLOW JULIAN SAVAGE TO CONTROL HER.

His mouth touched her neck, his breath fanning the pulse throbbing so frantically beneath her skin. Hunger flared in her, hot and erotic, like nothing she had ever known.

"This is exactly what we should be doing, *cara*," he breathed as his teeth scraped back and forth over her pulse, sending heat dancing through her.

Desari closed her eyes. His body, hot and hard and aggressive as he held her to him, turned her own into a living, breathing flame.

Savage was dangerous, a predator, a powerful Carpathian male, yet he held her protectively, kissed her as if she were the most precious thing in the world. How could she not fall under his spell?

She made a sound, a low moan of alarm. Her fists found his mane of golden hair and clung for support. He was stealing her soul, taking her heart. He was ensnaring her for all time…

…and she was giving herself to him without a fight.

Books by
Christine Feehan

DARK NIGHTS
DARK DESIRE
LAIR OF THE LION
DARK PRINCE
DARK GOLD
DARK MAGIC
DARK CHALLENGE
DARK FIRE
DARK LEGEND
DARK GUARDIAN
DARK MELODY
DARK DESTINY
THE SCARLETTI CURSE

CHRISTINE FEEHAN

DARK CHALLENGE

AVON

An Imprint of HarperCollins*Publishers*

This is a work of fiction. Names, characters, places, and incidents are products of the author's imagination or are used fictitiously and are not to be construed as real. Any resemblance to actual events, locales, organizations, or persons, living or dead, is entirely coincidental.

AVON BOOKS
An Imprint of HarperCollins*Publishers*
10 East 53rd Street
New York, New York 10022-5299

Copyright © 2000 by Christine Feehan
ISBN 978-0-06-201940-0
www.avonbooks.com

First Avon Books paperback printing: November 2010

Avon Trademark Reg. U.S. Pat. Off. and in Other Countries,
Marca Registrada, Hecho en U.S.A.
HarperCollins® is a registered trademark of HarperCollins Publishers.

Printed in the U.S.A.

10 9 8 7 6 5 4 3 2

For Francis and Eddie Vedolla Sr. for teaching my son, Brian and my daughter, Denise the importance of the dance. . . . There is a greatness in you both.

Special thanks to the staff at Konocti Harbor Resort and Spa who are always helpful, manage to come up with terrific concerts and genuinely are great people.

DARK CHALLENGE

Chapter One

Julian Savage hesitated outside the door to the crowded bar. He had come to this city for one last errand before he would choose a Carpathian's eternal rest. Almost an ancient of his race, he was weary of the centuries of living in a stark, gray world void of the intense colors and emotions known to the younger males of his kind, or to those who had found a lifemate. Still, he had one last goal to accomplish, one more thing asked of him by his Prince, and then he could meet the life-destroying dawn with an easy mind. It wasn't that he was on the verge of losing his soul, of turning vampire; he could hold out longer should he choose. It was the bleakness of his life, stretching an eternity before him, that had dictated his decision.

Yet he could not refuse this errand. In the long centuries of his existence, he felt he had given little to his dwindling race. True, he was a vampire hunter, one of the more powerful, which was considered a great thing

11

among his people. But he knew, as did most of their successful hunters, that it was the Carpathian male's killer instinct, not any special talent that made him so brilliant at what he did. Gregori, their people's greatest healer, second only to the Prince, had sent word to him to warn that this woman he now sought, this singer, was on the hit list of a fanatical society of *human* vampire hunters, who often mistakenly targeted unusual mortals, as well as Carpathians, in their murderous zeal. The society had very primitive notions of what made a vampire—as if avoiding daylight or feeding on blood alone rendered one soulless, evil, undead. Julian and his kind were living proof that nothing could be farther from the truth.

Julian knew why this task of warning and protecting the singer had been given to him. Gregori was determined not to lose him to the dawn. The healer could read what was in Julian's mind, realized that he had chosen to end his barren existence. But he also knew that once Julian gave his word to protect the human woman from the society of killers, he would not stop until she was safe. Gregori was buying time for him. But it would do no good.

Julian had spent many lifetimes, century after century, apart from his people, including his own twin brother. Julian was a loner even in a race made up of solitary males. His species, the Carpathian race, was dying out, their Prince desperately attempting to find ways to give his people hope. To find new lifemates for their males. To find ways to keep their children alive, to bolster their dwindling numbers. Julian, however, had no choice but to remain solitary, to run with the wolves, to soar with the birds of prey, to hunt with the panthers. The few times he walked among humans, it was usually to fight a worthwhile war or to lend his unusual strength to a good cause. But he had spent most of his years walking alone, unseen, undetected by even his own kind.

For several moments he stood still, reliving the memory of his childhood folly, that terrible moment he had stepped upon a path that had, for eternity, changed his life.

He had been but twelve summers. Even then his terrible, unquenchable thirst for knowledge had been upon him. He had always been inseparable from his twin brother, Aidan, yet that day he had heard a far-off call. A summons he couldn't resist. He had been filled with the joy of discovery back then, and he had slipped away, following the lure of an unspoken promise. The network of caves he discovered was honeycombed deep within the mountain. Inside he met the most amazing wizard— personable, handsome, and willing to impart his vast knowledge to a young, eager apprentice. All he asked in return was secrecy. At the age of twelve, Julian had thought it all an exciting game.

Looking back, Julian questioned if he had wanted knowledge so much that he had deliberately ignored the warning signs. He had mastered many new powers, but there had come the day when the truth hit him in the face with all its stark ugliness. He had arrived early to the caves and hearing screams, rushed inside to discover that his young, handsome friend was the most loathsome of all creatures, a true monster, a cold-blooded killer— a Carpathian who had yielded his soul and turned vampire. At twelve Julian did not have sufficient powers and skills to save the hapless victims as the vampire drained their blood completely, seeking not just sustenance, as a Carpathian would, but the subject's death.

That memory was etched in Julian's mind for all time. The streaming blood. The unearthly screams. The horror.

Then came the moment when the vampire's hand gripped him, the once-admiring pupil, and dragged him close enough to smell his fetid breath, to hear his taunting laughter. Then the teeth—fangs now—were tearing into his body, painful and vulgar. But, worse, Julian wasn't allowed death, as the vampire had given his other victims. He remembered the way the undead creature had slashed his own wrist and forced it to Julian's mouth, had brutally forced him to accept that tainted blood, to exchange blood with the most unholy of creatures, bringing him into his power, beginning the process that could make Julian his slave, that connected them for all time.

The shame had not ended there. The vampire had immediately begun to use the boy even against his will, as his eyes and ears, to spy on those of his former race he now wished to destroy. He had the talent to eavesdrop through Julian on the Prince or the healer when the boy was near them. He had taunted Julian that he would use him to destroy his own brother Aidan. And Julian had known it was possible; he had felt the darkness spreading within him, at times had felt the vampire's eyes looking through his own. Several times Aidan had escaped by a mere hairsbreadth from traps Julian later recognized he had inadvertently set himself, under the vampire's insidious compulsion.

And so, many centuries ago, Julian had made a vow to lead a solitary life, to keep his people and his beloved twin safe from the vampire and himself. He had lived on the fringes of their society, gaining a Carpathian's true strength and knowledge until he was old enough to strike out on his own. His people's blood still beating strongly in him, he did his best to live his life honorably, did his best to fight the gathering darkness and the continual assaults the vampire made on him. He had evaded further blood exchanges with the undead and had hunted and killed countless other vampires, but the one who had fashioned his life so brutally always eluded him.

Julian was now taller and more muscular than many of his race, and while most had dark hair and eyes, he was like a Viking of old, with long, thick blond hair he tied at the nape of his neck with a leather thong. His eyes were amber, and he often used their smoldering, mesmerizing fire to hypnotize his prey. Now, though, he gazed about the street, seeing nothing yet to account for his unease, and he moved forward like the predator he was, fluidly, muscles rippling beneath his sleek skin. When need be he could be as still as the mountains, and as relentlessly unyielding. He could be the rush of the wind, like flowing water. He had tremendous gifts, could speak in many tongues, but he was always alone.

In his younger years he had spent much time in Italy; more recently he had lived in New Orleans, in the French Quarter, where his aura of mystery and darkness alarmed almost no one. But not long ago he had given up his home there, knowing he would never return. At long last, after this one remaining task, his duty and honor would be satisfied. He saw no reason to continue his existence.

Julian heard the conversations, so many of them, from the interior of the bar. He felt the excitement of those inside. The patrons seemed enthralled by the singing group they were waiting to hear. Evidently the band was intensely popular, and recording companies were screaming for deals, but the performers refused to sign with anyone. Instead, they traveled like old-fashioned minstrels or troubadours, from town to town, city to city, never employing outside musicians or technicians and always performing only their own songs. The odd, reclusive nature of the troupe, along with the lead singer's voice, described as hauntingly beautiful, mesmerizing, nearly magical, had drawn the unwanted attention of the society of vampire hunters.

Julian inhaled deeply, and caught the scent of blood. Instantly hunger beat at him, reminding him he had not fed this night. He stood outside, unseen by the humans clamoring to get in or by the security guards silently standing at the entrance. He would go in, deliver his warning to the singer of the danger she was in, and get out. Hopefully the woman would listen, and his duty would be done. If not, he would have no choice but to continue to endure his terrible solitary existence until he could make certain she was safe. And he was tired. He no longer wanted to endure.

He began moving then, weaving silently through the crowd. At the door stood the two men, both tall and dark. The one with long hair looked like someone to contend with; he even looked vaguely familiar. Julian became but a rush of cool air as he glided past, hidden from sight yet walking confidently among the crush of humans. Still, the guard with the long hair turned his head alertly, black eyes searching restlessly, resting on Julian briefly even though Julian was invisible. The guard was clearly uneasy. Out of the corner of his eye, Julian saw him turn his head this way and that before his icy gaze swung back to follow Julian's progress through the crowded bar.

Julian's white teeth flashed with a predator's gleam. He knew he was unseen, so the guard had well tuned, radarlike senses, unusual for a mortal. Interesting that the band had him. He might be worth his weight in gold should there be an actual attack on the woman.

The cold air Julian pushed before him parted the pressing crowds; he didn't even have to slow down. He glanced at the stage set up for the performers, then walked toward the back rooms. As he did so the humorless smile faded from his face, leaving the familiar hard edge to his mouth. He knew there was a hint of cruelty there, the cold mask of the hunter. Then he smelled them. The enemy. Had they reached the singer before he had?

Swearing silently, eloquently, Julian moved with preternatural speed to the woman's dressing room. He was too late. She was gone, already making her way to the stage with the other members of the band. Only two beautiful leopards with spotted fur were curled up in a corner of the small room. Simultaneously their heads swung toward him, all senses alert. The animals were larger and heavier than most in the wild, and their yellow-green eyes, fixed on him, betrayed their superior intelligence. It was also unusual to see the two together, as leopards were generally solitary creatures. Like Julian.

"Where is she, my friends?" he asked softly. "I have come to save her life. Tell me where she is before her enemies kill her."

The male cat crouched and snarled, exposing long, sharp canines that could grab, hold, and puncture its prey. The female crouched even lower, ready to spring. Julian felt the familiar sense of brotherhood he always did when he encountered a member of the *Panthera pardus* family, and yet, when he reached for the leopards' minds, he found he couldn't control either easily. He succeeded only in confusing them a bit, slowing their reaction time. Then the male cat began its move, a slow stalking, head down, eyes fixed on him, its slow-motion manner preliminary to the explosion of speed preceding a kill. Julian didn't want to have to kill such a beautiful, rare creature, so he quickly slipped out of the room, closing the door firmly behind him, and headed toward the sound of thunderous applause.

The band began to play the opening to the first song. Then he heard the woman's voice. Haunting, mystical notes that hung in the air like silver and gold shimmering with fire. He actually saw the notes, saw the silver and gold dancing in front of his eyes. Julian stopped dead in his tracks, shock ripping through him. He stared at the hallway. The tattered, faded wallpaper was edged with red. It had been well over eight hundred years since Julian had seen anything in color. It was the fate of Carpathian males beyond their youth to lose all sense of color, to lose their emotions, to struggle in gray bleakness against their predatory natures, unless a lifemate appeared to balance their darkness with her goodness and light. Only then would color and emotion—powerful emotion—be restored to them. But females were rare, and surely one such as Julian would never be blessed with a mate. Yet his heart jumped in his chest.

He felt excitement. Hope. Emotion. Real emotion. Colors were so vivid that they nearly blinded him. The sound of her voice played through his body, touched him in places he had long forgotten. His body tightened; need slammed into him. Julian stood frozen to the spot. The colors, the emotions, the physical lust rising so sharply could only mean one thing. The singer possessing that voice had to be his lifemate.

It was impossible. Totally impossible to believe. The men of his race could spend an eternity hunting for the one woman that was their other half. Male Carpathians were predatory, with the instincts of dark, hungry killers, cunning, quick, and lethal. After their short time of growing, of laughter and adventure, it was all over as they lost the ability to feel, to see in colors. There was nothing left but a solitary, barren existence.

Julian's existence had been especially unbearable, alienated as he was from Aidan, his twin, whose inevitable closeness might have made the long, gray centuries a bit easier to endure. But he had known he was locked to Aidan through their blood tie, and every moment they spent together increased the vampire's threat to Aidan. Their very closeness endangered his brother. So Julian had fled his people, never telling any of them, not even his beloved brother, the terrible truth. He had done the honorable thing, as he had only his honor left to him.

Now Julian stood numbly in the narrow hall, unable to believe that his lifemate was close. Unable, in that dazzling moment of emotion and color, to believe that he could possibly deserve such a thing.

Many Carpathian males turned vampire after centuries of a life filled with no hope. Without emotions, power—the power to hunt and kill—seemed the only thing left to them. Others, rather than becoming a danger to mortals and immortals alike, chose to end their barren existence by greeting the dawn; waiting for the sunlight to destroy bodies meant to live in darkness. Only a handful actually found their other half, the light to their darkness, the one who could make them complete. After nearly a thousand years of bleak existence, after making the decision to meet the dawn before the predatory demon within him, now struggling for control of him, conquered him, Julian could scarcely believe he had found his true lifemate. But the colors and emotions and hope said that it was true.

The woman's voice—throaty, husky, erotic—held the promise of satin sheets and candlelight. It played over his skin like fingers, tantalizing, enticing, sinfully sexy. It mesmerized anyone within hearing distance; it haunted and captivated. The notes danced, pure and beautiful, weaving a spell of enchantment around Julian, around every listener.

Julian knew nothing of this woman. Only that Gregori

had sent him to warn her that she was in danger from the human society of vampire hunters. Evidently the Prince wished her and those traveling with her to be protected if necessary. The society of mortals who believed in the vampires of old legends and sought to destroy them had for some reason targeted this singer, Desari, with her haunting voice and eccentric ways. Most of the society's victims were killed, a stake driven through the heart. Worse, some victims were kept alive to be tortured and dissected. Julian listened to the beautiful voice. Desari sounded like an angel singing, her voice not of the earth.

Then a scream, high and piercing, interrupted the beauty of the song. It was followed by a second scream, then a third. Julian heard a shot ring out, then a volley of bullets thudding into flesh and musical instruments. The building shook with the force of feet pounding across the floor as the patrons raced to get out of the line of fire.

Julian moved so quickly that he blurred as he shimmered into a solid mass. The bar was in complete disarray. Mortals were fleeing the place as fast as they could, running over each other in the process. People were yelling in terror. Tables and chairs were smashed and broken. The three members of the band lay, bloodsplattered, on the stage, instruments shattered. The security guards were exchanging gunfire with six men who were also shooting into the crowd as they tried to escape.

Julian went straight for the stage. He pushed aside one male body and found the still form of the woman, Desari, sprawled on the platform, her masses of blue-black hair spreading out like a veil. Blood pooled under her, staining her royal blue dress. He had no time to examine her features further; the worst wound was mortal and would kill her unless he did something. Instinctively he fashioned a quick visual barrier, blurring the stage from watching eyes. In the pandemonium, he doubted if any would notice.

He lifted Desari easily into his arms, found a weak pulse, and placed a hand over the wound. Blocking out the chaos around him, he sent himself seeking outside his body and into hers. The entrance wound was small, the exit wound quite large. The bullet had torn through her body, ripping internal organs and tissue. He sealed the wounds to prevent further blood loss before taking her deeper into the shadows. With one lengthening fingernail, he opened a wound in his own chest.

You are mine, cara mia, *and you cannot die. I would not go quietly to my death without avenging you. The world could not conceive of such a monster as I would become. You must drink*, piccola, *for yourself, your life, for me, for our life together. Drink now.* He gave the command with a firm compulsion, not allowing her to squirm away from his iron will. Before this moment, before Desari, he had chosen to destroy himself rather than wait until it was too late and he had become one of the very monsters he had spent centuries hunting and destroying. For tying Desari to him now, he might deserve death a hundred times over, but he would take what destiny offered him.

After long, empty centuries, in a single moment, everything had changed. He could feel. He could see the brilliance of the colors in the world. His body was alive with needs and desire, not simply the ever-present gnawing physical hunger for blood. Power and strength ran through him, sang in his veins, flowed through his muscles, and he felt it. *Felt* it. She would not die. He would not allow such a thing. *Never.* Not after centuries of complete loneliness. Where there had been a yawning black chasm, an abyss of darkness, there was now a connection. Real. *Felt.*

His blood was ancient blood, filled with healing strength, filled with power. His life flowed into her, forging a bond that could not be broken. He began to whisper to her in the ancient language. Ritual words. Words that would make their hearts one, words that would weave the tattered remnants of their souls back together and seal them irrevocably for all time.

For one moment time shimmered to a standstill as he struggled to do the honorable thing, struggled to give her up, to allow her to live without the terrible burden he carried. But he wasn't strong enough. The words were wrenched out of his soul, from deep where they had been buried. *I claim you as my lifemate. I belong to you. I offer my life for you. I give to you my protection, my allegiance, my heart, my soul, and my body. I take into my keeping the same that is yours. Your life, happiness, and welfare will be cherished and placed above my own for all time. You are my lifemate, bound to me for eternity and always in my care.*

Julian felt tears burning in his eyes. Here was another dark sin for his soul. This time against the woman he should protect above all else. His mouth brushed her silky hair, and very softly he issued the command that she cease to drink. He was already weak from lack of feeding. Healing her wounds and giving her a large volume of his blood weakened him further. He inhaled her scent, took it into his lungs, his body, imprinting her on his mind for all time.

The warning came to him as nothing more than a brush of fur against a chair, but it was enough. Julian sprang away from the unconscious woman, whirling to meet the threat, his snarl exposing gleaming white teeth. This was a huge leopard, a good two hundred pounds, and it sprang at him, its strange, inky eyes fixed on him with lethal malevolence. Julian leapt into the air to meet the beast, shape-shifting as he did so, his body stretching, contorting, golden fur rippling over heavy muscle as he took another form to meet the deadly threat.

They met in midair, two huge male cats in their prime, at full strength, rending and tearing with claws and teeth. The black leopard seemed determined to fight to the death, but Julian hoped to save its life. The black cat arched in a half circle, swiping at Julian, and Julian felt the rake of razor-sharp claws ripping into his side. He lunged for his opponent and managed to score four long furrows on its belly. The panther hissed softly with hate and defiance, with renewed determination, with retaliation, vengeance.

Julian reached for the beast's mind. It was in the red haze of a killing frenzy, a need to destroy. Agilely he sprung away. He did not want to kill the beautiful animal, and, the truth was, for all his own fighting experience, this creature was enormously strong and skilled. And it did not respond to his many attempts to seize control of its mind.

He swore as the panther crouched protectively over the woman's body, then began once more moving toward him in the slow-motion manner of the stalking leopard. The intelligent ebony eyes focused on his face in the unnerving, unblinking stare only a leopard could produce. The cat meant to kill him, and Julian had no choice but to fight to the death or flee. He had given the woman precious blood he didn't have to spare, and now the four long furrows torn deep into his side were dripping the liquid of life onto the floor in a steady stream.

The cat was too strong, too experienced a killing machine. Julian could not risk it. His lifemate's fate was now tied to his. He sensed no animosity toward her from the large panther, rather, a need to protect her. From Desari's mind he picked up memories of love for the animal. Julian forced himself to back away, his golden muzzle snarling, his eyes blazing defiance, not submission.

The black panther was clearly torn between following him and finishing the job and staying with the woman. Picking up that information from the panther reassured Julian even more. He backed away another two steps, not wanting to blunder by harming a creature his lifemate loved.

Then another attack came from behind him. A mere whisper of movement had him springing aside so that the second leopard landed where he had been. It snarled in rage. Julian bolted, leaping for the bar, then a table, his powerful back legs digging into the smooth surface for purchase. A third cat blocked the entrance, but Julian sprang and hit it squarely, knocking it off its feet. Then instantly he was gone, dissolving into thin air.

As mist, Julian streamed out into the night. He didn't fool himself, however; some of the droplets streaking toward the ocean were his blood. The cats could track him if he didn't put enough distance between them immediately. It took tremendous energy to put on a burst of speed while holding his image of insubstantial mist, energy that was fast leaking out into the night air. Julian summoned his remaining energy to close the wounds in his body to prevent further blood loss.

Totally bewildered, he went over every move he had made inside the bar. Why hadn't the black cat responded to his mind control? He had never before failed to mesmerize an animal. The panther's mind was not like any other he had encountered. In any case, he should have easily defeated a panther, but the black male was far bigger than any leopard he had met with in the wild.

And the cats had been working in unison, something not natural for the species. Julian was positive the large panther had been somehow directing the actions of the other two. And they had been protective of Desari, not treating her as prey.

Julian turned his attention back to the more immediate threat to his lifemate. Somewhere out there were six humans who had attempted to kill her, an innocent woman whose only crime was possessing a voice from the heavens. He could not rest this night until he had tracked them down and ensured they would never get close to her again. He still had the stench of them in his nostrils. The cats would take care of his lifemate until he returned to her. His job now was to defeat the assassins, bring Carpathian justice to them, removing the danger to Desari as quickly as possible.

He gave a fleeting thought to his need for blood, the wounds he had sustained, and the possibility of the mysterious panther tracking him, but decided all that didn't matter. He could not allow the assassins to go free. He turned back inland and streamed toward the bar, rising high to mingle with the fog. He hoped to avoid detection by the leopard's superior sense of smell, but if it found him again, so be it. As he moved through time and space, he touched the mind of his lifemate to see if she was coming out of her unconsciousness. She would need to heal, but he discovered that she was alive and being cared for. Pandemonium reigned at the bar, with police and ambulances everywhere. Likely by now the cats were locked up securely.

He found the first body in the thick brush not ten yards from the back of the bar. Julian shimmered into solid form, pressing a hand to the dripping claw marks marring his side, not wanting to leave any evidence of his presence. Though there was no sign of a struggle,

Christine Feehan

the assassin's neck was broken. Julian found the second body a few yards ahead, tucked in an alley. It was sprawled against the wall, half in and half out of a puddle of oil. There was a hole in the man's chest the size of a fist where the heart should have been.

Julian stiffened and glanced carefully around him. The assassin had been killed in a manner consistent with a ritual slaying of the undead. Not the human version, using stakes and garlic, but the true manner of a Carpathian. He studied the mutilated body. It almost had the look of Gregori's early work, yet it wasn't. These days Gregori would not have wasted time; he would have stood at a distance and simply killed all the evil mortals in one stroke. This was retribution. Someone had taken a personal hand in each death.

His own brother, Aidan, lived here out west and often destroyed the undead—there were few Carpathians as capable as he here in the United States—but Julian would have felt his twin's presence, would have known his work the instant he saw it. This was somehow different from the cool, impersonal work of Carpathian hunters yet still close to it.

Curious now, he sought out the other killers. Bodies three and four were side by side. One had buried his own knife deep within his throat, no doubt under an irresistible compulsion. The other's throat was completely ripped out. It looked as if an animal had done the damage, but Julian knew better. He found the fifth body only a few yards from the two. This one, too, had seen death coming. The horror was on his face. His eyes stared obscenely skyward, even as his own hand gripped the gun he had used to shoot himself—the same weapon he had used on the musicians. Julian found the sixth assassin lying face down in a gutter, a pool of blood surrounding him. He had died hard and painfully.

Julian thought for a long moment. This was a message, a clear and brazen message to those who had sent the assassins after the singer. A challenge from a dangerous adversary. *Come and get us if you dare.* Julian sighed. He was tired, and his hunger was becoming a gnawing, biting demand. Much as he shared the sentiment to brutally destroy any who dared to threaten Desari he could not allow this challenge to stand. It would place his lifemate squarely in deeper danger. If the society knew exactly how their assassins had been dispatched, they would be convinced she and her protectors were vampires and would redouble their efforts to destroy her immediately.

It took a few moments to collect the bodies into a heap in the privacy of the alley. With a little sigh he gathered energy from the sky and directed it toward the corpses now lying in the puddle of oil. Instantly there was a flash of fire and the stench of burned flesh. He waited impatiently, masking the scene from all eyes, even those of the police searching just down the road. When the dead men were little more than ashes, he directed the fire out and collected the remains. He then launched himself skyward and streaked away from the scene. Well out over the ocean, he scattered the grotesque, grisly ashes, watching the choppy waves, made hungry by a flick of his hand, devour them for all time.

Losing six assassins, not having a clue as to their whereabouts or fate, would be a huge blow to the society of killers. With luck, their directors would crawl into a hole to regroup and remain inactive for months to come, sparing innocent mortals and Carpathians from their malice.

Julian turned inland toward the small cabin he had tucked away in the mountains, his thoughts once more turning toward the strange behavior of the leopards. If he didn't know better, he would swear the large black panther was not really a cat but a Carpathian. But that was impossible. Every Carpathian was known to one another. They could detect one another easily, and all used a standard path of mental communication when necessary. While it was true that a few of the ancients could mask their presence from others, it was a rare gift.

Another thought disturbed Julian. His own behavior had assuredly thrust Desari directly into a new path of danger. By claiming her as his lifemate, Julian had marked her as surely as he had been marked in the eyes of the undead, his mortal enemy.

Swearing softly in his mind, Julian turned his attention back to the strange animal guarding her. Although Julian was a loner, he knew every Carpathian alive. And the black panther reminded him of someone, with its method of fighting, its fierce intensity, its complete confidence in itself. Gregori. The Dark One.

He shook his head. No, Gregori was in New Orleans with his lifemate, Savannah. Julian had seen to young Savannah's protection until Gregori had fulfilled his vow to allow her five years of freedom before claiming her as his lifemate. And Gregori was not the undead; his lifemate assured that. No Carpathian would attempt to destroy another who had not turned vampire. No, it could not possibly be Gregori.

Julian solidified at the entrance to his cabin and pushed open the door. Before he went in, he turned and inhaled the night; seeking the scent of any prey that might be nearby. He needed blood, fresh, hot blood, to fully heal his wounds. When he looked down and saw the tears in his side, he cursed, yet he felt a certain savage satisfaction in knowing he, too, had scored against the huge cat.

Julian had traveled the world. He had had centuries

to indulge his curiosity, his thirst and need for knowledge. He had spent considerable time in Africa and India studying the leopard, inexplicably drawn there time after time. He believed the cunning and deadly cats were possessed of superior intelligence. However, they were also wildly unpredictable, which made them all the more dangerous. So it had to be an unusual group of humans who had befriended the cats, let alone secured the required permits to travel with them in the United States.

Julian questioned again the unusual behavior of the cats themselves. Even if they had been hand-raised and trained, the coordinating of their efforts to bring down an intruder in their midst, especially when chaos and the smell of blood were all around them, was remarkable.

The huge black panther had not even licked at the woman's wounds or attempted to sample the blood of the other two fallen band members. The scent of fresh blood should have triggered the cats' instinct to hunt, to eat. Leopards were notorious scavengers as well as hunters. Something was off kilter, for these leopards were definitely protecting the singer.

Julian shook his head and returned to matters regarding his immediate attention. He sent himself into his own body, seeking the lacerations, sealing them off from the inside this time. The effort took more energy than he could afford, so he mixed an herbal drink that promoted healing. Drifting back outside onto the porch, he drained the liquid quickly, forcing his body to hold on to the unfamiliar nourishment.

It took a few minutes to gather the necessary strength to make his way into the forest. He was seeking rich soil, a blend of vegetation and dirt, that would best approximate the earth of the Carpathian homeland, which always aided the healing of a Carpathian's wounds. He found such soil beneath a thick layer of pine needles on the far side of a knoll. He mixed moss and soil with the healing agent in his saliva and packed his wounds with it. At once the blend soothed the terrible burning.

It was interesting to him, observing the different sensations and emotions pushing in on him. He had known that those Carpathians who reclaimed emotion and color found that everything they experienced was much deeper and far more intense than it had been when they were younger. Everything. That included pain. All Carpathians learned to block things out if it was necessary, but it took enormous energy. Julian was tired and hungry. His body cried out for nourishment. His mind was tuned to Desari's. His lifemate. Her mind was in turmoil now, but she was alive. He wanted to reach out and reassure her, but he knew such an intrusion would only make her more upset.

He closed his eyes and leaned against a tree trunk. A leopard. Who would have thought a leopard would score such a blow against him? Had he been so distracted by the presence of his newfound lifemate that he had been careless? How could an animal have outmaneuvered him? And what of the assassins and the way they were killed? No cat or even human avenger could have accomplished all that so quickly. Julian had supreme confidence in his own abilities; few of the ancients, and certainly no mere animal, could defeat him in battle. There was only one who could. Gregori.

He shook his head to try to clear his thoughts. The way the cat had battled, so focused, so relentless, was all too reminiscent of the Dark One. Why couldn't he shake that thought when he knew it was totally impossible? Could another ancient have hidden from all of his own kind? Gone to ground for a few hundred years and emerged undetected?

Julian tried to recall what he knew of Gregori's family. His parents had been massacred during the time of the Turk invasion of the Carpathian Mountains. Mikhail, now the Prince and leader of the Carpathian people, had lost his parents the same way. Entire villages had been destroyed. Beheadings were common, as were bodies writhing on stakes, left to rot in the sun. Small children were often herded together into a pit or a building and burned alive. Scenes of torture and mutilation had become a way of life, a harsh, merciless existence for Carpathians and humans alike.

The Carpathian race was nearly decimated. In the horror of those murderous days they lost most of their women, a good number of their men, and, most important, nearly all of their children. That had been the most violent and shocking blow of all. One day the children had been rounded up, along with mortal children, and driven into a straw shack, which had been set on fire, burning them alive. Mikhail had eluded the slaughter, along with a brother and sister, Gregori had not fared as well. He had lost a brother around six years of age and a new baby sister, not yet six months.

Julian took a deep breath and let it out, going over each and every male Carpathian he had encountered over the centuries, trying to place the unusual black panther.

He recalled the legends about two ancient hunters, twins, who had disappeared without a trace some five or six hundred years earlier. It was believed one had turned vampire. He inhaled sharply at the thought of that. Could he still be alive? Could Julian have escaped relatively unscathed from one so powerful? He doubted it.

Julian searched every corner of his mind for information. Had there been a child he didn't remember? Wouldn't any Carpathian, male or female, from Gregori's bloodline be far too powerful to miss? If there was a chance that any relative of Gregori's existed somewhere, anywhere, in the world, wouldn't the rest of their people know it by now? Julian himself had traveled near and far, in new lands and old, and had come across no strangers of their kind. True, there were rumors and hopes that Carpathians as yet unknown to their people might well exist, but he had never found them.

Julian dismissed the matter for the moment and sent forth a call, luring prey in close to him rather than wasting valuable energy hunting. He waited beneath the tree, and a light breeze carried to him the sounds of four people. He inhaled their scent. Teenagers. Males. They had all been drinking. He sighed again. It seemed that was the favorite pastime of young mortals—drinking or using drugs. It didn't matter; in the end, blood was all the same.

He could hear their conversation as they stumbled almost blindly through the forest toward him. None of the boys had permission from their parents for this camping outing. Julian's white teeth gleamed in the night in a slightly mocking smile. So the boys thought it was funny to make fools out of people who loved and trusted them. Their species was so different from his own. Although his race was often more predator than man, a Carpathian male would never harm a woman or child or be disrespectful to those who loved or protected or taught him.

He waited, his intense eyes molten gold, easily piercing the veil of darkness. His mind continually strayed to his lifemate. Every Carpathian male knew the chance of finding a lifemate within their dwindling race was nearly impossible, their numbers being repeatedly decimated by the vampire and witch hunts in the Middle Ages and during the bloody Turk and Holy Wars. To complicate matters, the few remaining women had not given birth to a female child in years, and the rare children born in recent centuries nearly all died within their first year. No one, not even Gregori, their greatest healer, nor Mikhail, the Prince and leader of their people, had found the solution to these grave problems.

Many had tried in the past to turn mortal women Carpathian, but the females had either perished or become deranged vampiresses, feeding on the lifeblood of human children and always killing their prey. Such women had had to be destroyed to protect the human race.

Then Mikhail and Gregori had discovered a rare group of mortal women who possessed true psychic ability who could survive the conversion. Such women could be turned with three blood exchanges, and they were capable of producing female children. Mikhail had made such a match, and his daughter, Savannah, had been born as Gregori's lifemate. A new surge of hope had spread among the Carpathian males. But though Julian had traveled throughout the world—granted, preferring the wilds of the mountains and the freedom of the open spaces to long periods spent among humans—he had never come across any women possessing the rare abilities required.

Julian had long since ceased to believe or hope the way the others had, even when his own twin brother had found such a woman. Julian knew he was a cynic, that the darkness in him, calling out to the undead, was like a stain spreading across his soul. He had accepted it, as he accepted the rest of the ever-changing universe, as he accepted the sin of his youth and his own self-banishment from his people. He was of the earth and the sky. He was a part of it all. And as he neared the time when he was dangerously close to the change, he accepted that, too. He knew he was strong; he was willing to walk into the sun before he became a demon with no soul at all. For a very long time he had had no hope, had had nothing to hold out for.

Now everything had changed. In one heartbeat, one instant. His lifemate was out there. But she was wounded, hunted. At least she had a decent bodyguard, and her cats were obviously protecting her. Still, he could not get it out of his head that the huge male leopard was not what it had seemed. And there was the way the assassins had been dealt with, not in the human way but that of a Carpathian hunter. If there was a powerful Carpathian, another male, that Julian wasn't aware of, he did not want the man anywhere near his lifemate.

The teenagers were traipsing closer, their voices loud in the stillness of the night. One stumbled repeatedly, having consumed far too much alcohol. They laughed raucously, and from the deep woods, the golden eyes watched them, the white teeth gleamed. Julian stepped out slowly from behind the trees. His face was hidden in the shadows. He smiled at the boys. "You seem to be having a good time tonight," he greeted softly.

All of the boys stopped abruptly. They could not make him out in the dark. And they were suddenly aware that they were somewhere deep in the forest, far from their campsite, without a clue how they got there or how to get back. They exchanged puzzled, alarmed looks. Julian could hear their hearts beating loudly in their chests. He prolonged the suspense for a moment, his teeth gleaming, allowing the faint red haze of the beast within him to be reflected in his eyes.

The boys stood frozen to the spot as Julian emerged from the shadows. "Has no one ever told you the forest can be dangerous at night?" His beautiful voice purred with menace, and he deliberately deepened his foreign accent, evincing a danger the boys could feel moving through their bodies.

"Who are you?" one of them managed to croak. They were sobering up fast.

Julian's eyes were glowing a feral red, and the beast within, always crouching so close to the surface, fought for release. He allowed hunger to sweep through him, the terrible emptiness, the biting, gnawing craving that was never fully sated, could never be sated until he was with his lifemate in every way. He needed her dwelling in him to anchor the raging beast. He needed her blood flowing in his veins to stop the horrendous craving, to bring him back for all eternity into the light.

One of the boys screamed, and another moaned. Julian waved a hand to silence them. He didn't want them terrified, only scared enough to remember their fear and modify their behavior. It was easy enough to take possession of their minds. He erected a veil to cloud their memory of the event as he stepped forward to drink his fill. He needed a large volume of blood and was grateful there were several boys so none of them would be left too weak. In each boy he planted a slightly different memory, wanting confusion to reign. At the last moment, smiling sardonically, Julian planted a firm command in each boy to blurt out the truth to his parents every time he intentionally sought to deceive them.

Julian melted into the shadows and released the teenagers from the thrall paralyzing their minds and bodies. He watched them as they stirred to life, all sitting or lying on the ground. They were dizzy and scared, each remembering a close call, an attack that came out of the deep forest, but all remembered it differently. They argued briefly but without much spirit. They just wanted to go home.

Julian made certain they made it back to their camp without incident; then, as they huddled together around the fire, he began mimicking the hunting cries of a pack of wolves. Laughing, he left them throwing things helter

Christine Feehan

skelter into their car and racing away from the terrors of disobeying their parents.

Feeling much better with the soil pressed into his wounds, and the biting hunger appeased for the time being, Julian slowly returned to the cabin. Beneath the wooden planking of the floor was a small crawl space. With a slight wave of his hand he opened a plot deep within its earth floor. It beckoned him, the soothing peace of the ground, calling to its own.

Julian floated to his resting place and lay still, his arms crossed lightly over his wounds. He pictured Desari as he settled into the soil. She was tall and slender, her skin creamy white. Her hair was luxurious, shining like a raven's wing, masses of curls and waves falling in a shimmering cascade to her hips. She had small, delicate bones, making her classically beautiful. Her lips were luscious, sexy. He loved the way her mouth had looked, even in her unconscious state. She had a perfect mouth.

Julian felt a smile softening the hard edge of his chiseled lips. A lifemate. After all these centuries, after never believing. Why in the world would he be chosen for such a thing? Out of all the Carpathian males he knew, men who religiously followed the rules, why would he find a lifemate? He was practically an outlaw.

He gave more thought to the mortal woman now stuck with him. It took three blood exchanges to convert a human. And he would have to ensure that she was truly psychic. Still, excitement beat at him. A lifemate to make the world beautiful and mysterious, a wonderful, intriguing place, when for so long it had only been barren and dark. Unfortunately, for the woman, things would have to change. Singing before crowds would be impossible. Desari. He remembered now that she also used a nickname. Dara. Something, some recognition shimmered for a moment in his mind. Ancient. Persian. *Dara. Meaning from the dark one.*

Julian felt his heart jump at the connection. Could such a coincidence be just that? Gregori was referred to as the Dark One. As his father had been before him. The bloodline was pure, ancient, and very powerful. Why was her nickname Dara? Was there a connection? There had to be. But how?

Julian shook his head slowly, discarding the idea. No Carpathian lived unknown to the others of his kind. And certainly no Carpathian female could do so. Since the decimation of their ranks, the females were closely guarded, given from the father into the care of the life-mate at an early age to ensure the continuance of their race. Otherwise every unattached Carpathian male around the world would be following her, pressing his suit. And Mikhail would have her under the mantle of his protection.

Julian put the puzzle aside for the time being. He closed his eyes and concentrated on reaching Desari. Dara. Ordinarily, a blood exchange was needed to keep track of another, but Julian had studied and experimented for many years. He could do incredible things, even for one of his kind. He built the image of Desari in his mind, focusing on every detail.

Then he aimed and thrust his will into the night. Seeking. Drawing. Commanding. *Come to me*, cara mia, *come to me. You are mine. No one else will ever do for you. You want me with you. You need me. Feel the emptiness without me.*

Julian was implacable in his pursuit. He ruthlessly applied more pressure. *Find me. Know that you are mine. You cannot bear another's touch*, cara mia. *You need me with you to fill the terrible emptiness. You are no longer happy and content without me. You must find me.*

He sent the imperious command, his entire focus bent on finding her mental channel. He did not stop until he was certain he had connected with her, that his words had penetrated any barriers separating them and found their way to her soul.

Chapter Two

The police were everywhere. Desari carefully sat up, dizzy and sick. She felt strange, different, as if something inside her had changed for all time. There was an odd, yawning emptiness, a void that had to be filled. Her brother and bodyguard, Darius, had his arm around her. He examined every inch of her with his ice cold black eyes. There was blood staining her dress, and her insides ached.

"They shot me." She made it a statement.

"I do not know how I failed to detect the danger to you in time." Darius looked gray and drained.

Desari stroked his strong jaw. "You need to feed, brother. You have given me too much blood."

Darius shook his head, then glanced surreptitiously toward the police. "I gave to Barack and Dayan. They were hit also. Six mortals, Desari, all wanted to kill you."

"Barack and Dayan? Are they all right?" she demanded quickly, worry in her soft, dark eyes. She looked around frantically for the other two members of the band. She had been raised with the two men and loved them nearly as much as her own brother.

He nodded. "I have sent them to ground. They will heal more quickly. I had little time for proper mending, but I did my best for them. The police were pouring into the bar. I made certain they could not see us. We have trouble though. It was not me who gave you blood. It was another. He was strong and powerful."

Alarmed, Desari stared up at her brother. "Someone else gave me blood? You are certain? There is no mistake?"

Darius shook his head. "I would not have reached you in time. You were already unconscious. You did not have time to shut down your heart and lungs as the others did, so you bled profusely. I examined you afterward, Desari. You would have died of your wounds. He saved your life."

She dragged up her knees and burrowed closer to him. "His blood is in me?" She sounded lost and forlorn, frightened.

Darius swore eloquently. For centuries he had looked after his family. Desari, Syndil, Barack, Dayan, and Savon. The only others similar to their kind they had ever encountered had been the undead, the evil ones. This creature had slipped past him as a strange, cold wind that had pushed its way through the bar. Darius had been uneasy, worried; he had felt the presence of another, yet he had not caught the stench of evil. The undead. Vampire. He should have acted, he had been sidetracked by the vicious mortals emerging from the crowd.

Why had Desari been suddenly targeted by these people? Had his family members somehow given themselves away? He knew that from time to time throughout history there had been eruptions of hysteria among humans, particularly in Europe, about vampires. And over the last seventy-five years a string of murders in Europe had been attributed to members of some secret society hunting down these alleged creatures of the night.

Darius had purposely kept his family from that continent, not wanting to expose them to either these dangerous humans or to what could be the tainted blood of vampires. There was plenty of room in the world without going near Europe. His memories of his original homeland were vague and terrible. Marauders driving stakes through women and children still living, hanging them in the sun to die a death of excruciating pain. Beheadings, burnings, torture, and mutilation. If any of his race had survived, they had long ago turned vampire. If any other children had escaped as they had, they were probably better left unfound.

"Darius?" Desari clutched at his shirt. "You did not answer me. Am I going to turn? Did he make me the undead?" Her beautiful voice quavered with fear.

He circled her with one strong arm to comfort her, his face a hard, implacable mask of resolve. "Nothing is going to harm you, Desari. I would not allow it."

"Can we remove his blood, replace it with yours?"

"I sent myself into your body. I could find no evidence of evil. I do not know what he is, but I was able to mark him as he marked me." He lifted the arm he had clamped to his side. His palm came away from his belly coated in blood.

Desari gasped and went to her knees. "Seal your own wounds now, Darius. You have already lost too much blood. You have to tend to yourself."

"I am tired, Desari," he acknowledged softly.

The confession startled her. Shocked her. Terrified her. She had never once, in all their centuries together, remembered her brother admitting such a thing. He had gone into battle countless times, had been savaged by wild animals, wounded by mortals, had hunted and killed the most dangerous of all, the vampire.

She slipped her arm around his broad back. "You need blood, Darius, right now. Where is Syndil?" Desari knew she was far too weak herself to help her brother. She looked around the scene of chaos and realized her brother was still shielding them from the sight of the mortal policemen. He must have been maintaining the illusion for some time. That in itself was very draining.

She clenched her teeth and dragged him to his feet. "We will call Syndil, Darius. She must be hiding deep within the ground not to have been aware of this disturbance. It is time she came back to the world of the living."

Darius shook his head, but he leaned his towering frame against Desari. "It is too soon for her. She is still traumatized."

Syndil, we are in much trouble. You must come for us. You must heed our call. Desari sent for the woman she regarded as her closest friend and a sister. She felt sorrow for Syndil, outrage on her behalf, but they needed her now.

There had been six of them, children thrown together in a time of war and cruelty. Darius had been six years of age, Desari six months. Savon had been four. Dayan had been three, Barack two, and Syndil a year. They had grown up together, depending only on one another, looking to Darius for leadership, protection, and their very survival.

Their parents had been caught just before the sun was at its peak, weak and lethargic, paralyzed in the way of their race. The marauders had overrun the village and killed every adult, including the Carpathians attempting to aid them. Children had been herded like cattle into a shack and the building set on fire.

Darius had noticed a peasant woman escaping unseen by the attackers. Since the sun did not affect Carpathian children as severely as it did the adults, Darius had awaited his opportunity, hiding five younger children from the murderous insanity. He managed, through sheer force of his will, to cloak the presence of the human woman and the Carpathian children, even as he planted the compulsion in her to take them with her. Unaware of their race, she had led them down the mountains to the sea, where her lover had a boat. Despite their terror of the ocean, they had set out, more afraid of the cruelty and sheer numbers of the marauders than of sea serpents or sailing off the edge of the world.

Hidden in the boat, the children remained quiet. Afraid of the war, knowing of no safe shore, the man took the boat much farther than he ever had. High winds pushed it even farther out to sea. There a terrible storm buffeted the vessel until it broke up and went down, the mortals sinking beneath the rolling waves.

Darius had once again saved the children. Even at six he had been unusually strong, his father's blood pure and ancient. He took on the image of a powerful bird, a raptor, and, clutching the small ones in his talons, had flown to the nearest land mass.

Their lives had been extremely difficult in those early days, the coast of Africa still wild and merciless. Carpathian children needed blood but were unable to hunt. They also needed herbs and other nutrients. Even then most children did not survive their first year of life. It was a tribute to Darius's strength of will that all six children had survived. He learned to hunt with the leopard. He found the little ones shelter and soil and began to learn the healing arts. None of the lessons had been easy. He was sometimes wounded in his hunts. Many of his experiments failed or backfired. But he persevered, determined he would not allow any of them to die. He often poisoned himself trying new foods for the children, and he learned to force the poison from his own body.

Over the centuries they had stayed together, a family unit, Darius guiding them, always acquiring more knowledge, devising new ways to hide their differences from the humans they encountered, and even to invest money. He was powerful and determined. Desari was certain there was no other like him. His rule was unquestioned; his word was everything.

None of them had been prepared for the tragedy two months earlier. Desari could hardly bear to remember it. Savon had elected to lose his soul, giving himself over to the crouching beast, choosing to be completely dark. He had hidden the spreading evil stain even from those closest to him.

He had bided his time, awaited his opportunity, and then he had viciously attacked Syndil. Desari had never seen such a brutal assault on any woman. The men had always protected, treasured, and cherished the women. No one dreamed such a thing could happen. Syndil was sweet and trusting, but Savon had beaten her that day, mauled and raped her. He had nearly killed her, draining her of blood. Darius found them, directed by Syndil's frantic mental cries for help. So shocked that his closest friend had committed such a monstrous crime, he was nearly killed himself when Savon had attacked him.

Afterward, Syndil had been so hysterical, she allowed only Desari near her and only Desari to replace the blood she had lost. In turn Barack and Dayan had supplied Desari and Darius. It had been a tragic, horrible time, and Desari knew none of them had fully recovered yet.

Syndil now spent most of her time in the earth or

shape-shifting into a leopard. She rarely spoke, never smiled, and did not allow discussion of the attack. Dayan had grown quieter, more protective. Barack was the most changed. He had always seemed a playboy, laughing his way through the centuries, but for a month he, too, had stayed in the earth, and lately he was moody and watchful, his dark eyes following Syndil wherever she went. Darius was different, too. His black eyes were bleak and cold. He watched over the two women even more closely. Desari noticed he had also distanced himself from the men.

Syndil, come now! This time she gave the order in a firm, decisive voice. Darius was far too heavy for Desari, in her weakened state, to move. What had happened to Syndil was not her trauma alone. They had all suffered, all had been changed forever by it. They needed her. Darius needed her.

Syndil materialized beside them, tall and beautiful with her enormous sad eyes. She paled visibly when she saw the bloodstains on Desari, when she noted Darius swaying unsteadily on his feet, his face gray. Quickly she caught him, taking most of his weight. "The others? Where are they?"

"Darius gave them his blood, blood he could not afford to give up," Desari explained. "We were attacked by mortals with guns. Dayan and Barack were both hit too."

"Barack?" Syndil's pale face whitened even more. "And Dayan? Do they both live? Where are they?"

"They are in the healing earth," Desari assured her.

"Who would want to shoot you? And what happened to Darius?" Syndil urged Darius forward toward the troupe's bus. Under cover of darkness they made their way inside where Darius had left the two leopards after they aided him.

45

Christine Feehan

The moment they had Darius on the couch, Desari ripped away his shirt to expose his wounds. Syndil pushed closer. Her gaze narrowed speculatively. "A leopard did that."

"Something did it," Darius corrected grimly. "But he was no true leopard. Nor was he mortal. Whoever he was, he gave Desari blood." He shook his head and looked up at his sister. "He was strong, Desari, stronger than anything I have ever come up against."

Syndil bent to him. "You need blood, Darius. You must take mine." She refused to let her fear of being close to a male, the strongest in her family, allow her to shirk her duty. She was already ashamed that she had removed herself so far from the others that she had been unable to detect the danger to them all.

Darius's eyes, so dark they were black, drifted over her face. He could see everything, see into her very soul, see her aversion to touching a man. He shook his head. "Thank you, little sister, but I would prefer that you give your blood to Desari."

"Darius!" Desari protested. "You need it desperately."

Ashamed, Syndil hung her head. "It is for me he does this," she confessed softly. "I cannot bear to be touched by a male, and he knows it."

"If it were not necessary to dilute the blood of the intruder in Desari's veins," Darius objected softly, his voice soothing, "I would gladly accept your offering. If it is distasteful to you to do such a thing for me, then the offer is all the more valuable, and I thank you."

Darius, Desari warned, careful to use their own private mental wave, *Syndil is not strong enough to dilute the blood.*

This is a small thing to do for Syndil, Desari. Darius closed his eyes again and sank into himself, sealing off the worst of the claw marks and beginning the ritual to

46

heal each of the deep wounds from the inside out.

Syndil watched Darius's face, waiting until he was far from them in spirit, not heeding their conversation, before she spoke. "Is he lying to me?" she asked.

Desari stroked her brother's arm, choosing her words carefully, thoughtfully. "There was another besides the mortals. We do not know what he is. He saved my life, sealing off my wounds and giving me his blood. Darius attacked him; they fought. Apparently neither came out the victor."

Syndil studied Desari's face. "You are afraid. It is true then. You have this intruder's blood in you."

Desari nodded. "I feel different inside. He did something." She whispered the words aloud, for the first time admitting it to someone other than herself. "I am changed."

Syndil put an arm around Desari. "Sit beside Darius. You look as if you are going to fall on your face."

"I feel like it, too." Desari buried her face on Syndil's shoulder for a moment, hugging her tightly. "What would we do without him?"

"He will be fine," Syndil said softly. "Darius cannot be killed so easily."

"I know." Then Desari confessed her worst fear. "It is just that he has been so unhappy for so long. I am always afraid he will one day allow something or someone to destroy him so that he does not have to continue."

"We all have been unhappy," Syndil pointed out as she firmly pushed Desari to a sitting position. "How could what Savon did to me, to all of us, leave us unchanged? But Darius will not desert us. He would never do such a thing, not even in the guise of a carelessly received wound."

"Do you think he was careless then?" That frightened Desari even more. If Darius had been careless, it meant her fears were closer to the mark than ever.

"Take my blood, Desari. It is freely offered to you and Darius. I hope that it provides both of you with strength and peace," Syndil replied softly. She opened her wrist with one sharp nail and held it to Desari's mouth. "For Darius, if not for yourself."

Desari fed, then leaned down to her brother, whispering softly into his ear. "Take from me what is freely offered, brother, what you need. Take it for yourself and for all of us who depend so heavily on you. I offer up my life that you might live."

"Desari!" Syndil protested sharply. "Darius might not know what he does. You cannot say things like that."

"But it is true," Desari said softly, stroking back her brother's hair. "He is the greatest man I have ever known. I would do anything to save his life." She pressed her opened wrist to her brother's mouth. "What he has done for all of us, no other could have done. No other six-year-old could ever have saved us. It was a miracle, Syndil. He had no training, no one to guide him, yet he managed to keep us all alive. The life he gave us has been a good one. He deserves so much more than he has."

"You must take more of my blood, Desari," Syndil insisted softly. "You are so pale. Darius would be angry with you if he knew you did not feed properly. I insist, Desari. You must feed." To force the issue, Syndil reopened her own vein with her teeth and pushed her wrist to Desari's mouth. "Do as I say, little sister." She gave the order in her firmest voice.

It was so unlike Syndil, Desari was startled into obeying her. Syndil had a gentle, soft-spoken, and loving nature. She rarely did wild, unpredictable things the way Desari did. Desari was forever getting reprimanded by her brother, not that it did him much good. She always found something new and different to try. Always amazed at the beauty of the world around her, she found everything exciting, people intriguing. She was not content, as Syndil was, to do as the men instructed.

It wasn't as if she set out to defy Darius. She would never do that; no one would dare. She just ended up in trouble over lots of little things. For instance, Darius did not want Desari wandering off by herself, but she liked her privacy, and she enjoyed running in the forest, taking to the skies, swimming with fish. Life was bubbling over with so many opportunities for adventure, and Desari wanted to try everything. Darius, however, believed that vampires might be lurking anywhere, waiting to carry off the women, and he guarded them accordingly.

Desari closed the wound on Syndil's wrist, careful to leave no mark, then very gently pulled her own arm away from her brother, closing the laceration with the healing agent in her saliva. "Do you think he looks a little better, Syndil?" Darius was in the deep sleep of their people, his heart and lungs already shut down.

"His color is not so gray," Syndil agreed. "We must get him to ground, where he will have a chance to heal. Where did he send Barack and Dayan?"

"I do not know," Desari admitted. "I was unconscious."

"In any case, you need to go to ground to heal also. I will have to handle the inquiries with the police. I will tell them Darius spirited you and the band out of harm's way, that all of you were injured but the attack on your life did not succeed."

"They will want to know where we were treated," Desari objected. She was very tired, and the uneasiness in her was growing. She felt restless and unhappy, near tears, something unheard of for her.

"I can plant memories as well as any of you," Syndil

said firmly. "I may prefer solitude, but I assure you, Desari, I am every bit as capable as you."

Desari stroked back her brother's long dark hair. The silken strands fell past his broad shoulders in a shiny fall reminiscent of her own. Darius always looked so harsh and implacable when he was awake, a hint of cruelty about his finely chiseled mouth. Yet all that was gone when he was asleep. He looked young and handsome, without the tremendous responsibilities he always shouldered when he was awake.

"I do not like sleeping so close to mortals, especially when we are hunted," Desari said softly. "It is not safe."

"I am certain Darius took Barack and Dayan into the woods and ensured their safety. We will do the same for Darius. Desari, he may be wounded and tired, but he is powerful beyond even our knowledge. He can hear and feel things even when he is sleeping the sleep of our people."

"What do you mean?"

Syndil pushed at the thick braid falling over her shoulder. "That night Savon attacked me, Darius was deep in the ground healing from a wound. The rest of you were far away, hunting, and I had stayed to watch over his resting place. Savon called to me to met him in a cave to see a rare plant he had found." She bowed her head. "I went. I should have stayed to watch over Darius, but I went at Savon's call. I screamed for all of you to aid me, but you were too far to make it back in time. But Darius heard. Even from deep within the earth. Even from the healing sleep of our people, he heard and knew every detail; I felt him lock on to me. Wounded, he rose and came to save me."

"Darius heard you while he slept?" Desari, like the others, had assumed Darius had risen while they hunted. By the time she and Dayan and Barack had returned,

Darius had already destroyed Savon and was healing Syndil's terrible wounds even though he himself was weak from loss of blood.

Syndil nodded solemnly. "He came when I believed there was no hope for me." She bowed her head, her voice soft, filled with tears. "I feel so ashamed that I cannot control my sorrow and ease his pain. He feels guilty. He feels he failed me."

Desari lay her head protectively over her brother's chest. She knew Syndil was only half-correct. Darius believed he had failed Syndil, but he did not feel guilty. He did not feel at all. He hid his lack of emotion from all of them, but Desari was so close to him, she was well aware of it and had been for some time. It was only his intense loyalty and sense of duty that kept Darius fighting for them. It was not feeling.

She knew Darius feared for their safety should he ever turn as Savon had. She was certain, as was he, that neither Barack nor Dayan could defeat him in battle. She doubted even their combined strengths could do so. She believed Darius was invincible. He could not turn. To her, it was that simple. Whatever darkness in him that was growing, spreading, whatever the lack of feeling in him, he would never allow it to turn him. His will was far too strong. Darius had shown that from the very first. Nothing could sway him from his chosen path.

Unless, perhaps, he simply allowed himself to be honorably killed. That was Desari's prime concern, her deepest fear. She was frightened for all of them. Carpathian men had natures completely different from the women. They were dangerous, powerful predators, even when protective of women and mortals, they were dominating, arrogant, and thus truly perilous if they turned. It wasn't in Syndil's feminine nature to chafe under the males' constraints or to rebel against them. Desari alone did what she wanted and damned the consequences, which only served to make the men more dominating and protective. Yes, they would all be in grave danger if Darius were to die or turn vampire.

"You will have to drive the bus, Syndil," Desari instructed. "I will guard the rear to ensure we are not followed."

Syndil wished she could navigate the big vehicle and also cast an illusion over it to hide from the mortals, but it was impossible for her. She would have to leave it to Desari, even in her weakened state, to fashion as many blockades as possible to any that might follow them. They were evidently in danger from some murderous group of mortals.

"Go, Syndil," Desari said, making her way to the back of the bus.

Who was it that had saved her life, she wondered. Why had he done so? Darius said he could detect no evil, no tainted blood in her, and he should know. He had hunted and killed the undead often enough down through the centuries. He knew better than any of them the stench of tainted blood. He said it burned skin, raised blisters, and ate through flesh if left in contact too long. Darius had learned that bit of important information as he had everything else: the hard way.

Desari knelt on the bed at the back of the bus and stared out at the scene of dwindling chaos. Ambulances and police cars were pulling away, the crowd was beginning to disperse. She hadn't thought to ask Darius if any of their attackers had escaped. Knowing Darius, she doubted it, but he might have been so concerned with her, Barack, and Dayan that he had allowed some of those guilty to escape his particular brand of justice.

Syndil drove the bus with surprising expertise, and Desari kept her eyes glued behind them, watching for any lights trailing the vehicle. Suddenly her heart was in her throat, pounding in alarm. For some reason she didn't want to leave the bar. She felt she was leaving behind her destiny. She needed to be where he could find her. *He?*

Desari gasped and sank back onto the bed.

"What is it?" Syndil demanded, looking into the rear-view mirror. She could hear Desari's increased heart-beat, her sudden gasp of alarm. The blood was pumping through her veins far too fast. Syndil couldn't see any-one behind them. "What is it, Desari?" she repeated.

"I cannot leave this place," Desari said softly, sadly, sorrow in her heart. She pressed her hands to her pound-ing temples. "Let me out, Syndil. I must stay here."

"Breathe, Desari. Just breathe your way through it. Whatever happened to you, we can fix it," Syndil as-sured her, stomping harder on the gas pedal. She was not about to leave Desari anywhere in her condition.

Desari? The faint stirring in her mind was Darius. She recognized his touch, the natural arrogance in his voice. *Do you have need of me?*

I cannot go away from him. The creature who gave me blood has tied us together in some way. Darius, I am so frightened.

Syndil has given you good advice. Remain calm and think. Breathe. You are powerful, maybe every bit as much as this creature who is attempting to ensnare you. Use that power now. If you fear leaving him do not. He will come for you again. And this time I will be waiting.

There is a terrible emptiness in me. I cannot bear to go away from him. He is calling to me.

You hear him? Darius's voice in her mind was stronger, his interest caught despite his need to rest and heal. *You hear his voice?*

Desari shook her head, forgetting for a moment that her brother couldn't see her. Her arms were across her

Christine Feehan

stomach, and she was rocking herself back and forth for comfort. Her battered body was not nearly as painful as her aching soul. *No, it is not like that. Only a terrible wrenching, a feeling of being ripped apart. He is so strong, Darius. He will never let me go. Never.*

I will rid you of this creature, Desari.

Again she shook her head. *I do not think you can, Darius.*

I will not fail you.

Desari pressed the back of her hand to her trembling mouth. "You cannot," she whispered softly aloud. "If you kill him, he will take me with him when he goes."

Syndil gasped, her acute hearing picking up the thread of sound and sorrow from Desari. She had known Darius was communicating privately with his sister even in his deep sleep; Darius was strong even in the worst times. "Tell him, Desari. Tell Darius if you really believe that. You know no one can defeat Darius. It is impossible. He must know if what you say is true."

"He cannot help me this time. No one can," Desari said.

Syndil called to Darius inside her own mind, something she had not done since the violent attack on her. *Desari believes that if you kill this creature, he will take her with him from this world. And I believe that if she thinks he can do such a thing, she is in danger.*

There was a short silence, then Darius sighed softly. *Do not worry, little sister. I will think on what you have said and not move too quickly. Perhaps we need to learn more of this creature.*

Huddling on the bed, Desari cut herself off from the others. With each mile that took her farther from the bar, the oppressive dread seemed to increase. She could feel perspiration beading on her forehead. Her breath came in short, uncomfortable gasps. She had to find him.

She had to be close to him. He had somehow stolen the other half of her soul.

Desari bit down hard on her lower lip, welcoming the stinging pain that helped her to center herself. She closed her eyes and sought inside her own body. She could not find the stench of evil. She found her heart whole and strong. She found her soul complete. But she was no longer simply Desari. A stranger dwelled within her. A stranger who was somehow very familiar, more familiar than even her family.

After the first shock, she studied the evidence of his work. He was strong and powerful. Self-confident. Even arrogant. Very, very knowledgeable. And he meant to have her. She could feel his deep resolve. No one would stand in his way. Nothing would stop him. He would never give her up. And deep within him dwelled . . . a dark shadow.

Desari swallowed the fear choking her. Why was she so afraid of this unknown man? She was not without her own power. No one could force her to do what she did not want to do. Nor would Darius ever allow it. And she had Barack and Dayan to support her as well. Even Syndil would fight for her if the need arose. Why was she so afraid?

Because there was an excitement in her that she didn't want to admit even to herself. She was intrigued by the stranger, drawn to him. Her body wanted his, and she had never even laid eyes on him. How could he have wrought such a thing? Was he so powerful?

She didn't want Darius to harm him. The thought came unbidden and was, she felt, on the verge of disloyalty. She should not even think such things. Desari rubbed her forehead with the heels of her hands. Whoever he was, he would come for her, and she had to decide what to do. She could never leave her family.

Especially not now, when Darius was having such a hard time with his own darkness.

"Oh, God," she murmured aloud. "What am I thinking?"

You are in pain?

Desari's head snapped up, and she looked around the bus cautiously. The voice was clear, arrogant, a velvet purr. Not Darius. Her throat closed convulsively, making it nearly impossible to breathe. She felt a strength, a male's touch, his heart beating steadily, his lungs working easily, in and out, regulating her breathing as if they were one being. His voice was beautiful, and reached something deep in her soul. Yet he was using a mental path unfamiliar to her. The experience unnerved her.

Go away. She tried the path he was using.

She heard soft laughter, taunting male amusement. *I do not think so*, piccola. *Answer me. Are you in pain?*

Desari glanced around guiltily. Syndil was busy maneuvering the large motor home down a winding ribbon of highway leading deep into a wooded area. Desari felt as if she were talking to the devil himself, allowing him access to her family and their whereabouts through her. But she couldn't stop herself from feeling the sweeping excitement.

Of course I am in pain. I was shot. Who are you?
You know who I am.

She shook her head, her long mass of blue-black hair flying in all directions, catching Syndil's attention.

"Are you all right, Desari?" Syndil asked, a worried catch in her voice.

"Yes, do not worry," Desari managed to respond.

She felt his touch, his palm brushing her cheek. *You fear me.*

I fear no one.

There was that laughter again. Male amusement that made her want to strangle him.

What is the Dark One to you? he asked. There was no amusement in the question. It was an imperious command to answer him. He even pushed at her with a compulsion.

Furious, Desari cut off the contact. He thought her a mere mortal he could so easily command? How dare he? She was of ancient and powerful Carpathian blood. She deserved respect. No one, not even her brother, the leader of their family, would treat her with such disdain. Taking a deep breath, Desari calmed herself. Two could play at his game. She could track him as well. His blood was in her veins. If he could find her and try to "push" her, she could do the same. Desari went very quiet, allowing her mind to become a tranquil pool. She took her time searching each path until she found the one that would lead her to the stranger.

Who are you? She pushed him, gave a good, hard compulsion.

There was a silence. Then his infuriating laughter. *So, you are like your guard. Carpathian, not mortal after all. We have much to find out about one another. You are Carpathian, yet different.*

You did not take my blood. How is it you can track me? In spite of herself, Desari was impressed. She knew Darius could do such a thing, but Barack and Dayan could not. Nor could she. Yet. But she was always learning things from her brother.

Know this, cara, *you belong to me.*

Only if I wish it, she corrected him, angry all over again. His arrogance was astounding to her.

The bus shuddered to a stop, and Syndil turned in her seat. "This is a good place for us to hide, Desari. Can you help me get Darius to earth?"

Christine Feehan

Color swept up Desari's neck and into her face, and
she avoided Syndil's gaze. She did not want anyone to
know what she was doing. "Yes. I am feeling much
stronger now, thanks to you, Syndil," she answered.

What a little liar you are, the taunting male voice
informed her.

Stay away from me.

You want me. His voice was a drawling caress.

You wish. Desari forced herself to her feet and staggered down the aisle to her brother's side.

Desari and Syndil focused their attention on Darius
and lifted him between them, using only the power of
their minds. The cats pushed close, trying to see for
themselves that Darius was fine. Without warning, Desari's strength increased. Startled, she looked at Syndil.
But she knew it was the stranger lending her his power.

Go away. Just go away. Desari stumbled on the bottom step but recovered. Darius's body didn't so much
as waver.

"You are practically carrying him by yourself," Syndil
said admiringly.

I injured him. The words were said with a deep satisfaction, but the stranger continued to provide Desari
with the necessary strength to keep from dropping Darius to the ground.

She refused to acknowledge his statement. Angry with
herself for her disloyalty, for even wanting to converse
with the stranger, Desari waved a hand to open the
ground for her brother's body. She knew the stranger
was dwelling in her, but she was fully aware of her own
power. He could not read what she did not want him to
know as long as she remained on the alert for his invasion.

Darius floated into the earth. Healing soil poured over
his body. Sasha, the female leopard, lay on top of the

58

spot. Desari opened the earth beside her brother and entered, grateful for the soothing tranquillity nature offered as it healed her body and mind.

"Sleep well, little sister," Syndil whispered. "Do not fear. I will take care of all the details and loose ends before I seek rest this night. Heal, Desari, and be safe."

"Watch yourself, Syndil. There may be other assassins," Desari cautioned. She closed her eyes and let the earth surround her.

The last thing she felt as she shut down her body was a male hand brushing her face in a slow, heart-melting caress. The last thing she heard before her heart ceased to beat was his voice. *I will come to you,* piccola. *I will always be near should you have need of me.*

Chapter Three

Security was tight at the singing troupe's next sold-out concert. Policemen and security personnel were visible everywhere. No one was taking any chances this time, treating Desari as if she were a national treasure. Every entrance was heavily guarded and each person checked with a metal detector before being admitted. Dogs roamed the aisles with their handlers, and Darius oversaw it all. He was not about to allow assassins a second chance at his sister.

The police had searched for the suspects in the attempted murders during the past week, but they could not find a trace of them. A good amount of blood had been discovered leading from the tavern, but no bodies. The police were certain that at least one suspect had died and his companions had removed the corpse, but Darius knew better. He had killed every one of the assailants and left them in plain sight for whoever had sent them to discover. Someone had interfered, and he suspected just who it was.

Darius continually scanned the crowd, his black eyes moving unceasingly over the people pushing to enter the building. Besides the assassins he had to worry about, he knew the creature would come tonight. Desari hadn't said anything of the sort to him, but she was restless and emotional, completely unlike herself. Several times he had reached to touch her mind with his, only to find it closed to him. He could have pushed past the barrier with some effort, but he respected her right to privacy.

Julian, dressed in faded blue jeans and a sleeveless black T-shirt, moved with the crowd toward the doors. He spotted Desari's security guard instantly and took a few minutes to study him. More than ever the man reminded him of Gregori. He was tall, as Carpathians tended to be, but he carried more muscle than most males of their race. Gregori was muscular also. The security guard's face was a chiseled mask of harsh beauty, very reminiscent of the healer, but his eyes were black ice, where Gregori's were silver.

The guard's eyes glinted with menace and seemed to miss nothing as they moved over the crowd. Julian did not want to call attention to his own presence by using any kind of power. Already the security guard had spotted him, those soulless black eyes resting thoughtfully on him as the line he was in moved closer to the entrance. Julian made certain his brain patterns were the same as a mortal's. A grim smile of amusement touched his mouth. It was like a game of chess. The thoughts he presented to a mind probe were those of any human male about to see an impossibly beautiful, sexy singer performing in person.

He felt the presence in his mind, the sharp thrusting,

the quick scan, then the release. Julian nearly laughed aloud, but he kept his face a blank mask. Even the light, decisive touch was reminiscent of Gregori. Whoever this guard was, Julian was certain he was related to the healer, the one all Carpathians referred to as the Dark One. The guard had to be of the same bloodline. The puzzle intrigued him. The man's presence irritated him. He didn't want any Carpathian male near Desari until the ritual mating cycle was complete.

The probe came again, a direct, powerful thrust into his mind. The attitude was so like the Dark One's, Julian was astonished. The guard was not swallowing his innocent act. Julian kept his mind in the human pattern, evincing only anticipation and harmless if somewhat erotic wishing. It was irritating to allow someone into his mind, but he reminded himself that the intruder was picking up only what he was deliberately broadcasting.

Julian carefully avoided looking at the guard. The male was far too sharp. Even after two mind probes to assure himself, he sensed power. Julian was suspect, and the guard was intuitive enough to keep coming back to him. Julian felt the weight of those burning eyes. This man held real power. He had to be one of the ancients, with the blood and strength of centuries of learning. Julian wished he were in a position to probe the guard, but it was imperative to appear human until he knew more. He had once spent centuries searching, accepting his solitary existence even as he scanned the earth for remnants of their kind. Now, when he had nearly ended his life, he had found a band of his people. The mythical lost ones? They must be.

But Desari belonged to him. And if the other male thought differently, he was in for a hard lesson. Julian moved into the building and away from those black, prying eyes. Only then did he realize he was excited. He liked challenges. He had always craved knowledge. And he could feel the power and strength he had accrued pursuing information and skills of every kind. A contest with this other powerful male could prove quite interesting.

He moved easily, maneuvering through the crowd down toward the front. Instead of seating himself, he took up a position along the wall near an exit. Inhaling, he scented the presence of two jungle cats, the same two that had worked in conjunction with the huge black panther. Julian was now certain that the guard had shape-shifted into the form of the large predator. Although the guard showed no evidence of the wounds Julian knew he had inflicted, he was still certain the man had been the panther directing the others in their attack on him.

Desari. He found himself smiling. Their brief mental exchange had been a revelation. She was Carpathian! How she had managed to run around the world undetected was still a mystery. There were remnants of their race, and he had found them! He had always wondered if some of the children had escaped the Turk invasion and scattered. On behalf of their race, at Gregori and Mikhail's urging, Julian had sought them, particularly the females, in hopes of finding a way to save his people.

And he had found Desari, his own lifemate, when he had been seeking lifemates for others. And she had a temper, this woman. He found himself laughing aloud, remembering her "push" at his mind. She was much stronger than he had anticipated. He had gone from a stark, barren existence to one filled with excitement in the blink of an eye.

The mood of the crowd was almost electric, the air

thick with anticipation. Desari's performances were always sold out. It didn't matter where she played, whether a small tavern or a huge stadium. And with the publicity following the recent attempt on her life, she was even more of an celebrity. Reporters, too, were out in numbers.

Julian listened to the conversations in the arena, sifting through them, looking for a whisper of conspiracy. He knew the fanatical nature of the human vampire-hunting society. Desari was a marked woman now. They would not stop with one attack. But Julian was fairly certain the society would need time to recover from the huge blow they had so recently received. He was more concerned now with the threat from vampires. The presence of a Carpathian woman nearby was sure to draw the creatures. And her safety was now of paramount personal importance to him.

Without warning it struck. An intense need to leave the dome, to get out. The feeling, a dark, oppressive dread, beat at him, swamped him, and for a moment he could barely breathe. Furious that he had left himself open for such an assault from the guard, he allowed himself to slump against the wall, the heel of one palm pressed to his forehead in a manner of distress while he carefully sought out the position of the guard.

Only then did it hit him. The touch was feminine, not masculine. Desari. He countered the compulsion to leave with a search of his own. He gathered his strength and waited. She was in a dressing room, seated on a stool. Julian inhaled her scent, taking it into his body. She was nervous. Not about her performance, but because she knew he was there. She was afraid of what he might do.

Julian smiled, his white teeth gleaming like a predator's. He fed her fear a bit. Not sharply, but with a simple, gentle flow of information. He was there. He was strong. Invincible. Nothing, no one could stop him. She could not possibly send him away.

Desari's right hand went to her slim throat in a gesture of protection. She knew the stranger was close by. Waiting. Watching. She could feel the weight of his presence. She could feel Darius's uneasiness. She was afraid. What was the stranger going to do? She couldn't bear it if Darius and he got into another fight. Someone would die. The stranger was so strong, he might kill Darius.

Her head jerked up, fury washing through her. No one could defeat Darius! That cad. He was amplifying her fears, her agitation. *Stop it, you!*

That irritating, mocking, male laughter echoed in her mind. *You started it. If you want to play games,* cara mia, *I am more than willing.*

I do not want you here.

Yes, you do, Julian countered calmly. *I am in you. I feel your excitement at my presence. The same excitement is in me.*

You feel my agitation. I have a job to do. Your presence is unsettling.

Only because you are afraid of your future. You know it lies with me. A major change in life can be frightening. But I can do nothing other than to make you happy.

Desari pounced on that. *It would make me happy if you left this place. I do not want you and Darius to fight.*

The first is a lie, cara. *You seem to be able to tell untruths easily. But I will respect the second. I will avoid a confrontation with your guard if it is at all possible.*

You do not understand. Desari was beginning to feel desperate. She had to find a way to make him leave. She didn't dare risk his presence, even if what he said was true, that she secretly wanted him there. She had never felt so alive. Every cell in her body was like her music, wild, free, soaring. She didn't understand it, but it was exhilarating. And he knew it.

I understand, piccola. His voice was tender, almost caressing. It slipped under her skin, producing an unexpected curl of heat in her bloodstream. *Trust me.*

Desari was battling unfamiliar emotions. In all the centuries of her existence, she had never felt such a sizzling chemistry. She had actually feared that nothing would ever make her feel the erotic longings she had heard and read of for so many centuries. Her body had been cold and unresponsive until now. She had never laid eyes on this stranger, yet he easily evoked this reaction. *I do not know you. How can I trust you?*

You know me. He said it in that same soft, arrogant voice. A statement of fact. Simple. Easy.

A loud knock on the door of her dressing room set her nerves jangling. She should have known someone was right outside. She had never before failed to be aware of the presence of the others. She rose and smoothed the silken sheath that fit her every curve. The slit up one side was nearly to her hip. The fabric was white with a garden of red roses. Her hair fell in a cascade of ebony silk past her hips and moved with a life of its own. For the first time in her life, it mattered that she looked good.

"Desari! Get a move on!" Barack rapped his fist against her door a second time. "The crowd is beginning to get restless."

Taking a deep breath, she stepped out into the hall. Barack's arm instantly swept around her shoulders. "What were you doing in there?" He glanced around, then lowered his head toward hers. "You are not afraid, are you? We are all on alert this time, even the cats. Those assassins will not have a second chance at you."

"I know." Desari's voice came out low and husky. "I

will be fine, Barack. Please do not say anything to Darius. He is already jumpy enough."

"Do not mistake Darius. He does not fear a return of the assassins. He thinks the other creature will return for you this night." Barack matched his longer strides to hers as they moved through the hall toward the entrance to the stage.

Dayan fell into step on her other side. "Darius will destroy this creature."

Desari's dove-soft eyes darkened to black opal. "Why do all of you insist on referring to him as the creature? Have you become as intolerant as the mortals now? I thought we were one with all of nature, with the universe itself. Because he is something we do not know, must we hate him? Reject him? He saved my life. That should count for something. Or would you prefer that I had died?"

Dayan caught her arm. "Little sister, you need not defend this creature."

Instantly she heard a soft growl of warming in her mind. The stranger was not happy with another male touching her. Now they were all annoying her!

Desari pulled her arm free, gave Dayan a look of pure disdain, and swept out onto the stage. The roar of the crowd was so tremendous, it filled the dome and burst into the sky. She smiled, her gaze wandering over the mass of people rising out of their seats to pay homage to her voice, to her music. But she was looking for one man. Only one.

Unerringly she found him, her gaze locking with his, and her heart stood still. For a moment she couldn't breathe as her dark eyes met molten gold. He was standing against a wall, in the shadows, but his face was a carved creation of sensual beauty. His gaze was hot,

Christine Feehan

burning with possession. Desari's mouth went dry, and her body seemed to go up in flames.

Do not look at me that way! The words formed in her mind on their private mental path before she could censor them.

I cannot help how I look at my lifemate, he responded. *You are so beautiful, you take my breath away.*

The way he said it, the way his voice brushed at her insides, tugged at her heart and brought sudden tears to her eyes. He was so intense, his voice truthful and hungry. Her entire being responded to him. She almost missed her cue as Dayan and Barack played the notes to her opening song. But then she sang for him. To him. Each note a haunting blend of mystery and magic.

Each note sank into Julian's pores, seeped into his soul. Desari was incredible. She captivated the entire audience. The arena was so silent, not even the shuffling of feet interrupted her song. The crowd could feel each separate note, see it shimmering like a flame dancing in the air. They smelled the sea she sang of, felt the rise and fall of the waves. She brought tears to their eyes, peace to their hearts. Julian couldn't take his eyes off her. He was mesmerized by her, enthralled completely. He found himself painfully aroused and surprisingly proud.

Darius's black gaze strayed often to the man leaning with deceptive laziness against the far wall. He was tall and handsome. Power oozed from him, radiated around him. At the moment his strange, molten-gold eyes were fixed on Desari, his attention seemingly consumed by her performance. But Darius was not deceived. This was a predator. Not necessarily evil, but he had come here hunting. And his prey was Desari. There was a hard edge to his mouth, a stark possessiveness reflected in the depths of those burning eyes. Darius knew this man was a dangerous adversary.

Julian's eyes never once wavered from Desari's face. She was the most beautiful woman he had ever seen. On stage, in the midst of the rising theatrical fog and floodlights, she looked ethereal, mystical. A woman of erotic dreams, of fantasies. His body was completely still, nearly a part of the wall behind him, as if she had somehow absorbed every bit of his energy.

Darius moved closer, cloaking his presence as he did so. He stalked with the silent advance of the leopard, counting on the stranger's being caught up in the spell Desari wove around her audience. He was within four rows of his destination when a soft warning growl stopped him in his tracks. He knew no one else had heard that low rumble. It was directed solely at him. The stranger hadn't changed position, hadn't taken his eyes off the stage, away from Desari, but Darius suddenly knew the stranger's complete attention was centered on him.

On stage, Desari faltered, missing two lines of her song. Her heart was beating in her throat. *Oh, God, please do not do this.* Terror was in her voice, concern for him, for both of them.

Julian deliberately turned his head toward Darius and smiled, a show of gleaming white teeth. He straightened, his body fluid and supple. Two fingers touched his forehead in a mock salute directed at Darius. Muscles rippled suggestively beneath the thin T-shirt. He sauntered unhurriedly to the exit, arrogance in every step. His amber eyes glinted with menace until he swung his gaze back to Desari. Then his eyes burned possessively, intently, a molten gold that turned her to liquid heat.

For you, cara mia. His voice moved through her body with the same inflammatory heat of his gaze.

Desari wanted to run after him. She stood on the stage and sang to a crowd of several thousand, but her mind and her heart and soul were somewhere else. Dayan and Barack were watching her closely, puzzled, worried by her strange behavior. Desari had never faltered, never missed a beat in all their long centuries of singing on stage.

Darius followed the stranger out of the dome. The man was gone, dissolved into mist in the night air. Darius sensed him, felt the power in the air, but dared not leave his sister to pursue her pursuer. Something about the man gave him pause. He looked at Desari with more than lust in his gaze. More than possession. He looked at her protectively. Darius was nearly certain the stranger was not out to harm her. He was also certain the man had not left out of fear. Nothing would scare him. He walked with the confidence born of many battles, much hardship, and enormous knowledge.

Darius looked up into the night. Whoever the stranger was, he had left out of deference to Desari's wishes, not because he feared a battle with Darius. Darius sighed and turned back to the dome. He did not need this worry at this time. The assassins stalking Desari required his full attention. It bothered him that his intruder had arrived on the very day someone had tried to kill her. And to make matters worse, Darius had been convinced for some time that the most evil of all enemies stalked his beloved sister—the undead.

Desari saw her brother return. Anxiously she studied his face. It was the same mask of harsh sensual beauty he always wore. He had no visible wounds. She was certain she would have felt the disturbance if the two men had fought. Her singing had always flowed from her, a beautiful creation as mysterious and wonderful to her as it was to everyone else. Now it was difficult to create, with her mind in chaos, her throat closing off, being so near to tears.

70

Where was he? Was he alive? Was he all right? She wanted to scream, to run off the stage, away from the thousands of prying eyes, away from her family who watched her so closely. She was uncertain for a moment if she could continue the concert.

Sing for me, cara mia. *I love the sound of your voice. It is a miracle. You bring me peace and joy when you sing. You make my body burn as it never has before. Sing for me.*

The voice was low and husky, brushing away her inner chaos as if it had never been. Just like that her voice soared free, rising to fill the dome, to burst out into the night to find him. The feelings in her body, the pent-up passion, the wild hunger, the need of centuries poured into her voice. She was a living flame, moving across the stage like flowing water. Nothing could touch her; she was not of the earth.

Somewhere her lover waited. His eyes were on her. Watching. He was burning, too. She could feel the heat of his skin, the hungry eyes never leaving her face. He had left the dome, but he had returned because he needed to see her. Nothing else mattered at that moment. Not the danger to him, not her family, only that he see her perform. She sang for him, to him, the strength and intensity of her need in each note. The burning flame heating her blood took her music to new heights. Wildly erotic heights, whispering of silken sheets and candlelight.

Julian could not take his eyes from her. She was so beautiful, he could barely find it in him to breathe. This was the one? His lifemate? No one, least of all him, deserved such a woman. She reached into his dark soul and touched something good in him, something he hadn't known existed.

In all the world, no one sang like she did. Her voice

was mesmerizing, enthralling; it wrapped one up in a silken web of passion and held him there. Julian's body reacted in a savage, primitive manner. He wanted her as he had never wanted anything else in his existence. He wanted the concert over, yet he wanted it to go on for all time.

The walls of the dome seemed to have fallen away as she created the illusion of a dark, mystical forest, of cascading waterfalls, deep pools, and hungry fire with her voice alone. The images would never leave his mind, the erotic picture of her swimming to him, her arms eagerly outstretched to greet him.

The audience rose to their feet, their applause thunderous. Julian knew the reviews would be raving. He was proud of her, but at the same time he objected to her performance. Such publicity went against his every instinct. It would only serve to draw more unwanted attention to her. He knew what reporters would write. That she was an enchantress, weaving a spell over the audience.

Desari returned for one encore, tired but exhilarated. This time it wasn't simply because she knew she had performed well, had shared her extraordinary gift with others. It was because, somewhere in the darkness, a man waited for her. A stranger already familiar to her. It was terrifying yet exciting. She took her bows, her body humming with life. She wanted to run off the stage, to join him.

She wanted to see those eyes. Those beautiful, unusual, oh, so hungry eyes watching her. Staring at her. Those eyes that saw only her. Desari waved to the crowd and hurried off stage, moving down the hall to her dressing room. Barack and Dayan paced at her side, uneasy because of her strange behavior. Both had felt the presence of power in the dome. Who could not? But they had complete confidence in Darius. They would follow his lead, and so far, he was not hunting down the creature.

She didn't look at either of them as she firmly closed the door to her dressing room. Sinking into a chair, she slipped off her sandals. She could feel him. Somewhere close. Desari rinsed off her stage makeup and waited, her heart beating, her lungs barely breathing. She knew he was near. Darius must know it, too.

A fine mist streamed under the door, collecting in a spiral close to her. She held her breath. Instantly the handsome, ruthless stranger shimmered into a solid mass beside her. Her heart slammed. Up close he was frightening. Enormously strong. His finely chiseled features were sensual, hard. His countless victories in battle over the centuries were in the set of his broad shoulders, in the grim composure of his face. He was strikingly handsome yet immeasurably intimidating at the same time.

Desari's tongue touched her suddenly dry lips. "You should not be here. It is too dangerous."

His body clenched at the sound of her voice. It was so soft, it seemed to seep through his skin to wrap around his heart. "I could do nothing other than see you tonight. I think you know that."

"Darius would destroy you if he found you here." She believed it, and her fear showed in her soft, charcoal eyes.

His hard mouth softened, his golden eyes warming at her needless concern. "I am not so easily destroyed. Do not worry, *piccola*, I have made a promise to you this night, and I fully intend to honor it." His voice dropped another octave, his eyes consuming her as he spoke. "Come with me."

She felt her heart jump again. Every cell in her body cried out to go. His gaze was a smoldering heat she could not resist. There was so much hunger in him, such dark intensity, burning for her. The devil tempting her. Resolutely she shook her head. "Darius would—"

Julian stopped her words by simply enveloping her smaller hand with his. His touch sent darts of fire racing up her arm and through her torso, taking the very breath from her lungs. "I grow weary of hearing of this Darius. You should be more concerned with what I will do if he attempts to stop me from taking you with me."

Temper flared in her eyes. "No one can take me anywhere I do not wish to go. You have as much arrogance in you as my brother does. I happen to know he has earned the right to it. Have you?"

A small, satisfied smile curved his mouth. "So this Darius is your brother. I find that something of a relief. As you hold him in some esteem, I did not want to have to destroy your illusions of his greatness."

She glared at him, furious, until she caught the glint of humor in his golden eyes. He was teasing her. Desari found herself laughing with him.

"Come with me tonight," he said. "We will go for a walk. Dance somewhere. It does not matter, *cara*, and we will be hurting no one." His voice was black velvet. A sorcerer's whisper of temptation. "Is this so much to ask of you? He does not allow you to choose your own friends? Do as you wish?"

Julian had looked into her mind, seen her need for independence, her constant chafing at the restraints put on her. Still, no self-respecting Carpathian male would ever allow a woman to wander around unprotected. He did not blame Darius; it was his duty to protect Desari. In his place, he would do the same. There were many unanswered questions to ask Desari, but right now, the only thing that mattered to him was her answer to the one he had posed.

She was silent, long lashes concealing her warring emotions. More than anything she wanted to go with him, have just one night of freedom to do as she liked. But she knew Darius. He would never allow such a thing. There was nowhere they could go that he would not find them. And that only served to make her want to go all the more. Her mysterious stranger had struck a nerve. She hated being constantly told what to do or not do. She wanted this one night just for herself.

Desari looked up at him. "I do not even know your name."

He bowed with Old World elegance. "I am Julian Savage. Perhaps you have met or heard of my brother, Aidan Savage. He and his lifemate reside in San Francisco." His white teeth gleamed. His golden eyes burned her.

Something in that intense, possessive, hungry gaze made her knees go weak. Desari pressed backward until she was against a solid wall to help hold her up. "Savage. Somehow it suits you."

He acknowledged her words as if they were a great compliment, bowing once more at the waist in his courtly manner. "Only to my enemies, *piccola*, never to those under my protection."

"Is that supposed to put me at ease?" she asked.

"You have nothing to fear from me, Desari."

His hand brushed her face in the lightest of caresses; she felt a jolt of electricity right down to her toes. He was too intense, too hungry for her, his eyes burning with need. Desari lowered her lashes, trying to shut him out, trying to prevent him from trapping her with his power and need. This was so dangerous. Could she risk his life? Risk Darius for a momentary pleasure? Could she possibly be that selfish?

"I scare you to death." He said it with certainty, his

voice soft and hypnotic, beautiful and soothing. "More than your fear for your brother or for me, you fear what will happen if you part from me."

She took a deep breath, found her hands were trembling, and put them behind her back. "Perhaps you are right. Why risk so much for so short a time?"

His hand framed one side of her face, his thumb feathering over her soft skin, absorbing the perfection of it before finding a resting place over the frantically beating pulse in her neck.

Desari's heart nearly stopped. Her words came out strangled. "You cannot touch me like this."

His thumb moved back and forth in a hypnotic rhythm over her pulse. "I can do no other than touch you, Desari. I am, after all, a Carpathian male. You cannot see yourself, in that dress you wear, with your hair tumbling around you. You are so beautiful, it hurts to look at you."

"Julian, please do not say such things to me," she whispered into his palm.

"It is only the truth, *cara*, nothing for you to fear. Come with me."

His voice was such temptation. She had never wanted anything more in her life. The pull between them was electric. She swore she could hear it sizzle and arc. She stood there in silence, his hand against her skin sending waves of heat rushing through her blood. In all her centuries she had never experienced such a thing.

"Desari, you know it is right. You feel it. I promise to return you to your family safe and sound this rising." Julian was aware of the men gathering outside her door. Three of them. One was her formidable brother, the other two members of the band. "We do not have much time, *piccola*. The others are about to break through the door." He waved a hand in a peculiar pattern, then held his palm out toward the door.

"I cannot."

"Then I must stay here and convince you," he said unhurriedly, calmly. As if his death weren't imminent at the hands of her protective family.

She clutched his arm. "You must go before this thing escalates into violence. Please, Julian."

He could hear her heart beating wildly. He bent his head to hers, his mouth curving into a genuine smile. "Come to me. Promise you will meet me at the small tavern three blocks from here."

There was a loud popping sound from the other side of the door, and someone—it sounded like Barack—swore aloud. They could both hear Darius reprimand him softly, "I told you not to touch the door. Have some respect." His voice was low and hypnotic. "Desari?" He didn't raise his voice but rather dropped it to a whisper. "Open the door for us."

"Go out the window," Desari insisted, pushing at the wall of Julian's chest. It was a mistake to touch him; he instantly responded by covering her hand with his, trapping her palm against his heavy muscles.

"I came through the door, *cara*, and I intend to leave the same way. Do you meet me later, or shall we stay together here?"

She could feel the beat of his heart beneath her palm. Steady. Solid. Not in the least affected by the fact that he was hunted by three powerful predators just a door's width away. His thumb was feathering back and forth across the back of her hand, feeding the flames already leaping in her body. Desperately Desari attempted to shake him off. He was a rock, unmoving. "What am I going to do with you?" she demanded.

"Say you will meet me. Do not allow your brother to

rule your life." He could smell the leopards now, knew they had joined the three men and were pacing restlessly in the hall.

Desari knew it, too. "All right. I promise," she capitulated. "Just go before something terrible happens."

He bent his head and brushed her soft, trembling mouth with his. It was the lightest of kisses, but a gentle lingering, yet she felt it touch her heart, her soul. He smiled at her, his golden eyes burning with molten heat. With need. "So, *piccola*, open the door."

Desari's fingers curled in his cotton T-shirt. "No, you do not understand. You cannot go out there."

"Remember your promise to me, Desari. Come to me." Julian bent his head one last time to her because he had to. She smelled fresh and clean, a breath of air from the highest mountains he loved so. Her skin was softer than rose petals. His body was making harsh urgent, relentless demands. Julian controlled them, but he needed to touch her, to feel her response, to feel the burning flames in her matching the firestorm in him. For he was on fire.

His mouth found hers. Hot. Demanding. Dominating. His hand went to the nape of her neck, holding her perfectly still so he could explore her sweetness. He was lost instantly, feeding on her, his posture aggressive. His arms swept her into the shelter of his body, so close it was impossible to tell where one started and the other left off.

A rumbling growl from outside the door had Desari struggling, pushing at him, her eyes wide with fear for him. "He will kill you. Please, please go while you can."

She looked so beautiful, for a moment he couldn't breathe, couldn't think. Slowly a smile took the edge of hunger from his mouth. "Come to me, *cara*. I will keep you to your promise." His hand slid slowly, reluctantly from the nape of her neck, and he stepped away.

"Desari." It was Darius's soft, compelling voice. "He has safeguarded the door against us. Only you are safe from its harm. You must open the door for us. Once you touch it, you will break his spell, and we will be allowed entry. Do as I bid."

Desari watched as Julian's solid form shimmered, then dissolved into nothing. She looked around quickly. He had to be something. Somewhere. Her frantic gaze searched her dressing room. There was no mist. Nothing. She walked to the door, her hand hovering over the knob. Where could he have gone? He had not left by way of the window. It was still closed tightly, the blinds drawn.

Very slowly she opened the door. Her brother's shoulders filled the door frame. His features were dark and merciless, his black eyes icy cold. "Where is he?"

Barack and Dayan were solidly behind him, cutting off any escape route, and what was worse, the two leopards prowled behind them, back and forth, a low warning rumbling in their throats.

Desari's chin lifted. "I want him left alone. He saved my life."

"This man is more dangerous than you think," Darius informed her softly. "You do not know anything about him." He walked into her dressing room, his probing eyes searching restlessly, missing nothing. "He is here, in your room. I can feel his presence, his power." Darius abruptly caught Desari's arm and pulled her close to him, inhaling sharply. "Did he take your blood?" He gave her a little shake.

Desari shook her head as she struggled, trying to jerk away. Darius unexpectedly released her, cursed softly, and put his hand to his mouth. His palm was singed. The black eyes continued scanning the room.

Barack and Dayan crowded in, gaping at the damage

done to Darius. "He is here. I feel him," Dayan echoed, a bite to his voice.

How could you do such a thing? You hurt Darius, Desari accused Julian, near tears. She had never been so emotional in all the centuries of her existence. It was like being on a roller coaster. Disloyalty and guilt were now pushing in hard and fast.

He is already healing his palm. He should know better than to grab you like that. It is unacceptable to me. Julian's voice was lazy and confident. He sounded complacent, as if he found it all amusing while she was afraid.

I should tell him where you are, Desari snapped, exasperated at his tone, his arrogance. Men were so irritating sometimes.

You do not know where I am. But if you wish it, by all means, tell your brother what you think. I give you my permission.

Desari's teeth clenched, but a hiss of complete annoyance escaped. It was a good thing he had dissolved; otherwise, she would be tempted to strangle him with her bare hands.

Darius flicked his cold gaze over her. "He speaks to you. What does he say?"

"Enough to make me want to slap him," Desari snapped. "Come, let us leave this place."

Barack yelped triumphantly. "He is the dust in the room. Look at the way it falls in an unnatural pattern around the floor and along the windowsill." Secretly he was proud of himself for spotting it before Darius or Dayan. "Perhaps we should do some cleaning up in here." He had his own burned palm from touching the door.

Desari paled visibly. "No. I told you, I want him left alone."

Barack deliberately stepped on a pile of dust particles and, ground them into the floor. "He cannot walk in here and think to have you. He has beguiled you in some way, Desari. It is our duty to protect you from one such as this."

Darius dropped an arm around his sister's shoulders. "Do not fear for this one, Dara. He is far too cunning to be caught in the dust on the floor. It is too obvious a ploy. He set it there to deceive us. Come, let us go. He is even smaller than what you see on the floor. Probably only tiny molecules in the air, and impossible, at this moment, to destroy." He looked around the room and up toward the ceiling. "I have used just such a method to escape detection myself on a few occasions. We will leave this place. I trust you have said your good-byes."

Desari went with her brother, confident he would not lie to her. Dayan and Barack, just to make sure, swept up the dust and ran it under water until it dissolved down the drain. Satisfied they had rid themselves of the "creature," the two of them left to hunt for sustenance, leaving Darius to deal with his wayward sister.

Chapter Four

Desari slipped out of the bus dressed in soft, faded blue jeans. Her shirt was ribbed cotton, V-necked, and form fitting. Deliberately she had not fed this night and kept hunger uppermost in her mind, knowing Darius might scan her. He had gone off to feed and might occasionally check on her.

His lecture had been long and severe. Desari was feeling especially defiant and a little bit desperate. She had promised Julian she would meet him, and she knew if she didn't show up, he would come for her.

This is very dangerous. She searched for him, sending out her exasperated distress. *Darius and the others will be watching me.*

There was a moment of silence, just long enough that she thought perhaps she hadn't connected on the correct path with him. Completely unperturbed, totally arrogant, Julian responded. *If you prefer, Desari, I will be more than happy to meet with them and discuss this rationally.*

*You belong with me. They cannot interfere. And just who
are those other two clowns? Do not try to convince me
that they are also your brothers.*

*I do not think I know you well enough to tell you my
family's business,* she replied haughtily.

*Do not deliberately provoke me, cara mia. I will admit
to being a jealous man. Our males have never been famous for allowing their women to associate with other
men.*

I do not belong to you. I belong to myself.

Desari sighed as she made her way from the motor
home down the street toward the tavern where she had
promised Julian she would meet him. She shook her
head. This was so ridiculous. Darius could track her at
will. Men were beyond her understanding, even after
centuries of trying to figure them out. Not one of them
made any real sense.

*Darius does not have the right to rule your life any
longer, piccola. That is the right of your lifemate, not
your brother.*

Desari stopped dead in her tracks. He sounded so
complacent, so insolent. Conceited. Overbearing. Arrogant. What was she doing?

His laughter echoed softly in her head and brushed
little flames over her skin. *You want to come to me. You
know you have to come to me. Nothing can stop you. It
is inevitable, like the tide. There can be no turning back.*

Her feet were moving of their own volition, pulled
inexorably toward the bar. She moved several yards,
reaching the corner before she realized she was under
compulsion. His voice was low and beautifully pitched,
a blend of the night and seduction itself. He was using
his voice alone as his weapon, and she, like a rank fledgling, was responding. Desari forced herself to stop moving by grabbing a lamppost and hanging on.

His laughter was low and taunting. *Desire is more powerful than I realized. And it is the same for you.*

You wish it were, she responded, her chin up, eyes flashing. *I refuse to play these childish games with you. Go away, and do not come back.* He was right, though. She had never felt this way before. Every cell in her body was hot and heavy and aching for release. She wanted him. Pure and simple. But that was all. It was just sex. Hot, steamy sex. Absolutely nothing else. Who would want such an arrogant jerk?

"You." The single word was breathed against her neck, against the pulse beating so strongly there. His body was suddenly so close, she could feel the heat emanating from his skin. Although she was tall, his large frame seemed to tower over her. Up close, she could feel his power, the intensity of his emotions. His gaze drifted over her with stark possessiveness.

Desari stood perfectly still, afraid to move. There was something about him she couldn't seem to resist. It was his eyes. The way his eyes burned a molten gold. So intense. So hungry. How could she resist his eyes? It was in his mind. He had been so alone. He *needed* and only she could provide. His hand moved down her shoulder to rest on her slender waist. His touch was possessive. His palm was burning a hole through the thin material of her shirt.

Julian exerted a little pressure, taking her with him as he moved toward the tavern. She was still uncertain, her brain at war with her instincts, her emotions, the chemistry of her body. He was well aware, having now shared her mind, that Desari was no one to trifle with. She had lived centuries, had acquired tremendous knowledge and strength. This was a situation that required more than a little finesse—not his strongest point. Julian was used to having his way in all things. More than anything he believed it was his duty, his right, to protect and care for his lifemate. But Desari did not seem to follow the path of the women of his race in temperament.

"I heard your brother refer to you as Dara. How did you come by such a name?" he asked, his straightforward curiosity completely throwing her off the track.

"I have long been called Dara. It is a nickname. Darius said my mother often called me that," she answered, moving with him automatically. His body was very close to hers, so that she felt the brush of his thigh, his chest, the heavy muscles coming into brief contact with her, then moving away. Her tongue touched her lips, moistening their sudden dryness. She was intrigued by the way Julian could make her feel so aware of herself as a woman.

"Do you know what Dara means?" Julian asked softly.

Desari shrugged. "It is old Persian. It means, of the dark one."

Julian nodded. "Do you remember where you came from? Where you were born?"

Desari moved away from him, a subtle retreat from the heat of his body. What she really needed to do was run from the heat in his eyes. No one had ever looked at her as he was doing. Julian slid his arm around her waist and gathered her under his shoulder.

She put her hand on his rib cage to push him away, but somehow her palm lingered against his thin shirt, savoring the heat of him. It drew her like a magnet, in the same way his eyes drew her. She lowered her lashes. This was insanity. But for a few brief hours tonight she would indulge her dreams, allow herself a fantasy that might have to last her for all time.

Julian's larger frame urged her into the small tavern. The band was playing something soft and dreamy, allowing him to step around and take her into his arms. The moment he enclosed her against him, he knew it was right. Her body fit into his perfectly. They moved with the same rhythm, matching heartbeats, matching gliding, swaying steps. Her head fit in the niche of his shoulder; her hand belonged in his.

"We should not be doing this," Desari said. In spite of her determination not to allow him to control her, she couldn't stop herself from moving in the erotic dance. His thighs were hard columns against her softer ones. He smelled woodsy, mysterious, dangerous. She inhaled, taking in the scent of his blood.

His mouth touched her neck, just a feather-light caress, but the jolt sent shock waves through both of them. Hunger flared in her, hot and erotic, like nothing she had ever known. She felt the warmth of his breath fanning over the pulse throbbing so frantically beneath her skin.

"This is exactly what we should be doing. I have no other choice, *cara*. I need to hold you in my arms." His lips were velvet soft, his tongue a rasp of heat stroking her pulse. His fingers enveloped hers, curling her wrist so that he could hold her hand tightly against his heart. "Do you have any idea of how beautiful you really are, Desari?" His teeth scraped a gentle rhythm back and forth over her pulse, sending flames dancing through her body.

Desari closed her eyes and gave herself up to the sheer physical pleasure of the moment. His skin was hot and rough against the softness of hers. She could feel his strength, his muscles like steel. They moved together in such perfect rhythm. She wanted it to go on for all time. His arms made her feel protected and cherished. The burning hunger in his eyes made her feel desirable. His words made her feel beautiful. But most of all, the way his body moved, hot and hard and aggressive as he held her to him, turned her own body into a living, breathing flame.

"It is the way you are inside, Desari, not just the outside package, that makes you so beautiful." His tongue tasted her throat, his lips sliding up to her chin, to the corner of her mouth.

"You cannot possibly know what I am like," she protested, even as she turned her mouth blindly to his. She had to taste him, had to know if this was real, this black magic spell he was weaving so effortlessly around her.

Desari expected a savage ravishment, his hunger ran so deep and strong. The first touch of his lips was incredibly tender, his mouth moving over hers, memorizing the feel and shape of her, as if he were being swept away, as if he loved the taste of her. It disarmed her as nothing else could. Her legs went rubbery, but he simply gathered her tightly against him, protectively, as if sheltering her with his heart. His hand encircled her throat lovingly, his fingertips moving in a tender caress that sent heat pooling low and a wave of weakness flowing through her body. She made a sound, a low moan of alarm. He was stealing her soul, taking her heart with his gentleness. Desari found his thick mane of golden hair with her fists, clung to him for support. He was ensnaring her for all time, and she was giving herself to him without a fight.

He was a dangerous, violent predator, yet he held her protectively, kissed her as if she were the most precious thing in the world. It was as if he needed the taste and feel of her just to breathe. How could she not fall under his spell? His voice was low and seductive, a murmur of Italian that took possession of her heart, stole it right out of her body. The world was dissolving into a strange mist around her, the earth shifting beneath her feet. Their bodies were swaying to the music, the shadows hiding them from prying eyes. Desari had the strange feeling he was making love to her. Not sex, but making love to the one woman in the world who mattered to him. Everything in her rose in response to the gentleness of his possession.

His kiss deepened so that he was feeding on the sweetness of her mouth, his hand spanning her throat, his body trapping hers against a wall, holding her still while he ignited the fire in her blood and turned her body into a living flame.

"Come with me away from here," he whispered, his beautiful voice raw with need, a sorcerer's seduction.

Desari rested her head on his shoulder, confused and vulnerable. She wanted him, wanted to be with him. The need was so strong, it was almost a compulsion. She couldn't understand it. Nothing in all her long centuries had prepared her for the force of his magnetism. "I do not even know you."

Julian's fingers stroked her silky hair, a small, masculine smile softening the hard edge to his mouth. "You insist on believing that, Desari, but you have been in my mind as I have been in yours. I know you are beautiful from the inside out because I hear it in your voice, see it so clearly in your heart and mind. You are a little troublemaker, but you would never hurt a single soul. You are the light to my darkness, my lifemate."

She shook her head. "I do not know what you mean."

"You feel it. Do not try to deny it." His thumbs were rubbing silky strands of her hair against his fingers. His burning eyes were molten gold, alive with hunger, relentless need, fierce possessiveness.

"What is a lifemate? I have not heard such a term."

Julian studied her upturned face, shaped her classic bone structure with his palms. "How is it that you are Carpathian and you do not know this? We have much to learn about one another. Tonight I will explain to you what lifemates are to the people of our homeland." His hand slipped to her throat, then glided down her shoulders and the length of her arm to lace his fingers through hers. "But we are hunted, *piccola*. Let us leave this place and go elsewhere to talk."

Her breath caught in her throat. "Darius? My brother? He is hunting us?" He had not yet called to her, demanding her return, as she had expected him to do when he found her gone. She thought she would have time to lay a false trail away from Julian. "I must leave you. He can track me straight to you."

Julian pulled her toward the door of the tavern, and Desari felt almost helpless under his spell. It was insanity to defy Darius like this. He would find this man, and there would be a terrible battle.

"Come with me, Desari. There will be no battle unless you choose to force the issue by staying here. I have a need to talk with you. You promised me this night, and I will not release you from your word."

They were moving quickly now, out the door and into the darkness of the night. Had she promised him? He had her so bemused, she couldn't remember exactly what she had said. "There is no way to deceive Darius," she pointed out. "My blood flows in his veins. He can track me at will, and he is very powerful."

Julian slipped an arm around her slender shoulders. "It is true he presents an interesting challenge, but we can give ourselves time if you wish it, Desari."

Despite herself, the possibility intrigued her. She had never really tasted freedom. Darius and the others watched over her as if she were a mere fledgling. At times it was galling. "I do not wish to put you in danger." Her large velvet eyes didn't meet his hot gaze as she made the admission. She felt she was giving away her true feelings.

Julian's hard mouth curved in satisfaction. "I am pleased you worry for my safety, *cara*," he said, a seductive caress in the deep timbre of his voice, his Italian accent very much in evidence. "But there is no need. I am not without power of my own. I know this man is someone you love. There will be no real confrontation between us. Perhaps a game of cat and mouse."

Desari shivered, the cool of the night wreaking havoc with her heated skin. It had to be the air; his voice alone couldn't possibly cause the fever in her blood. And it wasn't just the strong chemistry between them drawing her, she decided, her chin going up, it was the knowledge he could impart to her. This was a true Carpathian, raised in their homeland. He knew things she desperately wanted to know, things that could be important to her family.

"Tell me how we can do this."

There was a natural haughtiness in her voice, a note of imperious demand. Desari was used to getting her way when she chose to push it. Julian's arms circled her small waist. Electricity sizzled and crackled between them. She might try to deny it to herself, but he could see her response in her eyes, feel it in her body, in her scent calling to him. "Merge your mind fully with mine, so that there is nothing of you he can find."

She tried to jerk out of his arms. "No! I cannot."

That infuriating smile was curving his mouth, taunting her. "What are you afraid of, *picccola*? My resolve? I have made no attempt to hide my intentions from you. I want you in every way. I am relentless when something is important to me, and you are the most important thing in my life, in all the centuries of my existence. Merge with me. We will fly far from here and talk of important things."

It was a dare of sorts. He was making no secret of his amusement. Desari's dark eyes flashed at him. "I do not fear you," she snapped. "I am powerful in my own right. You cannot seduce me if I do not give my consent. I will go with you to learn from you." She sounded like a princess bestowing a favor on a peasant.

Julian knew better than to allow his triumph to show on his face. He caught both her hands in his. "Now, *cara mia*, come with me, merge with me." His voice was a caress that sent flames moving through her, flames she had no way of dousing.

His blood ran in her veins. She reached out with her mind and immersed it completely, decisively into his so that she could not panic and change her mind. At once she knew she was lost. He had enticed her into an erotic world of heat and hunger and fierce need. And he was every bit as ruthless as Darius. A loner. A great warrior with centuries of battles behind him. He appeared to hide nothing from her. Nothing, not even the terrible, relentless darkness. He had always been alone, even in his own world. Always alone. Until now. Desari moved into that darkness, suddenly uneasy.

Shape-shift, piccola. *Use the image I give you*. His words held an urgency she couldn't ignore. Darius was close.

They launched themselves skyward simultaneously, their hearts beating as one, feathers iridescent even in the night sky. Wings beat strongly, lifting them quickly up and away. They wheeled in the air in perfect synchronization, flying toward the distant mountains.

Julian shared the beauty of the night with her. He had not seen color in centuries, so it was all new and wonderful to him. The silvery leaves of the trees glittering below them, the sheen of water from the large lake nearby, the haunting shriek of an owl as it missed its prey, and the rustle of gray mice scurrying through vegetation on the forest floor.

Darius would be unable to track Desari while they were merged so fully together. The moment they were apart again, he could find her. The trick was to take her far away, set up as many blinds as time would allow, so that Darius would have no choice but to turn back, seeking safety before the dawn broke upon them.

Desari faltered for a moment when she read Julian's intentions. She had not considered being away from her family during the day, when she would be completely vulnerable. At once Julian sent her waves of warmth and reassurance, the implacable resolve of the Carpathian male to protect his mate above all else. While she was with him, nothing would happen to her; he would never allow it.

And what of you? Am I safe from you? She asked it softly, well aware of the fierce needs of his body, her body. The terrible, insatiable hunger he had for her alone. No one else would ever be able to fulfill the demands his body was making on him. No one else could ever assuage the fire burning deep within him. The knowledge only served to weaken her resistance to him. His need was a terrible thing.

Always, Desari. I would protect you with my life. You feel it, I know you do. I can do nothing other than ensure your safety.

Julian felt the disturbance in the air, waves of power echoing through the sky, seeking the prey the hunter was determined to find. In the raptor's body he smiled. Darius was very dangerous, a true ancient with a will of iron. Merged as she was with Julian, Desari was masked from her brother. Still, Darius was a brilliant adversary, and he was not so arrogant that he discounted his enemy. He knew he faced one his equal, or very nearly so.

The waves of seeking power receded, and the air was quiet and fresh. Then, without warning, Darius struck again. Julian felt the pain slam into his head, into Desari's head. She made a noise, just a soft cry in her throat, but Julian instantly took the full brunt of the sound wave, blocking it from her.

Hear me, stranger. I know you feel me, you know what I am. If you hurt her in any way, there will be nowhere on this earth you will be able to hide. I will find you, and you will die—a long and painful death. The voice came on the wings of the night, broadcast on every possible wavelength so there could be no doubt it was heard and clearly understood.

Julian was astonished at the power the bodyguard had. He seemed as adept as Gregori, every bit as dangerous. Perhaps Darius did not have Gregori's elegant grace— he seemed more earthy and raw—but he held very real power. Few could accomplish what he was doing, holding a painful note in Julian's head even though they had never exchanged blood and Darius had no real idea of where he was. And he meant what he said. He was determined and ruthless and without an iota of mercy.

Julian inhaled sharply and brought Desari out of the sky with him to the small snug cabin nestled high in the mountain peaks. As he landed, shape-shifting, he held Desari's mind merge so that she did not inadvertently give their position away, but he changed the tone of the sound so that it no longer raked at him with such sharp edges.

It took a little doing, to turn the trap back on its master, especially since he was shielding Desari from the battle between the two Carpathians. She didn't need to know they were posturing at one another. He turned the note around, reshaped it, and sent it slamming back through the night sky. There was a certain satisfaction in knowing that he had scored on the powerful Carpathian. Only then did he release Desari from his mind, allowing her to withdraw completely.

For the very first time Desari found she was really afraid. What had she done? Followed a complete stranger away from the protection of her family, and for what? Sex. Pure and simple. She was so attracted to Julian Savage, she had willingly thrown away her values and rules and placed Darius in an untenable position. He would worry about her. She had trusted Julian because she had never once in all her existence felt so deeply about anyone, yet now she knew he was manipulating her. And he was a master at it. Perhaps he was manipulating all her other emotions as well.

Julian moved away from her, giving her space, his body fluid and powerful. He shoved a hand through his thick mane of golden hair, his eyes drifting over her possessively. "You would have me allow you to feel pain when it is not necessary?" His voice was strictly neutral.

She knew he was making a point. He was not compelling her. She either trusted him or she didn't. It was that simple.

Julian folded his arms across his broad chest and leaned one hip lazily against a porch column. "I know you felt it."

"For a moment," she conceded, knowing he meant the blast of pain that had blossomed so suddenly in his head. It had been gone in an instant.

"And I removed it immediately. It was your brother. A warning."

"I heard his warning. I have worried him unnecessarily. I intend to tell him I am coming home this night."

She said it defiantly, more for her own benefit than his. She didn't want to go. Julian was so enticing, with his hungry molten eyes. The intensity he felt for her was overwhelming, exhilarating.

"Then we will both return. But do you really believe we can get to know one another in the company of your protectors? It will be unnecessarily difficult." He waved to a chair on the porch. "Sit for a while and talk to me."

It was a soft purr of menace. He fully intended to go with her if she left, walk casually into the den of those who would seek to destroy him. His voice was so beautiful. Pure and gentle. It held a hint of tenderness, a trace of arrogance, and more than a little masculine amusement.

It felt like a dare. As if she were a small child, a fledgling, afraid of her shadow and of being away from her big brother. Desari tilted her chin and glided regally up the stairs to the chair on the porch. She seated herself, her dark eyes remaining on his face.

He grinned at her, suddenly dispelling the dark danger that clung to him like a second skin. For one moment he looked almost boyish. "I am not going to hold you prisoner, Desari. There is no need to look at me as if I were a monster."

Desari found herself relaxing. A slow, answering smile lit her face. "Is that what I was doing? I am feeling guilty for defying my brother and making him worry. Perhaps I was taking it out on you. It is so much easier to blame someone other than oneself."

Julian shook his head. "Do not worry for your brother. He knows in his heart I will not harm you. It is more that he must relinquish his control over you."

"What is a lifemate?" Desari asked, knowing it was important. She had been in his mind, knew he believed her to be his lifemate.

"Every Carpathian male is born a predator, dark and deadly. True, we have strong instincts to protect those we love, but there is a darkness in us that grows stronger with each passing century. Without a lifemate we lose all emotion, even the ability to see colors. It is an empty existence. Every day the beast within grows stronger, and the darkness inches across our souls. You have not observed this in the males of your group?"

Desari tapped a long fingernail against her cheek. "Actually, yes. At least with Darius and Dayan. Barack was always filled with joy until recently. He is quieter now. And there was another, Savon, who turned into someone none of us recognized."

"If we males do not find our true lifemate, the other half of our souls, the light to our darkness, disappears. We cannot regain our emotions. We are lost." Julian sighed softly, watching the gathering dismay on her face. "We have two choices. We can walk into the sun and end our barren existence, or we can choose to lose our soul. We can become the undead, vampires preying on the human race for the ultimate rush, the power of the kill. It is the only feeling left to us."

Desari knew he spoke the truth. Savon had chosen to become vampire. Darius had destroyed many such undead over the centuries. She swallowed hard and looked up at him. "How do people know for certain when they find their lifemate?"

Julian's smile was like a physical touch, a soft caress. "I have lived centuries without seeing color or feeling emotion. And then I found you. The world is now beautiful again and filled with life, with color, with so much intense emotion I can barely process it. When I look at you my body is alive. My heart is overwhelmed. You are the one."

"What happens if the woman does not feel it also?"

Desari asked, curious. This was an entirely new concept to her, one she had never considered.

"There is only one true lifemate for each of us. If the male feels it, so does his mate." His white teeth flashed at her. "Perhaps she might wish to be stubborn and not admit it right away, not wanting her freedom curtailed for all time. Because there are so few of our women, they are guarded carefully from birth and given into the care of their lifemate as soon as they are of age."

"What do you mean, her freedom is curtailed for all time?" Desari suddenly felt restless. Just watching the easy way his body moved could make her feel hot and achy. She didn't like the sound of his voice, soft and arrogant, faintly amused when he'd said those words. It sounded as if the woman had no choice in the matter.

He grinned at her, then moved suddenly with astounding speed, fluid and graceful, looming over her when she thought herself safe. "You have no need to worry, Desari. I could do nothing other than see to your happiness." He held out his hand. "You hunger. I feel your need inside me as if it were my own. There is no need for you to be uncomfortable."

Her hand was enveloped in his before she could think, an instinctive reaction to the allure of sex that surrounded him. He was drawing her to her feet, his arm circling her small waist before she had a chance to protest. His body was hard and hot, the scent of him filling her mind. When she inhaled, she took him into her lungs so that he rushed through her body like a strong drug. Whatever the chemistry was between them, she could not deny to herself it was hot, inflammatory, and instant.

"I cannot take your blood," she whispered, afraid if she tasted him she would be lost for all time.

Julian's white teeth gleamed for an instant above her head; then he bent slowly, almost languidly toward her soft throat. His golden eyes were hot with desire, holding hers for a long moment before his lashes descended and she felt his mouth move against her skin.

Desari's entire body clenched in reaction. His arms tightened like steel bands around her, yet his hold was oddly protective. His body swelled against hers with need, a raging demand he made no attempt to hide. His lips were firm and soft as they nuzzled her pulse. His teeth nipped gently; his tongue provided a rougher rasping that teased and enticed. "Would you deny me then?" he asked softly, his mouth against her satin skin.

She could deny him nothing. Her body was no longer her own, but his other half. Desari pressed closer, needing to give him whatever it was he needed so desperately. There was no room for thought. She felt his breath, so warm and enticing, his tongue stroking her skin so that heat pooled low within her and she ached for him. She closed her eyes, her arms sliding up to cradle his head. White-hot heat pierced her throat, a pleasure so intense it was almost pain. She heard herself moan, felt his mouth feeding on her, taking the essence of her life into his body, sealing them together in some erotic way she didn't understand.

She had fed every night for centuries; she had given blood numerous times when it was needed. It had never been like this. Fire racing through her body, hot, leaping flames demanding relief. She felt like a living flame burning in his arms, her body moving restlessly, aching and impatient for the hard aggression of his.

Julian sealed the marks on her throat with a caress of his tongue, at the same time opening the buttons on his shirt with one hand while the other palmed her nape. He murmured something to her in Italian, something soft and aching and sexy, and the smoky need touched off a wildness in her she had never known. He pressed her to his heavy muscles, reached down to gather her small, jeans-clad bottom into his hand so he could urge her more closely into the thick evidence of his arousal.

He smelled fresh and masculine. Her body was on fire for him, her skin so sensitive her breasts ached, her nipples chafing in the thin, lacy bra that confined her. Hunger was swamping her, sexual as well as physical. She couldn't begin to tell where she began and he left off. His heart beat strong and fast, waiting for her, needing her, wanting her. Hunger was a raw ache between her legs, in her stomach, her breasts, gnawing mercilessly at her until she felt her teeth pierce his skin.

At once pleasure beat at her; it took hold and rushed through her body like a wall of flame, a firestorm of beauty and ecstasy. Sweet and hot. Immeasurable. Like nothing she had ever known. It was addictive, consuming, eternal. There would never be a Desari without Julian. Never a Julian without Desari. She would need his body, his blood, and his soul for all the rest of her days. He would need hers.

Gasping, terrified, Desari closed the tiny pinpricks and held on to him, the only solid anchor in a world that seemed to be disintegrating around her. At once his arms were there, real and strong, his chin nuzzling the top of her head so that silken strands of her hair were caught in the golden shadow on his jaw, weaving them together like threads. "Do not fear this, *piccola*. I know what to do. I am ancient and powerful and know the ways of our people. This is natural for us."

She shook her head, her heart pounding. "Not for me. You do not understand at all, Julian. I cannot leave my family. I have been in your mind and know your intentions for us. You are a loner, even a bit of a renegade. You like to set your own rules and go your own way. You follow your Prince, but rather loosely."

Julian's hand again came up to caress the nape of her neck, easing the tension out of her. "We have time to get used to one another."

"I sing, Julian. I love to sing. I like the crowds, the sharing, the excitement in the audience, the connection with them. And I love my family. If we have a prince, a leader, it is Darius. He had dedicated his life to us, lived for us, protected us. You do not know what he has done for us. I cannot leave him at this time, when he is so close to the edge of destruction."

The night whispered to them, enfolding them in its dark cloak. Julian lifted his face skyward, staring at the stars spread above them like a glittering blanket. "Tell me about him. Tell me how it is possible that no other Carpathians know of your existence. If you managed to escape notice, perhaps there are others, also. This could be very important to the continuation of our species."

His voice was so gentle and tender, it turned her heart over. Yet she could sense his implacable resolve. Like Darius, he had a strong and relentless will. He chose to follow his own path, make his own rules. He coaxed the entire long-ago story out of her. The terrible massacre. The precariousness of the ship. The terror of the children in a savage, lawless land surrounded by predatory animals.

Julian soon realized that Darius and Desari were indeed living relatives of the healer, the Dark One. They had to be Gregori's younger brother and sister, presumed murdered by the Turks. Perhaps others had escaped as well. The moment he knew the truth, he reached across time and space. *Gregori! I have found what I long sought. There are others. Your bloodline. They survived the massacres and escaped far away.*

It was no wonder that Darius reminded him so much of the healer. Darius was every bit as resourceful and powerful as his older brother. He would make a bitter, relentless enemy, dangerous beyond imagination. He would make a loyal, protective friend despite his inability to feel emotions. His word was his law. He recognized no other. Julian found himself respecting Darius where he respected few others.

I thank you for sending me word of Darius and Dara, Julian.

I also feel your need, Julian. Desari is your lifemate. Attend to her. There was great satisfaction evident in the healer's voice even over the distance. *Have you need of me at this time?*

No, healer. I welcome the challenge your male kin provides. And Julian did. The wonder and beauty of the world was within his grasp.

I will contact Mikhail and inform Savannah. We will come if you have need of us; otherwise, we will all meet at a later date.

I have no need, Julian assured the healer. He had faith in his own abilities. He didn't want or need the healer's interference or presence. Gregori doubtless knew the exact nature of the darkness crouching in Julian's soul, a fact Julian had successfully kept even from his own twin. Gregori believed in his honor, but he also knew Julian was shadowed, and might decide such a one had no right to Desari, no right to her at all.

Julian had no intention of giving up Desari. It would be impossible even if he were inclined to do so. They were tied together for all eternity. The ritual words had been spoken. Although they had not completed the entire cycle of the ritual, the ancient words themselves were binding, and Julian knew the consequences. They would be unable to be apart without intense grief, without dire physical discomfort. And the waves of Carpathian heat would eventually overcome them, demanding they unite.

It was a protection for the male's sanity, for his soul, that he could bind his mate to him for all time regardless of her fears. Fears could be dealt with; the destruction of one's soul was for all eternity. Desari believed she could control her destiny, that she had a choice, but Julian knew better. She belonged to him, was a part of him. Not even Darius could change that without destroying her. And if his own honor demanded he do the right thing, release her from one such as him, it was already too late. He had tied them together in the heat of their first meeting. It was done.

Julian sighed softly and held her close to him. "Your brother is Carpathian and blood kin to you. I would not wish harm to him. If it is necessary that we remain with him to ensure that he does not allow harm to come to himself, then that is what we will do."

Desari knew Julian believed he was making a great concession for her, but he wasn't doing her any favors. Darius would not accept him easily into their circle. Neither would Dayan or Barack. The males were difficult at best. For hundreds of years they had depended upon one another, interacted with one another. They would not willingly allow a stranger into their midst.

Chapter Five

Desari lifted her head from the warmth and temptation of Julian's chest. Her enormous eyes were soft with sadness. "I know you do not understand, but I can do no other than return to my family right now. I refuse to continue being irresponsible, selfish, when my brother has given so much."

She expected Julian to argue with her, and her hand, positioned over his heart, trembled. Julian's golden eyes drifted possessively over her upturned face. His burning hunger, so intense, so blatant, took her breath away, stole her resolve. How could a man need her so much? How could he show that need to her without ego or fear that he would be totally vulnerable? How could she turn away from such an honest burning need? "Julian." She whispered his name, an aching desire, feeling torn between two strong men, two loyalties, one she didn't even understand.

"We have a few short hours until the dawn, *cara*. If

you insist on returning to Darius, then we must do so."
His voice was a soft, mesmerizing spell, seductive and
masculine. Just the sound of it threatened her precarious
will. His words said one thing, while his blatant, sexy
heat whispered something altogether different.

"Julian, you have to stop looking at me like that," she
cautioned him, something blocking her throat so that it
felt impossible to breathe. She tried to pull her gaze
away from the intensity of his. "I cannot think when you
look at me like that."

His hand moved over the silken mass of her hair, his
fingers rubbing the strands against the pad of his thumb
as if he couldn't help himself. "Have you always been
an entertainer?"

There was a note in his voice, a drawling caress of
admiration and sorcery that set her heart beating fast. He
disarmed her entirely with that lazy, Italianate drawl of
his. His question also threw her off track. It felt like a
seduction, though it was innocent enough. "Yes, I always sang. We traveled to different continents every
twenty-five years or so. That way no one ever noticed
we did not age." His hand, the one that had been so
innocently fingering strands of her hair, had somehow
slipped to her shoulder. Those fingers were now rubbing
heat right through the thin material of her top so that
she felt as if his skin were connecting to hers. Her voice
faltered as she lost her train of thought.

Julian bent closer as if to soothe her. "Please continue.
This is extremely interesting. I searched centuries for
lost Carpathians but had given up hope. How all of you
accomplished what you did is extraordinary." His fingertips moved to the neckline of her shirt absently tracing its delicate embroidered edge.

Desari swallowed as little flames licked at her skin,
as her breasts reacted to the pad of his thumb sliding

sensuously over the soft swell. She glanced up at him, determined to reprimand him, but he was looking intellectual and earnestly interested in whatever she had been telling him. Except for his eyes. His eyes were molten gold and burning with a liquid fire that seemed to consume her, to mesmerize her.

"I have no idea what I was saying," she finally admitted, her voice so husky it was an invitation.

His body crowded closer to hers, not touching, simply so close his heat and masculine scent enfolded her, surrounded her, swamped her. It called to her as nothing else could have. "You were telling me about traveling around from place to place singing." His voice was aching with need.

She heard it clearly, and her body responded on its own, dissolving into liquid heat. Desari cleared her throat. "We simply became our own ancestors if someone remembered us. It was seldom necessary, as we made certain we stayed away from areas for decades at a time. Dayan is a poet, a master with words, and no one is better on a guitar. Syndil, too, is a wonderful musician. She can play almost any instrument. Actually, Barack is the same way. He seems to really enjoy playing for our audiences." She gave him the information, but her mind was on the fact that his fingers had slipped inside her neckline and were moving hypnotically back and forth as if he were memorizing the feel of her.

"Barack and Dayan." Julian repeated the names softly. There was the smallest bite to his voice, his perfect teeth snapping together, reminiscent of a hungry wolf. "Those two act as if they have certain rights where you are concerned." There was a cruel edge to the set of his mouth, a darkness in his golden eyes. "They do not. In lieu of your father, Darius is the only one you are answerable to until your lifemate claims you. I have done so." He leaned forward as if drawn beyond his own will and touched her collarbone with his lips, the harshness in his face at once softening. The touch was feather-light, but it penetrated her skin and made straight for her heart, setting it pounding with some emotion she didn't want to try to understand.

His mouth moved, a trail of fire running from her collarbone up to the pulse beating so frantically in her throat. Her soft mouth trembled, long lashes sweeping down to cover the luminescent glow in her dark eyes. She should stop him. For her own sanity, she should stop him. But his mouth was moving slowly, gently, a heated exploration not at all aggressive.

Desari tried desperately to marshal her thoughts. "You have claimed me?"

His fingers tangled with hers. He brought her hand to press against the muscles of his chest, his thumb feathering with false innocence over her pulse. He felt it jump as his lips drifted lower, pushed the limits of the neckline of her shirt, where the creamy invitation of her breasts swelled in anticipation. "I have. You are bound to me." He whispered the words into the valley between her breasts, and her entire body clenched with such need that Desari felt weak.

She swore there were flames dancing over her skin. She actually looked down, expecting to see little orange tongues of fire licking along her skin. She shivered and tried to withdraw her hand, tried to put some much-needed space between them. "You believe I am. I do not." Desari found that where her head was certain she wanted to move, her body refused to cooperate.

His laughter was low and husky with male amusement at its worst. "You cannot possibly think you could get away from me now." Julian transferred his attention to her arm. His lips skimmed along her bare skin, stopping to dwell in the sensitive inner elbow before moving on along her forearm. Then he was doing something to her inner wrist, his teeth scraping over her skin, making every muscle in her body clench until she thought she might have to scream with need. "I would not be much of a lifemate if I could not hold what is my own, now, would I?"

As he bent forward over her arm, his golden hair was brushing against her skin, and she closed her eyes against the waves of heat rising so sharply between them. In spite of herself she smiled. "You are every bit as arrogant as Darius." She liked the feel of his hands, the molten gold of his eyes burning over her. She even liked his arrogance.

"Mmm," he murmured rather absently, clearly distracted. "Am I?" His hand glided over her rib cage until he found the edge of her shirt. "You know you love everything about me." He buried his face in the waves of ebony silk cascading around her shoulders and down her back. "I love the way you smell." His hand slipped beneath her thin cotton top, his fingers splayed wide to take in as much satin skin as he could.

The sensation was beyond her wildest fantasy. So hot. Reaching into her insides and simply melting everything. "I thought we were going to talk," she said a little desperately. Her arms seemed to have a will of their own, sliding around his neck. For a moment she closed her eyes, savoring the heat of his body in the coolness of the night.

"I am talking to you," Julian whispered. "Do you not hear what I am saying?"

His voice moved like velvet over her skin. How could she not hear him? Inside her body, Desari felt a volcano of molten heat erupt. It raced through her, thick and heavy and hot and aching. She wanted him, and he needed her. Could it really be that simple? She turned up her mouth to the demanding invasion of his.

Julian swore the ground moved beneath his feet. Desari knew she heard the roar of thunder and felt the blue-white lash of lightning. Julian kicked open the door to the cabin and managed to make it inside, his body raging. The beast within, ever present, fought for supremacy. Julian fastened his mouth to hers, a little out of control, a soft warning growl emanating from deep within his throat as she tried to lift her head.

His hand spanned her throat, holding her to him, holding her as if she were a part of him. Holding her as if she was the most precious thing in the world and he couldn't be without her. His other hand skimmed her waist, then stopped to rest there, hot and urgent even though his palm was lying quietly against her skin. Desari was so aware of it, aware of how close it was to the most intimate, sensitive parts of her body. She ached for him. Wanted him. She was beyond thinking rationally; she wanted his hand to move. Either direction, it didn't matter. His mouth was hot and hard, yet velvet soft, demanding her complete surrender. And then his hand did move, finding the tiny catch at the front of her lacy bra, and her breasts spilled free. It was such a small thing, but her entire body felt wild and untamed and in need.

She felt the moan rising from deep within her soul as his hand caressed the full rounded underside of her breast. It amazed her that he could make her feel such intense pleasure when his palm was simply cupping the weight of her breast. Her mouth was open to the invasion of his, her body receptive to his every advance. When his hand encircled her breast, his palm pushing against her erect nipple, she gasped and pulled her mouth free so that she could taste his skin, so that she was free to do her own exploring.

She could feel his hand shaping her, tracing the curve of her breast, the soft, swelling invitation, her nipple, aching and hard, pushing into his palm. Desari slid her own hands under his shirt, found his heated skin, the ridge of defined muscles, the golden hair spreading across his chest. He made her feel so alive, so completely feminine. He made her feel restless and hot, her body a cauldron of creamy liquid fire.

Julian caressed her breast, marveling at the sheer perfection of her body. It was amazing to him, the satin texture of her skin, the silken feel to her hair, the heat rising between them, how small and delicate she felt beside his own strong body, yet her every muscle was firm and supple. Her hands were driving him crazy, threatening not only his tenuous control but his very sanity. His body was raging at him, so hard with the need for release that his clothing felt tight and unbearable against his flesh.

Desari tugged at his shirt, heedless of the buttons flying in all directions. She needed to burrow as close to him as possible. Julian's body trembled, driven beyond the boundaries of endurance. The feel of her hands on his heated skin only served to arouse him further. His body went rigid as her mouth moved over his chest, began to trace a path down the fine trail of gold hair.

Julian caught at the neckline of her shirt, easily parting the material, tossing the lacy scrap of bra aside so that her skin gleamed invitingly in the darkness. His breath caught in his throat at the perfection of her. His hands spanned her waist, bent her backward so that her breasts rose up to meet his descending mouth. She was luscious, beautiful, everything good and perfect in the world.

His mouth was hot and moist, closing around her, all heat and fire so that flames erupted inside her, inside him, like a firestorm. With each strong pull of his lips as he fed on her, there was an answering rush of hot, creamy liquid as her body called out urgently to his, a rush of swelling heat from his own body.

Julian's hands slid down along her waist to the slender curve of her hips, pushing her faded jeans and silken panties ahead of them. Her legs were satin smooth, firm to his touch yet so soft as he trailed his fingers back up along the inside of her thighs. His mouth left her breasts for just a moment so that his tongue could trace the tiny indentation of her belly button, then once more returned to the temptation of her full, soft breasts. His hand slipped between her legs to find moist heat.

Desari cried out, a soft, musical note that reached inside his body and ignited a blazing inferno in him that began licking at her skin, his skin, her body, his, their very insides. Without thought her hands worked at the confines of his trousers so that he burst free, hot and demanding, his body enflamed beyond redemption. She could feel his hand pushing against her, so that her body felt heavy and unfamiliar, hot and aching with urgent need. She moved her hips, seeking release from the building torment. Julian's fingers delved deep, testing her readiness, pushing her temperature up another ninety degrees. Hot cream met his caresses, and her nails raked his broad back. Her breath came in convulsive gasps.

"*Dio, cara mia*, you are so hot, so ready for me." His voice was raw and hoarse as he tugged her with him farther into the cabin, his mouth still on her breast, his teeth gently stroking her tender skin, his tongue easing the slight ache.

She went with him, every step nearly impossible when she was going up in flames, his fingers stroking rhythmically, his mouth pulling at her, his teeth an erotic teasing that made her so wild and uninhibited she was moving urgently against his hand.

Julian's teeth moved along the curve of her breast, his tongue lapping gently in the deep valley. His hands caught her and carefully, gently, lowered her onto the thick quilt of the bed. Kicking aside what was left of his clothes, he immediately knelt over her so that her slender body was trapped beneath his.

Desari's breath escaped in a long gasp as his massive frame descended on hers, skin to skin, as she felt the hard strength in him, and the long, hot, thick length of him pressing aggressively against her thigh. Her heart seemed to stop beating. Fear or anticipation, excitement or apprehension, panic or impatience—she had no idea what she was really feeling. Everything all at once.

Julian's knee nudged between her legs so that he could press his sensitive velvet tip against her heated, moist entrance. At once her body bathed his with hot cream, sending waves of urgency spreading through him. His mouth captured hers, and he eased a little deeper inside of her. His breath slammed out of his lungs. She was so tight, a sheath of fiery velvet gripping him, taking him into her body. The feeling was so close to ecstasy, he had to clench his teeth, to use every ounce of control to force himself to go slowly, to allow her body time to adjust to the invasion of his.

Desari moved her hips restlessly, mindlessly, needing all of him, wanting so much more. At once there was pain, and she gasped and went rigid. Julian became perfectly still, not withdrawing, holding her close to him, his arms strong bands of protection. He framed her face with his hands, his eyes burning molten gold, so intense, so mesmerizing she couldn't look away. "Look at me, *piccola*. Look only at me. Merge your mind with mine."

"You are too big, Julian. We do not fit together." Desari wanted to pull her gaze away from the heat of his, but she was drowning in his naked hunger. "Julian." She just said his name, a whisper of sound, a blend of fear and aching desire.

"We are meant only for one another," Julian reassured her gently. He bent to kiss the corner of her mouth. "Merge with me, fully merge with me." His mouth moved down her chin to her throat. Her pulse was calling to the wildness deep within him. Teeth traced a path along her throat to the swell of her breast, stopping to rest over her racing heart. "Relax for me, Desari. When you look into my eyes, you see into my soul, and you know you can trust me with your life, with your body. Relax for me." The words were hypnotic, his voice so beautiful and pure, so husky with desire. His golden eyes met hers, a blaze of searing heat, and then he gathered her hips into his hands. His body surged forward, one powerful stroke, and his teeth pierced deeply making her cry out with the exquisite fire of it, tears glittering like jewels in her eyes. He filled her completely, filled the terrible emptiness in her soul. As his body withdrew and thrust a second time, she felt his mind take hers.

The intensity of his feelings, the burning pleasure he was experiencing, were there for her to share, just as he could feel the rapture of her own body, reveling in his possession. He began to move, surging into her with sure, hard strokes that seemed to build in intensity, causing a fiery friction between them so hot they were consumed with the flames.

Desari clung to him, her safe anchor, as he transported them higher, ever higher, to a place of such ecstasy she wasn't certain she could stand it. His mouth fed at her, his hips drove into her, a frenzy of lust and love, of reverence and craving. It went on and on until her body seemed to belong to him rather than her, until she heard herself give a soft cry of sheer shock as her body seemed to fragment into a thousand pieces, to shatter, as wave after wave of fire rocked her, convulsing her muscles so that she tightened around him even more, gripping and demanding.

Julian swept his tongue over the curve of her breast, closing the tiny evidence of his assault, yet deliberately leaving his brand on her soft skin. "I need you, Desari," he whispered, his voice erotic and hoarse with his husky demand. "I need you."

She was merged deeply in his mind and knew what he craved, what his body longed for. It was almost too much, the hard thrust of his hips, driving him so fiercely into her. With each hard stroke he was delving deeper and deeper into her body, her very soul. She knew it was happening but felt helpless to resist, unable to deny him anything. Her tongue tasted his damp skin, swirled over the heavy muscles guarding his heart. She felt the instant response, his body, buried within her tight sheath, swelling, hardening even more, the leap of his heart beneath her seeking mouth.

Julian gripped her slender hips tightly, crushing her to him, his body so hot and hard and slick with her fiery cream that he was drowning in pure, scorching heat. He could feel her surrounding him, tight velvet fire, a steamy, torrid passion beyond anything he had ever conceived he could feel. White-hot lightning lashed him as her teeth finally pierced his skin. His throat convulsed, his body in a frenzy of pounding, merciless need. He threw back his head, his golden eyes blazing at her with both possession and a fierce commitment. His mind held hers, and his body grew hotter and harder as she took the very essence of his life's blood into her. Her sheath gripped him, milking insistently so that he erupted into a torrent of passion, spilling his seed deep within her. All around him her body was fiery hot and tight, rocking with its own response to the deep fever raging between them. The earth itself seemed to rock, a rolling quake, the atmosphere split apart; their world narrowed until there was only one another. Two beings merged so deeply, locked so closely together, they had become one, as they were meant to be.

Julian held her tightly, his face as harsh and relentless as time itself. "I can never let you go away from me. You must know that."

Desari was too stunned by the fire in her body, by his addicting taste, by the little erotic aftershocks in her sheath that made her body refused to release his, to reply. It felt so perfect, so right, with Julian buried deep within her. She reached up, touched his mouth with a trembling fingertip, and traced his lips. She could drown in the molten gold of his eyes, live forever sheltered in his heart. "I had no idea we would be like this, that it could ever be like this."

Julian slowly lowered his head, his long hair sweeping across her shoulders, brushing the swell of her breast, touching his mark on her. "You are so incredibly beautiful, Desari, you turn me inside out."

A soft smile curved her mouth. "I want you to remember that when I do something you object to." His hair on her sensitized skin was fanning embers still smoldering deep within her. She was shocked at her abandoned behavior, deliberately tightening her muscles so that she was tormenting him, teasing him, her body already slick with their combined liquid heat and the faint stain of innocence. "I have the feeling, Julian, that you are the type that objects often to things."

His eyebrows shot up. Her body was doing delicious things to his. He kissed the corner of her mouth, then found the fullness of her breast. He could feed there forever. The feel of her was so exquisite, so perfect, her body created exclusively for him. He reveled in that knowledge, that she was his alone, that no other male, human or Carpathian, could satisfy her. With the ritual words he had bound them together, body and soul. He had taken her blood, given her his, and claimed her body. The ritual was now complete. She could never escape him, not for all eternity.

And he had placed her in terrible danger. He closed his mind to that thought, to the echo of a warning uttered centuries earlier. Julian wanted to lose himself in Dara's body, in her soul. He needed to burrow deep into her, to bathe himself in her light so that, at least for a time, the shadow would recede from his soul. His tongue lapped at her nipple, part playful, part possessive. Her body was his to explore, to arouse, to satisfy, to complete.

Julian was driving her crazy with his lazy, slow-handed exploration. His palm was moving deliberately over every inch of her body, finding every curve, memorizing every hollow. Desari was already restless again, but when she would have caught his hips with demanding hands, he shook his head, his golden hair brushing her skin, inflaming her even more.

"I want to know every inch of you, *cara mia*," he whispered, sliding his thick heat out of her.

"Julian!" Desari's dark eyes censured him, her slender hips moving on the quilt beneath him, determined to entice him back to her. Just the feel of him, hard and hot, against her thigh was erotic. She wanted him.

His hands simply caught at her and turned her over so that his lips could follow the flawless curve of her back. He took his time, kissing the nape of her neck, her shoulders, kissing his way down her spine. All the while his thighs trapped her beneath him, his body swelling, pushing against her buttocks, the tip of him so hot she was squirming against him, needing him.

Julian was determined not to allow anything to shatter his tenuous control. He would know her body as well as his own, know every secret point that could arouse her, every curve and hollow that ached for his touch. His teeth found the rounded muscle of her buttocks, felt her jump beneath his caressing hands. His palm beneath her found her moist invitation, so hot with urgent need he smiled, satisfied with his knowledge now. He simply lifted her hips and pressed against her waiting entrance, waiting a heartbeat until he had the reaction he craved. Desari pushed back, frantic for his invasion.

He caught her hips and surged forward, penetrating deeply, burying himself in that tight, wet, velvet-soft sheath that fit him so perfectly, so uniquely. The feel of it was unlike anything he had ever experienced in his long centuries of existence. He found his hands moving over her beautiful body, cupping her breasts, caressing her bottom, his mouth tasting her back. Her long ebony hair cascaded in waves to pool on the quilt around her, and it was a sight he knew he would never forget. And then the fire took hold, so hot, so fast, he found himself gripping her hips and plunging into her, harder and faster and deeper until the fiery friction was poised on the knife edge between pleasure and pain. Her body wound tighter and tighter, and she cried out to him for release. He wanted to stay, poised forever on that edge, her soft body burning with his, her mind sharing the ecstasy of it all. The savage demands of his race erupted to the surface, and he bent over her smaller body, completely dominant, his teeth finding her shoulder to pin her submissively in place.

Desari allowed it, feeling the compulsion riding him

so hard. There was a desperate need in him she could nearly touch, nearly see, hidden deep but swirling close to the surface, an elusive shadow she couldn't quite catch. Then she lost her train of thought completely as his body swelled even more in hers, so thick and hard he was driving out all sanity, and they exploded together into time and space. Colors burst around them like the most wondrous fireworks imaginable. There was no room for air in their lungs.

Julian would have collapsed on top of her, but he was far too conscious of how delicate she was. He rolled to one side, taking her with him because he couldn't tolerate the slightest separation. He had seen as much of her mind as she had seen of his. She thought, incorrectly, that she would now go back to her family and meet with him every now and then. Or, worse, that he would leave her because she refused to go off with him. His arm was heavy over her narrow rib cage; his thigh held her still. Lazily his hand cupped her breast, his thumb feathering gently, first over her nipple, then tracing the curving fullness.

Desari felt her body clench in reaction. It would always be that way. She knew it. Julian Savage had some dominion over her body, some perfect union with her no one else could ever match. She had read about sex, knew every detail, every position, every intriguing intimacy that could possibly be shared. Yet her body had never once felt desire. It was as if that part of her had been dead. She simply assumed most Carpathian women did not have urges and desires like human women. But her body had been waiting for this one man. Her other half.

Julian kissed her gently. "I will not allow you to leave me, Desari." He said it softly, his voice a hypnotic spell of enchantment.

She could feel it brush at her mind like butterfly wings. Pure and gentle. Almost tender. So insidious that for a brief instant she did not recognize the elegant touch of compulsion. Desari sighed, not wanting to shatter such a perfect interlude with a disagreement. She might never have such a moment again. Still, she had a duty; she could not be selfish no matter how perfect this seemed.

Julian was a renegade, someone who rarely recognized authority, preferring to go his own way. He intended to take her away to some remote place, somewhere far from her family and her singing. But that was not even remotely possible. A soft smile curved her mouth. She knew him, knew what he was. Julian had merged his mind with hers. She knew there was a dark place, a shadow she had not yet entered. Still, she knew he was not capable of allowing her to be unhappy.

He was definitely an outlaw. He had pushed the limits of Carpathian laws many times in his existence in his relentless quest for knowledge. Julian had an active brain; he was quick and intelligent. He was so used to his own power, he wore it like a second skin. He knew things of which many of his kind were still ignorant. He was an extraordinary warrior, a hunter of vampires, and he had destroyed many of them.

Deep within him she touched on the darkness. He seemed to believe he was different from most Carpathian males, that his darkness had not developed over centuries but had always been present in him, had begun to grow even when he was a child. Desari believed that whatever the difference that set him apart from those of his race was also in her own brother. It was what allowed them to possess the iron will and relentless drive to continue without turning when others would falter.

Desari had touched the emptiness of his life, the sense

of meaningless, barren existence. He had made his choice to end it all, had believed there was no chance he would find his lifemate. For one moment she touched on the strange shadow in his mind. There was a shimmer of regret at not succeeding in his mission to self-destruct, but then it was gone, as elusive as before. She felt his joy in finding her, the intensity of his feelings for her. He had a possessive streak a mile wide. Desari had never before heard of a lifemate. She didn't even know if she believed in the concept, but Julian did.

Julian lay stretched out on the bed, propped up on one elbow so that he could study every expression that crossed Desari's face, taking it into his being like the very air he breathed. It was incredible to him that this woman, so beautiful, could be his. It seemed a dream, a fantasy he had somehow brought to life. He had never allowed himself the luxury of wishing or hoping. From the beginning he had known he would make the choice to walk into the sun. This was a priceless gift of life itself, a treasure beyond the realm of his imagination. *And he had brought her into a world of darkness and danger when she had only known light.*

Desari could hear the steady rhythm of his heart. She was very aware of his hard muscles close to her, his posture somehow protective and possessive at the same time. Skin to skin. The door was still open, allowing the night breeze to swirl through the room, to cool the heat of their skin. She smiled, her breath stirring the fine golden hairs roughening the roped muscles along his arm. "You changed your clothes for me." He had come to meet her at the tavern elegantly dressed.

His hand moved over the line of her back, unhurried, his palm simply savoring the feel of her. "You were so beautiful in your white dress, and I was in jeans and a T-shirt. I thought I should come up to your standards."

119

His hand moved up and over her rib cage to cup the soft weight of her breast.

"And I changed into jeans for you," Desari admitted. "I think you look sexy in jeans." She pressed her bottom snugly into the curve of his body. "But I must admit you are dynamite dressed up."

He pushed aside the sweep of silken hair to brush his mouth over the nape of her neck. It was extraordinary to be able to touch her like this. "*Dynamite* is an interesting word, *cara*."

His voice sounded so distracted, Desari turned her head to look at him. His golden eyes were burning hot, moving over the length of her. She felt the heat searing her insides despite the cool breeze. She was very aware of his hand caressing the soft roundness of her breast. "We have to think, Julian. You know we do."

"I have already made up my mind, Desari," he answered her, a purr of menace creeping into his voice. "You have no other choice but to stay with me. We are lifemates. I could allow you to go back to your family without me so that you would know that I speak the truth, but it would be painful for you. I can do no other than to ensure your comfort."

Desari sighed, her long lashes sweeping down to cover the sudden pain in her dark eyes. She needed more time with Julian, to savor this night with him. To end such a beautiful interlude with an argument was the last thing she wanted.

"There is no need for an argument," he murmured gently, obviously still nestled in her mind. "I have no choice but to ensure your well-being at all times. You are hunted. Aside from the discomfort of separation, I would never leave your side without first eliminating the danger to you." *And what of the danger he had brought with him?*

"Julian." She turned over, shivering a little as flames danced unbidden over her skin where his fingertips trailed. "If you believe what you say, then you must see that I cannot bear a fight between you and my brother. I have never defied him before, and he is responsible for my safety, the safety of all of my family. What I have done is truly wrong." She held up a hand. "I am not sorry, Julian. Please do not misunderstand me. I would not trade this night with you for all my days."

Julian bunched a mass of ebony strands in his fist and crushed it to his face, inhaling the fresh, clean scent of her. "I will deal with Darius."

"That is the point I am trying to make. I do not want you to do so," she objected patiently.

"So what do you want, Desari?" he inquired between his white teeth. "A one-night stand? This is it?" Instead of the anger she expected, his voice was slightly mocking, and his male amusement set her teeth on edge.

Her charcoal eyes went black with smoldering fire. "You know that is not so. But I do think it best to ease into things."

He laughed out loud, then rolled over to stare up at the ceiling, his broad shoulders shaking with humor. Desari glared at him, coming up on her knees, heedless of her bare skin gleaming so invitingly in the night. "What is so funny?" she demanded.

He touched her face, a tender caress meant to soothe. "I would not call this night easing into anything, *piccola*. It was more along the lines of a wildfire consuming both of us." His smile was all male satisfaction.

"Wipe that smirk off your face." Desari touched his perfect lips with a fingertip.

"I deserve to wear it," he contradicted her solemnly. "You know I do." His eyes were hot and molten again, touching her so deep inside that Desari nearly forgot what had been so important just moments earlier.

"You are deliberately distracting me," she chided, but her hand found his heavy chest muscles and lay directly over his heart. "We should settle this."

His hand covered hers so that her palm was pressed tightly to his skin. "We have settled it. I go where you go. You go where I go. You are no longer under Darius's protection, although all male Carpathians guard our women as the treasures we know them to be. He will understand."

"In time, Julian," she agreed a little desperately, "but not right away. I will go back and talk to him. If he agrees to our relationship, the others will have no choice but to do as he says. Give me a few risings to convince him."

Desari was well aware of the hard edge to Julian's mouth. He was nowhere near agreeing with her.

Chapter Six

Julian felt his breath catch in his lungs, his throat constricting to the point of closing off completely. Dara was so beautiful, on her knees, her silken hair caressing her body, pooling on the quilt around her. Her skin was flawless, her narrow rib cage and small waist emphasizing the fullness of her breasts. He loved the sound of her voice, so pure and true, like nothing he had ever heard before.

Desari could not escape him; he felt quite complacent in that regard. Her expression, as she glared down at him, trying to be exasperated with him, could not erase the softness of her dark eyes. She didn't have a mean bone in her body.

Julian simply reached up, caught her waist, and lifted her easily with his extraordinary strength. He shifted his body at the same time, a fluid motion that settled her directly over him. Her long hair brushed his thighs, his hips, dancing over his skin as erotically as the most skilled fingers. When he lowered her gently, his body had already surged to life, hot and hard, eager for the feel of her velvet sheath tightening around him.

Desari gasped as he filled her, driving every thought from her mind but the need of her body to match Julian's insatiable appetite. Her eyes went wide, and Julian reached up to cup her breasts while his golden eyes held hers captive. They were sharing more than their bodies, Desari knew; she was looking into his soul, and he so clearly could see hers. He moved his hips, rocking her gently, telling her more about him than his wild, untamed possession had.

"There is no one more beautiful than you, Desari," he whispered softly, "not in all the world."

Her smile was slow and seductive, the smile of a woman certain of the power she wields. She traced the definition of his muscles, ran her fingers through the mat of golden hair on his chest. Time seemed to stand still as they went on a lazy, sensuous exploration together with mutual silent consent. His hands followed the satin contours of her body, lingering in every intriguing place, memorizing the feel of her.

His hips picked up the pace a little more aggressively, and she could feel the hot, slick passion rising with every stroke. Deliberately she began to ride him, tightening her muscles so that the friction increased, so that hot velvet gripped and teased him. She loved watching his face, the way his amber eyes heated to molten gold, the way his breath became labored, the way passion emphasized his dark sensuality. His hands gripped her waist hard, his teeth clenching, a harsh cry tearing up through his body as she exploded around him, ripple after ripple, taking him with her. They soared together, climbing higher than either would have thought possible in so short a time.

Desari lay over him, safe in the protection of his arms, content to be still, uttering no words to mar their remaining time together. She could hear the branches of the trees brushing against the side of the cabin, see the moon lighting the room with a silvery glow. Dawn was approaching faster than Desari would have liked, but they still had time to be together for a while longer.

The wind blew through the open door into the room, filling the air with tales of the night. All at once Julian's hands on her waist gripped her hard, keeping her motionless. The warning came to her from his mind, a silent urging to quickly clothe herself, while he rolled off the bed, coming to his feet in one fluid motion. Everything about him suggested menace. He made a motion with one hand, instantly providing his muscular body with civilized trappings.

You stay put, he ordered without looking at her, already moving out of the cabin and down the steps, determined to meet any intruder as far from Desari as he could safely get. He had been an arrogant idiot to take her from the protection of her family unit when she was hunted. The darkness in *him* provided an even brighter beacon for the undead, for his sworn enemy. Whatever was out there, stalking them in the night, was close. He felt it, sensed it, although he could not identify the threat.

He inhaled sharply, studied the sky, the woods, the very ground itself. He looked every inch of what he was, a dangerous predator. *Dara, if an attack comes, call to your brother to meet you, and go to him immediately.*

Desari had no intention of doing any such thing. If anything threatened them, she was not going to run like a rabbit and leave him to face an attack alone. *What is it?* she asked.

Desari's soft tones eased some of the tension in Julian.

What do you *feel?* He demanded her answer, his demeanor reminiscent of her brother's.

There was a moment of silence while Desari's senses flared out into the night. She felt no threat. None at all. Crossing her arms protectively across her breasts, she went to the door to lean against the frame, inhaling the night air. Nothing. *Are you certain there is a threat to us? I detect nothing of the kind. I can assure you, Julian, I am not without my own power. I think I would know if danger were near.*

If a Carpathian as powerful as Desari could not feel a threat, there was only one reason. She was not the one being threatened. Julian took several steps out into a clearing, circling cautiously, waiting to meet the menace. It was there. Somewhere close. He felt the oppressive channeling of energy directed at him. It was strong, much stronger than he had anticipated, beating at his mind with thoughts of defeat, an attempt to tear down his self-confidence. Julian had used such a mind trick himself on many occasions. It angered him that his adversary would think him such a rank amateur.

It was easy enough to reverse the apprehension, sending it winging back through the night air, reinforced with his own power and strength. There was a moment of complete silence. The very insects seemed to hold their breath, as if his retaliation had struck and the recipient was in a cold, killing fury. The attack came from his left, a blur of motion impossible to see. It was Julian's heightened senses that saved him from the slashing, raking claws. The leopard materialized out of thin air, going straight for his belly with a terrible ferocity. The claws came within a hair's width of nailing him. Julian actually had to hold his breath to prevent the cat from laying his belly wide open.

Cursing, Julian took to the air, shape-shifting as he

did so, acquiring razor-sharp talons, a wicked, curved beak, and a six-foot wingspan. He dove straight at the muscular black leopard, talons outstretched.

The leopard somersaulted to avoid the lethal charge, heading toward the cover of the trees, knowing its huge, feathered opponent would not have easy maneuverability in the canopy of branches.

Desari stood perfectly still on the porch, her eyes fixed on the terrible battle. *Julian. Darius. Her worst nightmare come true*. She took a deep breath and let it out slowly. Then she lifted her hands toward the moon and began to weave an intricate pattern, even as she sang softly.

Notes sprang to life in front of her, notes of silver and gold, spilling toward the two combatants. Her voice swelled with purity, with beauty, took wing, and rose above the clearing, spreading outward into the forest. The song was a whisper of sound yet perfectly clear. The notes danced like whirling eddies of stardust, spinning around and between the leopard and the owl.

Desari's song carried far into the night, and everyone and everything within hearing had to stop and listen. The song was of peace and understanding among all species. Her voice was not of the earth but a blend of musical notes so in tune with the universe that even natural adversaries, anything within range of the music, could not possibly be at odds. Caught in the mystical enchantment, Darius was unable to hold the shape of a stalking leopard, and Julian nearly fell out of the sky as his body regained its original form. He landed rather heavily, quite close to Darius.

The men stared at one another, astonished at the power of Desari's voice. It held them easily within its spell, two strong Carpathian males unable to find the aggression to continue their battle. Her voice continued, drawing the notes into a net of silver and gold shimmering brightly in the moonlight. The net enveloped the two men, weaving tiny radiant threads between them. They could only stare at her, captivated by the sheer magnificence and power of her incredible gift.

Darius could feel the depth of his sister's emotions, her need of this man, her body's demands for him, her uncertainties and fears. He could feel the fierce, protective nature, the possessive streak, the deep hunger and desire for Desari, the passion running so deeply in the Carpathian male. He felt the melding of their two souls into one solid unit, shared between two separate bodies.

Julian could see clearly into Darius's heart. The demands of his very soul to protect his sister, to see to it that all within his family remained safe. The man feared that Julian was vampire, the undead, luring his sister to her doom. He would fight to the death, take anyone who threatened her with him. There was no peace for Darius. He fought the terrible darkness the males of their race were forced to battle toward the end of their existence. He fought it and with only the sheer force of his will survived each rising.

The silver and gold notes began to shimmer, their luminescence slowly fading with the whisper of her voice falling away. There was silence. It was loud, almost obscene after the beauty of her song. Darius continued to stare at his sister. Julian was frankly awed by her display of power. He, like most Carpathian males, generally thought of power as a destructive force. Desari had as much power as any male, but of a completely different kind.

"I did not take her away to harm her," he offered, his voice low.

Desari's dark eyes flashed. "No one could take me,

Darius. I go where I desire, not where someone takes me."

"I can see you have made your choice, little sister," Darius replied evenly. "But this man will not be an easy companion." He could smell the combined scent of their lovemaking, the male's blood mingling with hers. However the golden-haired stranger had done it, Desari was locked to his side for all eternity. "I am Darius," he introduced himself reluctantly. "Desari is my sister."

"Julian Savage," Julian returned, gliding to the porch to take up his position at Desari's side. His very posture screamed possession, yet was protective, almost tender toward Desari. "Desari is my lifemate."

"We have never before encountered another like us. All have been the undead and had to be destroyed." Darius's dark eyes, so like Desari's yet so coldly lethal, measured Julian. Whether Darius found Julian lacking or not was hidden beneath the impassive mask he wore.

"There are a few of us left," Julian said quietly. "We are often hunted by those who have turned vampire as aggressively as we hunt them." His hand found the wealth of silken hair tumbling down Desari's back and crushed a fistful of the ebony strands in his palm almost absently, his touch tender. "Did you know she could do that?"

"I do not even know what the hell she did," Darius admitted.

"I am here." Desari sniffed indignantly. "And I know exactly what I did. If the two of you were not so arrogant and conceited, you might have considered that the women of our race would have endowments equal to those of the men."

Julian glanced at Darius, just a quick flash of golden eyes, but Darius caught a glint that might have been amusement.

"Arrogant? Conceited?" Julian reprimanded with a grin. "Desari, that is a little harsh."

"I do not think so," she told him severely. "You are like two territorial male animals, circling each other threateningly without even knowing what the other is about. How intelligent is that?"

"Desari . . ." There was a distinct warning in Darius's voice.

She glanced down at her bare toes, then blushed, realizing that Darius knew exactly what had taken place in that cabin. How could he not? Julian's scent clung to every inch of her skin. Julian's hand went to the nape of her neck, his strong fingers beginning a slow, soothing massage. He was linked to her mind, and he felt her discomfort at her brother's knowledge of their intimacy.

The protective touch on her neck provided her with courage and conviction, and her gaze leapt back to her brother's face. "I hold you in the highest respect, Darius, you know that. No sister could love her brother more. I do not know exactly what this thing is between Julian and me, but it is strong and compelling. The two of you will have to get along without further physical violence. I mean it. I ask little of you, but this I will insist on from both of you. You must promise me. You must give me your word of honor."

Darius's dark eyes smoldered in warning. "Do not put too much faith in him, little sister. You do not know him. A stranger comes into our midst, heralding an attack on your life, and you trust him completely. Perhaps you are far *too* trusting."

Julian's breath eased out in a long, furious hiss. His golden eyes glittered with menace. "You are quick to judge those you do not know." His voice was soft, even pleasant, but no one could mistake the threat beneath the surface. This Darius *was* like Gregori—he was of the

same blood as the healer, second only to the Prince—
and he sensed the shadow in Julian just as Gregori did.

"And you underestimate your enemies," Darius
pointed out, his voice like black velvet. "You are so sure
of yourself that you take too few precautions to safeguard the one you have claimed as your own. It was
unbelievably easy to unravel your pitiful attempts to di-
vert me."

Julian's white teeth gleamed in the waning moonlight.
"I knew you would follow; how could you not when
you are responsible for your sister's safety? In any case,
you could do no other after the assassins had been allowed to make their attempt on her life." He delivered
the blow smiling but without humor. They were indeed
playing cat and mouse.

Desari shoved Julian so hard and so unexpectedly, he
teetered for a moment on the edge of the porch. "That
is it. I have had it with the two of you." She tilted her
chin at them. "I will have no more of this nonsense. I
will not leave my family at this time, Julian. You can
accept my decision and remain with us as a member of
our unit, or you can go your own way. If you refuse to
accept him, Darius, then I will be given no other option
than to follow where he leads." Exasperated, she glared
at them. "Get over it already. I mean it."

Julian's mouth twitched, the amber eyes softening
with amusement. "Is she always like this? You are a
tolerant male to have raised such an impertinent
woman."

Desari shoved him again but this time Julian was
ready for her, laughing out loud at the eruption of her
temper, catching her wrists easily and pulling her into
him. "I gave your brother a compliment, *caressima*." His
voice was a tender caress, teasing, fanning smoldering

embers within her to instant heat. "Is that not what you wanted?"

She tilted her chin. "That is not exactly what I had in mind, Julian."

"I have not had much experience pleasing women these last few centuries. In truth, I had forgotten how difficult the females of our race could be," Julian told Darius with a straight face.

"Difficult?" Desari was outraged. "You call me difficult when you and my brother were trying to tear each other limb from limb? The males of our race are in dire need of self-control. You have too long had things your own way. It has made you arrogant and conceited and very spoiled."

Darius suddenly moved, his speed incredible even within their race, his body forcing his sister's into the shelter of the porch, down low. "Merge with Savage now, as you did before," he commanded, a hiss of sound in the stillness of the night.

Desari obeyed because she always obeyed Darius, merging her mind completely with Julian's. She expected anger, at the least smoldering resentment at Darius's high-handedness. Instead, she found him on the alert, moving to position himself alongside Darius to protect her. She submerged herself within Julian's mind so that any outside source probing and seeking a feminine touch would get nothing.

She felt the darkness sweeping over the land, the perverted aberration they called the undead. The vile touch of the vampire sickened her as it moved ever closer, searching, always searching. She smelled the stench of evil, the twisted, damned soul of one who always killed his quarry, drained his victim's lifeblood, often after torturing and tormenting the doomed creature.

Sheltered between the two powerful males, Desari

was unafraid, but the vileness of the vampire was making her body react, her stomach rolling and heaving. Julian enveloped her mind completely as he had done before, shielding her from the undead as it raced across the sky. Dawn was on the heels of the vampire, and it could not face even the first rays of the sun. It needed to find sanctuary immediately. It passed overhead and was gone, leaving a dark stain in the sky like an oily patch of evil.

"They seek our women," Darius hissed grimly. "Always they track us down. I know it is the women they sense." He sent an urgent inquiry traveling on the wind. *Is Syndil protected? The undead have once again found us.*

Julian reluctantly allowed Desari to surface from the total submersion, his arm circling her shoulders protectively. His heart was pounding in alarm. Had the darkness in him brought this vile creature straight to his lifemate? He had to destroy the demon.

The reply to Darius's inquiry came back on the mental path used by the family unit so that both Darius and Desari heard the news. *We felt his approach and took precaution. Syndil is deep in the earth where he cannot find her should he try another probe. It is near; he must go to ground soon.* The voice was Barack's. *Do not fear, Darius, no one will take Syndil from us, and no one will attempt to harm her and live.*

"There will be others," Darius informed Julian, once satisfied that all was well at home. "They have taken to traveling together in numbers, perhaps thinking those of us who hunt them will be more easily defeated." There was a natural self-confidence in Darius's voice that said plainly it didn't matter to him how many vampires tried to defeat him; it would be an impossibility.

"My brother has resided in San Francisco for many

years, hunting the undead in the western United States," Julian volunteered. "He, too, noticed a trend of late in northern California and up into Oregon and Washington of usually solitary vampires suddenly congregating. It seemed insanity to me that they would not simply avoid his area altogether."

Julian stepped off the porch, taking Desari with him, his fingers shackling her wrist. "What is the news of the rest of your family? The vampire did not detect the other woman, did he?" He knew Darius had contacted his family; he would have done the same.

Darius's dark eyes flicked over him. Julian was astonished at how much the man reminded him of Gregori, the healer of the Carpathian people. Although Gregori's eyes glittered silver with menace, Darius's black eyes could portray an equal threat easily. "Our family is safe," Darius replied softly, thoughtfully. "I will hunt this one now and go to ground when it is done."

"Do not risk yourself. Remember you are needed," Desari said in a low voice, betraying her fear.

"I am needed to hunt down these killers," Darius reminded her with great gentleness. "They follow us wherever we go. The reason vampires congregate in this part of the country, Savage, is because Desari prefers to perform in this region. Her favorite place to play is a small resort north of here called Konocti Harbor Resort and Spa. It is much to her liking. The people are friendly, the audiences receptive, the countryside is beautiful, and the place is small and intimate enough to suit her."

Julian circled her waist with one arm and brought her up against the heat of his body, needing to feel her for just a moment. "I should have known you were the troublemaker, Desari," he whispered against the bare skin of her neck, wanting to comfort her with his teasing.

"Do not do this, either of you." Desari's soft eyes were liquid with sorrow. "You are trying to distract me, both of you. You will hunt this vampire despite my wishes."

"I will hunt," Darius corrected firmly. "Savage will stay here to protect you."

"No. Desari is safe here for now. I will go with you," Julian stated in a soft voice, aware of his lifemate's silent terror, that her brother would choose to be mortally wounded, and achieve an honorable death, fighting a vampire. *Be easy*, cara, *I will ensure that your brother returns to you unharmed. No vampire could possibly defeat the two of us. Go to ground, and we will return to you after we destroy the undead*. He did not want not to leave the hunting of this vampire to her brother for reasons of his own, as well.

Her fingers clutched at his arm. There were tears in her mind. *You will probably end up killing one another without me to referee.*

I have given you my word on this, piccola. *You must trust me*. The deep timbre of Julian's voice in her mind was reassuring, sending waves of warmth and comfort throughout her.

"There is no need for both of us to go," Darius challenged softly.

Julian's white teeth flashed in answer, but the smile did not reach his eyes. "I agree with you, Darius. As Desari relies so heavily on your protection, it would indeed be best that you stay with her." He leaned over and brushed his mouth over the corner of Desari's lips. Cara, *do not fret*. Already his solid form was shimmering, evaporating, so that it was a prism of crystal fog rising toward the graying sky.

Darius swore under his breath, clearly outmaneuvered. He was beginning to feel a grudging respect for the stranger with the golden eyes. It had not been quite as easy as he had suggested to unravel Savage's trail, and he had been fairly certain the man knew he was following. Darius found him interesting. He didn't altogether trust him; he was a renegade, and there was something not quite right about him. Something buried deep. Darius intended to keep an eye on him.

"Go to ground, Desari. Do not argue with me, as I am giving you an order, not asking. I want to know your exact location so that I may sleep above you in the earth this day." His hand touched her face in a display of love and affection that he wanted to feel, that he should have been able to feel, yet could not. Nevertheless, he always granted her the gestures because he knew she needed them, knew she wanted him to feel those emotions that were no longer his to feel.

Without waiting for a reply, knowing the dawn's first light would render it impossible for the vampire to hunt Desari, Darius leapt skyward, dissolving into a fine mist that streaked after the stream of iridescent fog. Desari stared after the two male Carpathians, squinting slightly as the twilight before dawn began to replace the darkness. She didn't want to feel fear for either of them—they were both strong and powerful—yet she couldn't help but worry. On more than one occasion, she had seen Darius return torn and bloody from a vicious battle with a vampire. And they were braving the dawn as well, which would weaken them enormously, albeit not as drastically as it would one who had turned.

Darius had always tried to keep the women away from that aspect of their existence, but she was of his blood. The same power and intelligence ran as deeply in her, and she knew of Darius's terrible struggle. She knew he was slipping away from her. She feared for his soul, feared for her race and that of the mortal beings. She

truly believed in her heart that should Darius turn, there
was no hunter alive who could defeat him. All would
be lost, including Darius and all he had done, everything
he had sacrificed for them throughout the centuries.

She went into the small cabin and wandered around,
touching the things in the room. Works of art—unusual,
old, and unique. Julian liked beautiful things. She picked
up his silk shirt, brought it to her face, and inhaled his
masculine scent. *Julian.*

I am with you, cara. *Do not fret.* It was amazing to
her that the communication between them was so strong.
Just a thought of him, the worry for him in her mind,
and he was aware instantly. *I shall return to you soon.
Go to ground now.*

I will go to ground, she assured him, *but I will not
sleep until I know the two of you are safe.*

*You will not monitor me while I destroy the undead.
It would be upsetting—maybe even dangerous—for you.
Please do as I say, Desari.* He used the word *please* as
if he were asking her, but there was a subtle undertone
of command.

Desari had never considered that. When Darius
hunted, Syndil and she had always been secured in a
safe place, contact with him restricted. They had never
thought to defy Darius; in such matters, his word was
law. Now all was changed. Somehow, some way, she
was locked to Julian. The thought of him in danger was
so terrible, she could barely breathe. How could she do
as he asked and not touch him? Not reach through the
gray-streaked dawn and see for herself he was untouched
by the vampire's vile perversion?

After all, Darius was the ultimate warrior, a stone-
cold killing machine when the situation demanded it.
Julian was a man with emotion, which could confer both
weakness and strength.

Desari left the cabin. It was rare for her family to use a building to rest in; most of the time they sought deep earth. They had learned in early childhood it was the only real haven in a dangerous land. All of them felt uncomfortable, far more vulnerable than usual, if they slept above ground. In the hours of high sun, their great strength was totally drained. And if their bodies somehow came to be exposed to that intense light, they would burn. Early morning and late evening they could tolerate, although not always comfortably. Even dim sunlight affected their hypersensitive eyes, the burning pain driving through their heads like shards of glass.

Desari found an unobtrusive knoll covered in waves of green grass. She liked it immediately, feeling a sense of peace. With a wave of her hand she opened the earth and floated deep within its bed. Immediately she sent the coordinates to both her brother and Julian.

Close the earth and sleep. She recognized Julian's soft-spoken commands. He was like Darius in that he didn't need to raise his voice to convey either menace or authority.

Not until you return.

I do not want to have to force your obedience.

As if that could happen. You seem to forget I am no fledgling but your equal. Do not waste your energy attempting the impossible. Destroy this vampire if you must, then return to me quickly. We will discuss your conceit on the next rising.

There came the soft echo of his laughter. Desari relaxed, certain Julian understood she would take no nonsense from him. When he struck, she was completely unprepared, the compulsion strong and total, the need to obey him paramount. Before she could prevent herself from doing so, she relinquished control to him. Immediately Julian sent her to sleep, the deep sleep of their people, stopping her heart and lungs, covering her with the healing, soothing soil for protection and rejuvenation.

After his command to Desari, Julian turned his attention toward his goal. He would have to face Desari's wrath on the next rising, but for now she was beyond the reach of any vampire. She was safe. No vampire could touch her using Julian as a route.

Feeling the dark presence of the undead nearby, Julian settled to earth, his vaporous form shimmering into solid bone and muscle. Darius materialized a heartbeat after him.

"You should have raised her to obey those who protect her," Julian drawled in censure.

Darius's black eyes, as cold as any grave, flicked over him once. "I have never had need to force Dara's obedience."

They moved together, a slow, cautious hunt along the cliffside, all senses alert. The vampire would guard his resting place aggressively. "That is why she came away with me then? Because you approved?" Julian was running his hand lightly along the rock's surface.

Darius caught at him and jerked him back just as a boulder from above their heads dislodged itself and smashed into the very place Julian had been standing. "I knew she was in no danger. If you had wanted to harm her, you would have done so at the concert when the assassins struck," Darius replied complacently. He was examining a section of sheer rock wall as he spoke, his attention caught by the layers of compressed agate and granite.

"Ah, yes, the famous concert where you were guarding her."

"Do not try my patience too far, Savage. You are responsible for what happened at that concert. Had I not been distracted by the power you exuded, the assassins would not have made it inside. You opened the door for them." Darius stepped back and surveyed the cliffside. "This rock pattern looks strange, does it not?"

Julian studied the multilayered face of the cliff. "His safeguards perhaps. They are unfamiliar to me. Have you seen patterns like these before? I thought I had learned most of the ancient works."

Darius glanced at him. "You are fortunate that you had the advantage of being taught such things. Most of what I learned came from singeing my fingers when I made a wrong move. This is a relatively new theme, developed in the New World sometime in the last century. I believe it started in South America, where a group of vampires had quite a stronghold. They copied the pattern from native art. This seems to be some derivation of that." He paused. "In South America I saw evidence of others as well, perhaps like you. But I could not be certain they were not the undead; and with the women, I did not want to chance it, so I moved my family quickly from that place."

Julian glanced at him, then examined the rock face carefully, filing away for future reference the possibility that other Carpathians might exist in South America. He would relay the information to Gregori. The Prince would want to know, and what Gregori knew, Prince Mikhail knew. "Interesting. The pattern doesn't work on the reverse theory. It weaves back and forth."

"Exactly. When you unravel it, you not only have to reverse the pattern but also move up and down and back and forth. It is intricate, very complex to unravel. I am unsure if we have enough time to do it. The sun is climbing. Already I am feeling the effects," Darius admitted.

Julian studied his companion, his golden eyes seeing more than Darius might like. Most Carpathians could stand the early morning rays. Two things, however, made them hypersensitive. Feeding on blood from a kill, and moving closer to the time of turning. Darius had to be close. Very close. It was in the emotionless pits of his eyes, the total disregard for his own life. Darius didn't only fight with complete confidence in his abilities; he fought like a male uncaring of the outcome.

"Go back to my sister, Savage. Guard her well. I will do what I can here, as I am more familiar with this safeguard than you. If something should happen to me, perhaps you will take my place and provide leadership for the others of my family," Darius said casually, although the latter suggestion must have galled him at least a little. Still, his sense of duty made him want someone of power, even Julian, to protect his family should he seek his honorable death.

Julian shook his head. "I am strictly a loner. I do not have leadership qualities." He would not make it easy for Darius to leave his sister and break her heart.

"Desari feared that if something was to happen to you, it would also happen to her. Is that true?" Darius asked the question almost absently, as if he were not really paying attention.

Julian nodded. "It is so. I have bound her to me. If I were to die, she could very well choose the dawn rather than live on without me. You would have to send her to ground for a long while to safeguard her."

"It is far too risky. I am unwilling to chance Desari's life or the state of her mind. You are quite capable of leading should you choose. Perhaps you do not wish it, but if there is need, I am certain you would do no other than to step forward," Darius replied.

Julian had the feeling Darius was testing him again in some way. It didn't matter. Julian had lived long with the darkness crouching in him. He had cut himself off from his people, his own twin, even his Prince. He was used to being an outcast, used to being alone and distrusted. "Oh, no, Darius, you will not do this thing. Desari has feared that you intend to permit yourself to be mortally injured. This I cannot allow. Desari is not ready to leave her family, nor would the others accept me. We will both return to your sister now and take care of the vampire at sundown."

Darius went perfectly still. All at once he seemed every inch the predator he truly was. "I offered leadership over the family, Savage, not over me. I go my own way."

"As do I. I meant no disrespect to you; indeed, Darius, I wish to learn of your history. I believe you are the brother of Gregori, our healer. He is a great man, not unlike yourself." Julian grinned suddenly. "Gregori and I do not always get along either."

Darius blinked, the only evidence of movement. "I cannot imagine why," he muttered ruefully.

"I grow on you," Julian assured.

"I do not think you should count too greatly on it," Darius replied.

"The sun is rising, my friend. Let us go."

"It will not be so easy living within my rule," Darius cautioned softly.

Julian's eyebrows shot up. "Really? As I answer only to my Prince, I think I shall find it an interesting experience."

Darius began to dissolve into a fine mist. It was easier to travel without a body in the light of the sun. Even so, the brain insisted that the eyes were swelling, turning red, streaming in the terrible light.

142

Chapter Seven

The wind blew through the thick stand of trees, and the branches swayed, danced, and bent low to sweep the ground. The leaves rustled with a rush of sound, a glittering display of nature's music. Below the earth the notes resounded, luring the two slumbering hunters back into the world. The two hearts began to beat simultaneously. The sun was slowly sinking below the line of the mountain.

There was a muffled blast as dirt spewed high into the air, first one geyser, then, several feet away, a second one. When the dust and soil settled, two elegantly clad men stood facing one another. One was a golden menace, the other dark and dangerous. White teeth gleamed as they silently acknowledged each other.

"My sister?" Darius got down to his chief concern.

"She will sleep until this distasteful task is completed," Julian answered, his glittering eyes finding the exact spot where Desari lay beneath the earth.

"You are certain of this?" Darius arched an expressive eyebrow skeptically.

Julian's golden eyes iced over, cold and harsh. "I can handle my own lifemate—make no mistake about that."

If Darius had been able to feel amusement, he was certain this would be the moment. Dara was an ancient, a direct descendant of the original Dark One. She might be a female, one of tremendous compassion and goodness, but she was far more powerful than Julian was giving her credit for.

"Have you known many of the females of our race?" Darius asked with deceptive mildness.

"No. Very few remain. They are guarded at all times, as they should be. It is almost unheard of for a woman to be unattached after her eighteenth year."

Darius swung around to stare at Julian. "This is the truth? Eighteen is not yet a fledgling—in truth, yet a child. How can this be?"

Julian shrugged his broad shoulders. "With so few women, so few children born to our kind and surviving, with little hope and so many males on the verge of turning, it is the only safe thing to do. Any unclaimed woman is too unsettling."

"But the woman could not possibly hope to contend with a powerful male at such a young age. She would barely have had the time to learn the most simple of our gifts. How could she develop her own talents and skills?" Darius sounded a bit disgusted with the males of his own race.

Julian's golden eyes glittered for a moment. "If you found one who gave you back colors and emotions, who brought your dead soul to life and showered it with light, would you be able to walk away from her because she was yet a fledgling? Perhaps her skills are not developed, but her body is that of a woman, and any male under the circumstances would be more than happy to spend centuries aiding her in the learning." His body was beginning to shimmer, to dissolve into tiny droplets of moisture. "What are you waiting for, old man? If you did not get enough sleep, I assure you, I can handle this task on my own."

"Old man?" Darius echoed. He made his own transformation with astonishing speed. The sun, although it was sinking, was still bright enough to hurt his sensitive eyes. He had noticed that Julian blinked and squinted a bit, but his eyes weren't streaming in reaction as Darius's were. "I have to ensure you do not meet with any more near misses."

A layer of fog streaked across the sky, racing the sun toward the cliffs. Julian's iridescent colors intermingled with Darius's, and the cliff soon loomed before them, an intimidating sheer rock wall. Julian solidified, arms folded across his chest, watching with interest as Darius began to weave a strange pattern along the layers of granite. Darius moved unhurriedly, as if he had all the time in the world, as if he were unconcerned with the sun sinking or the vampire awakening.

The vampire was locked deep within the cliff wall, but he was very much aware of the two hunters prowling so close, aware of the exact position of the sun and of how much time he had before he could arise. His lips were drawn back in a snarl of hatred, his jagged teeth stained dark from killing while taking blood. His skin was waxen, ashy, drawn, stretched tightly against his skull. His arms were crossed over his chest, his long yellow fingernails like spikes. His venomous hiss was a vow of vengeance and loathing. He could only wait, locked within the prison of the stone and his terrible weakness, while outside the creatures hunting him scratched and sniffed at the entrance to his lair.

Julian was intrigued with the ease with which Darius unraveled the safeguards the vampire had set. Darius moved with great confidence yet was unhurried by even the setting sun. He seemed absorbed in his work, as if it commanded his complete attention, but Julian was not deceived. Darius was aware of the danger they were in.

As Darius continued weaving his strange pattern along the cliff, a faint line began to take shape, zigzagging across the face of the rock. With an ominous rumble the line began to deepen and widen into a crack. At once scorpions began to boil out of the crevice, thousands of them, large and hideous, rushing at Darius. As Darius moved to avoid the cascading fall of poisonous insects, the ground rolled, heaved, and buckled, throwing him directly into their path. Julian jerked him up and out of the way, launching them both into the air as the vampire's guardians swarmed along the ground.

Darius glanced skyward, and lightning arced from cloud to cloud. He gazed steadily at the sizzling streaks, building the energy until he could gather it into a bright orange fireball and direct it straight into the scurrying mass of scorpions. At once there was a stench as the insects blackened into charred ashes.

When Julian settled once more to earth, Darius went right back to work as though the interruption had never taken place. Julian watched the strange pattern, intrigued by the work he had not experienced in his long centuries of hunting. He had to admire the fluid grace Darius exhibited, his sureness and confidence, his lack of hesitation. His own heart was beating out a rhythm of excitement and dread. *Was this the one? Was a certain ancient evil waiting inside this lair, waiting to claim the pupil he had long ago so skillfully wrought?*

"The ground." Darius spoke the words softly. Julian

nearly missed them, even with his acute hearing, so deep was he in his dark memories.

"Excuse me?" Even as his own words slipped out, Julian was heeding the warning, studying the earth beneath them carefully. Darius had not looked away from the cliffside, working at the safeguards so that the crack expanded, the rock face creaking and groaning as it was forced to spread apart. Julian caught a movement—so fast and subtle, he nearly missed it—as it passed under Darius's feet, raising the soil a scant half inch as something streaked beneath the surface.

Then a tentacle erupted but three inches from Darius's shoes, wiggling obscenely, blindly seeking prey. Julian instantly battled the vampire's writhing demon root. He withered each appendage as it burst through the soil seeking Darius, who was seemingly oblivious to the entire battle, working efficiently even as the lashing tentacles attempted to wind around his ankles. Julian hastily destroyed the repulsive thing.

As the last wriggling tentacle withered into ash, a huge bulb erupted a few feet from Julian, its mouth yawning wide. A spray of greenish-yellow liquid spewed toward Darius, who held himself still, widening the crevice, revealing the hidden chamber within, relying on Julian to defend them from the latest menace. Julian blasted the bulb with a laserlike burst of fire from the sky, incinerating it before the acid spray could touch Darius.

"The sun," Julian reminded him, aware of its low position in the sky, seeing the reds and pinks of sunset stain the heavens.

"There is no way to hurry this procedure," Darius replied softly. "The undead is aware of us and sends his minions to delay us."

Julian reached out for the mind of their hidden opponent. *You are weak, evil one. You should not have challenged one so much stronger than you. I am of ancient and powerful blood, undefeated these centuries by those far more learned in the arts than you. There is no way to win. You are already defeated.*

Out of the darkened interior of the chamber rushed an army of large rats, leaping for the two Carpathians with a savage ferocity fed by starvation and compulsion. With his desperate, cunning mind, the vampire orchestrated the pack's vicious attack. Julian realized the rats were charging Darius. The vampire was prepared for this dark one, but perhaps he had not comprehended that another hunter, too, was stalking him. The rats were charging Desari's protector, suggesting that Dara *was* the undead's ultimate goal. With a savage satisfaction, Julian leapt over the thick mass of furred bodies and made his way into the belly of the mountain.

The ancient he had spent lifetimes searching for was not in the lair; he would have immediately recognized Julian, his voice, his blood, the shadowing. Still, the merciless fury drove him inward, seeking his prey. This one would not escape.

The walls of the narrow tunnel bulged with razor-sharp, jagged spikes, erupting unexpectedly right, then left, as the vampire threw obstacles in his hunter's path to delay him. The vampire was aware of the peril approaching *and* of the sun sinking. He felt he had a fighting chance if he could hamper the progress of the hunter long enough to allow the sun to set and his own strength to rise.

Julian simply thinned and elongated his body, sliding easily through the maze of sharpened spikes, continuing deeper within the bowels of the mountain. He smelled the evil stench, the lair of the beast. It stank of death and decay. As Julian stepped into the chamber itself, thousands of bats rushed at him, emitting high-pitched squeals of alarm. His mind automatically reached to calm them and sent them retreating back into the depths of the cave so they wouldn't be caught in the light, prey for more aggressive species.

The vampire lay staring at him with red eyes hot with hatred, his thin, bloodless lips drawn back in a snarl to reveal rotting teeth. His skin had shrunk to barely cover his skull; he already resembled a skeleton. Julian wanted to feel pity for the damned creature, but his revulsion at such proximity to evil was overwhelming. He detested the undead with a relentless, merciless drive he could never overcome. In his childhood he had come far too close to such a repulsive being, and the rotted, foul stench was forever etched in his memory.

The vampire lay in a depression in the earth, rotted clothes, once elegant and fine, covering his emaciated body. He looked grotesque. As Julian approached, the mouth curved in a parody of a smile. "You are too late, hunter. The sun has dropped from the sky." The vampire floated from the soil to an upright position.

Julian shrugged with studied casualness. "Do you not recognize me? We grew up together. You were once a great man, Renaldo. How is that you have sunk so low as to roam the earth in search of fresh kills?"

The head undulated back and forth in a palsied motion. "Why have you come to this place, Savage? You never concerned yourself with the politics of our race." The vampire's voice was an ugly hiss spewing from his throat.

"You chose to become something other than what you were born to be. I have long hunted those who chose to damn their souls and imperil others," Julian replied softly, almost gently. His voice was beautiful purity, its tones filling the cavern, pushing aside the stench of decay. "There was a time, Renaldo, when you hunted by my side. Even then you were not nearly of my strength and power. Why would you think yourself capable of challenging me now?" On the surface, it seemed an innocent enough question, but his voice was hypnotic, velvet, all the more powerful because it was nearly impossible to detect the hidden compulsion in it.

Darius had followed Julian into the mountain, remaining in the background to scan for other dangers, knowing from experience that the undead had many traps and deceptions and that they always tried to take those hunting them with them to their death. With the undead, nothing was ever as it seemed.

He found Julian's soft, gentle approach to the vampire interesting. Darius was more direct, hunting the undead down and quickly dispatching them in a brief, ferocious battle. Julian was a bit like the vampire himself—indirect, deceptive, undermining the confidence of his opponent, sidetracking him, throwing him off, reminding him of his earlier, better days. Darius shook his head but remained silent and unseen. His sister's mate was an interesting man, a renegade, going his own way in all things, a careless, sardonic humor spilling over when least expected. Julian appeared to be afraid of nothing, to respect few, and to be a law unto himself.

Darius's curiosity stemmed from more than merely wanting to become better acquainted with the man who claimed his sister for his own. There was something eluding him about his sister's chosen lifemate. Something dark and mysterious that nagged at him.

The vampire was moving in a circular direction, trying to position himself closer to the exit. Julian was not giving ground, merely turning with the monster in a strange, flowing dance. Julian could have been performing a minuet for all the stress he portrayed. "You know that I cannot allow you to live, Renaldo. It would be inhuman of me."

"You have no regard for humans, Julian," the vampire pointed out. "You follow no one, not even the Prince of all Carpathians. You think I do not feel the shadow lengthening and growing within you? You are of our blood. My challenge was not issued to you but to another, one not known to the people of our homeland. This one hoards more than one eligible woman for himself. This is against our laws."

Julian's white teeth gleamed in the darkness of the chamber. "And you follow those laws?" He asked it with deceptive mildness, but the vampire's words had struck deeply. *"You are of our blood."*

Even as he spoke, he felt the slight shift in the earth beneath his feet, the undead's next deadly desperate assault beginning. At once he moved with lightning speed, going from a loose standing position to lunging straight at the vampire, his hand diving deep into the chest wall, extracting the pumping heart as he leapt away.

His image was so blurred, his speed so swift, even for one of their kind, that Darius thought for the space of a heartbeat that he might have imagined Savage's skillful charge. The vampire swayed uncertainly, gasping from the blow, his grotesque features contorted into an even more grotesque mask. He fell in slow motion, landing nearly at Julian's feet.

Julian tossed the heart some distance from the body and immediately gathered energy in his hands to cleanse the blood from his skin. He then directed an orange flame at the still-pulsating organ, incinerating it to a fine gray ash. The flame then leapt from his hand to the body, instantly cremating the remains so that the vampire could not possibly rise again.

The earth beneath his feet rolled, heaved, and bucked.

There was an ominous creaking of rock, a grinding of layers of stone as slabs of granite began to slide toward one another. Darius appeared and sprang toward the shifting crevice, his hands weaving a strange pattern as he sang something softly beneath his breath, slowing the vampire's lethal trap. Julian didn't wait for an engraved invitation. Shape-shifting on the wing, making himself as small as possible, he streaked through the closing crack toward open air and the night, Darius right beside him. The two burst out into the freedom of sky, the open expanse of air, just as the two sides of the crevice thunderously crashed together.

"I thought you were planning on talking him to death," Darius informed the golden bat dryly as he himself·shape-shifted· from a black bat to a feathered and much more powerful predator.

"Someone had to do something while you were playing with your rock patterns," Julian replied easily, allowing iridescent feathers to erupt along his own body, becoming a raptor more than able to keep up with his companion's aggressive flight.

They began to fly side be side easily toward the forest where they had left Desari. "I could do no other than protect the man of my sister's choosing." Darius managed to make it sound as if his sister had a hole in her head.

Julian snorted. "Protect me? I do not think so, old man. You were the one standing back in the shadows while I destroyed the beast."

"I had to ensure you came to no harm through other traps and snares. You certainly wasted enough time with the undead," Darius replied softly. He veered to the left, winging his way above the canopy of trees. When Julian continued on his present course, Darius made a wide circle back to him. "You do not wish to return to my family with me?"

"I must awaken Desari first," Julian replied complacently.

"Desari rose an hour ago." Darius delivered the message in a tranquil, neutral voice.

Julian, within the owl's body, nearly dropped from the sky in shock. He could not conceive of Darius teasing him. Darius had no discernible sense of humor. He was closer to turning than any other Carpathian male Julian had ever met. It was an unsettling thought that someday he might have to hunt and attempt to destroy Desari's brother.

Desari. He whispered her name across the sky, somewhere between tenderness and rage. She had somehow managed to awaken on her own despite his forceful command. He should have known the moment she had risen. He was her lifemate. They were connected, two halves of the same whole. Darius had known Desari was gone. Had she contacted him? For a moment Julian's feathered body shook with anger. Desari didn't understand what it meant to be claimed by a mate. She was bound to him, heart and soul. She needed to learn much more of the man who was now her lifemate. Petty retaliation because he had forced her obedience would not be tolerated.

Tolerated? Desari's soft voice said scornfully in his mind. *I do not owe you obedience, Julian. I am no fledgling to follow your lead without question. You are the one who needs to learn more of the woman you claim you have bound to you. I will not be treated in such a manner.*

Julian slammed his mind shut while he wrestled with an unfamiliar, smoldering rage. He had never really experienced jealous anger. He had never had reason to.

And, as a powerful Carpathian male, he had naturally believed that his lifemate was the one who would willingly change her life for him. She would want to fit into his world, not force him to live in hers. Yet Desari appeared to have ideas of her own.

Julian deliberately turned away from Darius, working at repressing his unexpected temper. He needed time alone to get himself under control, to think things through. To try to understand that Desari was no fledgling to be guided by her mate. That she had lived many centuries, had many powers, and was used to making decisions and commanding a certain amount of respect. He winged his way toward the mountain peaks, where he always felt a semblance of peace. He would spend time there pondering the situation and the best way to handle it.

"You are of our blood," the undead had said. And it was the terrible truth. How had he thought he could claim a lifemate, live as an honorable Carpathian was meant to? Doubtless Mikhail, the Prince of their people, knew the truth. Gregori, too. And Darius certainly sensed it in him. Worse, Julian now realized, what Darius knew, so would Desari. *"You are of our blood."*

Desari wandered through the campsite Dayan had chosen. They were near other campers, human campers, yet protected from prying eyes. Still, for some reason, she was uneasy, restless. She found herself pacing back and forth until Dayan told her to stop or she was going to wear a new trail in the dirt. At first she thought it was because she was angry with Julian for sending her to sleep like a fledgling. Then she decided it was anger at herself for being vulnerable to such compulsion. Now she didn't know what it was. Her mind was in chaos, striving constantly to find Julian. That in itself was disconcerting. Maybe what she needed to do was feed. No, what she needed to do was find Julian. Touch him. See him.

She swore softly and flounced over to the picnic table. Forest, the male leopard that always traveled with them, was stretched out the entire length of the table. Irritably, Desari shoved at him. "Get down."

The cat answered her with a contemptuous raise of his lip, but he didn't budge. Dayan turned around to stare at her in surprise. "What is wrong with you?"

"Everything. Nothing. I do not know. The bus is broken down for the fourth time this month. Barack has no idea how to fix vehicles; he just tinkers with them all the time. No one wants to buy a new one, and I keep saying we have to either learn to fix the motor ourselves or hire a mechanic to travel with us. It is not like we cannot afford it." Desari began pacing again, unable to remain still.

"The cats would never tolerate a human around us," Darius said as he materialized beside the table. He reached out to shove the male leopard from his perch.

"They will have to tolerate it," Desari snapped, her black eyes flashing at her brother, then searching the sky and woods all around them. Where was Julian? *Where are you?* It slipped out before she could censor it, the cry for his mind touch. It was met with silence, and her agitation increased. Why did it matter so much? After all, what was he to her? A lover. People took lovers all the time. Barack was a hound dog. At least he had been for a couple of centuries there. Desari brought her mind up sharply. She couldn't think about this. Couldn't think about Julian and where he might be.

"Dara, be calm," Darius ordered softly. "Your state of mind has nothing to do with our vehicle."

"Do not presume to know my state of mind," she

snapped back. "I have told all of you over and over that we need a new motor home. Even the truck is breaking down now. Does anyone want to do anything about it? Syndil's too busy hiding from the world. Barack is molting somewhere. Dayan and you pay no attention to the details of our life."

"I get up on the stage every night," Dayan said, defending himself. "And I write the songs and the music for you. I do not know anything about motors, nor do I wish to know. We are not mortals to deal with such things."

Darius simply watched his sister without speaking. She was rubbing her hands up and down her arms as if she were cold. The night air was cool but not uncommonly so. She was abnormally pale.

"Getting up on the stage is not attending to the necessary details, Dayan," Desari informed him. "We have to book the tours, keep track of the accounts, plan the routes, see that we can always provide for the cats, ensure that we have adequate gas and stores for whatever could break down while we are on the road. We must look human, act human. Do you do any of that, Dayan? I say we need new vehicles or a mechanic. You others had just better choose which you prefer or shut up and live with any decision I make."

Darius raised an elegant eyebrow. "And what do you think is the best solution, Dara? A mechanic? The cats would probably eat the man before we finished interviewing him. But perhaps if you found someone the cats found unappetizing, we could allow him to travel with us."

"A human? A male?" Dayan was outraged. "That would not be tolerable around our women."

Desari's head snapped up, her dark eyes flashing fire. "We women are not your possessions, Dayan. We have the right to do as we please, to be around whomever—male or female, mortal, or immortal—we choose. You do not rule us, and you never will."

Dayan let out his breath in a long, slow hiss of disapproval. "This stranger you chose to consort with last night must have given you a virus. Your disposition has gone downhill, Desari."

"Dayan." Darius stepped between his sister and his second in command. "That will be enough. The 'stranger,' Julian Savage, is a powerful Carpathian, a hunter of the undead. We would do well to learn what we can from him. If he comes to this camp, you will treat him with respect as one of us."

Dayan shook his head, annoyed at the madness of allowing a stranger into their midst. "I will do as you instruct, Darius, but I think this man has somehow beguiled Desari."

"Why?" she demanded. "Because I am insisting you help with some of the details of our existence? You are not jungle animals, the male defending the pride and that his only requirement. You ought to help out more."

Dayan raised an eyebrow but refrained from continuing the argument with Desari. "Deal with this," he said to Darius. "You are the only one who can." And then he was gone before Desari could retaliate.

Desari was left to face her brother alone. "Do not say anything, Darius. I know something is terribly wrong with me. I do not know what it is, but I feel like I am losing my mind. It is more than just physical discomfort, it is mental as well."

"Call him to you." Darius gave the order softly, as was his way. It had no less impact. His voice carried centuries of authority.

She closed her eyes tightly, pressing her hands to her

rolling stomach. "I cannot, Darius. Do not ask this of me."

"I can do no other than demand it of you," he said. "Call him to you."

"If I do, he will believe he has the right to my obedience."

"You are suffering needlessly. Whatever this man has done to bind you to him we cannot undo until we know more." He forced a gentleness into his voice. "You know I cannot allow you to suffer, Desari. Call him to you."

"I cannot. Did you not hear what I told Dayan? Women have rights, Darius. We cannot be ruled by men simply because they believe it is so."

His icy black eyes captured her dark, sorrow-filled ones and held her gaze. "I have always been responsible for you and Syndil both. In this I must insist. I can feel your pain, the chaos of your mind. Do as I bid you."

"Please, Darius. I do not wish to openly defy you." Desari was actually biting her fingernails, the strain on her face terrible for her brother to witness. Her other hand nervously tugged its way through the mass of ebony hair cascading around her shoulders and down her back.

"You have done so repeatedly since this man entered our lives," Darius reminded her gently. "I will tolerate only so much defiance from you, little sister. I realize this is a new experience, one outside our realm of knowledge, but I cannot allow you to suffer. Call Savage to your side."

Tears shimmered in her eyes and on her long lashes. She sank onto the wooden bench beside the table, hanging her head in defeat.

"There is no need to call me." Julian's muscular form solidified beside her, close enough that she could feel his body heat. His arm curved around her shoulders. "I cannot take the separation from you, Desari." He made the admission without hesitation, uncaring that Darius was within hearing, wanting only to spare her further pain.

"What have you done to me?" There were tears in Desari's voice as well as her eyes. Her fingers curled into two tight fists so that her nails bit deeply into her palms. Her voice became a tragic whisper. "What have you done that I cannot be without you?"

Julian bent his head to hers, his grip gentle, tender as he pried her fingers open one by one. Very carefully he brought her hands to the healing warmth of his mouth, pressing a kiss into the exact center of each wounded palm. His golden eyes held her dark gaze captive.

Desari could feel the terrible knot in the pit of her stomach begin to melt from his molten heat. Whatever fire lay deep within him ignited a matching inferno deep within her. There was also a peace stealing into her soul and heart, filling the terrible emptiness. She was complete, totally complete again with him so close. Her lungs could work; her heart beat in a strong, steady rhythm.

"I can feel your fear, Desari," Julian said softly. "There is no need. I cannot hurt you. I am your lifemate, responsible for your happiness."

"How can that be if I cannot even be away from you for a short period of time?" Desari glanced at her brother, a silent plea for privacy. She had trouble enough accepting such a strange phenomenon without there being a witness to her humiliation.

Julian waited until Darius had signaled the two leopards to his side and disappeared into the dark interior of the trees to hunt. He palmed the nape of Desari's neck, his fingers caressing her silken hair. "Our physical bod-

Christine Feehan

ies can be in separate places, *piccola*, but our minds must touch often when we are apart."

"You knew this, yet you withdrew. I chose to assert my independence, and you punished me for it," she said, lifting her chin at him.

"You ignored your own safety, *cara mia*," he said softly. "You refused to believe the things I tried to tell you, even when I gave you access to my mind. I had no choice but to allow you to learn firsthand that what I say is true. I am your lifemate; there cannot be untruth between us."

Desari found one button on his immaculate shirt and twisted it nervously. "It was not as if I believed you lied. The things you believed—I did not doubt you thought them true. But it all seemed so unreal, like a fantasy, a dream. How could mere words bind us together for all eternity? How could one male have the power to so change a female's life?"

"We are connected from birth, *cara*," he explained, moving his body closer when he felt a shiver run through her. "Two halves of the same whole. There is only one true lifemate. I am fortunate that mine is so talented and beautiful. It is unfortunate, however," he added, "that you are so willful and have no knowledge of what is expected of you."

Desari leapt away from him, clearing the picnic table in a single bound. She looked wild and untamed, a sexy enchantress capable of taking his very breath away.

"You think me willful because I insist on taking control of my own destiny? Do not talk to me of this lifemate thing. It means nothing to me. Nothing at all. You breeze into my life, do something to tie us together, and then feel you have the right to dictate how I should live?"

Julian watched the expressions chasing across her

160

beautiful, furious face. Everything about her was a miracle to him. How small and delicate her bones seemed to be. The sheen and mass of her silken hair was so luxurious he could lose himself in it. "I am of the Old World, a male Carpathian. I did not take into account that you would not know the ways of our people."

"Is that supposed to be an apology of some kind?" Desari folded her arms across her body, shivering as if cold. "I do not care about the ways of your people."

"Our people," he corrected gently.

"My people are the ones I live with, share my life with. For instance, my brother, the one you tried to kill."

"If I had tried to kill him, *cara mia*, he would be dead." He raised a hand to prevent her indignant interruption. "I am not saying he would not have taken me with him; he very likely would have. But he was not really trying to kill me either. It was more a matter of being sure. Darius was not going to turn his beloved sister over to a stranger who was unable to protect her. It was a test."

"Darius was testing you?" she repeated slowly. "This is some kind of male thing I should understand? Approve of?"

Julian moved so quickly he was on her before she had time to run. He never gave a warning, never twitched a muscle. He simply was there, his body crowding aggressively close, his hand spanning her throat, his thumb feathering back and forth along her delicate jaw. "Desari, *cara*, we have no choice but to learn each other's ways. We are bound together. I would like to be able to say the pretty words you want to hear. That I was wrong to force your obedience—"

"Tried to force," she corrected with a flash of her eyes.

Julian bent to brush his lips across the tempting satin of her forehead as amusement crept into the deep gold of his eyes. "Tried to force. That is true. I am fortunate that my lifemate is so powerful. Still, *piccola*, I was well within my rights to see to your safety. I can do no other than ensure your well-being. Our people cannot afford to lose even one woman, Desari. The total extinction of our race is nearly complete. Our women are our only hope. I will admit that I do not always follow the laws of our people, but in this I have no choice, and neither do you. Your safety and health must be placed above all else. The other woman you have traveling with you must be guarded as well."

She swept a hand through her hair. "Are we meant only to provide children for our race, then? That is the sole reason for our existence?"

"No, *cara*, your existence is to bring joy to this world, as you have done for so many centuries. God would not have graced you with such a voice, such a powerful tool for peace, had he not meant for you to use it. But"— Julian shrugged his broad shoulders, his thumb tracing a pattern along her neck—"in time, that would be the hope, yes, that you and I would provide our race with more female children. I am uncertain what kind of a father I would make, as I never imagined myself in such a role, but I never thought I would find or be a lifemate either."

Something close to humor flickered for a moment in her eyes. "I cannot say you are a total success in that area." But his praise of her talents had warmed her, as had the drawling caress in his voice, the admiration in the depths of his eyes, the depths of his mind.

His hand found the nape of her neck and drew her inexorably to him as he bent his head to hers. His mouth descended with infinite slowness, then fastened to hers so that he could taste her sweetness. She felt her heart leap at his touch, and her body went into instant meltdown. She felt his great strength, the desire surging through him as the heat arced between them. His mouth moved to tease the corner of hers, to blaze a trail of fire along her jaw, her chin.

"I am, however, quite good at one or two other things," he murmured with casual confidence. His teeth nibbled at her chin.

"Is this supposed to get you out of trouble?" She asked it with her eyes closed, savoring the touch and feel of him. All at once it seemed imperative that they be alone.

"I should not be in trouble. I am as new at this as you are, Desari. Up until now I have spent my life entirely alone." His lips skimmed the silken column of her neck. "Trying to fit into this situation is as alien for me as it is for you. If your need is to be with this family unit, then I can do no other than be here with you. But you must recognize that I have needs also. I do not wish to find other males near you, nor do I want you to question my judgment when your safety is in jeopardy."

When she would have protested, he gave her a little shake. "Think what you say before you speak. I am in your mind. I know you do not want another authority telling you what to do with your life. I, better than most, understand this in you. But you would obey your brother in matters of safety. The same responsibility he accepted for your security is now mine. I require the same trust and loyalty that you have always given to him."

"Trust is earned, Julian," Desari pointed out softly. "And it goes both ways. My brother does not arbitrarily dictate to me what I can and cannot do. But I am in your mind. I feel the sometimes violent emotions you are contending with, your intense dislike of other males close to me. You do not even want me to feed."

He felt the words like a stab to his gut. Every muscle

clenched in protest as a vivid picture sprang into his mind. Desari luring a male to her with her beauty and mystery, bending close to him so that their bodies touched, so that her lips could drift along the male's neck to find the pulse beating there. Rage exploded in him, deep, nearly uncontrollable, certainly like nothing he had ever experienced before. It was wild and untamed, a berserker's rage.

Julian shook his head. It was illogical to feel such an intense emotion over something as natural as feeding. Nothing in his centuries of living had prepared him for such a thing. He didn't understand it. "You will not feed from any other than me," he declared, unable to stop himself from so commanding her.

Desari was watching him closely, monitoring his thoughts. Julian made no attempt to censor anything from her. He wanted total truth between them. It was not her fault that he was experiencing difficulties he hadn't been prepared for, nor did he want her to think so. Her soft mouth suddenly curved into a smile. "You are right, Julian, I will not. I have no wish to get so close to another male." Her fingertips brushed his jaw, her first real show of affection toward him without his prompting. "It will be no hardship to allow you to provide for me if that is what you need."

His relief was tremendous, the curious somersaulting in the region of his heart unexpected. "I will do my best to come to some kind of compromise over your family unit and your need to sing. It is a great gift, Desari, your voice and what you are able to do with it. I feel pride in your accomplishments, but I cannot lie. I fear for your safety. Your schedules are announced far in advance. I believe you will be safe from the human assassins for now, but we must explore the very real possibility that vampires are congregating in this region with the express hope of finding you and the other female." *Now more than ever it was imperative he succeed in his centuries-old quest to destroy his vampire mentor, or she would never be truly safe again. The ancient could so easily track her now through Julian.*

Desari winced at his last remark. "The 'other female' is Syndil. I love her as my sister. You have access to my memories. You can see that. You can also see why we are especially protective of her and why she chooses to take the leopard's form at this time."

"While she is in the leopard's form she does not have to cope with her trauma," Julian mused, "but you must see, Desari, that it is not right. It only prolongs her recovery. All of you think you are helping her, but she needs to be strong on her own. She can cope. Pretending the assault did not happen will not allow her to recover. She needs to be encouraged to start taking back command of her life."

Desari tilted her head to look up at him, astonished at his perception. "How could you know this when you have not even met her? Why did we not realize we were only lengthening her recovery?" Desari's anguish throbbed in her musical voice. "It was my negligence that this has not been attended to."

Julian smiled down at her. "You take far too much on your shoulders, Desari. All of you tried to shield her. I am certain in the beginning it was exactly what she needed. Now that has changed. Sharing your mind yet seeing things from a fresh perspective allows me to show you the conclusion you yourself would have come to in time."

Desari moved restlessly, wanting the warmth and comfort of his larger frame. Julian responded immediately by pulling her close to him. His strong arms enfolded her and held her tightly against him. "It will be all right, Desari. I promise you."

"Darius has told Dayan you are to be treated with respect," she whispered into his chest.

Julian shrugged carelessly before he could stop himself. He did not seek approval or protection from anyone.

Chapter Eight

Desari glanced up at Julian's face. It looked as if it had been carved from stone, an implacable mask, unreadable and stony. She sighed softly. Integrating Julian into their family was not going to be easy. He was not one to follow another man's lead. He walked his own path. Darius and he were bound to clash at every turn. The other men in her family were certain to treat Julian with distrust, and that very well could be like lighting a match to dry timber. Julian carried himself with arrogance and had a wry sense of humor often bordering on contempt.

His hand slid possessively up her arm, lingering for a moment on her soft skin before his seeking fingers twined themselves in the rich luxury of her hair. He bent down so that his mouth was close to her ear, his warm breath teasing her. "I can read your thoughts, *cara mia*, and you should have more faith in your lifemate. I can do no other than see to your happiness. If you wish us to live for a time, in peace, among your family," *rather overrun with territorial males*, "then I can do no other than offer my friendship to them."

Desari burst out laughing. He had tried to sound sincere but had ended up sounding pained. In any case, she could read his thoughts as easily as he could hers. " 'Territorial males'? What does that mean? We do not have our own territory, unless you count the coast of Africa, where we lived for so long."

"I spent some time in Africa, among the leopards," he said to get off the dangerous subject of her family.

Her eyes, so enormous and beautiful, sparkled at him. "You did? How incredible. We spent nearly two hundred years there, and we still sometimes return to visit. It would be funny if we were on the same continent at the same time and never met. Especially if you were running among our leopards."

He shook his head. "I doubt that happened. I sensed your brother's power as he sensed mine the moment we were in proximity. It would not have escaped our notice if we had come close in Africa. More important, you and I, born lifemates, would have sensed each other's presence in some way." But he did find it interesting that he had been inexplicably drawn to Africa, and the leopards there, in his search for other Carpathians. Perhaps some trace of Desari had called to him even then.

"Tell me more about your people," she said now.

"They are also your people. You have blood kin, Desari, still in existence. Your eldest brother is a great man among our people, very respected and equally feared. He is called Gregori, and Darius is much like him." He grinned suddenly, transforming his harshly beautiful features to those of a mischievous boy. "They are *very* much alike. Gregori, the Dark One, is often used as a bogey man to keep the young children in line. The only other immortal as great as your blood kin is Mikhail.

Mikhail is the acknowledged Prince of our people, the one who has kept our race alive and hopeful these many centuries. Mikhail and Gregori are as close as brothers in their own strange way. Each is so powerful that no one would dare to challenge either of them for fear the other would retaliate."

Desari nodded her head. "Like our family."

Julian thought about that. "In a way, though few of the Carpathians left alive have family units such as this."

"What of your family?" Desari asked innocently.

She saw him wince, and his golden gaze skittered away from hers. "I told you, I have a twin brother. Aidan. He resides in San Francisco. I have not spoken with him for many years, nor have I met his lifemate."

Her eyebrows rose. There was something dark swirling close to the surface again. She sensed a deep pain in Julian and did not attempt to probe his thoughts in so sensitive an area. She chose her words carefully. "Were there harsh words between you?"

"There is blood between us, Desari. As your brother can track you, so it is that we can track one another." Julian sighed and shoved a hand through his hair. "The majority of our males refuse to share blood with one another for the simple reason that each male knows it is inevitable, without a lifemate, that he must choose to end his life or lose his soul for all eternity and become the vampire. It is much easier to track those you have shared blood with, particularly for a hunter."

Desari took a deep breath. Julian had some terrible secret he wouldn't share with her. "Have you shared your blood with others, Julian?" She asked.

Julian grinned at her, his white teeth gleaming. "You have only to search my mind for the answer, *cara mia*."

He was tempting her, a blatant seduction to enter his mind and know him in the most intimate way. It bound them closer every time they merged. She could feel it, his mind becoming more familiar with each touch. Her mind craved the touch of his, the need growing inside her in the same way the need for sharing his body was growing. It was an ember smoldering, the flame spreading, a dark heat she knew she would be unable to resist. Yet somewhere in his mind, buried deep, was a shadow, too painful, that he refused to share.

Desari glanced away from him toward the thick forest. Freedom was so close. Julian wasn't touching her, not even in her mind; he was simply standing there beside her. Tall. Muscular. Sinfully beautiful. With a pain in him buried so deep, he could only wonder if she could ever find it and eradicate it. His golden eyes blazed at her with hunger and need, drawing her to him. Her heart turned over, and she knew she was lost.

"I have shared blood on more than one occasion, little one, although, because I am a well-known hunter, my help has been often refused. Should the one receiving it turn, I could track him with ease to destroy him." As he said the words aloud, he remembered anew, too, why few males with lifemates hunted the undead. To protect one's lifemate, the hunter could very well hesitate to go into a vicious battle that might destroy him and lead his lifemate, in inconsolable pain, to destroy herself.

An ideal hunter was one with longevity, knowledge, skill, ruthlessness, and power. Such a one had little hope of finding his mate, so the loss of his own life was not something to be feared. With a lifemate, if the male hunter were to be killed, his lifemate would likely choose to greet the dawn. And their race could not survive the loss of even one of their women. Julian had heard of only one case where a lifemate survived without the other. The female died, and the male became vampire, wreaking havoc in the Carpathian mountains, striking at everyone he held responsible, going so far as to murder his own son and attempt to murder his daughter's lifemate, knowing it would end her life as well.

Desari put a gentle hand on his arm, finally touching his mind to find what thoughts had made him grow so still and distant. She saw the memory of Julian slowly approaching a handsome man. The man had haunted black eyes, eyes that had seen far too much. The eyes of a man who had been tortured beyond endurance. Brutally wounded, dripping precious blood, he had watched Julian's approach with wary, dangerous eyes. She watched as Julian spoke softly, easily extending his arm to the man that he might live with the blood of an ancient flowing in his veins. *Jacques. Mikhail's brother. Lifemate to one whose father had murdered her brother, betrayed their people to human assassins, tortured her husband, tried to kill her.* She caught that much before Julian wiped the memory from his mind and caught her chin with his strong fingers.

Her dark eyes immediately were held captive by his golden ones. "We will work this out to both our satisfactions, Desari," he promised softly. "Come with me. You need to feed this night before we leave this place with the others. And I need to feel your body, touch you, know you are really mine and not someone I dreamed up in desperation."

There was such an intensity to his need, everything else was swept from Desari's mind. Heat sizzled and danced along her skin, arcing between them like white-hot lightning. Julian's hand slid around the nape of her neck, nestling her to him as he began to walk her away from the campsite. With every step they took together, their bodies brushed against one another.

Desari felt the burning need, too. But she also felt an inner peace, a completeness. She loved the way his body moved, rippling with power like a sleek jungle cat. The feel of his arm, so sure and strong, made her feel delicate and feminine despite the fact that she knew she was equally powerful in her own right. At the nape of her neck his fingers moved every now and then as they walked into the forest, away from the sounds of the others. She could feel him rubbing strands of her hair between his thumb and fingers as if he could never quite get enough of the feel of it. Then his fingers dropped casually to her neck, her collarbone, to move over her skin, stroking gently, almost absently, yet each caress sent liquid fire pulsing through her body.

How had she ever been happy without him? Before him her body had never been restless and hungry as it was now. She had loved her life, her singing, yet now she thought always of him, his strange, solitary life, his loneliness, and his terrible aching need only she could fill. And he seemed to fill her life as nothing had before. She was changed for all time, just as she had feared, yet now, as he walked so quietly beside her, she had no fear whatsoever.

Even as they walked together in perfect harmony, breathing in the fresh mountain air, listening to the forest creatures, the creak of the swaying branches, and a rushing stream nearby, Julian could think of only one thing. Before he went out of his mind, he had to bend down and find Desari's mouth with his. He wanted the taste of her lingering in his body for all time. He meant to be gentle with her—a caress, no more—but the moment he felt the softness of her perfect mouth, red-hot lava, molten and hungry, flared and consumed him. His muscles tightened to the point of pain. His arms, of their own accord, swept around her to pull her close. He imprinted his hard frame on her softer one, letting her feel his painful need, his body full and demanding, his mouth fastening on hers as if she were his very breath.

"You are my breath," he whispered into the softness of her mouth. "You are the only reason I am still living, Desari. I intended to greet the dawn after I had completed my errand and warned you of the impending danger to you." His tongue explored the heated velvet of her mouth, then moved to the slim column of her neck. As he continued to feed the fire between them, he was moving them deeper into the shadows of the forest. His hands slipped beneath her blouse to rest on her narrow rib cage, taking in as much of her soft skin as he was able to. Julian closed his eyes for a moment, just savoring the feel of her, the rose-petal texture of her skin.

Desari circled his neck with one arm, brushing at the wild strands of golden hair falling around his face before she slowly unbuttoned the tiny pearl buttons down the front of her blouse. As each slipped from its resting place, the blouse parted, and she drew his head down to her bare skin. Only a fine film of lace covered her full, aching breasts. Her nipples were hard and pushing through the lace, her need every bit as great as his own.

He whispered something soft and sexy in Italian, but the sound of it was muffled as he blazed a trail of fire from her throat to the valley between her breasts. She heard her own gasp, a soft cry of need as she arched to meet his wandering mouth. His tongue lapped at her nipples right through the lace, a hot, moist caress that created a hot, moist response between her legs.

"I need you, Desari. I was empty without you. And that kind of emptiness eats away at you, consumes you until your soul is dark and ugly and all that matters is sating your hunger. But nothing fills the void. Nothing. Year after year you endure the emptiness until life itself is a curse hardly to be borne. And all the while the darkness, the beast in you whispers, an insidious whisper

173

promising power from the kill, promises that wear away your belief in God, in all the things that are right and true and good. The monster inside you, so black and hungry for life, grows and grows until it has consumed everything you ever were. That is the curse borne by Carpathian males, Desari."

Julian's arms tightened around her until their strength threatened to crack her bones, but Desari only held him closer, listening to the anguish in his voice. She cradled his head to her, protective, feminine, his refuge and salvation.

"We have lost so many. I have hunted boyhood friends, dared not become too close to anyone in case I was called upon to end his existence." His hands moved over her skin, tracing each rib. The palms of his hands were hot as they moved to find her waist. Julian lifted his head to allow his eyes to drift slowly, possessively over her. His molten gaze ignited a firestorm of need in Desari. She loved the weight of his eyes on her, the hunger burning so intensely there.

She watched as he slowly lifted one hand, and stared at his perfect nails for a moment before one lengthened into a sharp talon. Very slowly he inserted it between her breasts, just touching the wisp of lace that hugged her body. One downward sweep sliced the material easily, spilling her breasts free.

Desari held her breath, afraid to move or speak, not wanting to shatter the moment, not wanting that look of hunger for her alone to ever leave his face. His hands moved upward, sliding over her skin to cup her breasts. His heated gaze went to her face, studying every detail, every expression, every emotion in her dark eyes.

"I will never deserve you, Desari, no matter how long we live, no matter how hard I try. I do not deserve a woman such as you." He whispered the words, meaning every one of them.

She smiled, tilting her head to one side. "Perhaps not, Julian," she agreed. "But I am not the angel you think me. You have only to ask my brother the trouble you are letting yourself in for. But I promise you, I do plan on showing you."

Her voice, soft and pure, straight from heaven, slipped over his body like the brush of her fingertips, touching him everywhere, teasing, stroking, promising the very things fantasies were made of. She wanted to end his suffering, take away the centuries of emptiness without hope, the terrible burden of the deaths he carried, forced to hunt his friends and end their lives in order to save mortals and immortals alike. She wanted to play and tease, be as mischievous as possible, teach him the meaning of her kind of "trouble."

A sound intruded. The others were still far too close to them. The campsite was some distance away, but Carpathians had exceptionally acute hearing. Julian could hear them breaking camp, starting up vehicles. He took a deep breath and forced himself to calm the raging storm within. He would not subject the other men, all so close to turning, to the sounds of their lovemaking.

Very tenderly he cupped the creamy fullness of Desari's breasts in the palms of his hands. His thumbs caressed her nipples into hard, beckoning peaks. "You are so beautiful, Desari, your skin so warm and soft." He bent his head to trace the valley between her breasts with his tongue, lingering over the steady beat of her heart. "I want you so badly I feel I might go insane if I do not have you at this moment."

She lay her head over his, rubbing his thick mane of golden hair with her chin. "But?"

Julian sighed softly. "I will have to be content with

looking at you in adoration." He reluctantly released her and stepped away. "I think I can manage to wait a short time." His golden eyes glittered at her dangerously. "If you do something to distract me."

Desari tilted her head, her long hair sliding like so much silk over her shoulder, partially covering her bare skin from his view. A small, feminine smile curved her soft mouth. Just the sight of it made him groan. "Distract you?" Her voice hummed with promise. "I can think of several interesting things we can try to distract you from thinking of my family." Her smile was sexy, enticing, a promise.

"You are not helping me," he scolded, his body an unrelenting ache.

Desari had slowly merged her mind with his. She saw his terrible need of her, the images of them intertwined. She felt the fire rushing in his blood, the heaviness pooling between his legs. The monster roaring for release, inciting him to take his lifemate with heat and passion and damn the strangers he was trying to be considerate of.

It was a measure of her own raging passion that she had not considered the men, their hearing, their ability to smell. The wind would so easily carry to the others what went on in the forest. "You are far more deserving of me than you believe," she whispered softly, pride for him making her want to throw herself into his arms.

The fire of hunger and need was on her. She wanted his body crushed against hers, filling hers, his blood running in her own veins. She needed the closeness with him to take away her fear of being separated from him.

Julian shook his head, his hand curling around the nape of her neck. "You cannot look at me like that, *piccola*, or I am sure to go up in flames."

Desari allowed her fingers to tangle in his golden

mane. "Thank you for thinking of my family when I could not." Her voice was a whisper of seduction, sliding over his hot skin. Just the sound of it made every muscle in his body clench.

Julian made another effort to breathe. Air. It was all around him, yet he couldn't seem to drag enough into his lungs. He took her hand in his and carried it to the warmth of his mouth. "We need to find a safe subject, *cara mia*, or I will not make it through these next few minutes."

Desari's soft laughter was like music in the wind. She perched on a large tree trunk that lay across the forest floor. The breeze tugged at her long hair so that it shifted around her like a veil, one moment hiding the temptation of bare, gleaming skin, the next revealing it. "A safe subject," she mused aloud. "What would that be?"

The air slammed out of his lungs once again at the sight of her. She looked so much a part of her surroundings. Wild. Sexy. Provocative. "You might try closing your shirt." His voice sounded hoarse and desperate even to his own ears.

Desari had made no attempt to button her blouse, and her breasts jutted toward him, a temptation he knew he would be unable to resist for long. Her button-fly jeans were partially undone, exposing her tiny waist and narrow rib cage. She continued to smile at him, a blatant seduction, while her fingers fiddled with the third button of her jeans.

His hot golden gaze touched her, then moved quickly away. "You are not helping me, Desari." His voice was husky with his terrible need. Much more and he might truly go up in flames, spontaneous combustion.

The tip of her tongue darted out to moisten her lush mouth. "A subject that will keep our minds off other things." She touched his chest gently, hardly more than a brush of her fingertips, but she felt him jump. "I am thinking, Julian," she said softly, innocently, her large dark eyes staring up at him. Her fingers slid the buttons of his shirt free so that the palms of her hands could find the heavy muscles of his chest.

Julian gritted his teeth. "You are killing me, Desari. My heart cannot stand much more."

"I am merely touching you," she pointed out demurely. Her nails slid lightly over his skin, tracing each well-defined muscle with exquisite care. "I like the way you feel." She bent her head closer so that her long hair brushed his sensitized skin, and a sound escaped his throat. "I love the way you smell, too. Is that so bad?"

He captured her hands and held them tightly to him. "You are going to get yourself into trouble."

"I wonder if you would be more comfortable if I just opened the front of your jeans. They seem a bit tight." Desari slipped her hands out from under his, wickedly tracing the path of golden hair down to his flat belly. Her fingers were already at work, parting the material before he could think to stop her.

"You are a tease, Desari," he accused, groaning again when his body burst free from the restraint of the denim.

Her eyelashes swept up so that he was staring into her dark eyes. Sexy, mischievous, intriguing. "Mmm, nice," she whispered, staring at the evidence of his desire. "Very nice."

He would be lost forever if he continued to look at her. He would never be able to stay in control. As if she could read his mind, her hands slipped even lower, brushing the strong columns of his thighs, moving up again slowly until he was once again unable to breathe. Then she cupped his heavy fullness in her hands, feeling the thickness of him, stroking the velvet tip with knowing fingers.

Julian couldn't help himself; his head went back as pleasure ripped through him, as fire raced through his veins. His teeth clenched. "What are you doing, woman? Trying to drive me insane?"

Desari's dark eyes trapped the moon and shone brightly. Her voice purred with innocence and laughter, silvery notes that danced over and caressed him. "I thought I was bringing you a measure of relief."

Her hands followed the images in his head, became more skillful, more persuasive, teasing and gliding over and around him until he was tempted to beg for mercy. "Is my family gone yet?" she whispered, intrigued by his reactions. She moved her head to brush his stomach with her mouth. Her hair cascaded around her face, fluttering against his skin, until his body was raging for release.

A low growl escaped his throat. "They are just now beginning to move their vehicles," he said between his teeth.

"Really?" Desari said, distracted by his hot fullness. Her hands slipped around his hips as she dropped even lower, finding the carpet of vegetation with her knees. She heard him gasp and looked up at his face, etched with harsh lines of need. She smiled slowly and once more bent her head to him.

Julian had never seen anything more beautiful in his life. The trees swayed and dipped in the wind. Her face was white and flawless in the moonlight, her long lashes and dark eyes so mysterious, her mouth so erotic he wanted to hold this moment for eternity. Her blouse gaped open so that her breasts were bare and inviting. She looked like a pagan goddess of ancient times.

Then her warm breath effectively knocked out his ability to think. Her mouth, moist and warm, took away all self-control. As her soft lips slid over him, he grabbed two fistfuls of silky hair and pulled her close. His hips began thrusting almost helplessly into her. Her nails raked up and down his thighs gently, urging him closer still. Her mouth tightened until he wanted to scream with pleasure. Her hands moved over his buttocks, lovingly tracing them, then moved to cup him once again.

"Thank God they are away," Julian gasped, his body thrusting into her hot mouth. Then he clenched his teeth and began to pull her to her feet. Reluctantly Desari left her erotic exploration and allowed him to tug her up against his rock-hard frame. His mouth fastened itself to hers, devouring her, dominating her, possessing her. His arms threatened to crush her.

Desari reveled in the strength of his arms, in his desire for her, his need of her. He was kicking his jeans away in a frenzy, forgetting in the moment his ability to simply will them away. She loved his wild, uncontrollable need, the fire and hunger in him for her. Only for her. She felt complete, feminine, powerful. She was lost in his arms, giving herself up completely to be whatever he might need or want. She wanted him with the same savage fury and need. Her body was going up in flames. His kiss alone was causing her bones to melt. She allowed her blouse to float to the ground, and her arms slipped around his neck. She pressed herself even closer.

Julian ripped at her jeans, jerking them in strips away from her legs. He lifted her in his arms so that she could wrap her legs tightly around his waist. She buried her face on his shoulder, breathing in his wild scent, gasping as he lowered her over him, filling her completely. It was a miracle to her the way her body stretched to accommodate his invasion, the way her muscles welcomed him in. The pounding of his pulse caught her attention, and instantly her hunger surged. She needed him flowing into her, his mind merging with hers, his blood flowing into her veins, his body taking hers with wild abandon.

Her tongue stroked his neck. Once. Twice. She felt his heart leap against her breasts. His hips thrust forward, burying himself inside her. Her teeth scraped back and forth over his skin, lightly, gently, in teasing bites until his hips moved in a savage frenzy and he growled a warning, his hands tightening on her bottom, urging her into a fiery, turbulent ride. Her teeth sank deep, and he cried out with ecstasy, somewhere between heaven and hell. She could feel what he felt, his mind a haze of heat and passion.

Julian moved closer to the fallen log so that he could lean Desari against it. The angle gave him the ability to deepen his stroke so that her body was forced to take all of him. He moved aggressively, hard and fast, burying himself in her over and over while lightning blazed through and around them. He wanted to make it last for eternity. She took away his terrible loneliness, the darkness crouching within him; she held it at bay with her velvet fire.

The wind rose around them, gusting at the branches overhead. She closed the tiny pinpricks at his throat with a sweep of her tongue. Very slowly she began to lie back against the tree, her breasts thrusting upward toward the sky, her hips filling his palms as he drove into her. As he stared down at her, he saw the triangle of silky black curls that met his golden down. He was mesmerized by the beauty of their bodies coming together.

Her muscles clenched, her moist sheath tightening and releasing him until the friction between them was so hot he felt flames dancing over his skin, her skin. He was swelling, growing, thick and hard, and still he wanted to go on.

Julian. It was the softest of pleas, Desari's beautiful, haunting voice shimmering for release in his mind. It sent him hurtling over the edge, taking her with him so that they clung together as the earth shook and the skies exploded.

Julian nearly collapsed on top of her, his great strength drained for a moment. His body gleamed in the night air, his golden mane wild around his face. Desari touched his mouth with the tip of her finger in wonder. "How can this be, Julian? How could it be that all these long, lonely centuries, I did not know of this? Why did I not hunger for such a thing?"

His eyes glittered at her, a warning menace, the ice cold of death itself. "You were made for me, Desari, only me. There was no need for you to seek another."

She refused to feel intimidated. His face was harsh, a hint of cruelty around his mouth. "Not now. But I have lived long. Why did my body not hunger for this? I read books, heard of things while among humans. Syndil and I talked of such longings, but I have never felt such a need. I have gone centuries without ever knowing the beauty of this. What if you had never found me?"

Julian's hands tangled in her ebony hair. "You are mine, *cara mia*, only mine. There is no other who could make your body feel the things I can. And if you tried to experiment, I would have to kill him. Make no mistake, Desari, knowledge is a good thing to acquire, but there is no need for you to go to any other. If you wish to try something new, I will oblige you, but I will not tolerate another male near you."

She shoved at the solid wall of his chest with her palms, glaring at him. "Oh, shut up. I was not contemplating running around with every male I saw. I was just wondering why I had to wait so long."

Julian refused to move an inch, his heavier frame pinning her beneath him, his body still firmly buried in hers.

"You waited for me, as you should have. For us there is only one."

Her eyebrows arched. "Oh really? Then why did Barack use human women in this way? Have you? Be warned, I will not accept a double standard."

Julian swept back the fall of hair from her forehead, the gesture tender as he bent to brush a kiss on her eyebrow. "Men feel for two hundred years or so, *piccola*. Some act on their urges, although they are a poor imitation of what we feel for our true mate. True sexual heat comes with the finding of our lifemate. It is more than infatuation or chemistry. It is stronger than love or sex. It is a combination of mind, heart, soul, and body. The emotion is so strong, one must always be in proximity to the other."

Desari was silent for a moment, suddenly aware of how vulnerable she felt. It wasn't just her body so open to his, or the depth of her desire, it was the emotions he evoked in her. Her long lashes swept down to conceal her sudden doubt.

At once, Julian's hands tightened in her hair. "*Cara mia*, do not fear our union so much. I will see to your happiness. I could never hurt you. Do you not understand yet?" He captured her hand, brought it to his mouth, and kept it pressed against his finely chiseled lips. "Even if you chose to be with another male, I would never harm you. It would not be possible for me to do such a thing. But I am being honest with you when I tell you I would kill the man. I am a predator. Nothing, not even your light, can change completely what I am. I will allow no one to take you from my side."

"Does it not scare you, Julian, the intensity of our feelings?" she whispered, her dark eyes clouded. "It frightens me more than anything I have ever encountered. I could not bear to be the cause of another's death.

I see you struggling with your emotions, those that I have brought to you. It is a battle within you that you cannot hide from me. And there is something else, something you struggle to hide even from yourself."

His teeth scraped the knuckles of her hand lovingly. "Yes, the emotions are new and strange, unknown to me these many centuries. And yes, they are difficult to learn to deal with, as they are intense and violent." The "something else" he could not yet share with her, could not yet face. "But we have centuries for the learning," he concluded. Reluctantly he eased his body from hers. "I feel your discomfort, *piccola*. Come here to me." He was already drawing her up so that he could examine her body for marks.

"I am perfectly fine, Julian." For some reason it embarrassed her that he was searching her fair skin for telltale bruises his passion might have left on her. "Explain to me why Syndil has experienced sexual feelings while I did not before you. Am I so different? Not feminine?"

Julian's head came up, his amber eyes heating. "How can you not know how desirable you are, Desari? Surely you see the effect you have on males, mortal and immortal alike."

Her fingers clung to his. "You are the first immortal I have ever encountered outside of my family. And just because human males find me desirable does not mean I am. Our race often has that effect on mortals. It is not me. Besides, I felt nothing in return."

"For which I am eternally grateful. Why Syndil has felt these urges, I do not know. Perhaps she has sensed her lifemate near but without recognition of him." There was a faint frown on Julian's granite features. "It is possible some women are able to have sexual affairs with men other than their true lifemate prior to their claiming. But I cannot see how, given how closely our women are guarded. I cannot see Darius allowing males near you or Syndil, even though he was not raised in the traditions of our people."

"That is true. Darius would never have allowed either of us to carry on with a male. Neither would Dayan or Barack. They watch us all the time. Since Savon's treacherous behavior, they watch one another just as closely," she added sadly.

"It is only Darius who fights the darkness so desperately," Julian answered grimly. "He has been drawn deep within the shadows because he has had to kill to protect you all. The others can hang on longer if they wish it. Darius's battle is a difficult one."

Tears swam in Desari's dark eyes. "I cannot leave him, Julian. He cannot think we can do without his protection. I have seen the same thing in him, and I fear for him constantly. More and more he keeps to himself. He rarely shares his thoughts with me. He is a great man, and I do not want to lose him."

Julian bent his head to brush each of her eyelids with the soothing touch of his mouth. "Then we can do other than see to it he remains with us."

Desari lifted her face to his, smiling up at him as if he had given her the moon. "Thank you, Julian, for understanding. If you only knew Darius, you would see how important it is."

"I have been in your mind many times, *cara*. I can see him as you do. I have also seen the iron will in him that allowed all of you to survive impossible odds. He is one truly worth saving." Then his golden gaze was sweeping the length of her body, and once again there was a hungry gleam in the depths of his eyes.

Chapter Nine

At once Desari was gone, leaping away from him like a gazelle, her taunting laughter floating on the wind as she alighted on the huge fallen tree trunk. She took his breath away, standing there naked in the moonlight, branches swaying all around her. The wind tugged at the waves of hair cascading around her body like a cape. A sound escaped his throat, something between a growl and a groan.

Julian was a hard man honed by centuries of a harsh existence. If he had ever had a sharing of laughter with others, it was but a vague memory of his youth. He had been damned to a life of solitude, yet now he wanted nothing more than to be with this one woman, to share his life with her, the mountains, the cities, the world. He didn't know how to play, didn't think of having a sense of humor other than an occasional strange amusement at the actions of another. But something new was rising in him. The sound of Desari's laughter was finding an answering playful note somewhere deep within him.

He leapt after her onto the fallen log, reaching for her waist, but she was already gone, her body shimmering in midair then changing even as she landed lightly on another log and sprang away. Sleek, glossy dark fur now covered bare skin; her muzzle was rounded and beautiful. The female leopard glanced back once enticingly, then was gone, running lightly through the forest, blending in with the foliage.

Julian grinned and followed her, his frame stretching and contorting into the heavy, well-muscled shape of a male leopard. He could smell her wild scent reaching out on the night wind to beckon him, and the wildness in him grew in response. To the male leopard, the female's scent was as alluring as the most expensive perfume. The female leopard's cry echoed eerily in the night, calling out to him. The male responded as if the call were a whisper of seduction.

He picked up speed, and moved effortlessly, a streak of golden fur as he silently stalked his prey. When he saw her, the wildness in him increased until he was more primitive leopard than modern man. She was rolling playfully on a soft bed of pine needles, her curves sensuous, almost serpentine. She was so alluring, the male leopard could only watch for a moment, until his age-old instincts triggered his rising need and he cautiously approached the female.

The female eyed him warily but did not rebuff his approach. He circled her, watching her every moment. She rolled again, moved closer to him so that he could touch her with his muzzle. She accepted his caress, returned it with one of her own. They looked at one another and then began to run together, leaping over logs and branches, winding through the forest with consummate grace.

Inside the body of the leopard, Julian reveled in the stretch of muscles and sinew, in the night itself and the freedom of the forest. He smelled her welcoming invitation, read it in the seductive playfulness of her body. He stayed close to the female, nudging her occasionally, enjoying the way his body thirsted after hers. He was patient. A female leopard's rebuff could be dangerous, and no male was going to risk her solid swipe. He simply stayed close to her, following his instincts.

She slowed her run, then began to circle him playfully, occasionally crouching in front of him in invitation. When his heavier body went to blanket hers, she growled a warning and leapt away, only to return with another seductive invitation. Julian could feel the male cat's rising urges; they grew stronger and more intense with each pass she took. She was so beautiful, her fur so sleek and soft, her muzzle perfect. Once more she crouched in invitation, tempting him. He blanketed her body, his teeth finding her shoulder to hold her still as he pressed closer to her, using his heavier weight to keep her motionless.

At that moment, he was so much a leopard, so much animal and instinct, he never knew afterward whether it was the leopard or the man that reacted. He sensed the dark shadow reaching for them just as the attack came. He used his considerable power to knock the female far from him to give her a better chance to run. At the same time he tried to roll, to take the oncoming blow on his shoulder.

The pain was intense as razor-sharp claws ripped through his shoulder to the bone. Instantly he cut off feeling to the area even as he melted out from under his attacker, shape-shifting as he did so. He faced the vampire in his human form, elegantly dressed, blood streaming from his wound, his golden hair a mane around his harsh face. *Was this the one? Had his blood called his tormenter, betrayed his lifemate?*

From across the short distance between them he assessed his enemy, keeping his human body placed squarely in front of Desari. He didn't look at her, didn't waste time warning her to obey him. His entire focus had to be centered on the vampire. A small smile curved his mouth, unreflected in the icy gold of his eyes, and he bowed slowly. "Very clever, I salute your timing." His words were soft, his voice gentle and pure. There was no recognition, this was not his archenemy. Julian didn't know if he was relieved or disappointed.

The vampire regarded him with hooded eyes. He was tall, taller than Julian, but without his heavy muscles. His face was flushed from a fresh kill. Some unlucky camper, no doubt. Julian was uneasy when the vampire refused to be drawn into a dialogue. The creature simply stared at him. It was unusual for one of the undead not to boast or brag when he had scored a blow such as Julian had just received.

Around Julian the forest seemed to blur, the ground rolling almost gently beneath his feet. Deliberately his smile widened, showing strong white teeth. "A child's trick. I learned that when I was but a fledging. I am insulted that you treat me with such a lack of respect." At no time did Julian's voice change pitch. It remained a hypnotic blend of mesmerizing compulsion and purity. His voice was grating on the vampire, he could clearly see. The vampire actually winced and shook his head in an attempt to stay free of the compulsion.

The soulless creature moved then, his steps a gliding pattern, a hypnotic dance. Julian remained still, not drawn into following the strange dance. He stayed alert, his body relaxed and ready, on the balls of his feet, his mind scanning the areas around him, even the skies. This behavior in the undead was totally unnatural. Julian was missing something, and, with Desari in danger, he dared not act too soon or make a mistake. His lifemate had not run, so he had to protect her.

You think there is another out there? Desari was a shadow in his mind, aware of his thoughts, of his unease. She had scanned but, had been unable to detect another being.

I am certain of it.

And it would be better to face the two of them together?

I would have a better chance to orchestrate the battle.

Desari had made herself small, wanting to give Julian as little to worry about as possible. Now she drew herself up to her full height and, with great confidence, stepped to his left. It gave her lifemate plenty of room to maneuver yet allowed him to see her so that he would not have to seek her with his mind. *Do not listen to the music I will make, Julian,* she cautioned, the words like the brush of fingers in his mind. She lifted her face to the blanket of stars and began to sing softly.

Julian's entire body clenched at the first silvery note. It took tremendous will power to force himself to shut out the sound. Her voice was haunting and beautiful, rising into the night air and spreading throughout the forest. It was carried on an unusual wind that seemed to swirl through the trees, reaching into the heights of the canopy and delving into the deepest ravines. It was a summons, a soft command to come forth, to come to her. All creatures, good or evil. Who or what could resist that otherworldly voice? It was pure and beautiful, the notes gold and silver, shimmering visibly in the dark night. Calling. Reaching out. Beckoning. A demand so soft and hauntingly beautiful it was mesmerizing, impossible to ignore.

Julian watched the effect of Desari's singing on the vampire. The face became gray and drawn, the skin shrinking over the bones until the undead looked like a skeleton. The clothes began to tatter and shred, rotting from his body like his skin. He could no longer keep up the illusion of youth and cleanliness. He looked a thousand years old, decayed, soulless, a parody of a living man. The notes drove him insane, beckoning him with the light of goodness and compassion, the things he had given up along with his soul.

Growling, spitting, fighting every inch of the way, the vampire hissed and dragged itself closer to Julian and death. Still Desari sang. The night air groaned with the effort to support the gathering weight of the owls flying in, settling on branches all around them. Deer, mountain lion, bear, even fox and rabbits, were drawn to the spot, circling the three upright figures.

The vampire covered his ears, grunted oaths, swore vilely, yet his feet continued to drag through the dirt toward Desari. From behind Julian another crawled forward from the bushes. His eyes were red and glowing with hatred. He was staring at Desari, his jagged teeth snapping together, his hot, fetid breath heralding his arrival. He was more ancient, more skilled than the first one, evidently using the other vampire as his pawn to draw out the hunter. He was fighting Desari's compulsion with every breath in his body. *But he was not the one.*

Julian knew immediately that he was dangerous and cunning. There was a ruthless set to the ancient undead's mouth and something alarming in the way his eyes never left Desari's face. *Take care not to look at him,* Julian cautioned her, a rush of fear invading his calm confidence. He cursed the fact that she was there, that his senses were divided by such overwhelming emotion—terror for her.

Julian struck without preamble, moving with the speed he was so famous for among his kind. But the vampire was not there. He had somehow broken the spell Desari had woven and was on her before she could move. Julian whirled immediately and went for the second target, his fist slamming into the wall of the chest, driving through muscle, bone, and sinew until he reached the one thing that could destroy the lesser vampire. The corrupt, pulsating heart was in the palm of his hand when he withdrew it from the chest, stepping back quickly from the screaming undead.

The tainted blood spewed everywhere as the vampire insanely spun around in circles before falling to the ground, where he convulsed hideously. Julian was moving again, drawing energy from the lightning arcing from cloud to cloud overhead. The bolt hit the writhing body, incinerating it immediately. The flames then jumped to the heart where Julian had tossed it. In seconds the lesser vampire was nothing more than smoking ashes. And Julian simply vanished as if he had never been.

Desari's breath slammed out of her lungs when the clawed fingers of the ancient vampire circled her neck. His touch was vile, making her skin crawl. The air around him was foul, and she didn't want to breathe it. Julian had destroyed the other vampire so quickly she was barely aware he had done so before he dissolved, leaving no trace of himself anywhere. She was completely confident in him. She didn't stop to think why, but she knew with a certainty beyond anything she had ever known that he had not deserted her.

"Why have you been stalking me, old one?" she inquired softly, using her voice as the weapon it was. The musical notes raked at the evil one.

The vampire flinched and hissed, his poisonous talons pinching her skin in warning. "You will not speak," he ordered, spitting and growling as the words burst out of him.

"I am sorry," she replied gently, her voice soft with innocence. She was determined to give Julian every advantage.

The vampire was turning her in every direction, using her slender body as his shield, all the while keeping a razor-sharp talon pressed over her jugular vein. The tip pierced her skin, sending a thin trail of blood trickling down her neck onto the white silk blouse she had donned on shifting. Her captor desperately scanned the forest around them. He could find no trace of Julian.

Above their heads, the owls began to shift their weight. Two of the mountain lions screamed, the human-sounding cries eerie. Other animals paced restlessly, outside the invisible circle Desari had created. Their eyes glowed fiercely as lightning continued to arc among the clouds.

"Your hero has deserted you," the vampire taunted her, his hate-filled eyes searching the night endlessly.

"You believe that I need him to save me? I am an ancient. I can defend myself. Besides, you do not wish to slay me. You have not stalked me time after time simply to rid the world of my presence." Her voice was like velvet, the notes musical. "You have challenged two of the most powerful ancients I know to get to me. You would do this and then slay me? I do not think so, old one."

His fingers tightened around her throat with bruising force, threatening to cut off her air. She laughed softly, tauntingly. "You think to frighten me with your empty threats? Your stench is more likely than your fingers to take my breath from me."

The undead hissed in her ear, spat curses and threats, but suddenly he screamed, dragging her backward and spinning wildly, attempting to escape the flames erupting all over his rotting clothing and flesh.

The vampire wrenched Desari's hair cruelly in retaliation for Julian's unexpected assault. But as he did so, the owls launched themselves from every direction, a hundred strong, talons extended, going directly for the vampire's glowing eyes. The beating wings created a swirling frenzy of leaves and twigs and pine needles, obliterating sight. Desari ducked as the owls rushed at the vampire's head. A huge owl, his feathers soaked in blood, materialized out of thin air, strong, curved talons outstretched. They bypassed the vampire's eyes and went straight for its chest. Even as the talons bore into flesh, the other owls were raking and slashing at the vampire's face, keeping him howling and off balance, unable to use his power and ancient skills.

Desari dropped to the ground and covered her head, but not one of the birds even scratched her. Julian had orchestrated the battle perfectly, giving the undead no time to harm her. She lay perfectly still, forgetting for the moment that she, too, could disappear. The sound of ripping flesh was terrible, the screams of the vampire unearthly. It wasn't until his foot touched her that Desari remembered to dissolve into droplets of mist and streak quickly into the safety of the trees. Perched in the top of one tall tree, she turned around and reappeared, biting her lower lip nervously as she watched.

The scene was like something out of a horror film. Darius had always sheltered her from his hunts, as had Julian when he put her into a deep sleep. This was brutal and terrifying. The vampire's stink of evil intensified; he was deliberately attempting to foul the air, making it impossible for beast or man to breathe. But as hard as the vampire tried, Julian countered every poisonous hiss, bringing forth a cooling wind of fresh air.

The undead was nearly blinded by the owls raking at his eyes. His chest cavity was cracked open and spewing a geyser of tainted blood that seemed to purposefully spray every creature in its path, burning like acid, even killing some of the birds. The animals were closing in tighter and tighter, a ring of restless, hungry beasts aroused to a fever pitch by the spectacle of violence and the smell of fresh blood.

Her gaze was drawn to the huge owl she knew to be Julian, her lifemate, terrible to see in his role as destroyer. Touching his mind tentatively, she discovered he had pushed out all thought of her, was as ruthless and merciless as the most efficient predator. He attacked from every angle, again and again, swift, deadly, wearing down the evil one with every razor-sharp slash, every deep laceration, always driving for the heart.

The vampire had no chance to dissolve and escape, but his claws and tainted blood were doing immeasurable damage. Even in the shape of the owl, Julian was still severely injured by the first vampire's surprise blow. She could see the feathered creature protecting one side, its wing never spreading its complete span. Desari realized he would have escaped even that blow if his only thought had not been of her. He was incredibly fast, moving like lightning, striking and moving, striking and moving, giving the ancient undead little chance to gather his energy and wield his considerable evil power.

Its howling was terrible to hear. The ugliness of it hurt her ears. She wanted to close her eyes, not see the dead and dying birds, the spray of blood shining black in the moonlight, hissing and sizzling as if it were alive.

She didn't want to see the grotesque vampire, covered in blood, his straggly wisps of hair greasy with it, his eyes pits of it. The deep gouges on his face added to the horror of his hideous features. He was ragged and torn with a multitude of wounds, yet he refused to go down, refused to acknowledge he had no chance of survival.

On the ground the tainted blood was moving, stretching out across the vegetation to seek a victim. Everywhere it touched, plants withered and blackened in the moonlight. Then Desari realized the blood was following the large owl's movements, waiting for an opportunity to strike.

The tiny spot where the vampire's talon had pierced her neck was throbbing and swollen, as if his claw had been dipped in poison. If that tiny wound hurt her, what did Julian feel from his bone-deep slash? She could not imagine it and again she touched his mind, but she found he had blocked all pain so that his entire focus was on destroying the evil one.

Desari wanted to rush forward and gather up all the fallen birds that had aided Julian in the fight with the ancient undead. Wounded as he was, he had no choice but to accept their help, yet she knew instinctively that he would feel sorrow over the destruction of such beautiful creatures.

Her heart ached for Julian, for her brother, for all those who had to fight and destroy a living entity. She knew the undead were wholly evil, that the only thing to do was rid the planet of them, yet those forced to do so risked their lives and, worse, their very souls, while they did so.

Desari attempted to calm herself, so that her mind was not in turmoil, so that it contained only confidence and strength. Then she sent herself into Julian's mind, giving him the rush of energy her ancient blood and power could supply. She was incapable of killing, could not end a life—compassion ran too deeply in her—but she prayed that she did not impede Julian's ability to do so.

Julian was grateful for the strength pouring into him. He had suffered tremendous blood loss, and the tainted blood of the vampire contacting his skin through the owl's feathers was burning deeply into his flesh. Still, he never hesitated but continued his relentless attack, beating back the powerful undead with his talons, driving deeper and deeper into the chest wall. Only when he was beyond the protective muscle and bone did he shape-shift back to his own body, his mind reaching for the remaining owls to release them of the compulsion to attack.

Desari gasped, her hand going to her throat as she saw the blobs of tainted blood on the ground rush together to form a large pool. The blackened liquid began to obscenely form the parody of an arm, then stretched farther into a diabolical, shadowy hand that began to furtively crawl across pine needles and over fallen branches to reach its goal. *Julian, on the ground!*

He didn't respond or acknowledge her warning; he simply faced the vampire calmly. His handsome face was lined with weariness, his golden hair flowing wildly to his shoulders. He stood straight and tall, his shoulders square, his amber eyes gleaming with a kind of fire.

"I bring you the justice of our people, old one. What you have done is a crime against humanity, against the very earth itself. I carry out the sentence pronounced on your kind by the Prince of our people and hope you find mercy in another life as I can give you none here." The words were soft and gentle, hypnotic and compelling.

Even as the vampire's body began to contort in a last effort to escape, as the tainted blood came within inches of Julian's shoes, the Carpathian hunter plunged his hand into the crack in the chest of the undead and extracted the heart. There was a horrible sucking sound as the pulsating organ came out of the shrieking fiend. Julian leapt away from the spray of blood and the grotesque hand reaching for his feet.

The vampire flopped to the ground, tried twice to rise, then began to blindly feel around him, seeking the only thing that could keep him alive. Julian dropped the heart a safe distance from the apparition, who refused to believe he had been defeated.

Desari felt the terrible weariness then, the pain throbbing and burning in Julian's body. She watched as he gathered the energy from the lightning and directed it first at the heart, then the body of the undead, and lastly into the ground itself, incinerating the dark blood that spread like a stain over the forest floor. Only then did he sink down onto a fallen log. Desari watched in fascination as he called down more glowing light to hold for a moment to cleanse his hands and forearms.

Desari leapt from her high perch and would have run to him, but Julian shook his head and pointed with his good arm toward the forest. Moving slowly but steadily, several humans were heading directly for the ring of restless animals. Desari instantly began to sing, soothing the large animals, releasing them from the enthralling spell she had woven. Growling and snarling, the animals slunk into the forest's dark interior, away from the group of humans.

"They must have been camping within the sound of my voice," she told Julian.

"We have much to do this night before we can seek rest," he replied. "We must find the vampire's kill and destroy all evidence. This ground must be cleared of any trace of the undead."

Desari could hear the weariness in his voice, feel it in

his mind. His blood loss had been great. "I will take care of those things. You return to our campsite and place yourself in a healing sleep while I complete the tasks."

A small smile softened the hard edge to Julian's mouth. "Come here, *piccola*. I need you close to me." His voice was a velvet heat she couldn't ignore.

Desari found her feet moving toward him before it registered that she was obeying his soft command. The moment she was within range, his hand snaked out, shackled her wrist, and exerted pressure so that she was forced to sit beside him on the log. "Hold still, *cara*," he ordered. "The vampire's claw was tainted. The poison is already moving through your system. I will drive it from your body, and then I must remove the memory of your song from these humans so that their lives will remain unchanged."

"You need healing far more than I do, Julian," she protested. "Do not worry about so small a thing as this scratch. We can take care of it later."

"I will not allow such a thing," Julian said. "Your health comes before all else. The vampire has been destroyed, but his poison is still lethal. Be still, Desari. I will do this. I know what it is to have the darkness growing and spreading inside, a thing that that cannot be removed. I will not allow such a thing to happen to you."

She read his determination, wished she could see the source of his grim resolve, but still it was hidden from her. Although she felt foolish having Julian attend such a tiny laceration when he was so badly wounded, Desari didn't attempt further protest. There would be no changing his mind, and she was not about to waste his time and energy on arguing.

Julian's golden eyes closed while he centered himself and once more disassociated himself from his own pain and fatigue. He sent himself seeking outside his own body and into hers. He found the foul drops of poison almost immediately. The thick black flecks were growing insidiously, spreading throughout her bloodstream and multiplying. He was light and energy, fire moving swiftly to overtake each and every speck of toxic venom and neutralize it. It was a difficult task. He took care not to overlook the minutest particle, delving into every artery, vein, and organ to ensure she was completely free of any residual toxin that might later grow and spread, causing illness or harm.

When he was finished, he made the journey back into his own body. Desari touched his face with loving, gentle fingers. He was gray and swaying with weariness. She pushed back his hair, her heart aching for him. She could feel the burning of his flesh, of his insides, the gaping wound in his shoulder. "You must rest. Let me do what needs doing."

Julian shook his head. "You would be a great help to me if you would take care of the humans. I cannot allow you near the remains of the vampire or his victims. You cannot trust the undead, not even in death."

"He is destroyed, Julian," she reminded him softly.

"Trust me, *cara mia*, I have dealt with his kind for centuries. Their traps often lie in wait long after they are dead." He brought her hand to his mouth. "Do as I say, Desari. Help the humans. You do not want them to live the rest of their lives as zombies. Go now. And then go through the air to Darius. Call to him, have him put you in the earth. I will go to ground as soon as I safely can."

Desari laughed softly at him. "Persist in your fantasies, my love. I am certain they will see you through this difficult time." She pulled her hand away from his and left him while she went to attend to the group of campers stumbling around the edge of the clearing.

Julian watched her walk away from the scene of brutal death. She looked so serene and beautiful, so untouched by the violence and ugliness surrounding them. He felt his heart lurch, and a curious melting sensation followed. He shook his head in wonder at his luck, pushed back his hair, and stood on shaky legs. He was weak, far weaker than he had allowed Desari to see. The wound in his shoulder was a fiery pain that encompassed his entire chest. He could feel poison spreading throughout his system, and each laceration of his skin throbbed and burned. But he had a duty; he was honor-bound to see to his lifemate first and then remove all signs of the vampire to hide their race from those mortals who would seek to destroy them.

He knelt beside the dead and dying birds. Those already dead he could do nothing about. Those that still lived were suffering. Gathering the live ones to him, he once more sent himself seeking outside his body and into the creatures who had answered the call to help him. No matter how difficult, he would heal every one that he could. Julian had a deep respect for wildlife. He ran with the wolves, soared in the sky with the birds, swam in the waters with the fish, and hunted with jungle cats in Africa. He lived as one with nature, and nature lived within him. Before Desari, wildlife had been his only solace in the long centuries of his existence.

Desari completed the task of masking the hideous scene in the forest from the humans and turned back to see Julian kneeling beside the fallen owls. He looked like a warrior of old, battle-scarred but undefeated. His golden hair flowed around him, blood dripped steadily, his face was set as if in stone, lined with pain and weariness, yet his hands were gentle as they touched the birds, stroked the feathers, and chanted the Carpathian healing ritual in words as old as time itself. She found tears swimming in her eyes. This man who stood so calmly and faced death, who could destroy an enemy mercilessly, ruthlessly, thought first to heal her and then the creatures of the forest. Pride rose in her for this man. She might never understand what his words had done to bind them together, but she was suddenly glad that he had done so. Julian was an exceptional Carpathian male; it was clear to her that he thought of others before he thought of himself.

I might just be falling in love with you. She brushed the words in his mind, her voice a stroking caress.

Julian didn't look up at her, but she felt his smug smile. *You already are in love with me,* cara mia. *You are just too stubborn to admit it to yourself. I walk in your mind with you. I know you love me.*

Keep on fantasizing, she teased, and turned back to the task at hand, leading the group of humans back toward their campground.

Julian was uneasy with her leaving his sight. *Call me if you feel in any way disturbed. Do not forget the recent trend of vampires traveling together in these parts. And you have now seen for yourself that lesser vampires, those who have recently turned, are often used by the more ancient and skilled undead. You must be very careful.*

I am beginning to think your lectures are even more tedious than my brother's, Desari replied, somewhere between laughter and exasperation as she led the humans away. She was no fledgling to be treated as if she weren't very bright. Sometimes the males of her race set her teeth on edge.

Julian could not hurry the healing of the owls. Each feathered body had to be entered and healed from the inside out. He tried to push away every thought but becoming energy and light so that he would make no mistakes. Still, he felt guilt for using the beautiful creatures—the price to be paid for once more feeling emotion. Sorrow and guilt over the owls that had lost their lives. Fear for Desari, for the separation forced on them through his own weakness.

Wearily he tossed the last owl into the air and watched the powerful wings lift the bird high so that it soared away. He was swaying now from the tremendous drain on his energy, from the volume of blood he had lost. He desperately needed to go to ground and seek the rejuvenating sleep of his people while the soil healed his body.

Julian turned and surveyed grimly the blackened ground strewn with the owls he could not save. With a sigh he once more called down the lightning from the clouds and sent a bolt slamming to earth to ignite the bodies. When the last of the forest floor was clean, he stepped away from the area to bring up the wind. It whirled around like a small tornado, sweeping ashes high into its funnel and dispersing them in all directions.

Julian shape-shifted slowly, his muscles and sinews protesting, his shoulder shrieking in outrage as he once again compressed his body into the shape of a bird of prey. One wing did not want to move correctly, so it required great concentration and skill to take flight. Once in the air, Julian soared over the forest, seeking the vampire's recent kill. It, too, was a grim task, and he did not want Desari anywhere near the site. He spotted her with her charges, returning the campers to their tents and motor homes.

He dipped low to ensure no danger threatened her before proceeding up the riverbank away from the main campground. Desari touched his mind with warmth and concern, and he attempted to feel strong and able so she wouldn't worry. He could feel her compassionate nature, her soft heart a beacon to guide her lifemate back from the edge of predatory madness.

Below him, he smelled the stench of death. He dropped low, and circled the riverbank twice before gliding to earth. He shape-shifted as he landed. At once his body protested again, this time the pain nearly driving him to his knees. He had never been able to abide weakness in himself. Swearing eloquently to himself in the ancient language, he walked to the bodies of two young gold-panners. They lay broken and discarded in the usual messy vampire manner, their faces rigid with terror. These two had seen the undead exposed in all his horror. They were young, not more than twenty-three or twenty-four. Julian shook his head, irritated with himself for not having sensed the ancient's presence earlier. Ordinarily, no vampire could approach within miles of him without his knowledge. His emotions were so new and intense, colors so vivid, desires so compelling, he felt almost blinded. He certainly had been occupied with his lifemate and his own needs instead of what was happening around him.

Desari? He touched her mind gently, needing to know she was not in any danger.

Everything here is taken care of, Julian. Shall I come to you? Her voice was a soothing breath of fresh air in his head.

No! His warning was sharp. *Do not*, cara. *Go to the others and the bus, and I will meet you there.* He was grateful for the beauty of her voice and longed to be away from the sight of evil and death, back in her presence, where he would find comfort.

She withdrew without argument, sensing his weariness, knowing he was hiding the true extent of his injuries from her. She fed, certain he would need blood, but took care to use only women. The last thing she needed was for her lifemate to go berserk on her.

Julian, still a shadow in her mind, found himself smiling at her thoughts. He might be too weary to go berserk at this precise moment, but he was grateful she was considerate of his feelings. He incinerated the human bodies and blew their ashes over a large area, leaving their camp scorched and blackened, as if it had taken a bolt of lightning in a ferocious storm. The authorities would never find the bodies, and would perhaps presume the campers had drowned, the currents carrying them off. Julian felt for the families, but he could leave no evidence of the vampire's handiwork or tainted blood to be analyzed by some human coroner. Protecting his race was top priority. He had no other choice. He took one last look around to assure himself he had done all he could to hide any evidence of the undead. Satisfied, he began to walk toward their own campsite.

Chapter Ten

Desari kicked the wheel of the bus. "The darn thing refuses to start. I knew it. I knew it would happen at the worst possible time." She kicked the tire again in frustration.

Julian stood in the shadows of the trees, swaying slightly, his eyes glued to Desari's slender figure. She was all grace, like flowing water, her ebony hair cascading around her like waves of silk. She was beautiful even in her fit of temper.

She swung around, her enormous eyes instantly locating him beneath the trees. At once her expression changed to one of deep concern. He was gray and drawn, blood coating his shirt. He looked so tired, she was alarmed. She instantly leapt across the space separating them, one slim arm curving around his waist in an attempt to support him. "Lean on me, Julian," she crooned softly. He had walked the distance, not flown or used his astonishing speed in any way. It was evidence of his ebbing strength.

He circled her shoulders, putting a small amount of his weight on her. She looked so anxious, he wanted to kiss her in reassurance, but the poison inside him was growing and spreading, and he wouldn't take the chance of infecting her. "You must call Darius to us, Desari," he ordered softly. He had given this much thought on his return to her. He had wanted to call Gregori to him, the healer he knew and trusted, but there was no time to lose. He would need to avail himself of Darius's strength and expertise.

She helped him up the step and into the bus. Julian went down the aisle on shaky legs and nearly fell onto the couch. "You need blood, Julian, and then, once in the ground, you will recover quickly." She sounded anxious in spite of her determination not to.

Julian shook his head. "Call Darius to us." His voice was a thread of sound, his lashes sweeping down as if he were fighting to stay awake and cognizant.

Darius. Can you hear me? Desari was alarmed now. Julian was not the kind of man to ask for help.

You have need? Darius was far away, but he could sense her fear.

Come to us now. Please hurry, Darius. I am afraid.

Julian laced his fingers through hers. "You have called him to us?"

She tightened her grip on him, afraid he was slipping away from her. "Yes. Feed now, Julian, and go to earth until he gets here."

"I will not take a chance on contaminating you. Go to the others. They will protect you until your brother and I are able." His eyes were closed now completely, his skin ashen.

Christine Feehan

Desari brought his hand to her mouth, but before she could kiss the lacerations on his knuckles, heal them with the agent in her saliva, he had snatched his hand away.

"Do not!" It was a sharp reproof.

"Talk to me. Tell me why you refuse what I offer. It is my right to heal you, to feed you and care for you." Desari was hurt and afraid, the emotions swirling around until she could not separate them.

There was a stirring in her mind, warmth, the impression of arms stealing around her shoulders, holding her close. His heart was beating abnormally slowly, she could feel it in her mind, hear the irregular pulsing. "This was an ancient, *cara*, one of the eldest vampires, much skilled in the old ways. His blood is extremely dangerous."

"You took it out of my system, Julian." She bent over him anxiously. "Take it from your own."

"I do not have the strength, *piccola*. Do not fear for me. I will not leave you. Go now to the others so that I know you are safe."

Desari sat up straight, suddenly comprehending. "You think more undead might come."

"I believe you and the other female—Syndil—are drawing them here. They seek mates, thinking that will guide them back to their emotions and souls. Go, Desari, while the sun is still far away." Julian feared *he* would come, his ancient enemy, feared he would be drawn right to Desari.

Julian's voice was nearly gone. Even his breathing was labored. Whatever was spreading inside him was taking a stranglehold on his lungs and heart. Desari stroked back the golden hair falling across his forehead. He was cold and clammy. She knew his fears for her were very powerful, but how could she leave him?

He had only been in her life a short time, yet he was the air she breathed. Her body recognized his. Her heart and soul were finally complete. She had to be wherever he was. *Darius, please hurry*, she whispered, knowing he was already in flight, powerful wings covering the distance between them in the shortest possible time. But he had to hurry.

What would she do if the vampire had other partners? She was not a warrior; how would she defend Julian in his weakened state? Again she had the impression of warmth and reassurance from Julian.

Just then something hit the outside of the bus with enough force to rock the solid vehicle. Her heart leapt in apprehension. At once, Julian struggled to his feet, his face harsh and merciless, carved in granite. "Sing the ancient healing chant, Desari. It is in your mind, I have heard it there. Merge with me while you sing."

His transformation from being nearly dead to this commanding presence was shocking. His head was up, and he was striding purposefully to the door of the bus. Desari sat still, her heart pounding. She could not send him off unaided. He would have her strength and courage, her belief in him, and any other aid he should need. Her voice began the ancient chant, as old as time, something they were born with, the memory already imprinted on them. It was soothing and peaceful, and her unique voice strengthened the power of it.

Julian listened to the notes as he made his way out into the night. Her voice was so pure, it pushed aside the effects of the vampire's poison enough for him to focus. Outside, shadows were moving under the trees, ringing the bus.

Julian breathed a sigh of relief. Not another vampire but merely the dead one's enslaved minions, the undead's ghouls. These former humans had tremendous strength and cunning—the vampire's blood ran in their veins—but they were not immortal. They slept in sewers and graveyards to escape the deadly sun, ate living flesh and blood. They lived to serve their master, hoping that one day immortality would be bestowed on them. Julian knew such a thing to be impossible. They were already dead, mere puppets, living only by the vampire's whim and tainted blood.

He stepped out of the bus and faced these living dead. Their target would be Desari. Though their master was destroyed, they had no choice but to carry out his orders to acquire her, and they would be brutal in their rage and fear. Julian's first task was to safeguard Desari, rigging the bus with the most powerful safeguards he was capable of weaving in the event the ghouls should defeat him in his weakened state. Darius would have to unravel what Julian had wrought.

Stall them until Darius gets here. Julian heard the plea in Desari's voice. She couldn't bear him to be in any more pain.

Sing for me, cara mia. *That is what keeps the pain at bay. I can do no other than what I do. You are my life. My only reason for existing. I will not fail to protect you.*

A storm then. I can bring in the mist, whatever you need. Allow me to take whatever burden from you I can. She had no wish to argue with him or distract him from those that threatened. She could hear the dark murmurs, the rustling of leaves and the breaking of twigs beneath their foul feet. The ghouls were advancing on Julian.

Sing for me, piccola. *Your brother will send aid in advance of his arrival. Be ready for him to use your sight.*

Desari had to be satisfied with that. She began the ancient chant once more as she moved to the window to be able to see whatever Darius asked of her. Julian looked so alone to her. Standing tall and straight, the wind whipping his hair around him, his body, so wracked with pain, relaxed and ready for the attack. Her pride in him grew.

Desari? It was Darius, his voice calm and unexcited as always, filled with complete confidence. He sounded strong, and close by. *Tell me what is wrong with Julian.*

Desari continued to sing for Julian but directed her thoughts toward her brother. She had been talking to him for so many centuries on their private mental path, she divided her attention with ease. *He says the vampire he battled was ancient, that its blood had powerful poison. Julian was wounded but he will not allow me to strengthen him through feeding. He is too weak to drive out the poison himself. He waits for you.*

You know what I will need, Darius responded. *Prepare the bus with the necessary candles and herbs. Have the scents in the air when we dispose of those who now threaten you. Call to the others. We will need them to join with us in the healing ritual. Insist that Syndil join, as she has tremendous healing powers.*

Darius broke off the contact with his sister and glided unseen and undetected above the circle of servants to the undead. Seven. This had indeed been a powerful ancient to sustain so many living dead on his blood at one time.

Darius felt a deep respect for the Carpathian standing his ground, looking every inch the intimidating hunter. The fact that he had not manufactured a clean shirt told Darius the extent of Julian's weakness. Yet even with the pain and weakness, Julian was ready to fight.

Darius dropped out of the sky, shape-shifting as he touched the ground, silently springing on clawed feet straight at his prey. The large male leopard sank its fangs into the first ghoul's throat, dispatching him with deadly efficiency. It dropped the body and padded noiselessly toward the next victim. This time the undead's servant was turned away from him, but the leopard merely vaulted into the branches above his head, then dropped on the fiend, burying its canines deep, crushing the throat.

Julian watched the abominations creeping toward him, seven strong, in various stages of decay, with the master dead and no longer sustaining their lives. Then a dark shadow moved behind the tree line, and Julian caught a glimpse of glossy fur. The large jungle cat quickly dispatched two of the zombies.

Julian let his breath out slowly. These ghouls were tainted with the vampire's infected blood, so it was more than likely that Darius also would be poisoned from his kills this night. Overhead, clouds were gathering, dark and ominous, blotting out the moonlight. Lightning began to arc, a strong, fast storm shrieking through the trees, sending limbs dancing and swaying. Julian knew it was of Darius's making.

One ghoul lurched forward, his burning eyes on the bus and his target. The only thing standing between him and his goal was Julian. Growling insanely, drooling and slobbering, he moved toward Julian, showing hideous teeth as he shuffled in close. His huge arms swung clumsily at Julian's head. The hunter ducked the blows and retaliated with one of his own. The head of the ghoul rocked, and the neck cracked audibly.

Julian sprang away to meet the second opponent moving in for the kill. This one swung an ax at him, the blade missing by a scant few inches. Silently cursing the fact that his arm hung uselessly at his side, Julian retaliated with a low spinning kick that swept the legs out from under the servant of the vampire. Then he swiftly delivered the killing blow to the head, crushing the skull just as the third zombie reached him. Despite its slowness, this monster was strong and cunning. He went for Julian's wounded shoulder, slamming into him like a charging bull. The pain was excruciating, exploding through Julian with the force of dynamite. It drove him to his knees before he could find the energy and strength to cut off feeling to the area. The air burst from his lungs so that he had to fight to breathe; his stomach clenched and knotted, rolling with nausea.

At once lightning hit his attacker, the bolt driving through the body. Smoke streamed from his mouth and nose, and his clothes and skin turned black. A ball of orange flame looking like a meteor from space then struck him in the belly, incinerating the monster, who howled eerily as he turned to ashes. The flames then jumped from body to body, directed by Darius's hand, dispatching the remaining ghouls with the ease of a hunter of long experience and at full strength.

At once his arm slipped around Julian and took his full weight. He carried the big man like a child, cradled gently in his arms. "Do you have the strength to remove the safeguards?" he asked. The voice was calm and confident, no change in breathing despite the long flight, the terrible fight, and the burden he carried.

Julian nodded in answer to Darius's question and began the complicated task of unraveling the safeguards, carefully making certain it was safe. Desari flung open the door and stepped aside so that her brother could carry her lifemate inside. Anxiously she followed them to the bed. The motor home was dark; only scented candles gave off flickers of light. The soothing aroma of herbs and candles filled the air, so that each time Julian took a breath, the healing scent entered his body to help alleviate the pain knifing through him.

"Is he going to be all right? Can you help him?" Desari asked anxiously, hovering behind Darius, trying to see around him to her lifemate.

"He is correct; the vampire's poison is strong and unusual. I want you to stay out of the way. Join with the others in the healing chant and lend your strength to mine. I will heal him and then myself."

Desari bit her lip, her hand going to her throat. "How were you infected?"

"The servants of the undead were tainted. A trap the vampire left behind for those who dared to thwart his plans." Darius spoke matter-of-factly, with no hint of alarm. His steady, calm voice, so familiar to her, was comforting.

Darius bent over Julian. The Carpathian hunter shook his head without opening his eyes. "You first, Darius. The poison spreads quickly and grows in strength. Heal yourself before it is too late. I will be unable to aid you. Do this for Desari, as I cannot watch over her as I should."

"Rest, Julian," Darius commanded, used to being obeyed. Few dared to question his authority.

Darius sent himself seeking within his own body, searching out every particle of venom advancing through his bloodstream. He studied the nature of the poison, its cells and behavior. Satisfied he knew how it worked, he began to destroy it, driving it from his body in the same unhurried manner in which he did everything. Julian was right. The poison was strong and fast-acting, destroying cells and multiplying swiftly. It was a tribute to Julian's incredible strength that he was still alive, that knowing what the venom could do, he had placed his lifemate and his duties before his own welfare. The healing chant, sung in Desari's beautiful voice, was lending strength to Darius, yet he found himself slightly dizzy when he emerged back into his own being.

"You are gray, Darius. Take what is freely offered that you and Julian can once again regain your strength." Desari quietly held out her wrist to her brother.

Darius took her hand and turned it over. His sister appeared fragile and delicate, yet her ancient blood ran strong and powerful. He bent his head and drank. At once he felt his strength returning. If it had been difficult and draining to remove the lethal venom from his own body after such a short exposure, it would be a monumental job to save Julian.

Desari touched her brother lightly, needing reassurance. Julian looked terrible, the lines in his face cut deep with his suffering. He was ashen and weak. His heart and lungs were slowed to impede the advance of the poison, but it was taking him over, she could clearly see. When she touched his mind to merge with him, his mind block kept her out. Julian was taking no chances that she would feel the gut-wrenching agony he was enduring silently.

"We will need all of our family to help," Darius said as he closed the wound on her wrist. "Take care none of you falter, no matter what I look like. You can always supply me with what I need when I am finished here."

Hear me, Julian. I will be with you. Wherever you choose to go, I will follow you. You are not alone. We will always be together. Desari whispered it solemnly in Julian's mind, making him hear her promise, understand her determination. She would not lose her lifemate, even if it meant following wherever he led. This life or the next, she would go with him.

Darius took a deep breath to inhale the aromatic herbs, to carry them with him as he gathered himself into light and energy and entered Julian's body. At once he could see the bloodstream was a mess. The poison acted like a virus, mutating quickly, reproducing, attacking the body's defenses. It was running wild, working at killing the Carpathian as fast as it was able to meet the demands of its master. The vampire must have long studied and experimented. This was a challenge Darius had never come up against.

Still, he was confident in himself and his abilities. He always found a way. He never gave up. He would triumph; he allowed no other thought, no other outcome into the realm of possibility.

He moved into the chamber of the heart and surveyed the damage. Julian had known what was happening to his insides, and the pain had to be excruciating. He had slowed his heart and lungs to slow the spread of the poison. As Darius worked to repair the damage, he studied the mutated strains. It was not so difficult to stop the original decay; he already knew the structure from studying it within his own body. The mutations were more aggressive and complicated. It was important to know which was moving faster and doing the most damage before he began to go after them.

By the time he had the walls of the heart repaired and the original strain destroyed, he had a good idea of how the virus broke up the cell, reshaped it, and multiplied. He moved into an artery to begin his real work. The poison was surging toward him, a solid army of cells on the offensive, rushing to overtake the threat to it. Darius became a general, manufacturing his own army of antibodies. He sent wave after wave toward the advancing poison. His creations began to pick up speed, moving quickly to destroy the vampire's last deathtrap. It took tremendous strength for Darius to hold his bodiless state, to be only light and energy, to keep up with the ever-

changing virus as it tried to mutate to escape the on-
slaught of warriors he had created to combat it.

He found himself admiring the vampire's work. It was
genius, this taint, somewhere between virus and poison,
fast-acting and lethal with a kind of programmed intelligence. Its entire reason for existing was to take over
its host and ensure its own survival. Darius's work was
complicated, but he did it with his usual confidence and
calm. The battle was strange and unfamiliar, but it was
simply a matter of unraveling what the vampire had
wrought. Nothing would defeat him.

At the same time, a part of him was analyzing the
Carpathian male his sister had chosen for her mate. Savage was remarkable in that he had known the extent of
the threat to himself, yet he had put Desari's health and
safety before his own. He had even healed the wounded
birds that had aided him in his battle with the ancient
one, a great cost in time and energy, and he had wiped
out all existence of the vampires and their kills to pre-
serve the secrets of their race.

Then Darius discovered a shadowing deep within Julian's body. He studied it a long time. The virus had not
tainted him thusly; this was something else, something
Darius had never seen. It made him uneasy. Julian, however, was extremely calm and accepting of Darius's
presence in his body, confident in his ability to heal.
There was no doubt, no adrenaline to cope with, none
of the body's defenses raised against him as he worked.
And Julian was aware he had discovered the dark
shadow.

The ancient healing chant, soft and melodious, gave
Darius added strength as his energy began to falter. The
familiar voices were all present: Desari, her voice itself
healing and soothing; Syndil, gentle and peaceful like
her nature; Barack, strong and sure; Dayan, the ever-

present second in command ready to aid him should there be need. Only when he managed to wipe out the last mutating strain and manufacture the proper antibodies to hold it at bay did Darius allow himself to emerge back into his own body.

His great strength was nearly depleted. He had worked for over two hours, an extraordinary time to be out of his own body. He was swaying with weariness, his body crying out for sustenance, and he could feel the first stirrings of unease at the approach of the sunrise.

At once Dayan thrust his wrist toward their leader. "Take what is freely offered," he said formally.

Desari touched her brother's shoulder. "You are gray, Darius. Please feed." She didn't want to tell him his appearance was nearly as alarming as Julian's. She was wringing her hands anxiously, afraid of touching Darius's mind to know if he thought Julian would live, afraid of asking the question aloud.

I live, my beautiful one. Julian's masculine voice brushed at her mind, enfolding her in warmth and comfort and a kind of exasperated amusement. *I live to teach my lifemate the meaning of obedience. Your brother is as adept as Gregori, and that, my love, is the highest compliment I could pay him.* He sounded weary and far away, as if the strain to reach her was weakening him even more.

"Julian," she whispered aloud.

Darius swung his icy black gaze to her face in clear reprimand. With careful courtesy he closed the laceration on Dayan's wrist and then bent his head to speak to Julian. "Hear me, lawless one. You are in no shape to oppose me. If you do not wish me to place you under compulsion, you will remain silent and conserve your strength to battle what is attempting to destroy both you and my sister." There was a hard authority in his voice, complete conviction that he would do as he threatened if need be. Darius never repeated himself; he often didn't even bother with a warning. He struck hard and fast. Those who knew him obeyed without question.

Julian lay as if dead, the action of his heart and lungs barely discernible, but incredibly, a faint grin eased the look of death on his face.

Darius glanced at his sister. "This one has no liking for authority. Go to ground, Desari, and stop making a nuisance of yourself."

At once the air in the room thickened with oppressive shadows. A warning, a promise of retaliation. Desari found herself holding her breath. She couldn't believe that anyone would defy Darius's orders, least of all a man half-dead and still in need of help from the very one he threatened. Surely Julian knew Darius would never hurt her. He simply bossed her around because that was his way.

Darius struck at the Carpathian lying so still on the bed with a powerful compulsion to sleep. In his present state, Julian had no way to combat such power. He had one thought before he succumbed to Darius's will: that this man was far more dangerous than any Julian had encountered in all his centuries of living, perhaps even more so than Gregori.

Desari reached around her brother and brushed Julian's hair from his forehead. Her hand lingered lovingly on his skin. "He was only seeking to protect me," she whispered.

Darius's teeth came together with an audible snap. "There is no need for his protection while I am with you. He knows that. He was warning me to mind how I talk to you." The black eyes glinted with menace. "He has enough arrogance for ten males." Darius inhaled sharply, taking the soothing aroma into his lungs. "Resume the chant and add another candle or two. It might keep you out of trouble."

Once more he simply blocked out everything and everybody until there was only the light and energy that was his strength and intelligence. He very carefully reentered Julian's bloodstream to examine the poisonous virus for any new threats. Sure enough, a new strain was attacking the antibodies Darius had configured.

Darius examined the cell structure, marveling at how it could wreak so much havoc. The original poison had carried the seeds to implant this far more virulent strain. It was fighting to reproduce over and over, replicating the monster that fought with such ferocity to carry out the vampire's last command of destruction. Darius sent out more of his army to fight the strain, leaving him free to begin repairs on the vicious wounds and lacerations in Julian's flesh. The newer poison had again weakened the artery walls and the chambers in the heart. Darius spent time restoring the systems. The shoulder wound was particularly bad, flesh and muscle torn to the bone. Darius slowly mended it, then meticulously returned to Julian's bloodstream to be sure it was completely devoid of the vampire's poisonous virus. He was taking no chances that his sister might be contaminated. He went through every muscle, tissue, and bone, every organ and vein, double-checking that he had removed every last vestige of the foreign cells.

Then he turned once more to inspect the odd shadowing. It was there in Julian's mind, in his body. It was dark. Tainted. The mark of a vampire. Darius studied it a long while. There was no way to combat such a mark. Julian had been in intimate contact with a vampire, and the beast was strong within him. A solitary Carpathian male's struggle to sustain his soul was hard enough without the taint of the vampire inside him; Darius could only imagine the fierce battle Julian must have suffered every moment of his existence. Still, he could do nothing to aid the Carpathian who had claimed his sister. With a sigh of regret, he entered his own body once again. He would keep a close eye on Julian to ensure his sister's safety.

Instantly his eyes reacted to the dawn. Light was beginning to slowly streak the darkness a soft dove-gray, heralding the morning. He closed his eyes to soften the effect. This recent weakness troubled him. Darius had never had to contend with weakness before. For centuries he had easily managed to stay above ground until ten, sometimes eleven in the morning, but the last few endless years, his eyes had become far more sensitive to any light. Darius had a will of iron. When he chose to do something, no matter what the difficulty, it was done. Yet he could not overcome this sensitivity to early morning light.

"Darius?" Dayan touched his shoulder lightly to bring him back to them. "It is done?"

"We must get him to ground, allow the soil to heal him. I will give him blood just before we place him under. My blood is ancient and should speed his recovery. Although why I should want such a thing, I cannot imagine."

"Darius, you have given too much of yourself this night," Dayan objected. "I will supply him."

Darius shook his head. "I will not take a chance with your life. If I have missed one cell of this venomous virus, there is a possibility it could infect you." The real reason was more complex. If Dayan ever turned, Julian should not be his hunter. Darius would take that responsibility on himself. And if the shadowing in Julian proved to be a beacon for a vampire, if it endangered

221

Desari, it would take Darius to destroy his sister's chosen lifemate.

Is there a possibility that you missed something? Desari demanded of her brother, not for one minute believing that. Darius was always completely thorough.

Do not be ridiculous. Darius sounded wearier than he intended. He realized it when he saw the alarm in her dark eyes. At once he held out his hand to reassure her. "Do not worry, little sister."

Dayan immediately offered his wrist again to supply the leader with whatever it took to aid him. By now Barack would have Syndil in the ground, safeguards strong to ensure her safety. It was always Barack who looked after Syndil, especially since the attack. Where once Barack had been easygoing and cocky, now he was much quieter, his eyes watchful, thoughtful whenever they rested on Syndil. Dayan had been the one to aid their leader in the healing of the stranger, while Barack had protected Syndil.

Dayan found himself sitting abruptly, dizzy from the volume of blood he had supplied this night. Darius was already compelling Julian to feed. Dayan could not help but admire the efficient way Darius did everything, his movements ever sure and powerful. The stranger had the same assurance about him.

Dayan studied Desari's choice of a mate. He looked dangerous even in his deathlike state. He glanced at Desari, a little mystified why she would choose a man so like her brother when she often chafed under Darius's stringent rules for the women.

"Go feed, Dayan," Darius said. "Desari and I will place Julian in the ground. I will lie above the two of them to protect both while he is healing. You must construct safeguards around our campsite to keep others out while we sleep this rising."

Dayan nodded. "No problem, Darius. Do not worry."

"Call to me if you have need of my assistance."

Dayan rose and moved silently out to the hunt. Desari sighed softly. "He seems very alone sometimes, Darius."

"Males are always alone, little sister," Darius answered quietly. "It is something we all must face." He touched her chin with a fingertip. "We are without your compassion and loving nature."

"What can we do to help?" Desari asked immediately, her eyes shadowed with worry.

"Your singing helps, the peace in you. You and Syndil are our strength, Desari. Never think you are not."

"Yet we are the ones responsible for the gathering of vampires in this region. They are looking for us."

Darius nodded. "That is more than likely. But it is hardly your fault."

"Yet you have to destroy them."

"It is my duty. I accept it without question or thought. Now, Desari, I am weary, and we must get this man of yours deep within the earth to complete his healing. Let us go."

Desari started down the aisle, then turned back to address him over her shoulder. "The bus broke down again, Darius. I intend to put an ad in some of the papers looking for a mechanic to travel with us. I realize it will change things a bit, but we can easily control a single human. I can even place a compulsion in the ad so that we attract the one we are seeking."

"If he is out there. If your chosen one is not going to get jealous. He appears to be somewhat possessive."

Desari turned away from her brother, pleased she was able to get that much of a concession out of him. Darius obviously believed she could never find such a person, but she was determined to try. She was tired of seeing to every detail of their travel by herself.

They stepped outside into the gray light of dawn and moved hurriedly into the deep forest to select an area protected from the sun yet with several escape routes.

Desari found such a spot and waved her hand to open the earth, revealing the healing coolness the soil provided to rejuvenate those of her kind. It beckoned her, whispering promises of sleep and protection.

Behind her, Darius floated silently to the site with his burden. Very carefully he lay Julian in the bed of soil. "Sleep deeply, the sleep of our people, chosen one of my sister, that you will heal completely and wake refreshed and in full strength." He spoke the words formally as Desari followed Julian to earth. He watched as his sister waved her hand, taking her last breath before the soil poured over them.

Darius stood a moment listening to the birds and the rustles of mice and small rodents foraging in the bushes. He was normally in the earth before the sun had risen this high; he had almost forgotten the sounds of morning. As he looked around at the black and gray world, he felt the utter loneliness the males of his race endured for most of their barren existence. Time stretched out before him, long and endless and ugly without hope. Nothing could change what was. It was but a matter of time before the black stain spreading in him enveloped his soul completely. It was only his iron will and strict code of honor, his responsibility for the protection of his family, that kept him from walking into the sun and ending the waking hell he existed in. How much worse had it been for Desari's lifemate, with the mark of the vampire consuming his soul, eating him from the inside out? Julian Savage was a threat to all he came in contact with. And now he was a part of Darius's family.

Chapter Eleven

The sun set slowly, hues of orange, pink, and red spreading across the sky. It sank behind the mountains, its colors radiating throughout the forest, casting dancing shadows on leaves and brushes. The wind blew gently, fresh and clean, renewing the cycle of life.

Most of the campers had long since left the area, disturbed by some unknown sense of distress, as if something dangerous lurked nearby. Two missing campers who had been panning for gold had never been found despite a search of the area on horseback, by helicopters, and with dogs. The search-and-rescue teams found themselves heavy of heart, an oppressive burden on their chests making it nearly impossible to breathe. All of them secretly wanted to get out of the area.

The barrier Dayan had erected was a good one, and Darius had reinforced it when he rose several nights previously. The bus had also finally been repaired.

Julian became aware of his heart and lungs beginning

to function, of the sound of another heart beating close to his. Carefully he scanned the area above and around him to ensure they were alone and free from danger. He checked for blank spots that might mask the presence of the undead. Then he opened the earth above them to reveal the swaying canopy of branches and the night that belonged to him. He moved in a slow, careful stretch to feel his body out. The movement brought him in contact with soft skin and silky hair. He inhaled deeply, bringing her fragrance into his lungs.

Desari. It was a gift, a miracle he had been given that he would never again wake alone. He would never again roam the earth, always alone. His fingers touched the ebony strands, brought them to his mouth. How would he tell her the truth? He could never give her up. Julian had been strong enough to separate himself from his twin, from his people, but he did not have the strength to walk away from Desari, even if every moment in his company would be fraught with danger for her. He turned toward her to bury his face in the wealth of her hair.

At once Desari responded, putting her arms around him, holding him with ferocious strength. He could feel her trembling against him. "I thought I lost you," she whispered softly against his neck. "It was far too close."

He tightened his own hold, molding her soft, pliant frame to his. "I told you to trust me, *cara*. You were worried needlessly."

Her hunger was beating at him along with his own. Both had stayed in the ground these last few risings while he healed and rejuvenated. Now both of them required sustenance. Julian took to the air first, rising swiftly to meet any potential danger to them, immediately. Desari followed only when he signaled all was clear. She closed the earth, leaving no sign of their occupancy, as she followed Julian across the sky in search of prey.

The forest seemed quiet, nearly empty of human quarry. In the bodies of owls, they circled above the trees, taking in a far larger hunting area than they could in other form. Upriver several miles from their place of rest, Julian spotted movement below. He dropped down into the canyon and made a single silent pass overhead. Two males were setting up a tent together, laughing at each other's jokes. Julian signaled Desari to find a tree on the rim of the canyon and wait for him. He continued to circle, scanning the area for dangers, ensuring she was safe before he flew to a tree near his prey. He tucked his wings under him and walked along a branch, his clawed talons digging into the wood. He studied the layout of the campsite, lifting his head to catch the wind's tales of the surrounding forest and river, making certain they were alone.

Desari waited patiently for Julian to feed for both of them. She watched him, finding pleasure in any form he took. What was it about him that drew her gaze like a magnet? He had somehow stolen into her heart and wrapped himself around it until there was no living without him. She didn't really mind anymore. Their species was of the earth and sky, a part of nature itself. She had learned centuries ago, in an ever-changing world, that nature was wild and free, making its own rules and as quickly abandoning them when it no longer needed them. One could not remain rigid. Like the changing seasons, the rising and setting sun, the spinning earth itself, everything changed. Including her life. Julian was now a part of it.

She watched him drop to the ground and shape-shift back into his human form. At once her heart somersaulted, and butterfly wings brushed inside her stomach at the sight of his tall, muscular form. He looked like a warrior of old, intimidating and dangerous, yet handsome and sensual. Desari followed his every movement, the casual, fluid way he moved when he approached the two campers, his friendly smile and softly spoken words hiding the instant enthrallment. He bent his head to drink. She noticed that he was careful and respectful, almost gentle with the first man as he helped him to sit beneath the tree before turning to the second man waiting so patiently for his turn to provide what the soft voice had commanded. Desari found herself marveling at the way Julian treated the humans, almost as if some part of him liked them.

She liked humans. There were many good people in the world. Darius and the other men considered each of them a potential threat, even though Carpathians had the ability to control human thoughts and even implant or wipe away memories if need be. Desari assumed all the males were similarly distrustful. It was nice to realize Julian felt gentleness toward the human race.

Do not credit your lifemate so much, cara mia. I do not feel the compassion and camaraderie you are capable of feeling. I wish it were so, but I am primarily a predator.

Desari found herself smiling even within the body of the bird. Julian was a shadow in her mind, monitoring her thoughts.

It is the only way I ever hear good of myself, he explained. *Aloud, you prefer to lecture me at every turn. Your thoughts are much more to my liking.*

I should be more careful. You are arrogant enough.

You are crazy about me. A wealth of smug male satisfaction filled his voice.

Desari tried to keep herself from laughing, but it was impossible. Julian Savage was everything she ever could have wanted. Even his warped sense of humor and over-bearing self-confidence were too endearing to pretend otherwise. *You wish I were.*

You cannot help yourself. Doubtless it is my good looks.

And your charming manner. She laughed again, this time dislodging herself from the tree branch. The owl circled lazily over the canyon before settling to earth, shape-shifting as she did so. *It is particularly your modesty that attracts me.*

Walk farther into the trees while I release these two from my command. I will not have them near you.

Desari's head snapped up, and her dark eyes smoldered dangerously. She walked away, but she was tired of all the orders the males of her race seemed determined to toss out as fast as they were able. *Has it occurred to you, Julian, that I can sing a binding song and leave you trapped in the body of a bird the next time you choose to shape-shift?*

Julian laughed softly in answer, that same male smugness that made her want to wring his neck. He had moved with his incredible speed and was keeping pace beside her with his easy, fluid strides. His arm circled her waist, and he bent to brush the side of her neck with the warmth of his mouth. "You might do so, *cara mia,* but you would not leave me in such a state for long. Your need of my company would be my freedom."

Excitement was rushing through her body at the touch of his. He smelled clean and fresh, his clothes immaculate, as if they had not been covered by earth these last few days. His veins were bursting with life, his heartbeat calling to hers. "Arrogant man," she sniffed with pretended indignation. All at once his playful boasting didn't matter. She hungered, her body crying out for sustenance, and mixed with that need was a bolt of lightning streaking through her, turning her insides to molten lava, spreading its heat low and wickedly.

Julian caught her up in strong arms and took her, airborne, through the forest, far from any other being, to a deserted emerald island in the middle of a small lake. He was already finding her mouth with his own, a fiery domination that was met with hot demands from Desari's silken lips. Her hands were everywhere, pushing at his clothes, insisting he be rid of them. She traced his shoulders, his chest muscles and ribs, the broad expanse of his back. Her fingertips explored his skin, assuring herself there were no lingering signs of his battle with the undead, that he was completely healed.

Her clothes felt heavy and cumbersome, an irritant to her suddenly sensitive skin. At once she rid herself of them so that nothing was between her and Julian's hard frame. He felt so right, his arms locking her close. She burrowed closer, needing to feel him, wanting to crawl inside him, wanting him buried deep inside her. After so many centuries without someone of her own, without a chance for children and someone to truly love her and want her, Desari woke with joy each rising.

Someone to need *you*, he corrected. His voice was husky as his hands did their own exploration. He dropped to his knees in front of her, looking up at her dark, smoldering beauty, the fire and flame in her. She was such a part of the night, of their world, shining like the moon and stars.

Julian caught her slender hips firmly in his hands and forced her forward so that he could trace every inch of her satiny thighs. He found each and every hollow, her body already committed to his memory for all eternity. It was as if time stood still for him, allowed him a moment from the universe, a moment that would last forever, to be consumed completely by the wonder of woman. The firmness of her muscles, the softness of her skin, the sheen and silk of her hair, the smoldering sexiness in the depths of her coal-black eyes, even her long eyelashes, inky and dark, and the triangle of dark curls that guarded heat and fire. She was so beautiful to him, such a miracle of light and goodness, that for a moment tears shimmered in his eyes before he could blink them away.

Julian rested his head on her thighs, inhaling her scent, while the wind whispered its secrets and teased their bodies. She was a creature of the night, as wild and hungry as he. She was his other half, and yet a part of him could not comprehend that she wouldn't vanish to leave him to be consumed once more by utter isolation, by total hopelessness.

His mouth found the warmth of one silken thigh, leaving a long trail of kisses, every one of them in thanks for what he had been granted. He was still awed by her whispered promise to him as he lay gravely wounded, her voice soft and husky, pure and compelling. There could never be untruth in her, not with her voice. She had meant that promise to him, meant it with all of her being. Had he slipped away to the afterlife, she would have followed him. *Always together. You are not alone. I will follow you.* Her commitment to him went beyond anything he could have hoped for. His hands tightened possessively on her small bottom, drawing her closer to him. Her heat beckoned, her wild scent calling to him to assuage her need. Julian wanted only pleasure for her, for everything to be perfect for her—the night itself, the touch of his mouth, his hands, his body inside hers, locking them together as they were meant to be from the beginning of time.

Desari cried out at the first touch of his lips. Her body seemed not her own but his to caress and touch. To kiss and explore. He was finding places so secret she hadn't known they existed, places of such pleasure that she could only stand helplessly while he swamped her body in waves of earth-shattering ecstasy. She had to curl her fingers in his thick mane of golden hair to keep herself anchored to earth. She was soaring out and away, high above ground while her body rippled with pleasure.

She was gasping for air when his mouth covered hers and he began pressing her down onto the soft ground. His body was hard and aggressive, his hands parting her thighs and wrapping her legs around his waist. His teeth grazed her neck, then traced a path down her throat to find the soft swell of her breast.

Desari pressed closer, wanting to take him inside her, keep him a part of her for all time. Her hunger was raw and aching, a need so intense, she dragged his head up so that her mouth could find his skin. She felt his body shudder, the hot velvet tip of him sliding into her. She thrust with her hips, intent on forcing his complete entrance, but he refused to move, his palm catching the back of her head to hold her face pressed against his chest.

Julian wanted it all, her complete union with him, heart and soul and body. Her mouth moved over his heated skin, sending flames licking over him so that he clenched his teeth and pressed her even closer in anticipation. Her teeth scraped over his chest, back and forth, until he thought he might go mad with need. His hips moved impatiently, but he held back, waiting, prolonging the moment. She bit him, a tiny bite followed by the soothing swirl of her tongue. *Desari!* Her name was wrenched from him, a plea.

He felt her tremble in response to his aching need, felt the moment in her mind. Even as he thrust himself deep within her, her teeth sank deep into his chest. White lightning flashed through them. Electricity arced back and forth, sizzling and melting until they were welded together, one being. He heard his voice shout hoarsely, the pleasure so intense he was unable to stay silent. His hands tightened, one in her hair, the other cupping her bottom. The deeper he drove, the wilder her body's response, the friction of fiery heat gripping and releasing him excruciatingly erotic.

Her mouth was moving in a frenzy of hunger and craving, the rich essence of his life's blood heightening her pleasure. Her body was moving restlessly, wildly, without inhibition, wanting him as deep inside her as possible. He was touching her in places that shattered her earlier, lesser ideas of eroticism. She closed the pinpricks her teeth had made with a stroke of her tongue. At once he caught her wrists and stretched her arms out away from her, pinning her beneath him while he bent his head to her full, creamy breasts. She cried out when his mouth closed over her taut nipple, already aching and sensitive with need. Julian responded by burying himself deeper, riding her harder, keeping them both on the edge of fulfillment.

"Julian, please," Desari found herself whispering, her body coiling tighter and tighter.

His mouth moved to her throat, his teeth nipping her skin, his tongue following. He laid a path of kisses to the underside of her breast, and his teeth found tender skin, gave a brief bite followed by the moist heat of his mouth. She gasped out his name, tried to free her arms so she could pull him to her, force him to relieve her of the flames licking along her skin, the fire blazing out of control between her legs.

Julian held her still, his body thrusting deeper, the lines in his face etched with hunger. The wildness was on him, the heat and need. He rode her long and hard, surging into her again and again. "I want you so much, Desari, just like this, so wild with need you cannot be without me. Feel it, the fire between us, my body in yours where I belong. I am part of you like your heart, like your breasts." He bent to lavish attention on her nipples, pulling strongly with his mouth. "I never want this to end."

He was so hard and thick, swollen with his seed and the fury of the fire between them, that her body seemed to be exploding, shock after shock ripping through her as if it would never cease, could never cease. She cried out with the endless climax, afraid if it continued she would die of sheer pleasure. Still he went on, his mouth nuzzling her throat.

"I want you like this, crying out for me to release you but wanting it to go on for all eternity," he whispered against her skin. "Pleading with me to end this, begging me to never stop. It is there in your mind. I hear you, see your fantasies. I know each of them, and I will fulfill every one." His teeth pierced her skin, in domination, in possession, white lightning streaking through her with blue heat.

He took her completely, her mind and heart, her body and soul, her very blood, staking his claim as he held her at her climax, until the firestorm consumed him and his body reacted to her desperate pleas. His hips thrust again and again, burying him deep as he poured his seed into her, as he took the essence of her life from her throat. His hand tangled in her hair, holding her still while his body raged its release, taking hers with it, spinning out of control until there was no Desari or Julian, until they were ecstasy and fire united as one.

Desari lay trapped beneath him, unable to believe the explosion between them, unable to believe he could create such a mind-shattering response in her body. Even now ripple after ripple surged through her, and her muscles convulsed and gripped at the thick length of him.

Julian lay for a moment, his mouth at her throat, before reluctantly closing the pinpricks. At once he bent his head lower so that he could take possession of her breast. She was soft and firm, and with every strong pull of his mouth, he could feel the answering rush of liquid heat between her legs from her very core. Her body was so aroused, the merest brush of his fingers across her breasts had her gasping. He moved his lips gently, without a hint of aggression, a soothing rhythm designed to ease her.

He could feel the grip of her velvet muscles surrounding him, the way her body clutched at his. He continued to move gently, tenderly, alleviating any soreness his rough behavior had caused. "I love the way you feel, Desari, so soft, your hair like silk. It is a miracle how you are put together." His hands traced the supple muscles beneath her satin skin. "And I love the way you respond to me."

She linked her hands behind his head and closed her eyes, giving herself up to the gentle rocking of his body, the velvet friction promising to relieve the terrible demands her body was still making. Julian rolled them over in one smooth move, afraid his weight might be too much on her. At once Desari sat up, shifting so that she could arch her back and ride him at her own pace. Each movement brought her closer to her goal.

She liked watching his face, the satisfaction in his smile, the admiration in his golden gaze. His eyes were riveted to her, taking in the line of her throat, her swaying hair and breasts. Julian made her feel infinitely sexy as she rocked her hips, taking him deep within her, watching him watching her. Her body was already rippling with pleasure. Desari threw her head back, her hair brushing across Julian's skin intensifying his own reaction, so that he thrust deeply inside her, over and over, increasing the friction between them until their next, even more shattering release. It was in perfect unison, tumbling them together in a sea of color and beauty.

Desari let out her breath slowly. "I cannot believe the way we are together. Surely we are going to burn ourselves out in a couple of years."

"The heat rises over the centuries, lifemate, it does not cool," he told her with a taunting, all-too-smug grin.

"I will not survive it," she warned, sweeping her hair over her shoulder, her dark eyes still smoldering with passion.

The gesture was sexier than she could have known, lifting her breasts, her narrow rib cage emphasizing her small waist and fine bones. Julian swept her down to him, finding her mouth with his because he had to find a way to thank her for simply existing, for being so exquisite and perfect.

Desari returned his kiss with the same tenderness he was showing her. He could melt her so easily, the way he could go from wild hunger to such gentleness. Reluctantly she allowed his body to be free of hers. It was almost too much to bear the separation. And Julian said it was only going to grow, this need she had for him, the intense emotion she was coming to know as what the humans called love. It was not an emotion she could name so easily. No words she knew could describe the strength, the intensity of what she felt for Julian. To keep from crying and making a fool of herself, she rose and walked to the lake, submerging herself in the shimmering water.

Julian propped himself up on one elbow to watch her in the darkness. She swam like a sleek otter, moving through the water with her hair streaming behind her.

He caught enticing glimpses of her rounded bottom, of her breasts, her small feet. Just watching her took his breath away. He ached inside with some unnamed emotion. Then he was on his feet and striding toward the lake, unable to keep still when his insides were twisting in knots with so many unfamiliar feelings pushing in. He hit the water running and did a shallow dive toward deeper water.

He surfaced close to her, needing the nearness. He had failed to read the danger to them several risings earlier because he was so aroused. It was a difficult lesson, one that could have taken Desari's life, had almost cost him his own. It would never happen again. A part of him continually scanned their surroundings. It didn't seem likely that there were many more vampires in the area. Most often those that traveled together temporarily were an ancient or experienced vampire and one or two lesser pawns. The undead, even the lowest of them, could not tolerate company for too long without a battle for supremacy. But somewhere out there was his archenemy, waiting, perhaps watching.

Although he felt certain the human society of killers would not strike again in the near future, either, he would not forget they had also made an attempt on Desari's life.

Desari had several concerts scheduled in the near future, but the troupe would take a well-earned break after this next one. Her family members were already setting up for it, waiting anxiously for her arrival. Desari and he had to cover the distance between them this night. As it was, she had missed her last stop. He wished they could miss all of them. But her concerts were advertised far in advance, and she hated to disappoint her audience. Still, it made Julian uneasy that anyone could know where they were going to be at almost any given time.

Julian glanced skyward. The night was gleaming with stars, clear and welcoming. Water lapped at his body, creating sound in the quiet. A slight breeze rustled the leaves of the trees; bats dipped and wheeled overhead. His world. The night. He glanced at Desari as she paced herself, swimming strongly across the lake. He did a lazy crawl after her, keeping within easy reaching distance of her. She was determined to do this next concert, to put herself in danger, just to entertain humans.

His fist hit the water hard, sending a geyser shooting into the air. It brought her attention back to him. He felt her in his mind before he could censor his thoughts.

"Not just to entertain, Julian. For myself, for my family. For Darius. He needs to keep busy. There has been such a change in him over the centuries. I cannot take the chance of quitting now, when he needs me the most. I told you I felt that way."

Julian had already told her they would stay with her family so she would not have to worry about Darius. "I am not changing my mind, *piccola*. I am simply considering what a pushover I have been with you. You could help me out a bit by learning what obedience is all about." In truth he was ashamed of himself for putting her in danger, for not being man enough to leave her. Was it not a matter of honor? He had lived for honor, yet now, when it counted most . . .

Desari's soft laughter added to the beauty of the night. "I would not hold my breath if I were you. This will be good for you, learning to deal with my family, interacting with the human race. It will improve your social skills significantly."

"You are saying my social skills need improvement?" There was a threat in his voice, and he began swimming toward her, his body gliding silently through the water like a shark, like the predator he was.

Desari splashed water at his face and dove deep to escape the arm snaking out for her. She felt his fingers brush her ankle. She kicked strongly, hoping to put distance between them before she surfaced. But the laughter welling up was making it difficult to hold her breath beneath the water, and she was forced to head for the top. At once strong arms captured her.

"I can always find you, *cara mia*," Julian reminded her, his mouth warm against her neck. "You cannot escape me."

"Do not count too heavily on that," Desari told him sweetly, and very innocently she began to sing.

Julian was enthralled by the notes skipping across the water, little silvery notes like leaping fish. He stared, intrigued by the display of power. Did all Carpathian women have special gifts? The few women he had known were far too young by Carpathian standards to have learned the more difficult skills. The notes rose into the air, silver slivers that danced and swayed as if alive. He felt peace stealing into him, surrounding him, so that his body relaxed and for a moment his mind refused to function beyond drinking in the soothing, peaceful lapping of the water and the purity of her voice. He had never known such peace, not since he was a child.

Julian deliberately ducked beneath the water to clear his head. He was furious with himself. Once again, he was so intrigued with everything about Desari, he had allowed himself to become distracted by the vivid new colors and the overwhelming emotions crowding in. It was much like being reborn. But he needed to be always alert, even when he thought they were alone. He could never forget they were hunted. She was hunted. His lifemate. Desari.

"Julian?" Desari swam back to him, her arms curling lovingly around his neck. "What is wrong?" She was

scanning the skies, the area all around them. His stillness, the glittering gold of his eyes, made her shiver.

"You distract me too much, *cara mia*. I cannot forget
what is most important. That is, above all else, your
safety. I will not allow you to be placed in danger
again."

His voice was quiet, that soft, black-velvet voice that
was menace personified. Desari could see that he meant
what he said. She had been playing with him, teasing
him, and just like that, he turned it into a lesson. She
didn't answer him, simply dropped her arms, her dark
eyes mirroring her hurt right before she closed off her
mind to him and swam away.

She had been teasing him, she admitted. But what was
wrong with having a little fun? She sensed his inner
turmoil, felt how difficult having feelings was on him.
He was experiencing everything anew, from sexual need
to jealousy, from fear for her to frustration with her an-
tics. And that strange shadowing he was so reluctant to
share with her. She had used her voice to provide a
concert for him alone, sharing with him her special gift.
It had been from her heart, something she never did for
another being. Was she so wrong to want to tease him,
to soothe him? She was his lifemate and had the same
need to care for him as he did for her.

Desari's movements were smooth and graceful as she
swam away from him, but Julian was not deceived. Hurt
was radiating from her as bright as any sun. He let out
his breath with a soft sigh. He had much to learn as a
lifemate. He knew the things necessary to ensure her
safety and health, yet what seemed so simple a task was
not nearly so easy to put into practice as it was in theory.

"I hurt you again, Desari. This seems to be a pattern
I do not like in myself. I have seen other males in similar
dilemmas, yet I thought them fools not to impose their

wills on their women. In truth, it was me who was so clearly the fool. I have much to learn." He meant every word. It bothered him that he had stored centuries of knowledge, knew how to move the earth and command the seas, direct the lightning and clouds, could hunt the most challenging of adversaries, be they animal or vampire, yet he could not meet his lifemate's needs without hurting her. It was ridiculous. The most important thing in his life, the one person vital to him, the only person who mattered in his existence, and he did not know how to communicate properly with her.

He swam after her, attempting to find words to express himself. How did one strike a balance between safety and play? Even making love out in the open seemed a risk. Yet even now, as they swam across the lake in unison, he ached for her, his body craving hers more and more. It seemed the longer they spent time together, the more intense his hunger for their merging became.

Desari retreated inward. She wasn't angry with Julian; she could even understand him to a point. She was a woman with deep passions and a quick, intelligent mind. She might choose to follow Darius's lead, because most times his way was her way. But no one else, not Dayan or Barack, could command her allegiance the way Darius did.

She did not want the same relationship with Julian as she had with her brother. She wanted a partnership, to be considered an equal with him. Desari instinctively knew she could never be truly happy with less. She wanted Julian's respect, to be able to discuss things and make decisions together, not have him lead while she followed blindly. She had powers of her own; she could be of use to him in times of need if he had faith in her.

Why was it she could see his strength yet he could not see hers?

"Desari?" There was an ache in his voice that sent butterfly wings brushing at her insides. "I know you are upset." He caught her arm in a gentle grip, halting her flight away from him. His legs treaded strongly in the water, holding them both up, one arm circling her waist, locking her to his larger frame. "Do not turn away from me. If I cannot read your thoughts and know what is important to you, I cannot provide for you."

Her teeth tugged at her lower lip. Her dark eyes did not meet his golden ones. Even with her face averted, Julian could read the confusion there. She did not want to merge her mind with his. His hand moved up the smooth line of her back to the nape of her neck, his fingers easing the tension from her tight muscles. "I have much to learn, Desari, about the relationship between lifemates. I have such intense emotions—wild and chaotic at times—I feel almost panic-stricken with the fear of losing you or allowing you to come to harm."

He wrapped his arms tightly around her, holding her against his heart. "Darius was correct when he said I was partially responsible for the success of the assassins' attack on you. I have replayed it a million times in my mind. In my arrogance, I assumed you and the rest of your troupe were human, and I gave no thought to the distraction my presence would cause. Darius felt my power and was busy trying to detect the undead. Later, when you began to sing, I was so caught up in the colors I saw and the emotions I felt, with the excitement of knowing you were in the world, my lifemate, I could not believe it. I think I stood there frozen, unable to move, in shock. If I had not been so caught up in my own emotions, I would not have allowed any assassin to get close to you."

His thumb traced the line of her jaw, then moved to brush her lower lip. Just the feel of her made his heart jump. "Desari." His voice was mesmerizing, playing on her soul so that she could do no other than listen. "I have failed you so often, failed to detect danger to you. In all the centuries I have existed, I have never made such mistakes. The last person I wish to fail is you. Can you not understand what I am saying?"

Chapter Twelve

Desari lay her head on his shoulder, uncertain what to do to ease the situation. "I am trying to be understanding, Julian, but it is not easy. Contrary to what you are often thinking, I am no saint. I haven't the patience of Job. What I want from my union with you is to be respected for what I am and for what I bring to this relationship. If I do not know more of your past, things that would help me better comprehend your fears for me, it is because I have respected your wishes and left your memories alone."

Julian felt as if she had punched him hard in the gut. His fingers tightened around her upper arms. "I have invited you to merge your mind with mine."

She straightened beside him, the water lapping at her waist. "Why are you shadowed, Julian? Why have you been alone all of your life? You have chosen a life of utter solitude when it is not your nature to be alone. You were born a twin. You needed another close to you, yet you cut yourself off from him. I know you love your brother, yet you will not speak of him, will not speak to him." Her dark eyes regarded him steadily. "I am no child to be shielded. I want a full partnership with you or nothing at all."

"My past is not what is haunting our relationship."

"Your past is haunting you, Julian." She gestured at their peaceful surroundings. "We are in a paradise, where I wish to make love with you often and in many ways. I see nothing wrong with it, yet you are afraid you bring danger to me. I cannot understand why you would choose to hurt me, to chastise me, rather than simply tell me what it is you are so afraid of."

She looked so beautiful there in the moonlight. She stole his breath as easily as she had taken his heart. "I have exchanged blood with a vampire." He said the words starkly, with no gentle explanations, the plain ugly truth that had haunted him all his life. The truth that had robbed him of his family and his birthright, the truth no other had ever been told.

Desari went very still, her face pale as she stared into his pain-filled eyes. The tip of her tongue wet her lips, her only sign of a reaction. "How terrible, Julian. When did this happen?" There was love in her voice, compassion. It was in the depths of her eyes. She moved to cover the distance between them, her arms wrapping tightly around his waist to press her breasts against his chest.

Julian actually felt tears in his eyes. He buried his face in her hair. "I would understand if you chose not to stay with me."

Her teeth nipped his skin, a small punishment for doubting her. "When, Julian?"

"I was twelve years of age. He looked young and handsome, and he knew all sorts of things I wanted to

245

know. I visited him in his mountain lair nearly every day, and I told no one, as he bade me. Not even Aidan, although Aidan suspected something was wrong." There was a wealth of self-contempt in his voice.

Desari pressed closer to him, kissing the hollow of his shoulder, running her hands up and down his broad back to comfort him. "You did not know he was vampire. You were but a boy, Julian."

"Do not excuse me." His voice was a whip of self-loathing. "I wanted what he had. I always sought to learn things I should not have known. He saw that in me. The darkness gathering. And one day, when I saw him make a kill, he leapt on me, and he took my blood and forced his tainted blood into my body. He tied us together for all time. He would know where I was, who I was with. He could use me to eavesdrop on others, to betray them. If he wanted to, he could even use me to kill. He was powerful, and I was not yet, so I had no choice but to leave, to stay away from everyone I had ever cared about." He rubbed his neck as if it burned him. "For centuries he tormented me, but I grew in strength and knowledge until he could no longer use his power over me. But then he vanished, and I could never find him to try to destroy him. I searched every continent, everywhere around the world, and I could not find him. He must use some special power I do not know to keep me from tracking him as I could others who do not have my blood in their veins."

"Perhaps he is dead." Desari circled his neck with her arms, holding him close.

Julian shook his head. "I would have felt his death. The shadow would have gone. I fear he will be drawn to you, through me, that he will come for you."

She stayed very still in his arms, taking comfort from

the strength of his body. "You are no longer a boy, Julian. You have grown very powerful."

He could feel the tension running through her like a fine wire pulled taut. His hand pushed at her back, a gentle guide toward shore. They had to complete the trip to the next concert site before the sunrise. "He was powerful when I was but a boy, Desari, not yet even a fledgling." Julian chose his words carefully. "For centuries I have chased the undead and destroyed them, removed all traces of their existence to protect our people. I have witnessed much death and horror, the cunning and destruction these soulless creatures cause. They victimize our people and humans alike. And they grow in power as they age."

"You were a child," she said softly. "He more than likely only seemed an ancient to you." Her heart ached for him, for the terrible loneliness he had endured. "Why did you not tell your Prince? Or your healer? Or your brother?"

"He said he would use me to kill my brother," he admitted without expression. That pain ran so deep, Julian couldn't totally share it. "Ever since I have dedicated my life to destroying the vampire. You have not seen, as I have, what they can do. I cannot let myself allow you into such dangerous situations to appease your desire for 'equality.' I have no choice but to protect you, even though it may mean at times we cannot agree."

Desari waded onto the shore and, automatically, without conscious thought, regulated her body temperature so she did not feel the cold of the night on her wet skin. She wrung out her long hair. "Is it so different then, being a hunter, a powerful male, than a powerful, ancient female who does not hunt?"

Julian shrugged his broad shoulders with a lazy ripple of muscle, striding easily after her. "We males are predators first, Desari. We have not a female's compassion and goodness in us. Our lives are ones of justice, right versus wrong. Those of us who are hunters see death continually, betrayal by old friends and even family members. We are forced to destroy those we once cared for or perhaps even owed debts to. We must protect the females from these horrors they were not made for."

"You are much like my brother. You and Darius think and react almost alike," Desari admitted as she donned clothing with a wave of her hand. Blue jeans and white sweater with pearl buttons down the front covered her, hiding her skin from his view. "I see why you think I should give you obedience, but I am no child, and I am not capable of returning to that state."

"*Cara mia*, I value your opinion in all things. But I am a hunter, a male Carpathian. It is imprinted on us, before our very birth, what our duty is. We know the ritual binding words, and we know we must protect our women and our children above all else. I cannot rid myself of this responsibility, nor do I know if I would want to do so."

Desari stood tall and straight, her long hair flowing in the slight breeze. She looked regal, like a queen. "It is shocking to me that males of your acquaintance have forced females no older than a fledgling to bind with them. I am no child or fledgling, lifemate. I am a woman with much power. I know who I am and what I want. I do not wish to be ordered about as if I have no common sense. Why would you think I would interfere in your battles with the undead? But it is my right as your lifemate to aid you, be it with strength or healing."

Julian clothed himself in matching blue jeans and a white shirt. He turned her words over in his mind and found himself agreeing with her. She deserved the same respect he gave to Darius. Were her gifts any less than her brother's? He did respect her; how could he not? He respected any woman strong enough to become lifemate to the Carpathian male, fledgling or no. He let his breath out slowly. Was this the dilemma of every hunter when he found his true lifemate?

"Julian?" Desari touched the back of his hand. "I am not trying to chastise you, but I feel you should know what I am. Who I am. I will never settle for a master. You will be my partner or we are never going to have a true relationship. I cannot be subject to your rules any more than you could be to mine. Do you not see that what I say is so?"

Julian sifted strands of her ebony hair through his fingers. "Do you believe I think you less than myself?"

Desari looked up at him. "I think perhaps you believe I have not the strength and wisdom to protect myself from harm."

"Do you?" He asked it seriously, his watchful gaze never leaving her face. He did not attempt to enter her mind, wanting to give her the courtesy of privacy in this matter.

Desari's first inclination was to tell him that of course she was strong and wise enough to defend herself and that surely she could prevent a vampire from taking possession of her. She even opened her mouth to say so but, then closed it again. Could she kill, even a vampire? The answer was no, she could not. She could not destroy even such an evil one. It was not in her to do so. Nor could she have fought the effects of the poison as Julian had. The vampire might have triumphed after all.

"I do not have the will to destroy," she answered honestly. "But that does not negate what I have said to you. I do not feel that just because I cannot do what you do I should be forced to obedience as if I were a child. I did not in any way impede you in your battle, nor would I have done so."

His fingers curled around the nape of her neck, gently, tenderly. "Your very presence was a hazard, Desari; my attention was divided. Every moment you were in danger, I could barely breathe. In the past when I went into battle, all there was was the vampire and myself."

"And what is so different now?" Desari's voice was soft and beautiful, its purity touching the darkness in him with soothing peace.

Julian found himself letting out his breath slowly. "The difference now is that if I am destroyed, so might you be. Desari, can you not see that the world needs your gift? The peace your voice brings to it, to all creatures of the earth and sky? To humans, to us, our people? We do not yet know but that your voice might even aid our cause, help find a way to provide female children for our dying race. Aside from the possessiveness I feel, the need to have you with me, I feel the responsibility for your safety even more upon my shoulders. I can understand the pressure on Darius all these centuries. You have a priceless gift, lifemate, one we cannot risk."

Desari smiled in spite of the gravity of their conversation. "Do not place me so high I am soaring, lifemate. I do not know if my voice can do the wonders you imagine, but I thank you for the honor you give me. The point is, Julian, I may not have the skills to destroy the undead, but I have wisdom to know not to engage him in battle. More importantly, Julian, I respect your ability and have pride in your strength. I am not illogical or the type of person to place myself in danger deliberately, out of defiance. And I must remind you, you should not try to force my obedience, particularly when your mind is divided. I will follow your advice in these matters because I choose to do so." Her chin tilted at him in a slightly haughty way.

Julian was used to being the sole authority in his world, and he had always viewed women as the gentler sex, to be protected and hidden away from danger. It had not occurred to him that a lifemate might wield as much power in her own way as he did. Desari was right. He should not force her obedience, even when their lives were threatened; she would obey only with her full consent. How arrogant the males of his race had become. Julian thrust a hand through his golden hair and arched an eyebrow at her. "There is something to what you say," he admitted, deliberately slowly, as if mulling it over.

Her dark eyes smoldered. "There is truth in what I say."

He rubbed the bridge of his nose thoughtfully. "I suppose I can concede there could be some truth in what you say."

She couldn't help but laugh at him. "You are deliberately provoking me because you cannot stand that I am right. It deflates your male ego."

"Not only mine, *cara mia*," he admitted with his mischievous grin, "but that of all the other hunters who find their lifemates. I will enjoy watching them learn this interesting fact of life when it is their turn. But in the meantime, Desari, should we be around other males, you could pretend that you obey my every word, lest we warn the others of their impending lesson."

Desari found herself suddenly relaxing, her dark eyes dancing. Julian wanted to see her point. And he had finally opened his memories to her of his own free will, allowed her to see the scars of his childhood. "Darius is much like you, Julian."

"That brother of yours," Julian said with his slow, taunting drawl.

"You like him."

Julian raised an eyebrow. "Darius is not a man you 'like,' *cara*. He is someone who inspires more emotion, to anyone who can feel emotion, than the word *like* implies. You might admire him. Respect him. Even fear him. But Darius is not someone you *like*. He is a hunter. Few, if any, would challenge him."

"You would," Desari said with complete conviction.

"No one has ever said I was brilliant," Julian answered.

"Do you think my brother is going to stay with us?"

Julian rubbed the bridge of his nose again, his eyes suddenly blank. "It is possible at some point, Desari, that you will want to establish our own family rather than stay with this unit."

She paced away from him, then returned. "You think he is close to turning vampire."

"I think your brother is a powerful hunter. He would make a lethal adversary, and I would not want the job of tracking him. Darius will hold on as long as he is able. He will not choose to lose his soul without a fight."

"Do you know any hunters greater than yourself?" Desari asked, curious. "Besides my brother, of course," she added impishly.

His eyebrows shot up, his grin slightly sardonic. "Do you wish to become a hunter groupie? I assure you, I am more than adequate for the job."

She burst out laughing. "You idiot. I was curious, that is all. Darius learned only through his own experience. Are his skills as good as those of your people?"

"Your brother is extremely strong and skilled. Perhaps it is inherited, in your bloodline," he mused aloud. "Remember, *cara*, Gregori, the Dark One, a most powerful hunter, second only to Mikhail, our Prince, is brother to you and Darius. We are of the same people."

Desari nodded, intrigued. "Do you think all hunters' skills are inherited?"

"The greatest hunter, as well as the greatest and most unique vampire, came from your bloodline. Those who choose the life of a hunter sometimes serve an apprenticeship under an experienced guide and are taught the rudiments of how a vampire must be destroyed almost from birth. But your brother did not have this information."

"But not all who hunt are guided?" Desari asked.

Julian shook his golden head wryly. "Some have not the patience for either the teaching or the learning."

Desari laughed at him. "I think I know what kind you were."

Julian looked into her dancing eyes, the beauty of them.

"Is hunting always a choice, or does your Prince order it?"

"It is by choice unless, of course, one stumbles upon the undead. It is kill or be killed in that situation. We have lost many males unprepared for such an event. The more ancient the vampire, the more dangerous he is. An unskilled hunter has little chance against a vampire who has survived many centuries. As our skill grows with experience and time, so does the vampire's cunning and knowledge."

"And my bloodline has both a vampire and a hunter famous for their skills?" She was uncertain she wanted to hear of the vampire. She wanted to hear that her bloodline was too strong to allow one of its own to turn. Her brother was becoming more deadly every day. She tried not to notice how distant he could be, how completely emotionless. He used to pretend, at least, that he could feel affection for her; now he seldom made the effort.

Julian's arm circled her shoulders with easy familiarity, the move comforting. His chin nuzzled the top of her head. "Darius will not choose eternal darkness, *cara mia*; he has lived in it far too long. Do not fear for your brother's soul." As always, he read her thoughts easily, a shadow in her mind.

Desari let out her breath slowly, his nearness easing her worries. He had experienced how Carpathian males changed over the centuries. He had lost feeling and colors until his world was one of bleak darkness, yet he had survived. He had even survived the mark of the beast, the vampire's shadowing of his soul. It could be done. "Tell me of my ancestors. After all these centuries of believing we were the only ones of our kind, it is interesting to know our family can be traced back to such legendary creatures."

Julian nodded. "There were two of them. Twins. Gabriel and Lucian. They were alike in everything. Tall and dark with eyes that could look straight through a person to his very soul. I saw them once, when I was a child. They were like gods striding through our village, visiting with Gregori and Mikhail for a brief time, then gone again. The wind went utterly still when they were near. The earth seemed to hold its breath as they passed. They were relentless, unswerving angels of death once set upon a path."

Desari shivered. Not so much at his words as at the pictures she glimpsed in his mind. True, they were the memories of a boy, yet she could see the images clearly. The two men very tall, elegant, their faces cruelly beautiful, as if etched in stone, their dark eyes merciless. Strong Carpathians trembled in their presence.

"They were loyal to the Prince of our people, but all

knew that should the two choose darkness, no one would be able to destroy them."

"Was the prince this Mikhail you speak of?" Desari asked.

"Mikhail's father was our leader when I was a small child. I believe the twins, ancients even then, had served Mikhail's grandfather long before that. In any case, they were always together, inseparable. It was said they had made a childhood pact, one with the other, that if one turned, the other would destroy them both. They were so close they thought alike, knew what the other would be doing at every moment, hunted and fought as a team."

"They were born together, like you and your brother?"

Julian nodded. "Some said they were demons, others called them angels, but everyone agreed they were the most lethal of all Carpathians, the most knowledgeable, the most skilled. What one learned through study or experience, he shared with the other, doubling their power and ability. Many of our race were terrified of them, yet they were much needed. In those days vampires were achieving a kind of popularity among humans, a disaster in the making for our people. Without the two angels of death, Carpathians would have been hunted to extinction, the vampires would have triumphed, and the world would have become a deadly, desolate place. There was chaos and war, the hunters of our race stretched beyond their capacity."

"Why would humans ever embrace the undead?"

"It was a time of great self-indulgence and decadence among the rich. They would have orgies of drinking and gluttony and sex. They would watch bloody, violent clashes and worship the victor. It was an atmosphere for the undead. They can be as cunning and charming as they need to be and influencing those already corrupt is not so difficult. We had to do something to change the course of history. It was Gabriel and Lucian who did so."

"Which was the vampire?"

Julian shook his head with his now familiar taunting smile. "Just like a woman, no patience."

She quirked an expressive eyebrow at him. "I am the one without patience? I think not, Julian. You are the one impatient."

His mouth swooped to take hers in a slow, leisurely exploration. He lifted his head, his eyes molten gold. "Then I will have to be more careful the next time to be slow and thorough. I want you to be completely satisfied in all things, lifemate."

Her slender arms circled his neck. "You know I am. And if you were much more thorough, we might both be dead."

He wrapped his arms protectively around her, pressing her body into his hard frame. "You are so perfect, Desari. For me there is no other."

"Nor for me. Before you, my world was not bleak and barren—I had emotions and colors, my singing to sustain me, my family to love—but I was alone. There was a part of me missing. A part of me restless and wild, searching for something. We wandered the continents to cover the fact that we did not age, but all of us were also looking for something to end the emptiness. We just did not know what it was we sought." Her hands were stroking his thick mane of hair, allowing the skeins of silken gold to run through her fingers. "I do not want to be apart from you, Julian. I want us to be always together."

He held her in silence for a time, breathing in the scent of her, trying to comprehend why he had been handed such a miracle, why he had been granted a reprieve at the last moment, been rewarded with a woman such as Desari. Julian tried not to think of the vampire who could destroy them both.

She felt his thoughts, the waves of intense emotion overwhelming him, things he could not put into mere words. Desari rested her head on his chest and listened to the steady beat of his heart, knowing hers tapped out the exact same rhythm. It was right. They were two halves of the same whole. She wanted to comfort him any way she could. He needed, and that was everything to her.

Stop wasting time, little sister. I can take only so much of this syrup between you and the one you have chosen. Have you forgotten you have commitments to fulfill? Darius's soft, emotionless reprimand echoed in her mind.

I am coming. She sent no more, unwilling to share her private thoughts. Again she mourned the fact that Darius felt no emotion, not even love for her.

I may not feel it, little sister, but I know it is there. Do not fear me now after all these long centuries.

I fear for *you, Darius. Do not go away from us.* She hadn't meant to show her deepest anxiety to him, yet it slipped out.

There was only silence. Desari found herself trembling, her breath suddenly hard to find.

Julian tipped up her chin to search her dark eyes just as he was searching her mind for what had frightened her. "He will not leave you, Desari, will not seek death until he knows he cannot hold out any longer against the darkness within him. If that should occur, you must willingly allow him to greet the dawn. He is far too powerful; if he became the undead, many of our hunters would die before he could be destroyed. He carries that knowledge with him. It makes his existence still more difficult for him, a two-edged sword. He knows he has a chance of surviving as a vampire, of feeling at least the thrill of the many kills he would achieve, yet he still has his memories of love and duty, his code of honor, which help him hold on. He knows those he loves would be destroyed first should he turn."

Desari broke away from him to pace restlessly across the pine-strewn forest floor. Her movements were graceful, her ebony hair gleaming as if a thousand stars were tangled in it. "Tell me more of my blood kin, Julian. Tell me of their fate."

He nodded. "You must remember, Desari, the twins had lived centuries longer than most of our people without finding a lifemate. They were hunters, having to kill often, the kind of double burden nearly impossible to long endure. As each century passed and their legends grew, more people feared and shunned them. It was rumored they were more powerful than the Prince, much more dangerous. It seemed not to matter that they followed him and protected those that could not hunt. Their lives were ones of nearly total isolation from all society. It had to have been torment." Julian knew the torment of isolation.

"Yet they continued, as you continued." Desari pressed back against a tree, her eyes enormous, searching his story for a shadow of hope for her brother.

Julian nodded. "Always they endured. They went after the vampires high society had embraced. The battles were long and fierce, as the undead were ancients with much power and now government backing. Rewards were posted for Gabriel and Lucian so that humans and the undead alike hunted them. They fought the many servants of the vampire, hosts of ghouls and zombies and demented creatures created at the undead's whim. Always they were the victors, and while our people were thankful, each time the twins emerged alive, the whispers grew of creatures half in our world and half in that of the darkness."

"How unfair!" Desari was angry at such treacherous behavior by those of her own race. What if Darius were to be treated in such a manner by those who followed Mikhail? Her fists curled at her sides until her knuckles grew white.

"Yes, it was unfair, yet not altogether untrue. As a male ages, as the hunter grows in strength and the number of his kills, he does live partially in the world of darkness. How could he not? They were powerful, and there were two of them, their pact strong. They would be invincible should they turn. Who could destroy them? Gregori was young then, as was Mikhail, though they sometimes secretly sheltered the two warriors when their wounds were severe. I know that Gregori and Mikhail both supplied blood on more than one occasion." Julian rubbed one eyebrow thoughtfully. "Gregori knew I saw them, but he said nothing to me. I was very young, you understand, no more than nine. I was very awed by the two legends, and, even then, by Gregori, who was rapidly growing in stature, and Mikhail, in line to be Prince. I would never have betrayed their secret, and I think they knew that."

"How sad the twins' lives must have been." Desari sounded as if she might weep. Julian was across the distance separating them instantly, wrapping her in his strong arms. "Really, Julian, to have the people so unappreciative of their sacrifices must have been a terrible thing. They were like men without family or country or even friends." As Julian had been. She suddenly realized the enormity of his sacrifice. He had been a man without family, country, or friends, and he did not even have his twin brother beside him. Love and compassion surged through her, strong and powerful. Julian would know

Christine Feehan

love. He would have a home, a family, everything she could give him.

"That is the danger inherent in the hunter's acquisition of power and skill and experience in centuries of battles. The two were lethal hunters, equal in strength, in intellect, in fighting ability. None was their better. And then the wars came. The Turk invasions that depleted the ranks of our people, destroyed our women and children. Our people had chosen to fight alongside those humans they had befriended and known for years, but we lost the ancient prince and most of those skilled in hunting."

"That is when Darius saved us," Desari offered.

Julian nodded. "During that period, yes," he agreed. "It was at that same time that Gabriel and Lucian really became legendary warriors, two against the Turk multitudes and the vampires thriving among them, driving the armies to do hideous things to their captives—the tortures and mutilations you can read about in history books. Some individuals slaughtered countless innocent women and children, drank blood, bathed in it, and feasted on living flesh while the orchestraters, the vampires, looked on and rejoiced. But Gabriel and Lucian were in constant pursuit of these enemies, and the body count the two of them achieved was so high, no one could believe they were real and not some mysterious death winds blowing in and out of villages, leaving little in their wake. Vampires disappeared by the dozens, and legions of their soldiers and demented creatures, mostly noblemen and women, were killed or exposed. War raged everywhere. The damage to humans and Carpathians alike was devastating. Sickness and death followed, homelessness and hunger, savage slavery of the impoverished. It was a hideous, merciless time for all."

"And my kin?"

"Few actually could claim to have laid eyes on them,

but they were everywhere, tirelessly destroying the enemy, saving our few remaining women, still without lifemates or hope of their own. It is said they consulted with Gregori and Mikhail at this time, and I witnessed one such meeting right after Mikhail's father was killed trying to save a human village. Shortly after, at Mikhail's order, I was taken from the region and placed in hiding with the remaining children. Mikhail was young to be a leader, but he had vision and realized our people were facing extinction. He and Gregori. the next oldest to survive, moved at once to protect the few surviving women and children. Gregori and Mikhail seldom spoke of the two ancients or that time, perhaps because both had lost—or thought they lost—their own families while trying to save their race. But their skills and accomplishments at such a young age were almost inconceivable."

"And what of the twins?" she prompted, intrigued by this history she had never known, her roots, her bloodline.

"When things finally settled down in Transylvania and Romania, throughout the Carpathian Mountains, it is said the pair traveled to Paris and London and anywhere else in Europe vampires were striving for a foothold. They hunted throughout the continent, always working together as a single unit. The stories of their unearthly powers grew beyond legends to mythology."

Julian moved away from her and shoved a hand through his golden mane. "The rumors started about half a century later. That Lucian had fallen to the dark side. That he was vampire, preying on the human race. No hunter could find him or even his trail. Only Gabriel would have been able. The hunt for Lucian went on for well over a century. It was unlike anything our people had known. Vampires are messy killers, leaving a trail of blood and death recognizable to any of us, exposing us to discovery by mortals and their inevitable mistaken assumptions that vampire and Carpathian are one and the same. In some ways it is fortunate for us that human police often label the murders and mutilations as the work of serial killers or cults. Otherwise we all would be hunted until we were no more.

"But Lucian was unlike any vampire ever known. There is no record of him slaying a woman or child, of creating servants or ghouls. He made hundreds of kills but only among the corrupt, the evil, the scourges of the earth. Many of our hunters were misled, perplexed, and came away thinking perhaps the twins were mythical, not reality. Only Gabriel recognized Lucian's work. Only Gabriel could track him."

"No one else would help him?"

Julian shook his head. "No one else could help him. Gabriel was a legend himself. An angel of death. No one approached him or dared try to ease his task. He pursued Lucian, often found him, but because they were equals, the battles were long and ferocious but never decisive, with both striking terrible blows, only to break apart and attempt to heal themselves for the next battle. It went on for years until, one day, they both simply seemed to vanish off the face of the earth."

Desari's long lashes fluttered for a moment. "That is it? The entire story? They just disappeared?"

"There are many stories our people believe. One is that Gabriel ended Lucian's life and then chose to greet the sun. I believe that is what happened. Ancient as he was, he would have been so close to the darkness himself, and without a lifemate or even his brother to hold him, long dead, I believe Gabriel simply laid it down. He had lived long and alone; he deserved release into the afterlife."

Desari shook her head. "I cannot believe that after

holding out for so long, fighting so many battles, Lucian would choose darkness and Gabriel would be forced to hunt his own brother, his twin. It is so terrible."

"It is a chance all hunters take. The kill triggers a sensation of power in us. For one who has no emotions, no other feelings, it can be tempting, addicting. There is also the problem of when to stop. If Lucian hung on to fight vampires as long as he was able, he might have been too late to make a rational choice. Some say Gabriel turned also, and when the two vampires fought for supremacy, both were killed. I do not think that is so, because there would have remained some evidence of the battle. Gabriel respected Lucian; he would have chosen to destroy all evidence of their battle and Lucian's defeat before he walked into the sun."

"You cannot hunt like these men any longer, Julian," Desari said, biting at her lower lip. "I cannot bear this to happen to you. It is a horrible story. Two men who gave their lives for their people, and no one cared for them, no one appreciated them."

His smile was tender. "*Piccola*, there is no need to fear. I cannot turn now. You are my light, the goodness to my darkness, the air I breathe and my reason for existing. The twins did not find their lifemates, but do not think they were unappreciated by our race. Though they were feared, they are also much revered, and many stories and songs have been written in their honor."

"A bit late for them," she sniffed indignantly. "It is hardly a happy story, and I do not like the ending. I do not wish this for my brother. We must find for him whatever he needs to survive."

"He needs to find his other half, *cara*, and there is no telling when or if that will happen."

"Maybe I will see what I can do. My voice is powerful; my words can weave enchantments. I have brought couples back to love and laughter, healed grief-stricken parents. I will try to draw to us the one my brother needs."

"If she comes to your concert, believe me, Desari, there will be no need of enchantments. Darius will recognize her instantly. He will not allow her to leave."

"He does not have this knowledge. Maybe I should tell him."

Julian shook his head. "No, it is better to allow nature to take its course in these things. If one is close to turning, one might try to force what is not there. If it happens for him, he will know what to do. Every male is born with the ritual words, with the instincts to bind his woman to him. It will be there for him when he needs it."

"What if she does not want him?" Desari asked.

"We have seen that ourselves," he teased.

Her hand cupped his face, her thumb lovingly tracing the hard line of his jaw. "I wanted you from the first moment I saw you." Desari shook her head. "No wonder the males of our species become so arrogant. They are able to tie a woman to them without her consent or even her knowledge. That must make them feel very superior." Her tone conveyed her annoyance.

"I think they are more inclined to feel humble," he answered sincerely. "When a male has survived so many centuries with no color or emotion, and he finds the one who brings him light and compassion, music and joy, he can do no other than revere her."

She quirked an eyebrow at him. "They still should not have the right to tie a woman without her consent. What is wrong with courting her? It might help to calm her fears and make her feel she is special to him."

"How could a woman feel anything but special when a man needs and wants her so much? A woman has only to touch her lifemate's mind to know what is in his heart. She knows who he is, his good traits and his failings."

"Even if she is a fledgling? Any ancient could hide whatever he wanted from one so young. I cannot imagine the fear a woman would feel tied without her consent to such a powerful being. She would not have a sense of her own worth, who she was or even what special gifts or talents she had."

Julian captured her hand, placed a kiss in the center of her palm, feeling her distress for the women unknown to her robbed of their childhood. It had been difficult enough for Desari, as strong a woman as she was, to accept that Julian had some kind of dominion over her. Even knowing she had the same dominion over him, it was still frightening to her. It was an admission of need. A need to be close to him always.

Julian's hand framed her face. "Never fear the need between us. Whatever you are feeling, *cara*, I feel twice as much. I was without color or song or emotion for far too long. I have had many bleak centuries to help me learn appreciation for my lifemate. You did not need my existence in the same way that I needed yours—even to continue my life, to save my soul. Had we never met, you would have lived far longer before the emptiness of your existence became too much to bear."

Desari lay her head on his shoulder, wanting to hold him close. "I think our need for one another is mutual, Julian."

Desari. The night is winging across the sky, and you two are still gazing into one another's eyes. This concert is yours. We have not yet rehearsed, and there is no way to plan without your presence. I will not repeat myself in this matter. Darius's black velvet voice was soft with menace. He demanded her presence, and she must comply.

Desari sighed. "We must go before it is too late to cross the distance this night. The others wait for us."

Julian's hand cupped the nape of her neck so that he could hold her still while he bent his head to find her mouth with his. She could sense his amusement at the order for their return to the family fold and her obvious need to comply with it.

"We must, Julian," she whispered, afraid he might attempt to defy Darius.

He smirked at her, his white teeth flashing. "Come along, little chick, we must obey the big bad wolf or something terrible might happen."

"You do not even know," she answered solemnly.

His laughter was his only answer.

Chapter Thirteen

The crowd was enormous. Julian inhaled deeply, allowing the air to tell him every story. The smell of excitement, of sweat, of rising tempers, and lust. It was all in the breath he drew into his lungs. He was looking out for danger to his lifemate. His amber eyes inspected the huge throng pushing to get into the building. He found himself tense, his every inclination to keep Desari far from these humans. He could hear myriad conversations even as he was scanning innumerable minds. Human security guards were using metal detectors on the people entering, but still he was uneasy.

Julian caught sight of Darius. He was an imposing figure, moving silently and swiftly through the crowd, his black eyes icy, piercing the crush of humans restlessly, in unceasing motion. He was every bit as alert as Julian, determined to protect his sister at all costs. Dayan, although he played in the band, was at a side entrance, as on guard as the others. Barack roamed inside the building, mingling with the crowd to add further insurance to Desari's safety. Both musicians were projecting images unrecognizable to the public.

The two leopards, Sasha and Forest, were locked in one of the rooms provided for the band members. Syndil, too, had taken her usual form of a female leopard and waited with the other cats. Julian wanted to protest the action, aware of the sadness in Desari at Syndil's withdrawal from reality. Julian had noticed that Barack was very edgy around all of them. He often placed his body squarely between the other males and Syndil. Clearly the terrible attack on her had shaken the males' faith in one another. With the assassins making their attempt on Desari and vampires threatening them for their women, the men were all on edge.

Darius paused briefly beside him. "Anything?"

Julian shook his head. "Nothing but a feeling of uneasiness. I do not like this, Desari exposed to all these humans."

"There will be no mistakes made this time," Darius said softly, confidently. "There will be no further attempts on my sister's life."

Julian had to respect the man's total conviction. It was difficult not to believe in Darius, power clung to him like a second skin. There would be no chances taken this night. Julian nodded at Darius and continued pacing among the humans, scanning minds, listening to the conversations around him. To his left a fight erupted between two men. Pushing and shoving, voices raised. But the human security personnel were there instantly, escorting the scufflers away from the building. Julian could detect no animosity toward his lifemate, so he ignored the incident, not wanting to be distracted from his
.primary task of protecting Desari.

Desari was in the dressing room, putting the finishing

touches on her makeup. She liked to put it on herself in the human manner. It soothed her somehow before she went on stage. It was also her habit before each concert to scan the minds of the crowd, and try to find those in need so that she could pick the songs most suited to healing and helping. It was important to her to seek the mood of the audience, listen for what they wanted to hear, their favorite ballads or the haunting new melodies she could produce. She liked to know which people had come to more than one of her concerts, who had traveled long distances to see her perform. Sometimes after her shows she would seek out those who had traveled far or often to hear her sing and introduce herself to them and chat.

For the most part, the crowd was eager, moving restlessly, excitedly, in their seats, eager to hear her sing. Desari tuned them out in order to prepare herself for the stage. At once her mind, of its own accord, sought Julian. She smiled as she felt an instant flood of warmth, strong arms surrounding her.

Julian was not thrilled with her family *unit*, as he called them, nor were they all that happy with him, but no one was snarling at each other. To his credit, Julian hadn't made even a single protest when she entered the theater to dress for her concert.

You are the lifemate of a sensitive, modern male. Julian's lazy amusement warmed her further, confirming what she already suspected, that he often stayed a shadow in her mind.

How fortunate for me. Desari smiled at herself in the mirror. Her dark hair cascaded in waves down her back. There was a sparkle in her eyes. She knew Julian had made her feel more alive than she had ever been. *Sensitive, modern men are so to my liking.*

Men? I am certain I did not hear my lifemate use the

word men. *The plural. No man is allowed to be to your liking other than myself.* He sounded stern, the fierce Carpathian male at his most menacing.

Desari laughed aloud. *I suppose I can see your point, Julian, but really, it is so difficult to keep from noticing all of those handsome hunks in the audience.*

Handsome hunks? His voice dropped low with the affront. *They are more like lovesick fops. If they could feel the vibrations in the air, they would show sense and run for their lives. It is bad enough to read their fantasies and hear them talk their trash, cara, but it is altogether worse to hear that my woman is looking back. One smile at the wrong man, lifemate, and trouble will find the man quickly.*

You sound jealous, she accused him, amusement curving her soft mouth.

The first rule for all women to know and never forget is that Carpathian males do not share their lifemates. Your brother has much to answer for that this was not drilled into you since birth. It was his job to prepare you for my coming. It was said somewhere between jest and complaint.

Desari drew in her breath sharply, finding herself wavering between laughter and exasperation. *My brother had no idea of your existence, you arrogant male. Besides, how could he possibly prepare me for your total ignorance of women? More likely, had he known you were coming to speak your ritual words, he would have been waiting to ambush you. I myself would have burrowed deep within the ground until you passed beyond my surroundings.*

You would have burst from the ground straight into my arms, cara mia, *and you know this to be true.*

Now he was laughing, that smug, taunting, male amusement that should have set her teeth on edge but instead made her laugh. *I think you are trying to find something to dictate to me about just so you do not lose your ability. Go away and practice this male art form on someone else.*

You will be singing to me tonight, piccola, *and to no other man.*

You are a spoiled little boy, not a grown man.

Should I come show you what a grown man I am? His voice was suddenly low and warm, so sexy she felt a rush of answering heat. She could feel the brush of his fingers against her throat, trailing down the valley between her suddenly aching breasts.

Go away, Julian, she laughed in answer. *I cannot have you getting me hot and bothered just now.*

As long as I know you are hot and bothered for me, I will do as you request and go back to work.

I can only hope.

Desari heard the familiar steps coming up to her door, Dayan knocking loudly with his usual five-minute warning. She knew Barack would be checking one last time on Syndil. Excitement was setting in, the quick rush right before she walked out onto the stage.

Desari paced across the floor once or twice, ridding her body of unused adrenaline. The second knock came three minutes later. Julian and Darius stood on the other side of the door, their eyes and minds continually scanning every inch of the building and the audience. Desari felt small wedged between the two larger bodies, suddenly aware of the potential danger to herself. That someone wanted her dead for reasons unknown was shocking to her. She moved closer to Julian for protection.

He touched her arm in a gentle caress, nothing more demonstrative, his mind obviously filled with security measures, tuned to the air around them. Yet Desari instantly felt comforted and safe. Dayan and Barack were waiting to enter the stage with her. As they moved forward, the roar of the crowd drowned out every other sound.

Julian began to pace the perimeters of the building, taking his time, getting a feel for the audience. He knew every nook and cranny of the interior, every possible hiding place, every entrance and exit. He knew every position, high or low, that a sniper could utilize. His gaze continually swept the areas that provided the most cover for an assailant.

In the recent past he had watched over Mikhail and Raven's daughter, Savannah, while she performed magic shows during the five years of freedom Gregori had allotted her before he claimed her as his lifemate. Several times her human security people had to prevent overeager men from rushing the stage to meet her. But Julian had kept his presence a secret there only to fight off the vampires who often stalked her without her knowledge. He had not had to handle the humans attracted to her.

This was different. Desari's voice itself was a lure, an enticement to all who heard it. And she was so beautiful up there on the stage, her long dress flowing fluidly around her slender figure one moment, then hugging her body the next. Her ebony hair glittered in the light and cascaded in waves down her back, brushing her shoulders and breasts, her waist and hips. She was irresistible.

Julian felt his breath catch in his throat. She awed him. The way she moved, the way her perfect soul shone so brightly for all to see. Desari was beautiful not only on the outside but also on the inside, and it showed. She was, literally, breathtaking. He dragged his gaze away from her, forcing his mind to remain alert, to scan for trouble.

Desari's voice poured into the air and flowed through

the concert hall. The silence of the crowd was complete. No shuffling in seats, not even soft murmurs. The audience was spellbound. There was enchantment in her voice, a soft, misty blend of laughter and tears, haunting, evoking memories, creating hopes. Feelings of deep, abiding love welled up in those listening. Older audience members recalled every wonderful moment with their spouse—holding hands, making love, creating children, their joy in being together as both lovers and parents. The younger ones dreamed of their perfect partners, that first sighting, the first touch, the first kiss. Couples growing apart were reminded of their vows and the love they felt for one another before resentments began to eat away at them.

Desari's voice gave them all comfort and hope. Julian was amazed at her power. She was not adding compulsion; she simply possessed a gift that was a treasure to the world. His pride in her grew with each song. It was as if instinctively she sensed what was needed by certain individuals or the group and was able to deliver it.

Julian turned toward the area just in front of the stage, a shadow creeping slowly but surely into his mind. At once he signaled Darius, who was closer. Darius was already moving, directing security in the same direction. Dayan and Barack closed in on Desari immediately, moving so quickly they were nearly a blur, placing their bodies squarely in front of her while two men clambered onto the stage. Slightly drunk, they reeled toward the band members. They had taken no more than two steps before a wall of security guards had them in custody and were ushering them out of the hall.

Desari's voice was soft with laughter, an invitation for the crowd to join her. "Poor boys, they have no idea what just hit them. But because of an unfortunate incident recently, my security people are treating me as if I were gold. Please bear with them."

She held the crowd in the palm of her hand. Julian could not believe how easily she did it, softly excusing the two overexuberant fans, teasing about her security guards, and making light of her vulnerability and her celebrity status.

Unfortunately, the shadow remained in Julian's mind. He glanced at Darius, whose dark eyes were as cold as ice. Darius shook his head slightly to indicate the danger to Desari was not past. The two of them began to move in opposite directions, circling the huge theater, covering ground slowly, scanning as they did so. Something was not quite right. Both felt it. Dayan and Barack felt it, too. There faces were expressionless, but they stayed positioned protectively near Desari, and their eyes moved restlessly, unceasingly, all of them seeking the source of that shadow.

The Carpathians on stage continued to play, and Desari's voice was more beautiful than ever, weaving such an enchantment on all within hearing that it was difficult for Julian to keep his attention fully on her protection.

Something malignant was infiltrating the building. It was such a soft, slow flow of tainted air it was barely discernible. Julian tried to find its direction. He had already scanned the crowd several times, and knew there was no real threat from that direction. It was something far more powerful. *Nosferatu.* The undead.

Desari and Syndil had to be the reason vampires were frequenting these parts even with Julian's brother, Aidan, living so close by. Aidan was a hunter renowned for his skills, yet lately this area seemed to be overrun with the undead. Julian could see no reason for it other than the presence of the two Carpathian females. Few would be aware that Desari had been claimed, and to a vampire, it hardly mattered. The undead were so arrogant, so bloated with their own power, they were certain they could gain possession of any woman for themselves.

Julian's gaze, a glint of glittering gold, shifted back to the stage. Barack suddenly stumbled on a note, his head going up alertly. At the same time, Julian felt the wash of hideous power pouring into the air around them, rushing toward the band's dressing rooms. Automatically, he blurred himself, streaking through the concert hall, as did Darius. But it was Barack who beat them both to the room where the leopards waited. Behind them, as if by design, Dayan went into a lively melody, his voice and guitar accompanying Desari, so that the audience went wild, clapping and stomping their approval.

It took both Darius and Julian to restrain Barack before he burst through the closed door. He snarled at them, his fangs savage, eyes red hot with killing rage. It was Darius who spoke to him, using the family's peculiar mental path that Julian was slowly becoming familiar with. The order was velvet soft, soothing, a promise of protection for Syndil. Barack took a calming breath and nodded his reluctant acquiescence, relaxing beneath the grip of the two hunters.

Julian dissolved immediately, flowing beneath the door into the room as tiny molecules in the air. The three leopards were pacing restlessly, low warning growls rumbling deep in their throats. He tried to touch their minds but found chaos and anger, the mood dangerous to any that might enter the room. Syndil had deliberately buried herself deep within the body of the leopard she had assumed to prevent the one who sought her from telling her apart from the other two real specimens. She paced along with them, every bit as moody and dangerous, raging in her mind at the evil threatening them. Even he could not tell which female was actually Syndil and which was the genuine leopard; he did not yet know her well enough to discern her spirit from where she had it buried so deeply within the spirit of the leopard.

Julian felt Darius's power filling the room, knew the moment he reached to calm the prowling leopards. The vampire was close, too close, stalking Syndil, but the undead was projecting his whereabouts from all directions so neither Darius or Julian could get a firm fix on his location. They waited with the patience of ancient hunters, still, calm, simply waiting for the moment when the aggressor must make his move.

The impact slamming against the door was tremendous, a huge bulging spreading inward. The door itself blackened even as thunder shook the building. A part of Julian remained connected to Desari, determined to always ensure her safety. She was easily holding the audience, projecting calm, her voice soothing as she sang a haunting ballad, Dayan accompanying her on the guitar. Dayan and the security people were close around her, the human guards uncertain how Barack had disappeared from the stage. No one had quite caught his exit. Yet they stayed close to Desari, directed by Julian without their knowledge. Desari and Dayan were incredibly smooth, Desari now perched on a high stool in the middle of the stage, her long dress flowing around her in graceful folds. Dayan played the soft, mesmerizing music on his guitar while the beauty of Desari's voice continued to fill the concert hall.

The leopards were pacing restlessly now, the male twice throwing himself at the door in agitation. Julian streamed back to the other side of the door, pouring out into the hallway with a rush of cold air. He knew Darius would stay behind to protect Syndil.

On the other side of the door Barack was in a fierce battle with a tall, gaunt stranger. The evil one had red-rimmed eyes and a vicious slash for a mouth. He raked at Barack with sharp claws, aiming for the jugular, but Barack eluded the quick strike and was ramming straight into the chest of the emaciated vampire. His fangs tore at the throat even as his hand bore straight to the heart. Easygoing Barack seemed lost in the ferocious beast that had taken his place.

Julian sought the man's mind and found a red haze of hatred and rage, directed not only at this vampire but at the one who had so violently attacked Syndil and left her so withdrawn. It took a few moments to find the mental path that Desari's family shared with one another. *Do not drink his blood, Barack. He is dead already. You have destroyed him. The blood is tainted.* Julian spoke softly into the mind of one gone mad with rage.

Do not interfere. He lives.

When Julian glided toward the struggling pair, Barack roared a warning, a growl that shook the hall. Julian stopped at once, not in the least surprised when Darius materialized at his side.

"Do not, Barack." Darius's voice was a soft menace. "You cannot drink as he dies. Not in the rage you are in. Release him and allow him to fall away from you."

Barack lifted his head, his fangs stained red, his eyes glowing hotly. The heart was flung aside, still pulsing wickedly. The rumbling grew louder, a clear warning to back away from him.

Darius and Julian glanced at one another with the same thought. If they joined together, they could force Barack to obedience, but he would never trust nor respect either of them again. Barack was definitely dangerous, and neither wanted to alienate him. He was a

Carpathian male, and it was his right to do as he was doing, protect the females in his family unit. Protect any female of their race. Not only his right but his duty.

Julian reached for the leopards' minds and found Syndil nestled in the smaller female cat's body. *Barack is in danger. We cannot reach him. You must do it. Call to him. Do it now before it is too late and he is lost to us for all eternity. He cannot consume the blood of the thing he is killing.*

Julian felt Syndil's immediate alarm. At once she shape-shifted, taking her human form, her slender, shapely figure shorter than Desari's but radiating the same inner light and beauty of the Carpathian female. She moved with fluid, elegant grace, her dark, expressive eyes touching him, then jumping away hastily as she gave him a wide berth. Her gasp was audible as she surveyed the bloody, violent scene in the hallway and the darkness so close to the surface in Barack, his own face nearly that of the beast within the Carpathian male. Darius was close to the undead, close enough to distract Barack from feasting on its blood. Still, power and rage ate at the younger Carpathian, allowing the beast within to take over his mind, so that all that was left was instinct and fury.

Without hesitation, Syndil approached Barack. "Do not step in the blood," Darius cautioned her, his dark eyes watchful. If Barack made one wrong move toward Syndil, there was no doubt in Julian's mind that Barack would be a dead man. Syndil was unafraid, ignoring both Darius and Julian as if they were invisible.

"Barack," she whispered softly, almost intimately. Her eyes were on the savage crimson streaks on his chest and face. "Come with me now. I have need to heal your wounds." Despite his ferocious growls, she laid her hand gently on Barack's arm, careful to stay away from the blood coating his clothing. "Come with me, brother. Allow me to heal you."

Barack's head swung around, red eyes glowing fiercely. For a moment his eyes switched between red and black, as if the man fought the beast within for their shared body and mind. "I am not your brother, little one," he hissed, struggling to overcome the killing rage.

For a moment Syndil hung her head, as if his words denying their relationship had cut her deeply. Then she stepped closer to him, so that her soft body brushed against his larger frame. Barack's hands immediately, instinctively, spanned her small waist and lifted her away from the thick pool of blood spreading across the floor. The moment he released the vampire, the body of the undead fell, thrashing around, head flopping and talons digging long, deep furrows into the wall.

"Barack, do not touch Syndil's skin with tainted blood on your hands," Darius cautioned with his black-velvet authority.

Julian was already gathering energy into his palms, taking it from the electricity in the air itself, rolling it into a ball to send it flaming into the vampire's pulsating heart so that there was no chance of the undead rising again. The sparks then jumped from the incinerated organ to the blood, reducing the thick pool of curling black ashes.

Barack reluctantly allowed Syndil's feet to touch the floor far from the hideous scene. He was breathing hard, struggling to gain control of the beast within, ashamed that Syndil should see him so out of control. At Julian's gesture he held out his hands so that the flames danced for a moment over his stained skin, burning the tainted blood from his hands and arms. Barack took possession of the white-hot ball of energy and ran it around Syndil's waist where he had touched her, cleansing her of any tainted blood staining her clothes. He tossed the fire back to Julian before turning his entire attention to the woman who had shown so much courage.

"Are you hurt?" Syndil asked him softly, ignoring the other two Carpathians as if they didn't exist. Her fingertips brushed Barack's arm, and she tried not to show how his denial of their relationship distressed her. If he chose, after all these years, to reject the ties between them, she was not going to let him see how bad it made her feel. She could only suspect it was because Savon had raped her, and Barack could not accept her anymore. Perhaps he thought she had brought the assault on herself in some way. Barack had not been the same since the attack on her. He had spent a great deal of time in the ground avoiding her and the others. Now he seemed sober and stern, so unlike his earlier, easygoing self. He watched her like a hawk, almost as if he didn't trust her, or as if she were a fledgling not to be trusted to care for herself properly. She wanted to weep and run off and hide again, but something in her refused to leave Barack in such a state, with so many lacerations.

Syndil lifted her chin but refused to meet his eyes. "Let me heal you, Barack. It will take but a few minutes."

Finally he took her elbow and led her away from the other two men. Julian and Darius watched them walk off. Julian glanced down at the body of the vampire and then up at Darius. "I guess we have clean-up duty." He directed the flames toward the undead. As he always did when the vampire destroyed was not the ancient he sought, he experienced a deep leftdown.

But this time he wasn't alone. From the concert hall Desari sent him warmth, love, her beautiful, haunting voice wrapping him up and holding him close to her heart.

Darius had been ensuring they were alone in the hallway, keeping humans away while Barack destroyed the vampire. "Barack has never before fought the undead. He has never even shown interest in hunting. Yet he was here before either of us."

Julian nodded thoughtfully. "Is it really a surprise?"

Darius shrugged his broad shoulders. "Barack has always stayed close to Syndil. He often protects her. As young children they were inseparable. Lately, though, she is so withdrawn that no one can get close to her, not even Desari."

"She spends far too much time in the form of the leopard. There is no way she will recover from her trauma if she does not face it," Julian replied casually.

Darius nodded. "She trusts no man. It seems a miracle she answered your call and aided us in persuading Barack to leave the vampire to his fate. She does not like to be close to any of us males."

"I do not think one can blame her," Julian said distractedly. Already he felt the need to be with Desari. He could touch her mind at will, see what she was seeing through her eyes, look into her mind, but he was still uneasy without her in his actual sight. Desari standing so vulnerable in front of such a large crowd brought out the worst in him. His need to protect her was so incredibly strong, he found himself fighting his own deeply ingrained primitive instincts. He went quickly to the concert hall.

She was so beautiful, she took his breath away. He watched the way she moved, gentle and flowing, her hips swaying, her long hair cascading like waves of silk down her back to brush around her slender body, drawing attention to curves and hollows. He wanted to carry her off to some secluded spot for all time, out of danger, away from prying eyes. He wanted to listen to her voice for eternity and watch her smile and light up the spaces around her.

At once, even in the midst of her laughing softly into the microphone, seemingly totally bonded with the crowd, he felt the brush of her fingertips at the nape of his neck, and hot flames engulfed his gut and clenched his muscles so that he stood still, shocked at the power of her touch over him. He had spent an eternity feeling empty, a gaping hole in his very soul, so that what little compassion and gentleness he had once experienced had slowly seeped away, lost to him. She had brought back his emotions, his joy in life. He had always thought he might resent the need for a lifemate. He was a solitary hunter, enjoying the animals and nature more than the company of others. But it wasn't so. Desari was a miracle to him.

There was a soft hiss in his mind, not the standard path Desari's family unit communicated on but a private, new meeting of the minds. Power. Authority. Male. It could only be Darius. Their sharing of blood had forged a bond, allowing Darius to communicate easily with him at will. *Stop daydreaming. We have a job to do. My sister has you wrapped around her little finger.*

I notice you have not stopped her from pursuing this dangerous career she has chosen. It was you who allowed such nonsense in the first place. Julian was more than happy to point that out. He was moving around the packed hall, his senses flaring out to read any signs of danger.

It is your decisions that should guide her now, Darius replied.

Do not attempt to push your failures off on me. It will take much time to undo all the damage you have done with your permissive guidance. I will have to work slowly, without her knowledge, ease her out of this in-

sane notion that she is allowed to make her own decisions. Julian could not help the humor creeping into his voice. The last thing anyone could do would be to put something over on Desari. She was no fledgling to be pushed around by an arrogant male.

Barack returned to the stage, his long hair pulled back to the nape of his neck, his face unmarked and handsome, his clothes immaculate. Julian sensed Syndil's presence in the hall, but she had made herself unseen to the human eye. It was Barack, looking sternly toward one corner of the stage, that tipped off her location to Julian. Barack had obviously dragged her there. Julian could tell he wasn't about to perform unless Syndil was where he could see her every moment. She was sitting on the edge of the platform, slightly behind and to Barack's right. She looked so sad, Julian felt an instant response, wanting to comfort her. Syndil appeared fragile and worn, a slight figure, almost childlike. Barack must have ordered her presence in such a way that she had chosen to obey him. Julian couldn't blame him or any of the others for their protectiveness. This was an explosive situation, one not easily controlled. Protecting two women in such a large crowd from human assassins, overeager fans, and vampires was difficult. They needed the women close together where they all could watch over them.

We are not children, Desari reminded him, taking her bow before the roaring crowd. *And Barack was quite harsh with Syndil. He should be more gentle with her. She didn't provoke the vampire's attack on her.* She smiled at the crowd, flashing the famous sexy grin that seemed to stop a few too many hearts for Julian's peace of mind. Her arm gestured back gracefully toward the two male Carpathians onstage, including them in the standing ovation.

Christine Feehan

Several females in the front row screamed and waved at the two guitar players, one throwing herself against the ring of security guards, calling for Barack and tossing a pair of red silk panties in his direction. The underwear landed almost in Syndil's lap. She picked them up gingerly by the tips of her thumb and forefinger, studied them for a moment, then, with absolutely no expression on her face, tossed them onto the neck of Barack's guitar. To the audience, red panties seemed to fly straight up into the air at him. They roared with delight, coming to their feet once again.

Syndil rose with her casual grace and started off the stage. At once Barack moved, cutting off her retreat. To the audience it simply appeared as if he had stepped away from Dayan with his back to them, his hips swaying provocatively. Several girls screamed louder, trying to rush the stage. Barack played his guitar solo for several chords, the music swelling, cresting like a wave racing toward shore, then crashing onto the sand. The audience was electric with intensity, yet every Carpathian's attention was on the scene taking place between the male and female.

Syndil glared at Barack, her body rigid with anger. Her eyes blazed at him. "You have no right to tell me what to do or where to go. As you pointed out earlier, you are not my brother. Darius is the leader, and he has not said that I must stay and watch you entertain these adoring women." She waved a disdainful hand at the screaming row of girls.

"Do not push me this time, Syndil," Barack warned softly, a growl rumbling deep in his throat. "I do not care what Darius has said or not said to you. You will not leave my sight until I know you are completely safe. In this matter you will obey me."

For a moment Syndil faced him in silent rebellion. It

284

was impossible to guess what she was going to decide to do.

"Please, Syndil," Desari said softly, persuasively, "we have an audience. Do not give Barack any reason to go berserk on us."

Syndil blinked once, her long lashes fanning her high cheekbones. Her large eyes moved over Barack with faint haughtiness. She swung her long hair over her shoulder and seated herself for the second set, her back to Barack. There was something regal about the way she held herself.

Barack finished his guitar solo, his body once more relaxed, but his eyes remained hard and watchful. Desari flashed a quick, relieved smile Julian's way. Dayan's guitar joined Barack's and Desari's voice soared into the air, bringing the spectators to their feet. Syndil began tapping her foot to the rhythm of the music. It was entirely involuntary, the first time she had responded to their music since the savage attack on her. She had always been musical, easily playing any instrument set before her, usually the keyboard and drums. The group had explained her absence to their fans by saying she had taken an extended vacation and would return soon.

Desari inwardly breathed a small sigh of relief. It was the first sign in a long while that Syndil might find a way to come back to them, to herself. Perhaps her love of music would bring her back. While her mind turned the matter over, her voice continued to keep the audience mesmerized. And it suddenly occurred to her that while she had had family close by all her life, Julian had been totally alone. To guard his brother in the best way he knew, to guard his people, he had been always alone.

Not anymore, Julian drawled, his voice a purring caress. *As you are my responsibility now, I suppose I have no other choice but to help your brother protect and*

285

guide this pack of fools. What I should be doing is haul-ing your beautiful little butt out of here. The Carpathian Mountains are our homeland. It is where we all belong, not here among so many mortals. In truth he was be-ginning to like the feeling of belonging to a family, of belonging to Desari.

Baby. She whispered it in his mind like the stroke of her fingers along his skin. Teasing. Loving. Their own private world.

Julian swallowed hard. His face was a mask of indif-ference, aloof, his hard, watchful eyes surveying the crowd mercilessly, yet inside he was melting with the warmth only she could produce in him.

Chapter Fourteen

Julian took Desari's hand and walked her out into the forest. The concert had seemed endless, and there had been so many people to talk with after the performance. Well-wishers, reporters, fans—far too many people for Julian's liking. It went on for most of the night. Now he allowed the peace of the mountains and the night breeze to push away the sounds of the crowd and the crush of so many humans pushing close to his lifemate. He was not altogether certain he would survive this life she insisted on. It was so foreign to the nature of a Carpathian male to allow so many near her, yet Desari took it for granted that he would just accept it.

"I do not, you know. I have never taken anything for granted," she protested, sharing his thoughts. "I know how difficult this is for you, and I appreciate the way you support me in my choice."

His dark eyes swept over her sincere expression, his eyebrows raised slightly. "You do, do you? Appreciate the way I support your choice?" He said the words softly, a hint of laughter in their depths. "And you look so perfectly honest and genuinely earnest with your far too beautiful eyes."

She tightened her hand around his. "I am completely sincere, Julian. I know this is hard on you, but it truly is my way of life."

"This century, *cara*. For only this century will I allow it."

She laughed softly. "You think."

"I know. My heart cannot take the constant strain of worry. So many males hanging around you with not-so-pure thoughts. It sets my teeth on edge. And we are not even counting the vampires who appear to be stalking you and the other female at every turn."

"Syndil," Desari corrected softly. "Her name is Syndil."

Julian heard the reproof in her voice, felt the tears in her mind. She loved Syndil as a sister, loved her and missed their close camaraderie. Even Julian filling her life could not take away the sorrow of what had happened. She wanted Syndil back again, whole and healed. Even her voice could not undo the brutality of what Savon had wrought. Syndil wouldn't accept her aid. Desari felt helpless and could only watch as Syndil seemed to withdraw more and more into herself.

He caught glimpses of Desari's memories. Syndil laughing, her eyes alight with the sheer joy of living. Syndil hugging her close, whispering womanly nonsense after they had teased Darius to distraction. The plots they hatched to attain a few hours of freedom. Secretly laughing at Barack's anger with Syndil and Darius's lectures when they were caught. They had had centuries together, so close, the only two females, with no other friends or confidantes sharing their innermost thoughts, fears, and joys.

Julian bent his head and rubbed his chin in the silk of Desari's hair. He loved her. *Love*. It was so small a word, and people seemed to use it for everything. To him it was sacred. Desari was joy and light. Truth and beauty. She was love itself. She was the world and what it should be. He felt complete and at peace with her, even when she was driving him crazy. It amazed him, her cool confidence and tremendous gifts. Of course their women would have extraordinary gifts. Why hadn't any of them realized? They had been so arrogant in their beliefs that the men had the powers, yet in truth, the males held only dark powers. How could that possibly compare to the gifts women brought to their world? Aside from the creation of life, obviously they had other things to offer, blessings of nature and peace, healing gifts far beyond the scope of the males.

Julian let his breath out slowly. "Syndil will be whole again, *piccola*, whole and happy once more. Time can heal where other things cannot. I feel it. I know it will happen. Do not continue to know such sorrow. She will return to you in a way totally unexpected. I do not know how I know this, but I do."

Her large eyes searched his face before her long lashes veiled her expression. "You are not just saying this to ease my mind?"

"I do not say things to ease anyone's mind. You should know that about me by now. Lifemates cannot tell an untruth to one another. Seek the information in my mind, Desari, and you will know I believe in what I say to you. And I will call her Syndil as you wish me to. If it is your desire that she be a sister to me, then it will be so."

"Why do you never speak her name?"

He shrugged with his easy, casual grace, the ripple of power he took for granted, the enormous strength she was coming to know. "Habit. We do not often socialize with unclaimed females of our race, and we do not personalize them. It is a protection for both parties. As males grow close to the end, we would not want any of them fixating on one of our eligible females and perhaps . . ." He trailed off, suddenly not wanting to articulate it.

Desari swept a hand through her hair. "Attacking her," she finished for him. "Syndil did not do anything to provoke Savon or lead him on. I know she did not."

"It never occurred to me for one moment that she did such a thing. A female does not have to do anything to entice a vampire. The undead are perverted, grotesque, wholly evil. In their warped imaginations, they think that if they find an unclaimed female, or perhaps make a widow of one with a mate, they will find their lost souls. It can never be. Once they have chosen such a path, it is for all eternity, until one of our hunters is able to properly destroy them. Most try at some time to find a mate. They use mortal women and sometimes are even able to turn them without killing them. But the woman becomes deranged and feeds on the blood of children. It is a terrible burden to be forced to destroy such a victimized creature. That is the worst of all our jobs." He stated it matter-of-factly, without looking for sympathy.

Her head brushed his shoulder, their bodies close as they walked together through the forest, winding their way aimlessly through the trees and brush. It was a small gesture, but the touch sent little shock waves through his body. She took away his distress. She gave him so much pleasure. Just being near her gave him pleasure. Breathing in her scent gave him pleasure.

"Julian, you give me the same feeling," she assured him, pleased she was able to lift his spirits.

"You are a miracle to me," he said. "You have no idea what you mean to me, what you are to me, and I can never find the words to tell you."

But she was in his mind. She could feel his emotions, and they were overwhelming to her. To be thought of as he thought of her! It was a powerful weapon the men of their race wielded. How could a lifemate possibly refuse to comfort and love such a man? She wanted this for Darius. She wanted a woman to love him the way she loved Julian. She wanted someone for Syndil and Barack and Dayan, as well.

Julian laughed and curved his arm around her, sweeping her beneath the protection of his shoulder. Of course Desari would think of all the others, wanting to share her joy. It only made him love her more. "Look at the stars tonight, Desari. Tomorrow night there will be a storm. I feel it closing in around us. But tonight we walk together in the open and have time to enjoy ourselves."

"It is nearly dawn," she reminded him, a little smile creeping into her voice.

"It is a few hours until dawn," Julian replied. "More than enough time to accomplish my task."

"You have a task?" she asked, her dark eyes dancing at him.

"Absolutely. I have to convince you completely that I am the only man you will ever want or need in your lifetime."

"My lifetime could be quite long," she pointed out in warning.

"It will always be my first duty in life to ensure your safety at all times, *cara mia*. I want you to live with me a very long time."

She turned to him, her body pressed close to his, her

arms sliding around his neck. "How long is a *very* long time?" she murmured, her teeth nibbling at the strong line of his jaw.

His arms closed around her tightly as joy swept through his soul and a tidal wave of need consumed him. Julian bent his head to find her mouth with his. The sweet perfection of it. Velvet fire swept over him, through him, electricity arcing between them so that flames danced up their skin and through their bodies. A low growl escaped his throat, a soft sound of possession. Desari responded by moving even closer to him, her smaller frame molding itself to his.

A sound intruded. It was barely discernible, the rub of fur against a leaf, but it was enough to elicit a frustrated groan from Julian. He leaned his forehead against her crown. "This family unit you have is driving me over the edge. We have no privacy, *piccola*, none whatsoever."

She laughed softly with the same frustration. "I know, Julian. But it is one of the small sacrifices we all pay for caring for one another. We help each other through any crisis."

"Who is going to help me through this one? Believe me, *cara*, I am definitely having a crisis. I need you before I start to go insane."

"I know. It is the same for me," she whispered, her lips against the corner of his mouth, teasing, tempting. There was an ache in her voice, an answer to the ache in his. "We will have our time."

"It had better be soon," he growled, meaning it. There was a hidden laughter in her, one he felt in her mind, in her heart. She found humor in the situation yet wanted him with the same urgent need. Julian found he was smiling in spite of his body's demands. There was something contagious about Desari's laughter, whether it was in her mind or aloud. It was joy. Pure and simple. There was joy in him now where there had never been before.

Desari kissed his hard jaw, his stubborn chin. "We cannot desert Syndil at this time."

"It is rather difficult to help her when she spends all her time in the form of a leopard."

"Shh. There is nothing wrong with her hearing," Desari cautioned, rising on tiptoe to kiss his eyebrow, rubbing at his frown with her cheek. "If she is willing to reach out for just a moment and talk to me as we used to, then I must be here for her."

"Fine," Julian agreed grudgingly. "But if that idiot Barack happens by with his hangdog look, tell him to keep going."

"He seems to be strutting around these days with a rather macho look," Desari pointed out. "He has gotten progressively worse since Savon's attack on Syndil. He has appointed himself her personal bodyguard, and he is not very nice about it. Julian," she added, her dark eyes lighting up with her brilliant idea, "maybe you should tell him to quit being so bossy. She needs him to be more gentle."

Julian snorted inelegantly. "As if that will happen. I absolutely refuse to interfere with anything Barack is choosing to do. Carpathian males cannot do such things. We believe in allowing one another to work things out alone. Especially anything that might have to do with a woman. Now that I am thinking about it, perhaps I should go and leave you two females to talk privately."

"Coward," she whispered, her teeth nipping his ear. "Do not go far, as I have great need of you."

Julian's tall, muscular frame shimmered, then became transparent in the night air. He was smiling down at her, that little smirk that always got under her skin. Desari felt her heart take wing, soar, even as he disappeared, becoming part of the night itself.

Desari turned as the female leopard burst out from the brush, shape-shifting as it did so. "Desari." Syndil's voice was a mere thread of sound. "I am going to go away. I need to be far from these overbearing males. I do not wish to leave you, but it is necessary."

Syndil was upset. Desari knew her so well, she knew every nuance of her voice. Yet, as always, Syndil appeared calm and unruffled. Desari reached out and took her hand. "It never bothered you before to have the males beating their chests like cavemen. We have always laughed together over their silly ways. Why are you allowing them to get to you now? If Darius has upset you, sister, I will speak to him myself."

Syndil pushed impatiently at the long strands of hair framing her face. "It is not Darius, although he is bad enough. And Dayan, too, watches me all the time. But at least he does not say anything annoying to me. Barack, however, thinks himself my boss. He is rude and obnoxious all the time. I do not wish to put up with his arrogance one more moment." She ducked her head so that her silky hair fell around her like a cloak, hiding her expression. "He denied I am his sister."

Desari felt Syndil's pain. Barack had really hurt her with that denial. They had been family, closer than family for centuries. How could Barack have said such a hurtful thing to Syndil? Desari had an unfamiliar urge to strike him. She put her arm protectively around Syndil's shoulders. "I do not know why he would say such a thing, but you know he cannot mean it. He must be so worried about you that he says things without thinking."

"Things to punish me because he thinks I, in some way, am responsible for what Savon did. Perhaps he wished Darius had killed me rather than Savon. He always looked up to Savon; you know that." Syndil shrugged painfully, staring up at the darkened sky. "Who knows, maybe I did do something inadvertently to provoke Savon."

"Absolutely not!" Desari denied adamantly. "You do not believe that, Syndil, and neither does anyone else. Julian says that the males turn after so many centuries without finding their other half. He says they have a choice, to meet the dawn or choose to lose their souls. Obviously Savon chose the latter. You cannot in any way believe you are responsible for anything that has been happening to the males of our race for hundreds, even thousands of years."

"They all treat me differently now, but Barack is the worst."

"Syndil," Desari said gently, her voice soothing and gentle, "you *are* different. We all are. It is a change we have to go through just like any other, but as always, we go through it together. Barack may be having a difficult time adjusting to what happened to you. He may even feel responsible. Maybe he noticed Savon pulling away from us and did not say anything. Who knows? I believe he is simply trying to protect you. Perhaps he is going a bit overboard, but it might be that we should cut him a little slack."

Syndil's perfect eyebrows shot up. "Cut him some slack? He should cut me some slack. You do not see how he is with me. He is rude and abrasive and totally out of line. Even Darius does not speak to me as he does."

Desari sighed and shoved a hand through her hair. "Do you want me to speak to him, Syndil?"

"I do not think it will be necessary. I meant what I said. I will be taking a vacation. It is time I went my

295

own way for a while." Syndil's voice was defiant.

"Darius will never allow you to go away unprotected," Desari reminded her gently. "He would send one of the men to look after you."

A male leopard, large and well-muscled, moved out into the open and leapt with casual ease onto a low tree branch. It stared at the two women, its eyes unblinking, its sides rippling with power as it breathed steadily. Syndil glared at the animal. Desari shook her head.

Barack, you must stop pushing her so hard. She is going to run if you keep this up. She used their common mental path, trying to convey the desperation Syndil was feeling.

She will go nowhere without the consent of Darius. And if he were to give it, there would be nowhere she could go that I would not follow. The voice was arrogant.

Without warning, Julian shimmered into solid form beside Desari, his arm dropping protectively around her shoulders. His eyes, molten gold filled with menace, were fixed on the leopard above them. The disturbance in Desari's mind had brought him instantly to her side. In that moment there was nothing easygoing about him, only a hard, implacable warrior honed by a merciless life.

Do not drive her away from us, Desari pleaded, *I beg you, be more gentle with her. You do not understand what has happened to her. She needs time to recover.*

I understand far more than you think, Desari. She is no longer living. She is merely existing. I cannot allow it to continue. Barack sounded cold and distant.

Desari's dark eyes filled with tears. She turned her head into Julian's shoulder. "Please, Syndil, do not leave me. Not now. I need you here with me. Everything is so different."

Syndil reached out and touched her hand. "If that is so, then he will not force me from my own family. I am strong enough to stand up to him." She glared at the leopard, who simply watched her without so much as blinking. Nodding at Julian, she moved away from them, disappearing into the trees. The leopard jumped sound-lessly from the branch and padded after her.

Desari glanced up at Julian. "Do you realize how really intimidating you can look when you want to? What did you think Barack was going to do?"

He shrugged with his casual grace. "It did not matter, *cara*. I did not like the way he made you feel. These other males seem to think they have the right to interfere with you women. Only your brother, as the acknowl-edged leader, has such a right and duty. The others can do no other than protect you, as Barack has tried to do with Syndil. He cannot chastise you. You are my life-mate and answerable only to me and the Prince of our people. In your case, perhaps to Darius as well. But not to Dayan. Not to Barack. Only to the leaders and your lifemate."

Her dark eyes flashed with fire. "I am answerable to you?" Her voice was even softer than usual, a velvet volcano waiting to erupt.

Julian rubbed the bridge of his nose, trying not to allow the smile creeping up from his heart to show in his mind or on his face. "As I am answerable only to you, my lifemate, and to the Prince of our people."

She studied the sensual beauty of his face for a long time. He was amused by her flares of feminism, she could clearly read that, although he wisely attempted to cover it up. Yet she found herself appreciative that Julian cared enough to try to put them on the same footing. Whatever rules he deemed necessary in his mind for his lifemate, he attempted to be fair enough to place the same on himself. Julian was in many ways a chauvinist, like most of the males she had encountered, yet he was at least attempting to make their relationship an equal partnership. She caught at his arm and slipped her hand into the crook of his elbow. "I seriously believe that I am beginning to fall in love with you."

His smile was pure masculine arrogance. "You are madly in love with me. Face it, *cara mia*, you know you cannot resist me."

Her small fist thumped him in the middle of his chest. "When you talk like that I can. Occasionally I think I must be insane to put up with you. 'Madly in love' is not a way I would put things."

His arm swept around her waist. "Sure you would, *piccola*, if you were not so stubborn." Julian bent his head to bury his face against the slender column of her neck. He loved her scent. She smelled so clean, so tempting. Beneath his wandering mouth, his stroking tongue, he felt the rush of life in her veins beckoning to him. Deliberately he nuzzled her neck, his teeth scraping back and forth over her delicate skin, an enticement that sent shivers down her spine and caused a trembling to start deep within her.

Desari moved even closer to him, her soft body pressing invitingly into his. "We might actually be alone if we move fast enough." Her smile was frankly sexy, her long lashes sweeping down in invitation.

Julian's arm tightened almost to the point of crushing her, yet he held her carefully, so that she could feel the power in his arm but know he was protecting her from bruises. She loved how he made her feel feminine, treasured and cherished, while taking nothing away from her.

"Why is it that I want you so much?" she whispered against his ear. "Why do I feel such a burning need that is so much more than mere want?"

His low laughter was all satisfied male. "Because I am so incredibly sexy." He was rising from the earth with her while all around them the night enfolded them in loving arms. The wind rushed past Desari's face, so she kept it buried against his chest, her arms winding around his neck.

"That may be true, arrogant one," she conceded with that soft rasp of velvet that turned his insides to molten lava, "but it is more than that. My skin cannot bear to be apart from yours. My mind tunes itself to yours. My heart and lungs do, too. Inside I burn for our joining. It grows stronger with every passing moment. Why is this?"

"We are lifemates," he answered seriously, his hands beginning a slow exploration of her back even as they flew through the air. "You know this area much better than myself; show me an image to guide me where we can be undisturbed." There was a gravelly edge to his voice that sent her heart somersaulting, as if he, too, was so impatient for their joining that he could not wait much longer.

Automatically she brought up her memories of the area and her private resting place deep within the bowels of the mountain. Her skin was so sensitive she could barely restrain herself from ridding herself of the clothes rubbing uncomfortably against her, keeping her from feeling his skin pressed tightly to hers.

"Lifemates have so close a bond, *cara*, that they must share one another's bodies and minds often. It is a need when our souls and hearts are so connected. Two halves of the same whole must be brought together very frequently or the demands become so great that control is no longer a possibility." He had picked the information he needed out of her mind and was descending into the very top of the mountain through a narrow crevice barely discernible to the eye even from above.

The relief in both of them was tremendous. Living with her family was as much a part of Desari as breathing, but the strain of not being alone with Julian was overwhelming. She raised her head even before they began the descent through the passageway that wound deep into the inner regions of the slumbering volcano. Their world. Their home.

Her mouth found his blindly. Clothes were simply wished away, tumbling off unchecked as their bodies continued to wind downward through the channel. At once Julian's hand moved to cup her bottom in his palms, urging her body to his.

Desari laughed softly, breathlessly, the heat of the mountain interior itself mixing with the fire burning in her body. She wanted him right at that moment, moving through the air with a languid pace. "We cannot do this, can we?" she asked him, her tongue stroking caresses over the pounding pulse in his neck. His entire body clenched in reaction so that she couldn't help but do it again, the erotic scrape of her teeth adding to the temptation of her bare skin against his. Her full breasts, aching with need, thrust temptingly against his chest, and she pressed the invitation of her hot, creamy entrance against his abdomen.

Julian groaned aloud, his hands lifting her over the thick evidence of his desire. "Do it, Desari, right now," he whispered hoarsely as he began to lower her over him, fitting them together like a velvet glove. "Do not tease me, *cara mia*. Let me feel my blood flowing into you as I take what I so desperately need."

Her power over him was all-consuming. To have this Carpathian male with his enormous strength, with all his skills and abilities, so completely enamored, so in need of her, was exhilarating. She lapped gently at his shoulder, tracing a trail of fire over corded muscle to his neck to find his strong, steady pulse. He groaned softly deep in his throat as she allowed her teeth to tease his skin.

Desari! Her name was a plea for mercy.

They were moving so leisurely now, Desari was barely aware they were still floating through the passageway. She could feel his body invading hers with exquisite slowness. Julian felt her tight, fiery sheath surrounding him, adjusting to his thickness, squeezing him with strong muscles so that he clenched his teeth to hang on to a vestige of control. Then her teeth sank into his neck, sending a bolt of blue lightning streaking through his body, slamming into him with such sexual ecstasy he had no other recourse but to surge into her with hard, sure strokes, to thrust decisively into her mind to share his erotic thoughts, the emotions and the sheer, passionate pleasure her body was giving his. He felt her pure, uncensored joy in the sharing of their minds and hearts, their bodies and souls, in the spice of his blood flowing like the finest wine into her. Desari's hair fell around them in a cascade of ebony silk, brushing their sensitive skin like millions of fingers caressing them. He tasted wild and untamed, an erotic blend of animal and man. Julian could taste the very essence of his life through her, and it was erotic beyond anything he had ever known. They hovered in the air, mating wildly, Julian plunging into her again and again, holding her body exactly where he wanted it, exactly where he needed it to be so that the friction building and building was fiery hot and gripping him almost to the point of pain.

Desari closed the tiny pinpricks in his chest with a slow, leisurely lap of her tongue clearly designed to drive him to madness. She threw her head back, exposing her throat in a clear invitation to him. Her arms circled his neck, and she began to move her hips, riding him almost helplessly with the same fast pace he had set. She looked beautiful, her dark eyes glazed with passion and her mouth a lush enticement impossible to ignore.

Julian's mouth wandered down her satin skin, between the soft swell of her breasts, his breath catching in his throat, in her throat, so that she gasped with pleasure. A small sound escaped, a low cry of need. Desari arced into him even as her hips matched his frantic rhythm. She wanted the whip of lightning flashing through her body, burning her with leaping flames. His tongue stroked her skin, the curve of her breast; his teeth teased her erect nipple gently while his body claimed hers with a fierce possessiveness he had never known he could feel.

"Julian," Desari whispered in an agony of anticipation, a siren's temptation, her melodious voice sending feathers of pleasure down his spine. "I may burn up before we have finished."

He answered her as only a lifemate could, sinking his teeth into the pulse beating so frantically over her breast. She cried out and clutched him tighter as white-hot heat pierced her skin. Incredibly his hips thrust harder into her, his hands holding her still while he drank deeply. The sensation of her body spiraling, gripping him tighter and tighter, went on and on until he could no longer think. There was only feeling, only pleasure, only the erotic taste of her. One skin, one heart and soul. They were soaring together through time and space, and it went on for eternity. How he loved her! How he needed her! She made him alive after centuries of such a bleak emptiness, and he could barely believe his happiness would last. He felt that at any moment it might be wrenched away from him. And he knew he would be far more dangerous than he had ever been in his life.

Savoring the taste of her, their combined scents, he was drowning in ecstasy.

He could feel her surrounding him, her velvet muscles rippling with strength, while she cried out to the very top of the mountain. The intensity of their shared climax rocketed them through the passageway, over cliffs and boundaries of time and space. She clung to him while he feasted, while his body remained locked to hers. Desari's soft little sigh of total acceptance brought him out of his daze, where there was only pleasure, only senses reeling out of control. That sigh brought him back to the here and now. Desari's head was pillowed on his shoulder, her long lashes fanning her cheeks. She looked pale beyond belief, her skin nearly translucent.

Julian swore as he impatiently closed the tiny wounds over her breast. His palm swept back the long hair from her face. "Desari. Look at me, *piccola*. Open your eyes." It was a clear order, delivered in a voice filled with compulsion, filled with naked worry.

She smiled drowsily, leaning into him so that he was bearing her weight. "You must feed, *cara*. I have taken far too much blood from you in my insatiable hunger. It is unforgivable that I would not see to your care even in the midst of such passion. I have no excuse, my love, but you must drink." He pressed her mouth to his bare chest.

Desari's head lolled back on her neck. She murmured something unintelligible, a sound of love. Julian took them both safely to earth and gently untwined their bodies. Her protest was more a slight frown passing across her dark winged brows, a faint pout to her lips, than anything verbal. Julian cursed himself and his utter lack of control once again. There was no censure in her mind or heart. She was as accepting of the animal side of his nature as she was of the Carpathian male side. He had taken far more blood than he should have, indulging his passion at the price of her strength.

Julian cradled her in his strong arms, bending to kiss the corner of her mouth. *Hear me*, piccola, *love of my life. I have taken far too much from you. You must replenish yourself with what I provide.* This was no soft plea; it was a strong and deliberate command, a compulsion sent mind to mind by a male of their species with tremendous powers. He gave no thought to it, simply issuing the order to ensure her health and safety. Julian slashed a line over the heavy muscles of his chest and pressed her mouth firmly to him.

He was angry with himself, angry that he had been so selfish in his passion. Had he spent so much time with animals that he had forgotten how to behave as a man? He was more beast than civilized. His newfound emotions were far more difficult to deal with than the most powerful of the undead he had ever vanquished. The lines in battle were always so clear to him, yet now his emotions rendered his unshakable control dust: He found himself tied up in knots, not wanting to hurt her feelings or do the wrong thing, that she might think less of him. He found himself constantly at war with his own instincts. He wanted to carry her off and keep her safe for all time and eternity.

Julian lay his head over hers. "It seems I need to keep you safe from your own lifemate."

Desari stirred in his arms even as she fed under his hypnotic command. Deep within the layers of compulsion she felt his fierce anger at himself for what he considered his abusive nature. She sent him her warmest love. She managed to project the gentle smile forming in her mind to share it with him, the deep feelings she had already developed for him. It was astonishing to Julian that she was already so much a part of him that she could feel the depths of his rage at himself and seek to soothe him.

And she had somehow managed to do so. He became more calm and accepting of his nature. He was what he was; he could never change that. He wasn't even certain he would want to if he could. Desari saw his strengths and allowed him to view himself through her eyes. It was another priceless gift she offered him, and he would treasure it always. He was finding out quickly why the male of their race so desperately needed the balance of their lifemates. Their women brought light and compassion to their inner darkness.

Julian lifted his head and regarded her carefully, searching her face for signs of recovery. Color ran under her skin, a much healthier glow. Breathing a sigh of relief, he allowed her to awaken slowly. His arms cradled her protectively. "I am sorry, *cara*. I should have been far more restrained in possessing you."

Her hand brushed his throat, sending heat coursing through him, a sense of belonging and acceptance he had never known. Her smile tugged at his heart. "You are my love, Julian. You would never harm me. I know that as surely as I know I would be incapable of harming you. I was quite satisfied, if you must hear me say it, although I suspect you know that you provided me with pleasure such as I could not have imagined before."

He stroked her hair, his eyes like molten gold. "It is more than giving you pleasure that I want, it is sharing something beautiful beyond compare, and that I cannot do if I cannot control my desire for you." His expression held infinite tenderness as he watched her face.

Desari found she couldn't breathe for a moment. Julian Savage was a beautiful male of their species, but he always looked so remote and rather harsh. She could not believe she was now seeing such tenderness in the depths of his eyes, in the curve of his mouth, in the touch of his hand. "Do you think that I would trade you for someone gentler?" she asked very softly.

He closed his eyes for a moment to hide the pain those words caused. "You have no choice who your lifemate is; we both know that, Desari. If you had, perhaps you would have wanted someone far different than me."

Her smile robbed him of air. "I believe in God, Julian. I always have. Living through the centuries as we have, I have witnessed many wonderful, miraculous things he has wrought. I believe we were created two halves of the same whole. I had no idea this was so until I met you, but I am now convinced. I would never want another, never fit with another. I can feel that we are right together, and I do not believe God would put together two creatures who did not suit one another." She rubbed at the frown on his face with the pad of her thumb. "I find your enthusiasm for me very sexy, Julian. You can want me like that anytime." Her smile was a siren's teasing enticement.

Effortlessly he shifted her in his arms so that he could press her against his heart, and he found himself breathing again after holding his breath. "I do not ever want to be without you, Desari," he admitted softly. The words were torn from his heart; he felt them leave his body, felt the truth in them.

She wound her arms around his neck, liking the feel of his long hair against her skin. "I do not expect you to ever allow us to be apart. I am counting on that, lifemate. Now stop talking so much and find us a place to rest this night. Tomorrow we will proceed to Konocti in the bus with the others. They will remain at the campsite we have established this night." A faint grin curved her soft mouth. "That is, if the bus will actually run. It is a disgrace that none of us have mechanical abilities.

Even I read the owner's manual, and found it too boring."

"We do not need mechanical abilities," Julian reminded her as he spun around, taking her with him as if she weighed no more than a feather. "We were meant to travel differently, under our own power."

"If we want to blend in with the rest of the world," she pointed out, "we can do no other than travel in the mortals' machines."

"It is much faster to travel our way through time and space."

She laughed softly, the sound a husky blend of velvet and wine pouring over him, into him, so that Julian knew the meaning of joy. It was a woman's laughter, her smile, the glow in her dancing eyes. "It certainly is less frustrating to simply join the wind and go where we wish without following those endless ribbons of highway," she agreed.

He took the right-hand tunnel entrance, drawing the directions from her mind. The path opened almost immediately into a wide chamber. At once he waved a hand to open the earth. "It is early dawn, *cara*, and I would spend more time enjoying your company, but you have performed in front of so many people, and you are tired."

"I do not mind, Julian," she told him. "I rather like the way you spend your time with me." She pressed closer to him, her naked breasts against his bare chest.

His answering kiss was slow and tender, a gentle exploration. "In this one thing I will have to insist. Your health must come before all things, even our pleasure. On the next rising we will have more time together. This dawn you must rest."

She tried to keep the amusement out of her mind. He was so positive he was giving her an order. "Of course,

Julian," she murmured softly, her long lashes feathering down to cover her dark eyes. Her body moved restlessly against his, her full breasts pushing into the heavy muscles of his chest. "If you say we cannot, then I must agree with you, but I am sorry to hear that it is so." Her hands were moving over his buttocks, her fingers tracing their defined muscles. Her fingers moved to his hips, caressed his thighs, worked their way to cup the weight of his rising desire in her palm. "I will do as you say, lifemate, if that is what truly pleases you." Her mouth drifted down over his throat and chest, following the pattern of golden hair to the taut muscles of his belly.

Beneath her caressing fingers, his body thickened and hardened in response, his gut clenched hotly, and the breath seemed to slam out of him. "You are deliberately testing my resolve, *piccola*, and I am failing the test miserably."

"That is exactly what I wanted to hear," she answered complacently, her mind already occupied with much more interesting matters.

Chapter Fifteen

The bus limped along, the engine sputtering and coughing, growing louder and louder with each passing mile, leaving thin trails of dark smoke. Even the air inside the vehicle seemed thick, making it difficult to breathe. The two leopards growled uneasily from time to time, the tips of their tails twitching in protest.

The entire experience was making Julian wary. He was restless in such proximity to so many of his kind. The leopards had to be watched and controlled. They had quick, unreliable tempers and even among the Carpathians they were quite capable of doing great damage if riled within such close confines. In any case, Julian felt a disturbance in the balance of power around him and knew the other males were also aware of it. The crowded dimensions of the bus gave him the feeling of being trapped, although he could easily dissolve into molecules and flow through the open windows if he so desired. The edginess of the males was communicating itself to the animals, making it all the more difficult to control their wild natures. Darius was wasting precious energy keeping the cats in check. Julian shook his head at the insanity of the way this family unit lived.

Desari drummed her fingers impatiently on the back of her seat, wanting to kick her brother. The entire mood inside the bus was one of intense frustration. Darius had insisted they travel together, leaving the other vehicles in a campground. It was uncomfortable to say the least. She wanted to be alone with Julian, and she knew he was unused to being so confined with others. He would be hating this.

Darius glanced at his sister just once, his black eyes empty. "I do not have to explain myself," he reminded her quietly. He didn't bother to point out the disturbance in the air. One of their kind was near, but one who had long ago chosen to trade honor, his very soul, for a few moments of high during a kill. Darius knew the enemy was far too close to avoid a confrontation, and the women were the target. All of them knew it. Desari also needed more time to be alone with Julian. The couple needed space to get to know one another. Darius watched Julian closely. He respected his sister's life-mate, his casual strength, the way he chose to keep Desari happy at the cost of his own comfort.

The troupe had taken so long trying to patch up their faltering vehicles again that they had little time to make their way to Konocti for their next concert appearance. Darius liked to get to concert sites a day ahead of time to scout around and be certain the security was to his liking. That balance of power was now gone, and the air was groaning with the presence of evil. All of them could smell the stench of a recent fire, the smoke and odor trapped in place by the absence of a breeze.

This time, at least, they would be in familiar territory.

Konocti was Desari's favorite place to perform. It was a smaller and more personal space than the huge stadiums she was usually booked to sing in. Desari liked the area, too, formed by volcanoes with hidden steaming pools and glittering diamonds scattered here and there. They had long ago established several bolt holes for each of them and could even have a semblance of privacy from one another.

"Stop the bus, Dayan!" It was Syndil who called out suddenly, urgency in her voice. "Take that little road off to the side instead."

"We do not have all night," Barack growled without looking up. "We are supposed to talk with the head of security, and, as usual, we are already late. Dayan, keep driving."

Syndil's slender frame began to shimmer. Desari gasped at the action. Syndil rarely defied the males, yet she was dissolving into mist, determined to seep through the open window into the darkened sky.

Barack reached out casually, a deceptively lazy-looking action when his hand had really blurred with speed. He caught Syndil's long hair before she could disappear completely. "I do not think so, Syndil. You have not scanned or you would feel the dark empty spaces that can only mean one thing. There is danger very close to us."

A small sound escaped Syndil's throat as she reappeared in her solid form. "Do you not hear the cry of the earth to me? I can do no other than answer," she replied softly. "Dark spaces mean nothing to me. Danger means nothing when the earth calls to me. Those things are for you and the other males to attend to."

Barack looped a fistful of her silky hair around his wrist. "I know only that you are placing yourself at risk,

311

and I am uncertain whether my heart can stand such a thing twice in two risings."

"In my head I hear the cries of the wounded land, the burned trees. I cannot continue without aiding that which is dying. I must go," Syndil said. "It is who I am, Barack." It mattered little to her what the others said at these times. She could do no other than heal the earth when it was crying out in pain to her.

Dayan sighed softly, a little helplessly, and, with obvious reluctance, complied with her demand, slowly turning onto the dusty road leading into the mountains. It appeared to be an old logging road. Barack sat quietly, no longer protesting, but he didn't let loose Syndil's flowing hair, ensuring that she did not run straight into trouble. The bus rounded a curve, and Desari stared in horror at the sight.

The entire west side of the mountain was a blackened ruin. Dayan slowly eased the bus to the side of the road and came to a complete stop. He had no choice in the matter. Syndil had risen, ignoring Barack's restraining hand. The male Carpathian sighed and rose with her, reluctantly allowing her hair to slide from around his wrist. Desari watched as Syndil pushed open the door to the bus. Her face reflected the same deep grief Desari had witnessed each time Syndil found the earth damaged in some way.

Julian stood, a frown on his face. He didn't like the blank spaces in the area around them. He glanced from male to male, outraged that they would chance one of their precious women out in the open when she was so clearly threatened. Desari touched him lightly, a warning to be still. He glanced from her small restraining hand on his arm toward Darius. As always, the man's expression was impossible to read. Darius was seeking outside of himself, obviously searching for anything that might threaten his family. It was out there. He felt it. All the males felt it, yet none of them seemed to want to stop Syndil.

Barack took the initiative, as he always did lately when anything involved Syndil. He shrugged his shoulders with his easy, fluid grace and sauntered with seeming carelessness after her. She was already moving through the twisted, charred acreage, her hands weaving a strange but fascinating pattern in the stillness of the air. She glanced over her shoulder at Barack, a slight frown on her face.

"Do you hear it, Barack? The ground is screaming in pain. This fire was set deliberately by something evil." Syndil's voice was soft and gentle, a mere whisper, yet all of them, with their acute hearing, could clearly understand her.

"Evil as in . . ." Barack prompted her.

"Not a fire-lover. Neither is it a human." She had already turned her attention back to the blackened trees and soil, dismissing the source as unimportant to her. If the men wanted to deal with such a terrible being, that was their right and privilege. She was of the earth, was part of it, as surely as it was a part of her. She loved the soil, the trees and mountains. All of nature sang to her, wrapped her in loving arms. It was as necessary to her as breathing. Nothing could have stopped her from going forward to help her beloved earth.

Julian watched as she bent down and touched the charred soil with caressing fingers. He swore the dirt moved around and over her hand, wanting the contact with her. He found himself holding his breath, shocked at what he was witnessing. Where Desari's gift was her voice, Syndil's was evidently much different. She held a deep affinity to the earth itself, could cure what was diseased or damaged. He moved to the door of the bus and watched in awe as her hands buried themselves deep in the blackened soil, weaving the same beautiful and intricate pattern beneath the dirt so that above ground ripples began to shape themselves in an ever-widening spiral.

Julian stepped from the bus and moved to one side, careful to stay out of Syndil's way. Desari laced her fingers tightly with her lifemate's. Darius and Dayan were deploying as they always did, guarding the perimeter of the area, their attention on the skies above them and the trees around them. Something was out there, something that had set a trap, something evil that had known Syndil would be unable to resist the screaming of the earth.

Part of Julian could not turn over guardianship of Desari to the other males even for a moment. So he remained at her side and simply watched Syndil, fascinated by the ever-widening circle of richness, spreading, growing. The color of the ground itself was slowly beginning to change to a rich, fertile, deeper black unlike the charred dullness that had been there before. He became aware that Syndil was chanting in the ancient tongue. It was melodious and beautiful, the words an ode to the soil, the essence of the earth. He understood the ancient language, thought he had heard every poem, every lyric, every healing art there was. Yet this chant was completely new to him. Julian easily interpreted the words, found them to be mysteriously soothing, yet joyful. The words spoke of rebirth, of green growth, and glittering, silvery rain. Of tall trees and lush vegetation. He found himself smiling for no reason. Syndil had never looked more beautiful. She shone. Rays of light surrounded her for all to see.

Desari slipped her arm around his waist. "Is she not as I said? Magnificent. Syndil can heal the worst scars on this earth. Anything will grow for her. I am so proud of her abilities when I see her like this. Anything of nature responds to her. Yet it can be so hard on her; part of her takes on the pain of the destroyed forests, the soil."

"Our women are truly miracles," Julian said softly, more to himself than to her. None of his people had known of this. Not a single Carpathian male alive had known a woman old enough to have gifts such as Desari and Syndil displayed. Their remaining women were miraculous in the light and compassion they brought to the darkness of the man, but they were far too young, mere fledglings, to have developed their own powers.

He glanced down at Desari. She was looking up at him with unmistakable love shining in her eyes. His heart seemed to stop. His breath caught in his lungs. She was beautiful beyond anything he had ever witnessed in his centuries of living. When she looked at him like that, he felt something close to terror, something he had never experienced before. He had faced experienced vampires numerous times, had fought in wars, had suffered grave wounds that he had somehow survived, yet he had never felt fear or actual terror. Now it never seemed to leave him.

Last dawn it had been so; this rising it was even more so. There was a price to be paid for happiness: the terror of losing it. "Women should be locked up and kept far out of sight," he growled, half meaning it.

Desari rubbed his arm in a soothing gesture. "I have survived many centuries, Julian, and I intend to survive many more. I cannot think why I would be in more danger now that you have joined with my brother in the guardianship of Syndil and me. I will be even more protected than before."

He stiffened, his face suddenly expressionless but his

eyes filled with pain. He *had* endangered her; he was marked, and they both knew it. "It does not change the fact that I would prefer you to be perfectly safe at all times," Julian said gruffly. He was shifting position subtly, automatically, without thought, his body crowding Desari's, shielding her. His eyes turned skyward.

Darius. He sent the call on the mental path he was becoming familiar with.

I am aware of it. Darius's answer was calm and unruffled, as if they had all the time in the world and would not be under attack at any moment. *Take Desari and get her to safety.*

I will return as soon as I know she is far from harm.

You will stay with her and protect her should I fail. Dayan and Barack will perform the same duty for Syndil.

Julian took Desari's arm. "Come on, *cara*, we must leave now."

Desari glanced from his harshly etched features to her brother's expressionless face. "The undead is coming," she said.

Julian nodded. He was watching Barack, now moving into position to protect Syndil. Dayan moved to flank her. It shocked him that they didn't just scoop her up and carry her off. Syndil seemed oblivious, her concentration total.

"They should get her out of here," he said aloud, his disapproval apparent in his voice. He found, as important as it was to him to guard his lifemate, he was torn, for the first time part of a family, unwilling to leave off protecting the others.

"She is no longer within her body, Julian," Desari said softly. "She is soaring free, moving through the earth to heal that which has been destroyed. Where there are blackened ruins she will coax small buds to life. They will grow lush and tall and spread quickly throughout this area. Trees will sprout and be strong. Wild creatures will aid in the recovery, flocking to this place the moment it will support life. The men cannot disturb her while she is out of her body."

Julian let his breath out slowly in a long hiss of irritation. His first thought was to get Desari to safety as Darius had commanded, but it went against his every instinct to leave Syndil so exposed. "This was a trap, Desari, purposely set to ensnare her. A lure meant only to draw her in. He is trying to use her skills against her."

"How do you know this?"

"I have seen similar traps, ones designed to snare a particular individual. He will try to take her without her body so that we must give it up to him to prevent her death. We cannot leave her." Julian sent the warning to her brother on their private path. *Darius, this trap is for Syndil alone. I have seen such things before.*

There can be no other explanation. I have tried to pull Syndil back to us, but she is too far spread across this land. He is drawing her away from us more quickly than I would have thought possible. There was no fear in his voice or mind, no expression whatsoever. "Julian," Darius continued aloud, "I have never encountered such a trap, but Syndil is slipping away from us far too fast."

"Barack," Julian snapped immediately, "you and Desari are closest to her heart. Desari can use her voice to hold Syndil to us; you must go after her and find her. She will most likely be difficult, disoriented, still half in the earth and half hypnotized by the trap that has been set. Darius, Dayan, and I will go after the undead. He is very skilled. Be very careful, this one is strong. He will not be an easy adversary."

Barack glanced at Darius for confirmation. The leader simply nodded his head. Unfamiliar with the technique the vampire was using, he was not above using whatever expertise was offered.

"You are certain you can track Syndil while you are out of your body?" Julian asked Barack, his voice deliberately without inflection. He had no intention of offending Barack, but he didn't know any of them well enough to know their abilities. Darius was the only male of the group Julian had absolute faith in. The leader was capable of defeating any opponent, and certainly he could track a member of his family unit out of his own body.

"I can find Syndil anywhere in this world, at any time," Barack responded, his voice low and confident. "And I can protect her."

Julian nodded. "Good." He turned back to Dayan and Darius, trusting that Barack could do as he claimed. "A vampire this cunning has been around a long time. He would not be making his move against four male Carpathians unless he believed he had a very good chance of defeating us. He must realize Darius has tremendous experience. He has studied this unit for some time, but he might not know about me yet. This trap took long-term planning, so it is safe to assume he has spent time setting it up. He has probably been counting on the fact that Syndil has been absent from the band these last couple of months and the link between all of you has weakened. It is why he chose her as his target and why he earlier sent the lesser of the undead to do his bidding, the one Barack, not an experienced hunter, so easily defeated."

"How is it you think that he has studied us without our knowledge?" Darius inquired, his voice devoid of inflection.

"I cannot answer that," Julian replied. "I can only surmise that we are dealing with a powerful being, patient as most of his kind are not. He will try to concentrate on destroying you, Darius, as he knows you are the most lethal to him. He will count on you sending Dayan away with Desari. He will strike at you the moment he thinks he has Syndil sufficiently enthralled in his web."

"Then it would be rude to disappoint this one," Darius answered softly, his black eyes empty, ice cold.

Julian nodded his agreement. "Dayan, I must ask of you that you stay with Desari and see that she comes to no harm should I be mistaken."

"Perhaps I could draw him out with my voice," Desari offered, suddenly anxious, not wanting to be separated from Julian.

You will not attempt to draw out the vampire. Dayan will keep you close. Stay linked with me unless I break off suddenly, and do not merge again unless you are in danger. Please do as I ask. Without your cooperation, I will be unable to help Darius.

Desari bit her lower lip. Dayan was moving to her side, his face grim and harsh. "I will concentrate on holding Syndil to us," she agreed as Dayan gently but firmly took her arm. "I will not fail her."

"It will be a struggle; do not think it will not be. The ancient undead will not give up his plan easily. It will take the combined strength of both you and Barack. Call her to you now, and hold her to you. Draw her back if you can do so. Darius and I will hunt this monster down."

Dayan can hunt with him. She couldn't help herself.

I must stay with Darius if I am to keep my promise to you. Dayan has not the experience to help should there be need.

Desari sent him waves of warmth and love, surrounding him for a moment in the wealth of emotion before she shimmered into transparency and allowed Dayan to lead her away from the danger zone. In his mind, Julian heard her soft, persuasive voice, a weapon powerful beyond imagining, a soothing, luring spell calling out to the woman who was like a sister to her. It was a call of need, of love, promising unity, sisterhood, and family.

Julian shook his head to rid himself of the powerful tug of Desari's enchanting magic. He glanced at Darius. "She is unique in my world. I marvel every time I hear her."

Darius was busy searching the area around them, all senses alert. "As I do," he replied sincerely. The women had extraordinary powers. Although he had had the privilege of knowing them for centuries, it had not lessened his memories of admiration of and awe at the women's incredible gifts. Darius remembered his pride and love for them and held tightly to that memory. No one would harm his women.

Julian's shape was already contorting as he launched himself skyward, wings spread wide so that the sharp eyes of the bird could catch anything unusual on the ground below. He had a much wider range of vision from above. He studied the blackened area, looking for anything that jarred the line of the landscape, no matter how slight it might be. He knew Darius would seek the vampire using the ability they all had to feel faint shifts in the air or land itself. Darius was a very dangerous male, one a Carpathian even as powerful and experienced and confident as Julian was would not want to have to battle. This vampire had not lived as long as he had without knowing it would be tantamount to suicide to go against one such as Darius. They were dealing with a truly powerful ancient.

Julian concentrated on blocking out everything but what he must find. The real threat to Darius would come from another direction. The undead would be wrestling the combined strength of Desari's voice and Barack's determination to reclaim Syndil. Julian believed in Desari's love for Syndil and Barack's determination that no one would ever harm her again. He was certain they could hold Syndil to them while Darius battled whatever the undead could throw at him.

Julian, within the body of the circling bird, caught a slight movement in a blackened tree a few feet from Darius. The bark, already wracked with pain, dying a slow death, seemed to ripple once. Julian fixed his eyes on it. It rippled again, and the tree trunk itself began to split apart. Darius was moving now, away from the tree toward the middle of the burned landscape. The twisted, blackened ruins of what had once been a beautiful forest looked suddenly sinister, as tree branches reached out- like eerie stick people. Darius was being drawn into the very center of the trap, the vampire deliberately showing a blank space where he wanted Darius to go. High above, the bird circled the blackened land and watched as several charred trees began to ripple like waves, the bark separating from the trunks, long black shadows moving silently to surround the tall, broad-shouldered man.

Darius, Julian whispered in the leader's mind.

I am aware of them. They are not aware of you. Has Desari anchored Syndil to us yet? Darius continued moving toward the center of the blackened forest. He looked neither right nor left, striding with easy, fluid steps, as if out for a mere walk. No one would have guessed he was communicating with another or that he had a single care in the world.

Julian noticed he had shifted his line of travel slightly so that he was veering toward the west. *Desari drew Syndil back toward us enough to give Barack a chance to merge his spirit with Syndil's. They are together, all*

321

*three matching their strength against the power of the
vampire. He must abandon his minions to their own fate
if he wishes to capture her.*

*He will go for her body if he cannot take possession
of her spirit.*

Julian knew Darius's assessment of the situation was
correct. Julian would have to keep the undead from Barack and Syndil's bodies. He could not afford to turn too
much attention to Darius's coming battle. He would
have his own soon enough. Barack and Syndil's flesh-
and-blood bodies must be guarded at all costs.

Above the bird, dark storm clouds began to gather.
They were large and ominous, filled to overflowing with
water and energy. The arcing of lightning lit the sky,
followed quickly by the rumble of thunder, as if heralding the opening to the great battle. *Not fire*, Julian urged
quickly.

*I am not completely without sense. These creatures
are honed in fire. Fire will only increase their power.*
Darius sounded as calm as ever, without expression of
any kind.

Within the bird's body, Julian found himself smiling
despite the danger surrounding them. Darius was a warrior. He had total and complete confidence in his own
abilities. Julian found himself believing that confidence
was well-founded.

Lighting flashed from cloud to cloud, long whips of
fiery energy. Thunder crashed directly overhead, slamming the earth with a roar of sound, shaking the ground
with tremendous vibrations. The black shadow figures
seemed to flinch at the sound, their strange shapes contorting, lengthening, so that they appeared to be thin
caricatures of humans clothed in long, hooded robes,
empty, staring sockets where their eyes should have
been, the slashes of their mouths gaping open and moan-

ing low and incessantly. The robed figures stretched their tree-branch arms outward and began to form a loose circle around Darius.

Still the leader did not look toward them. His pace did not falter, nor did he appear to hear the awful groans escaping from the ghouls pursuing him. Once he shook his head slightly so that his long ebony hair fell around his shoulders loosely, giving him even more the appearance of an ancient warrior. He looked what he was—a dangerous fighter, his face harsh and merciless. There was no pity in his black eyes, no compassion for those fashioned by the undead.

The shadow figures began to murmur softly, an ancient chant as they circled toward the left, the ring loose and flowing as they appeared to float above the charred earth.

Julian felt his heart slam hard in his chest. A binding from the depths of darkness. Could Darius possibly know a counterspell? It was difficult not to become too absorbed in what was happening below him, not to rush to aid. Julian's task was to watch those two bodies, to ensure that no harm came to them. He circled lazily above Barack and Syndil, watching the earth for signs of disturbance. His mind was still merged partially with Desari, that he might know the battle they waged with Syndil for her freedom from the undead's trap. The vampire was patient, pulling at Syndil relentlessly, bending his will to one purpose only. His best chance was to draw Syndil's spirit away from Desari and Barack, that he might triumph.

Desari was a formidable opponent, her beautiful voice casting a safety net of silver and gold for Syndil's spirit to wrap itself in. The tone was so pure that the undead, without soul, wholly evil as he was, found the voice diminishing his immense skills. He was unclean, and the purity of the notes was a gentle but powerful reminder of the foul, vile path he had deliberately chosen for himself. He saw himself as clearly as if Desari were holding a mirror to his face. The long centuries showed on his face, his skin rotten and decayed, peeling from his skull in long strips. Worms crawled through his body, and the vileness of his existence was laid bare for him to see. Poison blood, taken from dying humans and Carpathians alike, dripped like acid along his skin, pitting what once had been smooth flesh; it seeped from his flame-red eyes and oozed along the talons that were his fingernails. His fetid breath was a visible hue of green and yellow, and his hideous voice was a hiss of grating sounds in such stark contrast to the purity of Desari's beautiful voice that he pressed both hands over his ears and screamed in agony. As he did so, he lost, for one small moment, his hold on Syndil.

Immediately, as if he had been waiting for just such a reaction, Barack's grip on Syndil became more firm, his spirit so completely merged with hers that he felt her horror of the attack. It encompassed her mind, filled her with self-loathing. She believed she had somehow drawn the evil to her, that she was endangering the rest of her family by staying with them.

Julian felt the sudden hesitation in Desari, the small cry of denial as Syndil made an attempt to slip away from Barack. The Carpathian male, so much more easy-going than any Julian had ever met, suddenly displayed a will of iron. Syndil came up against the solid barrier of Barack's will.

The vampire roared his anger, the sound in competition with the cracking of thunder. Barack held fast. There was a quiet confidence in him. Syndil would not be taken from them. He was willing to die should it be necessary to prevent such a thing. The moment she felt his total resolve, Syndil once again threw her strength in with Barack and Desari's, moving backward slowly but steadily toward her body.

The bird watched the ground carefully now, could see the upheaval as the struggle intensified between the vampire's vicious resolve and Barack, Desari, and Syndil's stand. Movement caught the bird's eye as Darius reached the epicenter of the trap. At once the wind picked up in strength, wailing in protest as the circling ghouls moaned and clacked their branch-stick arms together in an old, rhythmic beat accompanying their chant. Darius stopped moving and raised his head slowly toward the sky, his arms wide-spread, as if offering himself to the distorted shadows. He stood in complete stillness, a marble figure without expression. The ghouls' voices rose horribly, the sound grating on nerves and tearing at the Carpathian's mind.

The ancient chant, which had been muffled before, now was audible to Julian, and he could understand the words. He had known deep within his soul what they were trying to do, but hearing the binding spell, seeing the shadowed figures closing the ring tighter and tighter around Darius, dismayed him. He had no real idea of Darius's understanding of the language or what the words could evoke. Darius did not seem in the least concerned with what the undead had wrought to slay him. He looked serene, completely at peace, and it instilled in Julian a new respect and deeper belief in Desari's brother's abilities.

When the attack came, it was preceded by a sudden chilling silence. The robed shadows with their sunken pits for eyes went motionless and silent, their upraised branches growing sharpened points, several knives protruding from each stump. Darius remained as still as a statue, the wind whipping his ebony hair around his face. He stood as straight as an arrow, his broad shoulders like an ax handle, his powerful body radiating strength and elegance.

Julian actually felt the gathering of power in the air. It vibrated around him. Below, the ghouls began their rush at Darius. Near the motionless bodies of Syndil and Barack, the ground swelled until it bulged ominously. Julian began his descent, forcing his mind to stay focused on his own battle. When it struck, the strength of the attack was enormous. For a moment Julian couldn't breathe, his lungs fighting for air, so that it was only his tremendous discipline that allowed him to remain calm. In the next heartbeat he realized the attack was directed at Desari. The undead had bypassed Syndil and Barack to trace Desari's beautiful voice back to the source. He was striking directly at her, projecting his will to choke the life out of the source of that voice. *The vampire knew her through Julian. He had betrayed his own lifemate.*

The ugliness, the shame, the horror of that childhood moment rose up to engulf him, so that for one moment he was a boy again facing an utterly terrifying monster. The vampire had whispered to him for over five hundred years, whispered of using him to harm those he was loyal to. His Prince. His twin. His lifemate, should he ever have one. Julian had studied, experimented, battled hundreds of years to prepare himself for this moment, certain he could protect those around him from the eyes of the shadow within him. But he had betrayed his beloved Desari.

No! Desari reached for him, her fear choking her but her warmth invading the coldness of his bones, of that terrible haunting moment that had changed his life for all time and driven him to a barren, lonely existence. *He found* you *through* me*! It is but a trick. Keep to your duty. Ignore the undead's grip on me.*

Every instinct in him cried out that that was illogical. He knew he had felt her panic, her throat closing. His mind was still partially merged with hers, and his body was so tuned to hers that he shared her pain and fear. But could what she said be the truth?

As her lifemate, his entire being, every nerve, muscle, and sinew in him screamed at him to go to her, to aid her, to join his strength with hers. He agonized over it for what seemed an eternity yet was but a heartbeat. He had waited for this moment, prepared for this moment, for centuries. He did the most difficult thing he had ever done. He closed his mind solidly to his lifemate.

Julian plunged straight toward the bulge in the soil, moving relentlessly toward the two helpless bodies. The undead had no choice when he realized his attempt to distract Julian had failed. The vampire had to release his grip on Desari and remove the energy holding his trap in place so that Syndil and Barack's spirits were free to return to their own bodies. He needed every vestige of power he had to fight the hunter. His merciless enemy. The enemy he had created.

He had sensed Julian's presence only when he had traced the source of the voice holding his prey with so much strength from him. Enraged, he had thought to destroy the woman, yet he had sensed the larger threat to him. He then recognized through her the boy he had made into a merciless, relentless solitary killer. For centuries he had tormented Julian from across time and distance. Until, one day, recently, without warning, he could no longer connect totally with the shadow within Savage. The boy had become far stronger than the vampire had imagined. Now he knew he had no option but to destroy Julian, or at least seriously wound him to give himself time to escape. For the first time in hundreds of years, he felt something close to fear.

The leader of the group was engaged in battle with his ghouls, but the ghouls' movements were directed by him. If he had to withdraw from them, Darius would certainly triumph and join this new threat to destroy him. With a vulgar cry of rage, the undead burst from beneath the earth, flying straight toward Julian with daggerlike talons stretching toward his enemy's eyes.

Julian was shape-shifting as he closed the distance to the vampire. He stretched into a long, scaled serpentine creature shooting out of reach of the talons and breathing a burst of flames over the half-man half-beast rushing toward him.

The vampire screamed as the fire poured over him, withering the twisted talons back into curled fingernails stained and blackened with the blood of his many victims. The undead whirled in midair and slashed at Julian's exposed chest.

Chapter Sixteen

Desari felt the touch of unclean hands wrapped around her throat. As the hideous grip tightened, she felt the shock of the monster's discovery. This was the ancient, the undead who had destroyed Julian's childhood. Whatever this evil thing had wanted before, it now wanted to destroy her lifemate. Focused on capturing the weakened Syndil, and busy studying the family unit, it had not even known that Julian was close until it had touched her.

The moment *Nosferatu* had traced Desari's voice back to her, he had scented Julian as surely as if he had been standing beside her. She was angry with herself for not masking Julian's presence in her mind or his scent on her body. She was certainly skilled enough to accomplish such a minor thing; she just hadn't thought of it. In all their talks of partnership, she always acknowledged Julian the superior in battle, yet she had considered herself up to whatever was necessary. Now she was ashamed and embarrassed by her failure to protect him.

As the all too real illusion of bony fingers around her neck tightened even more, she simply stayed still, her voice not coming from her throat but from her heart, pouring out of her like a silver stream of love and compassion, of fearless strength and eternal honor. The vampire could not maintain his hold for long from a distance. Her neck began to grow warm, distracting her for a moment until she realized the undead's fingers were being burned by the touch of her skin. Was that something Julian was doing? Desari detached herself from her body so that she would not feel the skeletal fingers attempting to choke the life out of her, attempting to silence the purity of her voice for all time.

She knew the vampire was not actually touching her. It was an illusion, one that could kill but still an illusion. Desari didn't falter with her song, not for an instant. She kept her thoughts centered on Syndil. *Stay with me. Stay with us. I will always need you in my life. Never leave us. Do not allow your precious gift to go from this world when it is so badly needed. Stay with me, Syndil. Beloved sister, my grief would know no bounds were we to lose you. Stay with me. Fight this monster who threatens to take you from your true family. Never deprive those of us who love and respect you of your presence in our lives.*

The notes of the music said even more than the words. They sang of deep emotion, of loving. They sang of compassion and understanding, of a need so great, of love that could never be shaken, the complete, unconditional love of a sister.

The notes and the emotion ensnared Syndil as nothing else could have. Syndil's guilt was overwhelming her, filling her gentle soul until her heart cried droplets of ruby-red blood. She believed she had somehow summoned this demon, this vampire who was determined to destroy her entire family. If she gave herself to him, if she sacrificed the rest of her life, perhaps she could save them. He was continually pulling at her, feeding her guilt. He was confusing her mind so that she didn't know what was real and what he had wrought with his trap. Had her soul cried out to his, begged him to find her, to release her from her endless existence, as he was insisting?

No! That was Barack. There was something different in him these days. He had denied a sibling relationship with her, ordered her around as if he had the right and she had not earned her place within their family unit. Yet he had put his life on the line, fighting one of the undead when it had come for her, wanting her to join its ranks of filth and vileness. Even now, Barack was not allowing this evil one to take her.

The voice in Syndil's head softened almost to the point of tenderness. A falsehood, she was certain. Barack could inject anything into his voice and his sensual features, make any woman believe he could care. But he was an ancient one, one who could not really feel anything. *You have done nothing to draw this evil one to you, Syndil. There is no evil in you, no wickedness. You are the light in our lives, as is Desari. Without you, there is no existence. I will not allow him to take you from us, from me. Know this, woman: if you do not stand with me, merge completely and allow our combined strength to fight his hold on you, then I will follow wherever he takes you and battle to the death for your return.*

There was such resolve in Barack's voice, Syndil could do no other than believe him. Yet merging her mind so completely would open to Barack every memory she kept locked away even from herself. She would never be able to look at him again, to face him, knowing he had seen the attack Savon had made on her body. He

would know her every thought. The humiliation and
fear. The degradation. Even worse, he would know her
secret, innermost thoughts, the ones she withheld even
from herself. A low moan escaped, and she felt the vampire tighten his hold. This she could not do. Not for any
of them, not even her beloved Desari. She could not
allow herself or Barack to read those secret desires and
needs.

Barack struck without warning, going from passive
restraint to swift and immediate action. His mind thrust
itself into hers, taking possession of her as surely as if
he had claimed her body for his own. Syndil found she
could not resist him, whether because she was just too
drained by the energy she had expended healing the
earth or because she was helpless before the determination, the single-mindedness of Barack. Perhaps all
along he had been far more powerful than she had imagined. Whatever the reason, he meant exactly what he had
threatened. He would follow her wherever she went and
fight to the death to return her to their family unit. He
would never give her up to the evil one. Syndil finally
took the least line of resistance and threw her strength
in with his.

Desari fed the two of them with her own power and
voice, applying steady pressure against the hold the
vampire had on Syndil. She could feel the undead's fingers slipping from around her own throat. He could not
sustain his energy in so many different directions. If he
was to fight to retain Syndil within his trap, he had to
release Desari. As the stranglehold lessened, Desari's
voice continued to pour out in a stream of beauty and
triumph, a songbird free to roam the skies, to aid all
within range of her voice.

Darius heard the silvery notes, joyous, a celebration
of life. Around him, in the nearby fields and streams, he

caught the reaction of the wildlife to her voice. It swelled into the wind and was carried easily across the blackened ruins of the forest. It held the ghouls silent as they began their charge. They thought him helpless, caught in the snare of their master's trap, the binding spell making him their prisoner, yet Desari's voice prevented such a thing. Her notes, resounding in his head, kept him safe as nothing else could.

His sister. She had always filled him with such awe. So beautiful from the inside out. Her womanly magic, a force for good, was far more powerful than what he wielded. Because he no longer was able to feel, he held fast to his memories of her. In this battle he relied on her voice. She would not fail to hold Syndil. Her voice could do no other than torment the vampire, weakening him further.

Darius felt the earth tremble, knew the struggle the undead was having with Barack, Syndil, and Desari. He knew the precise moment the monster allowed Syndil to slip through his fingers. Darius felt the hesitation in power, the shift. As the ghouls launched their combined attack, the vampire burst through the earth's soil in an all-out assault against Julian.

Darius waited until the last possible moment, holding himself still, arms outstretched, a seeming sacrifice to the evil one. His face was turned up to the heavens, the darkened clouds and arcing lighting, the wind whipping his jet-black hair around him. He slowly lowered his head so that his merciless eyes encompassed the rushing ghouls. Fiery flames seemed to dance in the depths of his gaze. He looked invincible, a phantom of the night, the prince of darkness, yet his outstretched hands were turned palms up toward the heavens in supplication.

The very heavens seemed to answer his silent prayer, opening the gates so that a flood of water poured down as if a dam had broken. Through the sheets of rain ran bolts of electricity that never seemed to seek the ground. Thunder crashed and rocked the ground, deadly as any earthquake. Seams burst open in the earth, ragged tears that allowed the water to rush along like ever-swelling rivers. The ghouls had reached the very epicenter of their master's trap, their stick arms reaching to gore Darius with so many knives, yet Darius was already gone from the center of their ghastly circle. Only the sheets of water were there to pour over the wailing creatures.

Steam rose from the thin, robed figures, hissing as it released the caricatures from their bondage. Black smoke melded with the white steam, the putrid mixture rising as vapor and dissipating. Darius didn't wait to see the results of his handiwork; he was already rocketing toward the two beasts in battle, one darkly evil, one a golden warrior, slashing at one another in the sky.

The vampire, raging at the destruction of his plan, ripped at Julian's chest with razor-sharp talons, hissing hideously, spewing tainted saliva along with his wrath. He screamed his disappointment as Julian somehow miraculously twisted away from his attack, the daggerlike claws missing by a millimeter. Julian was already maneuvering around for his strike. A raging vampire was a careless one. Julian shut out all thought, all reason, all emotion. His attack was swift and brutal, scoring long furrows across the unprotected belly so that blood began to run freely in four streams. Julian moved out of the line of assault, circling.

Darius exploded into the battle, his retaliation vicious and without mercy or fear. He drove in straight for the kill. His challenge was clear. The undead could elect to stand and fight, but either way, Julian or Darius would destroy him. It was kill or be killed. If Julian and Darius were inflicted with mortal wounds, so be it. The vampire would die with them. There were no half measures in either hunter, no pity or mercy. This ancient menace had dared to challenge them. He would be destroyed.

The vampire had not lived as many centuries as he had by tempting certain death. He might be victorious against one experienced hunter, but not both. He had lost his advantage. He dissolved as quickly as he was able, streaking away through the rain-washed sky, using the storm to hide the traces of his passing.

Julian immediately mind-merged with Desari to ensure she was fine. Even as he assured himself that she had come to no harm, he was trailing the vampire, using the droplets of blood to stay on the trail. The storm was diluting the poisonous brew, but Julian would know that scent anywhere. The stench was in his own blood, his soul, in the dark shadowing that had robbed him of his twin, his family and people. The undead had long tormented him, but now had committed an unpardonable sin, had attempted to harm his lifemate. As far as Julian was concerned, there was no other choice but to destroy him. His entire life's training had been for this moment.

Darius, too, was moving so quickly through the sky that he was a mere blur. He had no intention of allowing this vampire to go free. This evil one had challenged his ability to guard his family, and he was more than willing to pick up the gauntlet. The blood was almost impossible to trace now, so Darius allowed the fury of the storm to wane. The stick figures below were annihilated, the rain dissipating the dark shadows to vapor. Syndil's healing art did the rest, prevailing against what the undead had wrought against nature and the earth. Syndil called forth the energy of the universe and the being they revered as the father of all life. Already new life was struggling to take hold, small buds pushing through the soil, seeking the moisture of the storm.

Darius had the foul stench of the monster in his nostrils and was prepared to follow him all the way back to his lair.

Back off, Darius. This is no amateur. Do not follow him to his lair. He will be far stronger there.

Darius did not acknowledge Julian's softly spoken advice. He streaked through the sky after the fading trail of droplets. Julian swore beneath his breath in several languages, knowing full well that Darius could hear him. He had no choice but to allow the family leader to accompany him. The vampire might flee to avoid this confrontation, but if cornered, he would be extremely dangerous. Julian knew this vampire more intimately than most, knew him to be an ancient of great power. And ancients were never easy to destroy.

Julian? Desari's musical voice flowed into his mind to warm him. *Where are you going? I feel your worry.*

That arrogant brother of yours is more stubborn than anyone I have ever met, and that includes Gregori. He insists on chasing the undead back to its lair.

Darius is a tremendous fighter. There was a wealth of confidence in Desari's voice. *He would never leave a vampire alive that has shown itself to him. How could he do other?*

He could lure it out into the open, away from its lair, on the next rising. It is wounded, my love, and angry that it was thwarted in its attempt to acquire Syndil. It knows me and is afraid. Fear in these creatures only increases their cunning. Now it is returning to its place of safety. A vampire's lair is one of the most dangerous places on earth. I have cautioned Darius, but I cannot leave him alone to battle when I know he is moving into a trap.

Julian was winging his way through the air fast, hard on the tail feathers of Darius. The rain had slowed to a steady drizzle, but the air felt heavy and thick. Julian shook his head at the foolishness of what they were doing. Darius believed in the straightforward approach. At the same time, he was a lethal adversary, one fully committed to destroying an enemy even if it meant his own life. Julian understood, but through long experience he had learned to pick his battles. Darius had to attack anything threatening those under his protection, but some part of him was urging him to fight to the death, wanting to take the vampire with him to eternal rest.

The idea of losing Darius left Desari raw with fear. And Julian found he could not bear Desari's fear. He felt the presence of evil, the thick air surrounding them making it difficult to think. It was a common trick used by the undead to buy time. Julian simply directed his body on his instincts, trusting himself and his own strength and power.

Darius had often come up against the same snare, the effort to slow them down. He charged forward in a direct flight to catch up to their enemy.

The attack came without warning from behind both of them, two experienced hunters unprepared for the hurtling spear that zeroed in on the shadow in Julian like a heat-seeking missile. Neither knew whether it was Desari's cry of fear as she launched herself skyward or their own instincts, but as Julian turned to face whatever was threatening him from behind, Darius, flying slightly above and ahead, plummeted to place his body between his sister's lifemate and the incoming spear.

The streamlined weapon the vampire had fashioned was well made and deadly. It sliced through flesh and bone, catching Darius's body, imprisoned within the bird, just below the heart.

Dayan! Without conscious thought, Julian took over the leadership, calling the other Carpathian to their aid, then racing to catch Darius's body as it fell from the sky, at the same time searching around him for the vampire who had suddenly turned the tables and was now in the far better position to escape or attack. *Desari, breathe for him, now. Take a breath. I need you calm. Breathe for him, and keep him alive. The spear sliced his heart, and he had no choice but to cease breathing on his own. Merge with him and bind him to us.* Julian gave the order as a healer. He had learned much of the ancient art by watching Gregori, the Dark One, Darius and Desari's brother and blood kin, their people's healer.

Dayan reached them, cradling Darius in midflight, leaving Julian free to guard them as they raced toward their own safe haven, a mountain with pools of heat and fire within it. Julian's breath came out in a long, slow hiss. He could not continue to track his archenemy while Darius was in such need. Darius had saved his life and Desari's. Julian's sense of honor would never allow him to do other than what was right. The others did not have his powers of healing, although their closeness would help enormously.

Julian followed the others, guarding them from behind. His mind was already merged with Desari's so that he could better follow the patterns inside Darius's mind, so that he could examine the mortal wound even in flight. Darius had a strong constitution, a will of solid steel. Ultimately he would choose life or death for himself. No one would hold him to earth if he decided to go to eternal rest. It only strengthened Julian's own belief that Darius was blood brother to Gregori, the Dark One, the greatest hunter and healer of their time.

Barack and Syndil had already opened the mountain to make entry easier to the narrow passageway leading deep within the earth. Barack moved ahead of the group as their scout, his senses flaring out for every scrap of information he could ferret out. He looked for traces of the undead, blank spaces, strange smells, anything that might signal the presence of an enemy. Together he and Syndil worked to prepare a healing room. They found the richest soil. Syndil went down on her knees to add to the richness, chanting softly while Barack circled the cave, placing herbs and candles in a pattern along the wall.

Dayan placed Darius's body into the bed of soil so carefully prepared, and stepped back to give Julian room. Desari sank onto the edge of the sunken earthen bed, her entire attention centered on her brother. He was no more than a spirit while his body lay lifeless under her stroking hand. Tears were running unchecked down her face. She was well aware of Darius's strong will. If he chose to stay with them, it would certainly be his choice alone. She could not make him do anything he didn't want to do.

He will stay with us. Julian's calm voice was in her mind. Strong. Gentle. Certain. *Darius knows that all of you need him. He will not leave you alone until he is certain all of you will be safe without him.* Julian said it firmly, knowing Darius's spirit could easily read Desari's mind and hear his words. Desari needed reassurance badly.

Julian touched her shoulder, brushed her hair tenderly. Without looking at the others, he took a deep breath and released it, concentrating on losing himself, becoming pure energy, a white healing light that floated out of his strong body and into the body lying so still before him.

The wound was a terrible thing. The spear had entered just below the heart, tearing through sinew and tissue, arteries and veins. The tip had caught Darius's strong heart, slicing a wicked cut before driving on through almost to his back. This spear had been meant for Julian.

Most likely it would have killed him. And Desari would have died, too.

I owe you a tremendous debt, he murmured softly in his mind even as he began the difficult work of healing Darius from the inside out. Darius had managed to shut down his systems immediately, his spirit merged with Desari's that he might aid them if necessary. Julian could read the intentions of the leader as surely as if they were his own. Darius would not leave his family unprotected until he was certain Julian could take his place.

And then Julian was nothing but light and energy, pure white heat to be used for healing. He closed the terrible wounds in the artery that were draining the precious fluid of life from Darius. The heart required tremendous concentration. The gash was deep, and Julian could make no mistakes. He became aware, after a time, that the sound of chanting was surrounding them. The words were ancient and soothing to him, filling him with a quiet confidence for the work he had to do. This was the most extensive repair on anyone he had attempted, and the familiar words in Desari's beautiful voice gave him needed peace. She was there with him every step of the way, holding Darius to her, lending her strength to Julian even as her voice surrounded them with the healing words of the ancients. He was aware of the others joining in the melodious chant, lending their voices to the healing process.

Becoming pure energy tired any healer quickly. It was a difficult process to put one's body aside thusly. At the end Julian felt so drained that he slipped from Darius's body and found himself staggering, his enormous strength gone. He sank down onto the soft earth and allowed his head to fall forward so that his long hair hid the deep lines of strain in his face.

Desari stroked a long caress through the tangle of golden hair, her heart beating a steady rhythm to support her lifemate. Julian was so like her brother. He simply, masterfully, took control of a situation and did what had to be done. The two were very similar in character. She felt the stirring in her mind. Not the path she shared with Julian, but rather the familiar one she had known for so many centuries. Darius would live.

Dayan had moved into a position where he could watch the procedure closely. "He is going to live?" The question was addressed to Julian rather than Desari, a tentative olive branch from the second in command.

Julian glanced up at him, fatigue etching harsh lines in his features. "Darius will not leave this world until he is ready to do so. Then there will be no one who can stop him. He will live, but he needs blood and rest. All of us must feed well that we can supply him. He will need to be safeguarded at all times. The vampire is aware Darius is injured and thinks him vulnerable now. He will actively seek his resting place in hopes of an easy kill."

Beside him Desari stirred in protest, her slender body suddenly pressing itself against Julian's as if for protection. Julian responded immediately, his arm drawing her to him, shielding her from the world. "There will be no easy kill, Desari. Darius, even in his present state, is dangerous. His mind alone holds enough power for the kill. Do not fear for him. In any case, we will provide safeguards to protect him should the vampire get past any of us."

"He will come after *you*." Syndil spoke the words softly, her voice so beautiful it seemed to reach out and touch Julian's soul. "He hates you all, every male, and intends to use me to destroy you." She raised her eyes to Julian. "But he hates you most of all. He thought to

341

control you, and he cannot. I felt his rage."

Julian's glittering eyes examined the woman standing with her head bowed a little distance from the others. She was very pale, her eyes enormous. She looked fragile and vulnerable, as if she might break should the wind blow too strongly. He felt Desari twine her fingers through his as if to prevent him from speaking. Barack stirred, a restless, fierce movement the women misinterpreted as aggression. Julian read it as fiercely protective. Barack saw himself as a shield between Syndil's vulnerability and all others who might hurt her inadvertently or, worse, on purpose.

"He cannot use you against us, Syndil. You are our beloved sister and under our protection, just as the earth is under yours. Your power is too strong for this evil creature to corrupt." When he spoke, Julian chose each word carefully, adding a subtle "push" with his velvet voice. "He wishes you to believe you draw evil to you, but it is only one of his illusions. The undead have many traps they use in the hopes of ensnaring one of us. I have spent centuries hunting these creatures, and I have seen such traps targeted for specific individuals. You cannot be touched by his taint. It is impossible, as you are too pure. I know this through my mind merge with Desari. Every one of us knows this."

Syndil's long lashes swept her cheeks. "I do not know this."

Barack stirred again, a low growl rumbling within his throat. At once, Syndil's slender frame began to shapeshift, wavering somewhere between that of a human female and a female leopard.

Desari, you must tell Barack to give her more space. Julian knew better than to challenge the adult male. Darius might do so, but Julian doubted it. Sometimes Carpathian males allowed their protective natures to

overcome their good sense. Barack was not likely to
back off just because an older, stronger, more dominant
male told him to. Desari had a much better chance of
getting Barack to back off with her soft, winning way
and her magical voice. Julian didn't blame the man; Barack felt fiercely protective of Syndil and was still in a
dangerously combative state. Once the demon within
was aroused, it was difficult to overcome the savage,
predatory instincts of their kind.

Desari's answer was so perfect, it was all Julian could
do not to clasp her to him. She didn't so much as glance
at Julian or in any way act as though they had communicated. "Syndil." She whispered the woman's name
softly, lovingly, so that the leopard shimmered between
human form and animal. "Do not leave me as yet. I am
in sore need of your comfort." Desari projected just the
right note of weariness into her voice, and even Julian
was a believer.

How could she not be tired after her tremendous or-
deal? Of course she was. He could feel it in her now as
her body swayed slightly against his. Her large eyes
touched Barack's stone-hard features. *I know she wishes
to flee, Barack, but if you would, please step aside and
allow her to come to me. I have a great need to be with
my sister.*

You have the golden one to aid you, Desari. Barack's
words were harsh, but even as he sent the message winging through the air between them, he moved away from
Syndil, allowing her a clear path to Desari.

It was Desari who moved, rather than Syndil, covering
the distance between them in a few unhurried steps. As
they came together, their arms surrounding one another,
they simply disappeared from the men's sight.

Barack swore aloud and turned burning eyes on Julian. "There is the matter of the undead before us, and we have not fed, nor have our women."

Julian shrugged with his casual strength coming easily, fluidly to his feet as if he was as fresh as at first rising. "Then we must see to their needs," he responded quietly, sidestepping the bristling Carpathian.

Barack shoved a hand through his long hair, furious for no reason at all. He had never felt so edgy, so on the verge of violence before. He wanted to make the kill. To have such a foul, unclean creature as the undead come so close to capturing one of their family was unthinkable. There were four males to guard the women, yet the trap had been sprung, and Syndil once more had been the victim of an attack. It made him feel like clawing and raking the heavens above. It made him feel a failure. He had promised himself it would never happen to her again, yet that filthy abomination had managed to touch her mind, made her doubt herself, made her relive Savon's brutal attack and believe she was in some way to blame.

"Julian." Dayan was studying the Carpathian with knowing eyes. "It takes a tremendous amount of energy to heal a wound such as this one. Go with Barack and feed heavily, that the two of you can provide for our family. I will guard those here. Do not fear the task is too great. I may choose to follow my brother, but I am capable of fighting should there be need."

Julian waved a hand to close the ground over Darius, weaving intricate safeguards to ensure the leader's rest wasn't disturbed while he was gone. He nodded to Dayan, already rising to make his way from the mountain. If he didn't hunt prey soon, he would be sending his lifemate out to do it for him.

Soft laughter immediately enveloped him. *I heard that thought.*

I was certain you would, beautiful one. I will return immediately. Do not allow Syndil to disappear on us. Right now she is in more danger from herself than from any vampire.

Desari sighed softly, her breath whispering along the inside of his mind. *It is true, Julian. She feels as if she is responsible for placing all of us in danger. I am trying, but . . .* The thought trailed off, and Julian felt Desari's sorrow.

Piccola, do not worry so. We will not allow anything to happen to your family. A note of amusement crept in. *I cannot wait for your arrogant brother to rise. I will taunt him repeatedly over how I had to repair the damage to his family unit.*

I am sure you will.

Julian burst into the dawn air, the light striking cruelly at his eyes. A part of him was locked to Darius. He had been inside the man, a part of him, just as Darius had done for him. They were linked strongly to one another. And Julian was not altogether certain he had as much faith and trust in the other males of the family as Darius seemed to show. Either of them could be close to turning, and masking it. Leaving Darius so vulnerable, lying as one dead, where a trusted friend could so easily slay him, kept Julian locked to his lifemate's brother. Desari had given him what he had lost centuries earlier; she had given him a family. He would do all he could to protect it.

The wind brought the scent of prey to him, and he altered his course with ease. He streaked across the sky, uncaring whether or not Barack was following. He intended to make certain he was gone only a short time.

I thought you said Darius was still dangerous, even as he lies sleeping.

Julian sighed. He should have known Desari would

so easily read his thoughts, just as he could always touch hers. *It is so*, cara, *he is very dangerous. You can feel his power radiate from him. But I am not certain he would be expecting the attack to come from one of his own.*

There is no one who could surprise Darius ever again. Except perhaps . . .

Julian could feel Desari pause and give consideration to her statement. Then the little minx had a flashing thought, hastily censored. She was up to something, no doubt about it. Julian didn't mind—as long as her brother, not he, was the intended recipient of her scheming.

Chapter Seventeen

The call to awaken came not from within himself but
from outside. At the command, his heart took one beat,
and his lungs drew in air. There was pain with his first
breath, and Darius quickly assessed the damage to his
body without moving a muscle or flickering an eyelid,
without allowing anything else to intrude while he took
inventory. A thick wrist was pressed to his mouth, and
he felt, more than heard, the soft command to replenish
what he had lost. He knew immediately who was do-
nating so generously to him. The blood was ancient and
powerful, potent as it soaked into his starving cells,
carrying with it the energy and strength of a true ancient.

Darius slowly opened his eyes and stared up at the
blond stranger who was his sister's mate. Darius savored
the effects of the fresh blood pouring into his body,
strong, rich, ancient blood, and already he could feel the
healing powers working within him. He studied Julian
as he fed from the man's wrist. Julian was powerful and

enormously strong, equally confident. It showed in the way he carried himself, in the straight stare of his strange amber eyes and the set of his shoulders. It showed in the fluid way he moved and the quick decisions he made without hesitation. His leadership qualities were evident when he carefully sidestepped possible challenges by the other males, never allowing his own ego to get in the way. Julian knew he was infinitely capable; he had nothing to prove to anyone, or to himself. Right now he was wearing that sardonic expression Darius was familiar with, as if he were laughing inwardly, amused at life and those around him. As if he had some secret knowledge, of which none of them were aware. Darius decided he probably did. Aside from the knowledge already imprinted on them before birth, Julian had the advantage of learning from ancients. He also knew things about their own kind that Darius's family did not.

Very carefully Darius closed the wound, even in his weakness ensuring he left no telltale mark. He made no attempt to move. His heart was not yet completely healed. He knew what it had cost Julian in time and energy to repair such a near-mortal injury, and he had no intention of tearing the knitting gash before complete healing could take place.

"I am not yet healed, Julian," he said in his mild, expressionless tone.

Julian's mouth curved into a smirk. "No? Do you think you should heal so quickly, then? I put you in the ground only one scant hour ago. I awakened you merely to supply you with blood. Even you require more than one hour. And no, I have not yet tracked the vampire to his lair, but I will on the next rising. Be assured of that."

Darius's black eyes fastened on Julian's gold ones. "I have no doubt that you will find the one you seek. I know the kind of man you are." He was already tired, and his voice was fading, his thick lashes drifting down to cover the relentless, merciless, obsidian eyes. Even with the blood of such a powerful man, his body was so torn, the wound so savage, he was exhausted with just a small amount of effort.

"You did not want to stay any longer in this world." Julian crouched down beside the leader so that he no longer towered above him. "It was in your mind to seek eternal rest. You cannot hide that from me any more than I could hide what I am from you. What made you stay when you felt yourself so close to turning? I can feel your fight, every waking moment; your life is endless darkness. What made you stay when you wanted, needed eternal rest?"

"You did." The reply was simple, brief, yet Julian could read the truth in those two words. "I read some of your memories. I knew of your intention to seek eternal rest before you discovered what you call your lifemate, my sister. I do not know much more, only that she made it worth every moment of your struggle with the darkness devouring us. You have roamed the world and were certain you would never feel again, but you do feel. You laugh. There is a real joy in you that you cannot hide. I had no idea there was hope. I thought that for our males, once we lived a certain length of time, there would be only two choices. Eternal rest or the loss of our souls. Now that I have found this information, I can do no other than try to lead the way for Dayan and Barack. I will hold out as long as I am able to, until I know the crouching beast is close to overcoming my strength, and then I will seek eternal rest. If I can once again feel before I cross over, then it will be worth all the long, dark days." Darius's voice was very soft, a mere thread of sound, as if he could not find the strength to speak more strongly. "I would like to feel the love I have for my sister and my family, not simply remember that there once was such a feeling."

It made no difference to Julian that Darius's voice was fading. Like all Carpathians, he had incredible hearing and could turn the volume up at will.

"In any case," Darius continued, his long lashes hiding the dark depths of his eyes, "I will wait until there is no hope at all for me, so that Dayan will realize he must also have hope until there is proof otherwise. He grows weary of this earth and has spoken often of resting. And he will not follow you so easily."

"My charming personality, no doubt," Julian agreed.

"Dayan is a quiet soul. Not dark of nature like me or Savon. Dayan has always chosen the right paths instinctively. Yet as the darkness grows within him, the heaviness in his heart expands. Hidden within him is an explosive predator, all the more dangerous because he is so opposite to the man. Dayan struggles to understand that side of his nature while we simply accept it." He was deliberately imparting knowledge of his family to his sister's lifemate.

Darius's voice was so low now, Julian was unsure whether he was really speaking aloud or mind to mind. "You grow weak, Darius. Sleep. We can talk of such things when you are healed." Deliberately, Julian allowed his voice to drop an octave, to take on the low, hypnotic tone of his kind. Soothing, peaceful, healing. An underlying command, very subtle but nevertheless powerful.

Darius smiled, a mere flash of strong white teeth. He heard that "push" in Julian's voice and recognized it for what it was. Even in his weakened state, he would ordinarily have resisted such a mind touch, but Julian was going to do as he wished anyway. He would hunt the undead without Darius, and argument with him would be futile. And tiring. Darius planned to sleep for a long while. "I go under, golden one, but do not think you managed to make me overlook the fact that I must thank you for my continued existence."

"Or curse me." Julian stepped away from the black, rich soil, then watched as the breath ceased and the heart quit beating in Darius's chest. He waved a hand so the soil would fill in around and over the body, providing the healing balm to mend the terrible wounds. His hands wove the patterns of strong safeguards to ensure Darius would not be disturbed. He stood for a long moment, savoring the unexpected warmth that came with belonging to something. Once he hunted and destroyed his ancient enemy and knew all was safe, he would seek out his own twin brother. He ached to see Aidan again, to meet his lifemate and to present Desari to him. Though he dreaded having to admit the truth, that he had been marked by a vampire as a boy, he now longed for what interaction with others could bring into one's life. He wanted to be part of a family once again.

"You are already part of a family," Desari reminded him, her body brushing his, her arms circling his waist from behind. She had materialized out of nowhere, her presence filling the healing chamber.

She was there. Completing him. His air. His heart. The part of his soul that really lived and loved and mattered. Without conscious thought he sent up a quick prayer of thanks that he had been granted such a priceless treasure when he felt so undeserving of her.

Julian loved the way she smelled. He inhaled, and her scent washed over him, clean and sexy. "This mess? With all these males?" Julian allowed a low, rumbling growl to escape. "This is no family. This is a man's nightmare."

Desari deliberately moved against him, her body soft

and pliant with invitation. "Is that what you think?"

"What I think is"—Julian circled her slender throat with his large hand in mock threat—"you are deliberately tempting me when I have important, pressing business to attend to."

Her slender arms instantly circled his neck so that she could press her body against his hard frame. "I am a superstar, lifemate, yet you wish to leave me alone at every opportunity. There are men everywhere who would be happy to take your place by my side."

He bent his head, his teeth scraping a provocative rhythm over her pulse. Desari went liquid, boneless, her stomach clenching in anticipation. "No, they would not be happy to take my place at your side, *cara mia*, because I would promptly end their lives in a most unhappy way."

"You are such a caveman, Julian. You look tall and elegant and princely, yet you have not matured beyond the cave." Desari allowed her tongue a brief inspection of the taste of his skin. She closed her eyes to savor the moment.

"I have no intention of rising above caveman mentality," he growled in her ear, his breath teasing tendrils of hair and sending little flames dancing through her bloodstream. "There are so many benefits for the caveman."

"You like playing the part of the dominant male, no doubt," she whispered, her voice so husky with need that his body tightened in urgent, painful response. Her mouth moved over his throat, her hands seeking skin beneath his shirt. "I have a need of you, lifemate, and you are deliberately ignoring your sworn duties to me."

"Little minx." Julian curved his arm around Desari's shoulders and began walking from the chamber into the maze of tunnels carved from molten lava. They were numerous and deep, leading throughout the large mountain, deep within the earth. It was hot and humid, steaming, so that the heat soaked through their clothing as they walked together. Little beads of sweat formed and ran over their skin, following intriguing paths.

Desari's white silk blouse clung to her so that her breasts were dark, enticing shadows, her nipples even darker. Her long hair became damp and heavy as they descended deeper within the earth, and she stopped to twist it and knot it at the back of her neck.

Julian smiled faintly. "How do women do that?" His eyes were on her body, the way her breasts lifted in innocent seduction when she raised her arms to attend to her hair.

Desari turned her head to look at him. "Do what?"

"That thing with your hair." Julian leaned down to taste a small bead of sweat running down the back of her neck. He felt her shiver, felt the answering shiver deep within his own body. His hand slid under the edge of her silken blouse to find hot satin skin, his long fingers caressing each rib. "How do women tie up their hair without looking at it?" His voice was raw and edgy, reflecting the way his body was reacting to hers.

"Why does it feel like forever since you touched me like this?" she whispered. "It is hot, Julian."

"It is getting that way," he agreed. A thought took his shirt from his body so that his bare skin gleamed like bronze. In the blackness of the tunnels, to them it was as if it were daylight. The walls gleamed with yellow sulfur, and all around them was the beauty of nature, shimmering and glittering beneath the earth, ever moving, ever changing, the minerals that enriched the soil and made it fertile and healing, the very things that built the land masses themselves. Because their body temperature could regulate itself, enabling them to be inside the

353

earth, a part of its wonders, they saw it all happening where most humans never could.

Desari felt the intense heat, not from the earth but from deep within her own body, from Julian's fingers radiating just under her bare breast, along her side, lingering, caressing, bringing her body to life.

Julian stopped abruptly, his palm cupping the back of her neck, bringing her to a halt as his mouth fastened on hers. Molten heat raged between them. The taste of them, the moist heat of their mouths mingled. His fingers twined themselves in the thick ebony hair she had so carelessly secured, holding her to him so that he could explore her mouth with languid, lazy seduction and fierce, burning hunger. It was like creating a firestorm. The more they shared, the hotter the flames.

Julian pulled away first, trailing kisses down her throat to the valley between her breasts. Her breasts thrust so invitingly through the silk, his mouth simply found her nipple through the material. The sexual jolt slammed into her body hard enough that he experienced it also, and he answered by dragging her closer, his mouth drawing her breast into its velvet fire, his tongue stroking, his teeth scraping gently.

"There is something so beautiful about you, Desari," he whispered against her. "Something I could never resist even if I wanted to." His hand slipped across her stomach to her jeans. "Sometimes I think if I do not take you fast enough, you will disappear, and I will wake up and all this will have been a wild dream." He confessed it against her breast, his breath hot on her aching flesh. Already his hand had dealt with the fastenings of her jeans and pushed impatiently at the material so he could find the damp heat between her legs. She was always so ready for him, every bit as wild with hunger as he was.

He slipped two fingers into her, his own body reacting as her muscles clenched around him.

He closed his eyes and savored the way her body bathed his fingers in welcoming hot dampness. He felt there was no way to express the depth of his feelings for her, no way to find words for the intensity of his love and admiration for her, for his hunger and need for her. He could worship her with his body yet never find the right way in all eternity to say that same thing.

Her body was so hot and tight and welcoming. A solace, a comfort, a dazzling place of heat and ecstasy created for him exclusively. His mouth found her breast once more through the silken fibers, felt her body respond with another rush of liquid heat. She made a soft sound, moved her hips against his hand, arched her body more fully into his. She was restless with hunger and need, maybe even more so than he.

Julian loved the way it made him feel, to know that she wanted him, needed him with the same savage intensity he felt for her. He allowed himself the freedom of trailing kisses down her throat, of tearing the silken blouse from her glistening body. "You are so beautiful," he murmured again, awed that she was such perfection. His hands traced her skin, the shape of her, from her shoulders to her waist. It was easy enough to dispense with her clothes, and he did so, wanting to see every inch of her just because he could, because she belonged with him.

When he touched her again, his hand was trembling. "What you do to me, *cara*, should never be done to a male."

"Really?" She asked it with a hint of laughter, but her voice was husky with love for him. She read his thoughts as easily as he read hers. She knew the way he felt about her, words or no words. "Do you think it is too much to ask for a bed?"

His laughter bathed her throat in warmth. "You want a bed? You do not ask for much, do you, *cara mia*?"

"I thought we could try to make it to the lower caves before we go crazy here." She linked her hands behind his neck.

Julian responded immediately, swinging her into his strong arms. He moved with the preternatural speed of their race, taking her through the network of passages, following the map in her mind. He sent his command ahead, preparing the chamber for their arrival, lit candles throwing dancing shadows on the shimmering walls, rose petals on the ground leading to the large bed in the center of the room.

Julian lowered her gently to the sheets, blanketing her body with his own. He didn't want to be separated from her, not even by an inch. They had little time before they would have to seek the shelter of the earth, and he intended to rise before the vampire could escape.

Desari caught his face between her hands and held him so she could look into his eyes. "The way you love me, Julian, so beautifully, so much, that is the way I love you. You are everything to me. If only we have the next few moments together, everything that came before was worth the time we have had."

He could drown in her eyes. They were deep, fathomless, a siren's lure. Bedroom eyes. He had heard the term but had no idea of its true meaning until that moment. "I do love you, Desari. You know it is so much more than mere physical desire."

"Of course I know. I am of ancient blood, my love. Even one such as you would have a difficult time hiding the truth from me." She raised her head to reach his perfect mouth with her own.

They melded together, a living flame, coming together as if time and space ceased to exist. Everything fell away until there was just Desari and Julian locked in their own world, where violence and unhappiness could not touch them, would never touch them.

His hands moved over the satin of her skin, seeking every inch of her. The feel of her beneath the rough palm of his hands was incredibly sexy, adding to the fire spreading through their bodies. He savored her softness. She was exquisite, every hollow, every swell. He loved the triangle of dark curls guarding her damp, steamy treasure. His hand slid lower, caressed, lingered, once more found the heat inside her.

Desari moaned softly, finding his back with her hands. She needed something strong and solid to hang on to while her body rippled and danced with pleasure. She nuzzled the warmth of his throat, tasted his skin, caught a bead of sweat running over his chest with the tip of her tongue. She heard his heart, the strong beat, the rhythm that matched her own, that belonged to her. His fingers were buried within her, strong and sure, bringing ripples of pleasure to her so that her breath was coming in small gasps and she writhed against his hand, seeking relief.

Julian moved then, his knee parting her thighs to give him access. For just a moment as he lifted himself above her, he stared down into her dark, beautiful eyes. It was impossible to believe, even now, with her lying, waiting, beneath him, her body crying out for his, that she truly belonged to him. He caught her hips firmly in his hands and thrust deeply, burying himself completely in her tight, hot sheath. He heard the breath slam from his lungs at the intensity of completeness, her body tight and hot around his. He began to move then, long, hard, sure strokes, his hips surging forward, over and over, each time trying to bury himself deeper. She was surrounding him with heat and fire, a velvet sheath that locked him to her, that allowed them to become one, as they were meant to be.

Desari was moving with him, matching him stroke for stroke, her body clenching his, releasing, gripping again, until he wanted, even needed, to cry out with ecstasy, but his lungs couldn't get enough air to do so. He bent his head toward the temptation of her breasts. His incisors exploded into his mouth. Without warning, he sank them deep, so that Desari felt the white-hot pain and pleasure mingle together and flow from her to Julian and back again.

It was impossible to tell who was feeling what. They were locked together, body and mind, heart and soul, even their blood flowing together. He felt her body tighten around him; she was gasping, her nails in his back. "Julian." She whispered his name, or maybe it was in his mind. He felt her mind-shattering explosion as her muscles spiraled around him in waves like an earthquake. It was far too much to expect self-control as Julian's own body tightened to the point of pain. And then he was exploding outward, upward, convulsing with sheer pleasure.

He could not maintain the intimacy of feeding while his lungs were raging for air and his body was burning itself up. Julian held her to him, his arms possessive as they curved around her slender body. Very gently he stroked his tongue across the pinpricks over her breast. She was clinging to him as if he were her anchor in the center of a storm. It made him feel amazingly powerful.

Desari reached up to trace his lips. "You have a perfect mouth, Julian. An amazingly perfect mouth."

He arched an eyebrow at her. "Just my mouth is amazing?"

"You are such a man." Her eyes laughed at him. "You need constant reassurance that you are magnificent."

He nodded. "Magnificent. I like that. I could live with magnificent. Good choice of words, lifemate."

She circled his neck with her arms. "Arrogant male. Darius is right, you know. You are incredibly arrogant."

"But deservedly so," he pointed out. He bent his head once more to find her mouth with his. *She* had the perfect mouth. And she tasted delicious. There was something about the way she clung to him that turned his heart over every time. Desari shared herself with him without inhibition, without reservation. She gave herself completely into his keeping when they were making love.

Carefully, he eased his body out of hers and rolled slightly so that his weight was off of her. Her long lashes fanned her high cheekbones, making her more exotic-looking than ever. She snuggled closer to him, enjoying their time alone together and the silly conversations they always seemed to have.

"You grow sleepy, *cara mia*," Julian whispered, leaning down to kiss her forehead. "We should go to your brother's chamber. I will check him once more before we go to ground."

Desari refused to open her eyes. She made a soft purring sound, completely contented to lie in his arms. "Not yet, Julian," she protested softly. "I do not want to leave this place for a little while longer."

"I can feel how tired you are, my love. I can do no other than—"

"Do not say it!" Desari thumped his chest. "Just lie there and hold me. That is what I want. Men are such difficult creatures, Julian. I am beginning to realize this."

He rubbed his chin on the top of her head, her hair

catching in the shadow along his jaw. "Men are not difficult. They are logical and methodical."

She laughed softly. "You wish it were so. I must tell you, although I am taking a huge chance that you might become impossible to live with, that you are an extraordinary lover."

"Keep talking, lifemate. I am listening," he responded with a deep satisfaction. "Magnificent was only a starting place. Extraordinary lover is the perfect description. I see that now."

Her soft laughter washed over him, as gentle as a breeze. Touching him. Just like that. She could touch him with her breath. Julian wrapped his arms around her tightly and buried his face in her ebony hair. "Why is it you always smell so good?"

"Would you want me to smell like a cavewoman?"

"I do not know, *cara*. I do not know what a cavewoman smells like."

She opened her eyes at that, her long lashes fluttering in the sexy, flirty little way she had. "You'd better not want me smelling like any other, Julian, or you will find out what a real ancient woman can do when she is enraged."

"You do not know what rage is, my love." He rubbed his face in her hair once more before lifting his head. "There is no rage in you—nothing that can be called upon to save your life should there be need."

Desari immediately sat up, coming to her knees to face him, her long hair spilling around her, framing her slender body. "Where did that come from? Why would you worry about such a thing at this moment?"

He is still out there. My sworn enemy, the one who resides in me. And whoever sent the human assassins after you is still out there, and you are still insisting on singing in front of crowds. He tried to censor the thought

360

before she could read it, before it actually was in his mind, but it was too late. She was a shadow within him, just as he remained locked to her mind.

Desari smiled, her eyes loving and warm. "There is no need for this constant fear you are developing. I have survived centuries and will survive many more. I plan on having a family of my own someday, with my handsome lifemate. No one is going to take my future from me. I may not have what it takes to fight those who threaten us, but I am highly intelligent and have many gifts of my own to ensure my safety. And I can take care of you, too, should there be need. We are partners: I will lean on your strengths often, as I hope you will lean on mine."

"I have more faith in you than you can know," Julian replied honestly. "I just never had anything to lose before." He rubbed the bridge of his nose and gave her a faint smile. "I used to watch some of the human men, the ones I knew really loved their women, go through the agonies of fearing something might happen to take away their happiness. I always wondered what was wrong with them that they couldn't just enjoy what they had right then. Now I am like they were."

"If we were in your homeland and far from my people, would our life be so different?"

"In some ways. Many ways," he admitted. "You will have to come there with me soon. It is so beautiful, and the soil there is amazing. Nothing can match it. Syndil would be astounded."

"And what of your brother?" She rubbed her hand along his jaw, coaxing the shadows from his eyes, pleased that his invitation obviously included her family. "Aidan and his lifemate. We must go to see them very soon. I want to meet this man who looks as you do."

Julian was silent for a moment. "I, too, want to see him. I owe him an explanation."

"Then we will go." Desari pretended there was no vampire waiting to destroy her family. "Tell me what the people are like in the Carpathian Mountains."

Julian thought about that for a moment. A slow smile softened the faintly harsh edge to his mouth. "You always come up with great questions, *piccola*. To be honest, I never thought much about what they are like. Mostly they are hardworking people. They pull together in times of crisis. Mikhail and Gregori are very much like Darius. Leaders, hunters, protectors, healers. It will be an experience meeting your older brother, for you and Darius." His smile deepened, reaching his glittering eyes. "Raven is Mikhail's lifemate. She is very much her own person and quite a handful, from what I understand. You would probably become great friends."

"Try to sound like you might like that," Desari encouraged him, trying not to laugh at the pained expression on his face.

"I think the only safe thing to do is lock you up somewhere far from the rest of the world and keep you to myself." For one moment he was half-serious, wondering if there was a possibility he could get away with it.

"I might like that." Desari put her hands on his chest to push him back onto the bed. "We are never alone like this, and I think it is very necessary that couples have plenty of time for the things in life that they need. Like great conversation." Her hand moved through the golden hair on his chest to follow the path across his flat, hard stomach. "Do you hear me conversing with you?" she asked softly. Her nails were tracing patterns across his skin, moving dangerously low, tangling in golden hair, encountering the thick length of him.

The breath jolted out of him, and beneath her gently

caressing nails he grew harder and thicker, and the need began to build. "I thought you were listening," she murmured. "See what can happen when we take a little time to be alone? You should not spend so much time chasing enemies."

Desari shifted position so she could straddle him, slowly lowering her body over his. Even as she felt his body enter hers, the exquisite slowness heightening the pleasure, Julian suddenly sat up, his arms dragging her against him. He was aggressively male, his hips moving with powerful, sure strokes as Desari clung to him, her breasts pressed into his chest and her head on his shoulder. Julian held her tightly to him as he thrust upward into her. There was no greater joy than to merge with her, physically and mentally. There was no greater joy than to simply be with her, share her body and heart and mind. Julian took his time, wanting their time to last forever, wanting to be one for as long as they could possibly stay that way. In the end, they were gasping for air, clinging to one another, sated and exhausted.

The sun was obviously making its way to the highest point in the sky and their bodies began reacting as they normally did, protesting the time of day with tremendous fatigue. Soon, neither of them would be able to move. Even though they were already deep within the earth, the daylight still had the unwanted effects on them.

Julian raised his head first, all too aware of his growing weakness. "*Cara*, I am sorry, but we have little time, and I must see to your brother. I feel it necessary to sleep above him to ensure his protection."

Desari nodded wordlessly. She had never felt so tired before, her body like lead, yet her heart and soul were completely content. She wanted nothing more than to lie with Julian in the soil to allow rejuvenation. Secretly she was very pleased that Julian would care to protect her brother. She loved that about him, his willingness to accept responsibility for her family even though he decried it at every turn.

It took a few minutes to gather enough strength to get up and clothe themselves before moving back through the lava tunnels to the healing chamber. At once, Julian was aware Syndil had been there; he could smell her particular clean scent. The chamber was filled with aromatic herbs and candles and the rich healing soil so important to their race.

Julian opened the earth for Desari right above Darius's resting place. It beckoned to them, promising them soothing peace and restoration. Gratefully, Julian accepted what the earth offered. He lay beside his lifemate, one arm circling her, her head resting on his shoulder. She kissed him once, very briefly but tenderly, and at once her heart ceased to beat and the air left her lungs. He lay there holding her to him, astonished that his life had changed so drastically, that he was part of something involving so many others, and that he didn't dislike it as intensely as he made out to all those around him.

Once more he set the safeguards, ensuring that no one would disturb Darius and that the chamber itself was safe from any who might come seeking them in their time of weakness. Once more he waved his hand, and the soil covered him, covered Desari, closing over them so that there was no trace of their existence on the surface. Several feet below them, Darius rested, protected. The last thing Julian did before he succumbed to the sleep of the immortal race was to program his body to awaken just before sunset. He had his mortal enemy to hunt, one who would be trapped by the sun for a few precious minutes, giving Julian time to locate him.

Chapter Eighteen

The disturbance that awakened Julian was not one of aggression but of something within the soil itself. He felt the earth move around him, felt the properties of the soil enrich even as he lay within it. Above him, he could hear the soft chant, feel the vibrations spreading out in a ripple effect, one that moved on and outward, one that reached deep within the earth to find Darius and the soil blanketing his body.

Syndil was already up and working her magic. The sun was beginning to make its way across the sky, slowly toward the sea. Julian rose slowly, making certain Desari was aware of his intentions and would rise with him. He did not want to startle or frighten Syndil, a male Carpathian appearing beside her just before sunset.

Syndil sank backward, allowing Julian room as he burst through the topsoil. She was relieved to see Desari right beside him.

"Syndil," Desari greeted, hugging the woman to her.

"You have risen early to ensure our brother is well cared for. I am grateful to you."

"I felt his pain within the earth," she replied softly. "It has used much of its energy to aid him. I thought if I provided for the earth, it would aid in healing him faster." She was very pale after lending her energy to such a task. She brushed a tired hand across her forehead, leaving a smear of dirt in its wake.

"You know the earth will heal him quickly with your aid." Desari touched her with a gentle hand. "Your gift is one none of us could do without."

"I must go now," Julian said. "I must find the vampire's resting place before he has a chance to rise. I am already late."

"Julian, no," Desari protested. As she turned to face him, she raised her arms in a kind of objection, creating a slight stirring of air.

The wind she brought forth blew softly, a whisper really, tugging at Julian's long blond hair. He caught up the strands and secured them at the nape of his neck. Very gently his palm cupped Desari's face. "I have to do this, *cara*. You know I do. I can do no other than to see to your safety and that of your brother and the other female." At her quick frown he hastily made the correction. "Syndil." He glanced at the other woman. "I cannot allow this monster to continue to terrorize either one of you." *And you know he is the one; his shadow is growing within me, a stain I must cleanse from my body.*

"Why must you go now? Darius will be completely healed in another few risings. You are not at full strength. I know you must destroy him, but you can wait for a more opportune time," Desari protested. Her teeth worried her lower lip. She knew he was going to go despite anything she said, but she felt she had to try. She was in his mind, and it was written in stone that he would hunt the one that had threatened them all and so seriously injured Darius. The ancient vampire was Julian's mortal enemy; he had robbed him of his life and home, and now he threatened his newfound family.

A slow smile softened the hard edge of Julian's mouth. "You know very well I am at full strength, *piccola*, and that I can do no other than go. Do not give me a hard time over this."

Desari swept back her hair, her long lashes sweeping down to cover the expression in her eyes. "Then return quickly, lifemate. We have much to do in the next few risings. My concert schedule is already set, and we are expected. It would raise suspicion and cause unwanted attention if we did not show up when we are expected."

"I have little to say about your chosen profession, lifemate," he growled, catching her chin, forcing her to look up at him. His mouth found hers in a long, slow kiss filled with promise. "I will return quickly, *cara mia*. Have no fear."

She shrugged with pretended carelessness. "I have none. You will rid the world of this creature and allow us to continue with our schedule."

"Of course," Julian replied, as if he were going off to a banking job. He touched her chin with a gentle fingertip, the gesture so tender, Desari found herself blinking back tears as he moved away from her.

As Julian started out of the chamber, Barack materialized almost in front of him, blocking the way. "It is my right to do this thing. I will hunt."

Syndil, kneeling in the rich soil near Darius, swung around so fast she nearly fell over their leader's resting place. "What in the world are you saying? Have you completely lost your mind, Barack? What has gotten into you these last months? You have no business chasing monsters around." Her voice was the strongest Julian had ever heard it, a husky blend of sounds that made one think of bedrooms and satin sheets. That voice could easily stop a man in his tracks, and Barack was not immune to its magic.

The Carpathian male turned to look at her, his dark eyes cool and calm. "You will stay out of this business, Syndil, and behave as a woman should."

"I would think one kill on your hands would be enough," Syndil went on. "It is not your calling, or have you acquired a taste for such things?"

"The undead cannot be allowed to follow us or make another try for you or Desari," Barack replied without anger. "You will be protected."

For one moment Syndil's beautiful eyes came alive with a flash of brilliance quite close to anger. "You are taking far too much on yourself, Barack. You have no claim to make on my behavior. Our leader can chastise me if he so desires—not that it would do any good if I did not choose to follow him. I tire of these tantrums. Whatever I did to cause Savon to turn on me, I have paid for, many times over. You can quit punishing me for my sins. I refuse to tolerate it any longer."

"Is that what you think, Syndil? That I blame you for Savon's behavior?" Barack rubbed his forehead thoughtfully. "What am I saying? Of course you think that. I have been in your mind and have read the guilt you feel. But do not reflect such thoughts back on *me*, Syndil. I live to protect you, that is all. And I will do so despite your harsh judgments of my capabilities. It *is* my duty and my right."

Syndil stood up, her slender figure fragile and beautiful. Her chin was up, her eyes alive with pain and pride. "You wish me to be responsible for another death? I will not have such a thing happen to you. I will leave,

Barack, and when you come home there will be emptiness in my place."

A slow smile curved Barack's mouth. He crossed the
distance between them, ignoring Desari and Julian as if
they weren't witnessing the strange conversation. His
hand caught Syndil's chin and held her so that she was
forced to meet his steady gaze. "Do you not hear your
own words, Syndil?" His thumb rubbed gently, almost
tenderly over her skin. "You said *when* I return. You
know I will defeat this enemy, just as I defeated the
other. Do not fear for my life. I am not nearly so careless
as I pretend to be."

Her large eyes shimmered with tears. "Everything is
so out of kilter, Barack. I cannot find myself. I cannot
imagine existing if something were to happen to you."
She swallowed, then jerked her head away to shake it
as if denying her own words. "Any of you. We have
lived so long together, and now it is all coming apart."

Desari slipped an arm around Syndil. Barack's teeth
flashed again. "It is merely changing, Syndil, not coming
apart. We will weather this crisis as we have so many
others."

"We must go," Julian said. "The undead will rise any
moment now, and he knows we will be hunting him."
He turned abruptly and took the passage leading to the
chimney entrance, certain Barack would be with him.
Barack was correct—he had the right to hunt this demon
threatening his family—but Julian was a solitary hunter.
He had no real idea of Barack's abilities and felt responsible for the man's safety. Silently he cursed the
Carpathian male's sense of duty when it came to their
women. Even as he did, however, he knew he was
counting on Dayan to guard the women and Darius.
Should Dayan fail, he was counting on Darius to protect
them all, even wounded as he was.

Barack was silent, allowing the blond stranger to take the lead. Obviously an experienced hunter, the man was accepted and even respected by Darius. Julian was blasting upward through the narrow chimney toward the sky. Once out into the open, he shape-shifted, winging his way toward the south and the thick forest. Barack followed, a silent shadow, willing to do whatever it took to rid their family of this evil entity that threatened Syndil and Desari.

Julian blocked out all unnecessary intrusions and concentrated on the incoming data his senses were recording at a rapid rate. Immediately he turned slightly southeast and streaked toward the blankness in the air. The vampire was rising and radiating the stench of his presence, covering his tracks with a blocking spell. The very absence of data gave him away. Rising was always the most vulnerable, disoriented moment for any Carpathian or vampire, that one wrenching instant they came out of the solace of the earth.

Julian struck, even from the distance they were, hoping for a lucky hit, sending a bolt of light and white-hot energy slicing through the sky over the region of blankness. The sound was tremendous, a loud crack that shook the trees beneath them as the bolt traveled faster than sound. He was rewarded with a hate-filled cry of pain. The sword of light had tagged their enemy but had not disabled him.

At once Julian plummeted toward the ground, zigzagging, spiraling, moving so quickly it was impossible to see him. Barack broke away, realizing Julian was expecting retaliation. He followed suit, splitting off, taking a completely different route to make it more difficult for the vampire to score. At once the sky was lit with jagged bolts of lightning. Like arrows they fell in all directions, leaping from cloud mass to cloud mass and arcing toward the ground itself. Sparks rained on the earth, and the sky lit up, raining fireworks.

Within the display of white light, colors suddenly began to shimmer, blues and oranges and reds, tongues of flames like heat-seeking missiles. The colors raced back toward the oncoming vampire, swarming, gathering in number and strength. They raced through the sky, turning this way and that, obviously following an invisible trail. Again Julian was rewarded with a scream of rage. At once the ground shook, and trees were blackened as the monster retaliated.

Far away, both Carpathians heard the faint, feminine cry of pain. Barack swore. *He attacks her.* He used the mental path familiar to his family, hoping Julian was aware of it.

He is trying to draw her out. Can he do such a thing?

Barack considered that. He had been in Syndil's mind. She was of the earth, as they all were, yet her gift was an affinity the rest of them could never experience. She would feel the earth crying out, the death of the living plants as they withered in pain. *I am afraid it will be so. She will feel the earth's pain as we cannot. And she can do no other than attempt to heal it.*

Go then, stop her. I have instructed Desari to hold her there until you get there, and she has bound Syndil with her voice, but she says the pain in Syndil is torture to see. Go quickly, Barack, and know that I will destroy this monster while you keep her safe. Whatever promises you must make to her will be kept.

Barack believed him. There was something of Darius in Julian Savage. A quiet confidence that clung to him like a second skin. A second attack on the foliage below and Syndil's soft cry spurred him back toward the mountain.

Julian shut off his connection to Desari and the others.

This vampire was his ancient enemy, very dangerous and highly skilled. The vampire had found a young boy so many centuries ago, lured him into a world of knowledge and excitement, then betrayed him and marked him with the darkness of the undead. He had tormented Julian, whispered taunts and threats, forced him to endure the screams of his victims, to feel their terror before he killed them. And he had shamed Julian. Taunted him with the knowledge that he would forever be alone, tainted. Shadowed. The monster was finally before him, and they would face one another across the battlefield alone, as it was always meant to be.

Julian dissolved into a fine mist and spread out across the sky, moving in a semicircle toward the vampire's position. Three bolts of lightning slammed to the west of him, and he realized Barack was deliberately exposing his presence as he raced toward the mountain, hoping to give Julian more time to get in a position to attack. Julian immediately took advantage of the vampire's momentary distraction, streaking through the sky even as he built up fog on the forest floor so that it drifted in wide bands and began to rise in banks of mist.

The vampire was directing his attacks from a cliff above the forest floor. Julian could see him now and vaguely recognized the remnants of the once handsome Carpathian male. Now the face was sunken and gray, wisps of hair clinging to the scalp in tufts, the body old and gnarled. The vampire had not had time to feed.

As Julian materialized behind him, the vampire whirled around with a low cry. Julian smiled politely. "It has been long, Bernado. Much too long. I was but a boy, and you were telling me you were off to the libraries of Paris, in search of historical documents that might give our people a clue as to what really happened between Gabriel and Lucian. Did you ever find such a thing?" His voice was a soft blend of purity and confidence.

Bernado, monster of his dreams, his life. This cunning, crafty ancient who liked to consider himself a great scholar.

Bernado blinked, taken aback by the casual conversation. It was totally unexpected. He had not had a conversation with anyone in over two hundred years. "That is so. I was looking. I remember now." His voice was gravelly but thoughtful, as if he had to reach back to find the moment in time. "I found two entries that might have alluded to them. One was in a personal journal, that of a count. He wrote that he saw two demons fighting near the cemetery right there in Paris. That the fight went on for some time, a vicious battle but almost choreographed, as if each combatant knew what the other would do before he had done so. He claimed the two continually changed from one being into another. He wrote that both fighters appeared to have suffered terrible wounds, yet there was no trace of either fighter and no blood on the ground when he was able to get close enough to examine the cemetery. He told no one of his sighting for fear of being ridiculed."

"It does seem possible, then, that you uncovered something our people have searched centuries for." There was praise in Julian's soft voice. "And the other entry? Where did you find that?" It had been the excitement and lure of this mystery that had first ensnared Julian's interest in Bernado's studies all those years ago.

"It was a mere line or two in a record kept by a supervisor of the cemetery workers. A personal record, no more. It alluded to one of his workers, who he suspected had drunk far too much wine one night. It was the same date as that of the count's memory. The supervisor wrote that one of his men told of a fight among wolves and demons that ended in mortal wounds. He would no longer go into the cemetery and work, as he was certain the demons had risen from the graves."

Julian nodded. "You were once a man I thought had greatness in you. I looked up to you. To your learnedness. But you betrayed that trust."

The vampire blinked at him, uncertain about his mild tone. "You wanted knowledge. I gave it to you."

Julian could feel the power building in him, around him, in the very air itself. Century after century, each dark, barren rising, the aching need for his twin, the lost fledgling years. It was rising in him, the bleakness, the emptiness, the dark stain of humiliation and isolation. All he'd had left was his honor. His Prince and the healer had known and had recognized his need to be of value to his people, but this monster before him had altered the course of his life for all time.

"You gave me a living death, Bernado." Julian moved then, with blurring speed, whipping toward the ancient monster as the creature suddenly surged forward. His fist was outstretched and plunged deep into the chest cavity, using the vampire's forward motion to aid his attack. "I studied your methods, every kill." He whispered the words, his golden eyes gleaming savagely. "You taught me the importance of knowledge, of knowing your enemy, recognizing him, and I learned well." He wrenched the pulsating heart out of the chest and leapt away with the withered, blackened organ in his hand. It sickened him. There was no triumph as he thought there would be.

The vampire screamed in rage, a high, unearthly sound that hurt the ears and sent wildlife scurrying for cover. "You learned well the kill because I live in you," he hissed, poisonous saliva spewing from his mouth. "You are no different than me. You wanted to be like me, but you did not have the guts to embrace the life."

Bernado staggered toward him, his rotten teeth jagged and stained from thousands of kills, his body beginning to collapse in on itself. Julian stepped back farther, fully aware the aberration was still dangerous as long as the heart was in proximity to the body. He flung it away and directed a blade of light to incinerate it. At once the body began to flop around, spewing tainted blood that crept toward him relentlessly. Julian calmly sent the energy toward the body and then the blood, removing all evidence of Bernado's existence. At last he used the white-hot heat to sear away the taint from his hands. From his soul.

It was over. At long last. It was over. He had never felt such sorrow, an oppressive, nearly numbing force weighing him down. He found himself down on one knee, his body shaking, his chest burning. This thing had nearly destroyed his life, had taken so much from him. The vampire had made him believe it was invincible, and Julian had spent centuries, *centuries* acquiring knowledge for this one moment in time. It was over in seconds. Only seconds. When the vampire had cost him so much.

Bernado was right. He had turned Julian into the very thing he despised. A killer without equal. The shadow had grown and spread, consuming him. Julian's face was wet with tears as he looked up at the night sky. He was a monster without equal.

A hunter without equal. Come to me, Julian. Desari's soft voice washed over him like a cool, fresh breeze.

I do not think I can face the crowd there, beloved one. He answered her honestly. He was used to a solitary existence, and at this moment, when the weight of his life's sorrows hung on him, when he realized the numbers of his people he had slain, when the cost of losing his twin for all those long centuries burdened his soul and shattered his heart, when he felt like a boy, shamed and damned by his own reckless youth, he wanted to be away from others.

Would it help if I came to you, my love? There was the merest hesitation, as if she was afraid he didn't want her near.

Despite the stony ache in his heart, he found himself nearly smiling. How could he not want her at his side? His heart. His soul. The blood running in his veins. His other half. *It would help a great deal.*

He turned his head to watch her approach. Even in flight, her movements were wholly feminine. Whether on the wing, racing on four legs through the forest, or walking within her own body, she was the most beautiful woman he could imagine. He stood up as she landed lightly on the cliff beside him. She took his breath away. His tears away. She took the dark shadow and dispersed it for all time into the night.

Desari stood with the night sky at her back, her long hair cascading around her. Her smile held so much love for him, he could only stand spellbound, enthralled for all eternity by this one woman who completed him. She had given him his life. She had given him a family. She was his home.

Julian held out his hand for her. Desari's mouth curved invitingly. She placed her hand in his, her fingers entwining with his so that they were woven together as they were meant to be. She moved right into his arms, sheltered against his heart. She turned her mouth up to his, tasting his tears, his boyhood, the terrible burden he had borne for so long. She kissed him, her body molding to his, and in his mind her beautiful voice rose in song just for him.

The notes skipped from his mind to the sky, silver

and gold notes of joy and happiness, of courage and admiration. She sang of love between two people, sacred and beautiful. She sang of peace and happiness. Her hands moved over him possessively, lovingly, checking his body for wounds. Her warrior was home.

Whatever lay ahead for them, whether human assassins or vampires, it didn't matter. They were together, one and the same, and they were far too strong to allow anything to take what they had away from them.

At Avon Books, we know your passion for romance—once you finish one of our novels, you find yourself wanting more.

May we tempt you with . . .

- **Excerpts** from our upcoming releases.

- Entertaining **extras**, including authors' personal photo albums and book lists.

- Behind-the-scenes **scoop** on your favorite characters and series.

- **Sweepstakes** for the chance to win free books, romantic getaways, and other fun prizes.

- Writing **tips** from our authors and editors.

- **Blog** with our authors and find out why they love to write romance.

- **Exclusive content** that's not contained within the pages of our novels.

Join us at
www.avonbooks.com